TRANSCEND

TRANSCEND

SELFISH MYTHS
4

DARK GODS WORLD

NATALIA JASTER

Books by Natalia Jaster

FOOLISH KINGDOMS SERIES

Trick (Book 1)

Ruin (Book 2)

Burn (Book 3)

Dare (Book 4)

Lie (Book 5)

Dream (Book 6)

SELFISH MYTHS SERIES

Touch (Book 1)

Torn (Book 2)

Tempt (Book 3)

Transcend (Book 4)

VICIOUS FAERIES SERIES

Kiss the Fae (Book 1)

Hunt the Fae (Book 2)

Curse the Fae (Book 3)

Defy the Fae (Book 4)

To the smug gods who always get what they want.
Until now.

Go on.
Tell me to stop.

THE DARK GODS PANTHEON

Eros — **Love**

Psyche — **Andrew**

Icarus — **Anger**

Aphrodite — **Merry**

Hades — **Malice**

Persephone — **Wonder**

Narcissus — **Envy**

Oizys — **Sorrow**

THE DARK GODS
HIERARCHICAL CASTE

The Stars

|

The Fate Court

|

The Guides

|

The Crews
of Gods & Goddesses

AIM FOR THE BACK

Envy

Now he knows what pain feels like.

And maybe one other emotion, a persistent feeling that's been shadowing him like a pest, creeping up on him since the day he first lost his mind and touched her. That infamous moment in time when he'd traced the goddess's sarcastic mouth, those lips painted a brooding charcoal gray to match her hair.

In the past, her chronic scowls, dreary clothes, and perpetual middle finger used to nauseate him.

But hidden beneath the tough exterior? The watery texture of hurt. The sweet-and-sour taste of rapture.

Those are the parts he wasn't supposed to discover. Those are the parts that came later.

Yet his transcendence hadn't begun until asking her a question. *What's your pleasure?*

In return, she had thrown one back at him. *What's your pain?*

On this bloodthirsty night, the answers chip away at his soul. Standing opposite from each other, they face off across a chasm.

Rivals to lovers.

Lovers to enemies.

At some point, the two of them chose different sides. He can't remember how it came to this, how they've ended up fighting for different endings.

With the battle raging across the summit, his fingers tighten around the bow. On reflex, she nocks her own weapon. As they aim at one another, he smirks mournfully. This was only ever going to go one way, with only one outcome.

That's fate.

So now he knows what pain feels like, every shift of its curves, every sigh of its breath, and every glint of its irises. It's a permanent emotion, like a stain he can't rub off.

What's a god to do when his match is the last person he can stand? He resists.

And what does that goddess do? Naturally, she makes him regret it.

SIX DAYS AGO...

1

Sorrow

It's not the first time he's seen her naked, but it's the first time she makes him regret it. Sorrow dunks her head beneath the water's surface, fluid licking her calves and brushing her spine. Dammit. This secluded pond would be heaven if her least favorite god weren't spying on her.

She doesn't need to peek. After millennia of tolerating this male, his presence and posture are evident without having to guess. Nor does Sorrow bother gauging how long he's been standing there, since that requires more consideration than the conceited prick deserves.

She pictures the male figure casually leaning one bulky shoulder against the willow tree, its trunk sprouting from the depths, branches spreading like an umbrella. Likely, shadows are caressing his face, accentuating the high ramps of his cheekbones. A pair of insolent eyes are following her movements, the irises rich and molten, oozing conceit as he judges her from his pedestal.

Sorrow would bet the god's right nut that he's wearing cashmere. Preppy bastard.

The fucker is watching me. But he doesn't want to. Not anymore.

Accurate enough. He's spying against his will. This has nothing to do with enticement or attachment, the knowledge pinching her ribcage. Rather, he's checking on Sorrow out of obligation, making sure she doesn't cause trouble, as if she's a loose cannon prone to mishaps.

Offense prickles her flesh. She can take care of her fucking self. Of everyone in their crew, Sorrow is the last member to cause an uproar.

Gnashing her teeth, she cuts across the pond, her limbs beating eddies out of the way. All the while, his gaze trails her like a spotlight. But if it's too hard for him to look away, then it's still too easy for him to look away.

Hard isn't enough. She'd rather make it excruciating In which case, best not to let umbrage get the better of her. It will only make Sorrow thrash about and swim sloppily.

Submerging herself, she flips her eyelids open. Murk swirls before Sorrow, the gray strings of her hair weightless and floating. She slows her pace, breast-stroking with a lazy spread of her thighs, enhancing the motions to their physical advantage.

Let him see everything.

After a few taunting laps, her body shoots upward, breaking the surface with a deep, resentful arc. Sorrow's hair whips back, slapping her skin with enough force that it stings. At three-thousand years old, occasionally she forgets her own strength, the destructive impact she makes on herself.

While straightening, Sorrow sinks her bare feet into the spongy foundation. Despite the swim, the depth is shallow. The pond rises only high enough to cover her hips, the upper half of her naked frame exposed as she shakes out the sodden tresses.

Droplets sluice down her tits, the beads coursing an uneven path over the ruched nipples. Again, she feels that odious hyperawareness of an unwelcome audience, his condescending eyes raking across her drenched, unclad figure.

Strange. Sorrow wouldn't know if the water is warm or cold, yet her flesh pebbles, the onslaught rushing along her skin. The breeze could be the culprit, but she's not about to delude herself about its true source.

It's disgust, that's all. She hates when he stares at her for longer than three seconds. In the past, he did so out of hostility, assessing the physical traits that didn't meet his immaculate standards. Though these days, she can never tell what he's searching for whenever his gaze strays to her.

The sylvan woodland encloses this pond, encasing it in a dense oasis. It's isolated, yet with her ex-lover's whipcord silhouette filling in the gaps, the environment shrinks further. He idles by the willow tree, its roots clawing into the pond and sucking up moisture.

She grabs a few ropes of hair and twists them in a chokehold, excess liquid spilling from the strands. "Are you just going to stand there and gawk, God of Envy?"

His velveteen voice wastes no time. "Are you just going to stand there and let me, Goddess of Sorrow?"

Her feet are stalking in his direction before she realizes it, streams of water ejecting around her and splattering mineral rocks. His physique gets larger as Sorrow gets nearer, and she stops within smacking distance.

Burnished complexion. Long, mahogany hair tied in a low ponytail. Straight nose with an arrogant bump over the bridge.

Up close, Envy is what he's always been. An immortal douchebag. Tonight, he has indeed outfitted himself in cashmere trousers. A button-down shirt tucks into the waistband, the collar venting open at the throat and the sleeves rolled up his forearms, the white material a stark contrast to his light brown skin. Even while on a mission such as theirs, he can't resist sprucing himself up as if headed into a high-end brothel instead of enemy territory. Of all their kind, he's the only deity who dresses like the human version of a corporate hoe.

To avoid getting soaked, Envy's trouser hems are jammed up his calves. The effort is pointless, not to mention odd, since he's precious about defiling his wardrobe.

Case in point, Sorrow tilts her head at the ensemble. "Is that a wrinkle?"

It's a predictable shot to the ego. In record time, Envy's chiseled features condense into a dandified grimace. Like a reflex, he detaches himself from the tree trunk, his muscled frame rippling beneath the clothes as if he's made of rocks. Straightening, the god runs both palms over his thighs, attempting to iron out the invasive creases in the textile.

When that fails, Sorrow makes the mistake of snorting, which earns her a contemptible glance. Resuming his original position, Envy crosses his arms over that broad chest, the expanse of which requires its own map. Caramel irises carve a path down her nudity, from the pert nipples to the glistening patch of dark hair concealing her cunt. His pupils glint like a pair of firecrackers, then surge back to her face, the orbs gleaming with mockery.

"You should heed your own wrinkles instead," he patronizes. "Unless you'd like me to use my hands and smooth them out for you."

Because she's dripping, it would be hilarious to shake herself and spritz his outfit with algae. Except that would imply he's worth her time and energy. It would mean his words affect her.

For all she knows, he's come here to admire his reflection in the pond, but her presence has derailed that goal. Just like he'd ruined her skinny-dipping break. Although it's past midnight, nighttime excursions are her favorite.

"You're neglecting your beauty sleep," she chides.

Captain Ego scoffs. "As if I need it."

"Based on the grass stains tarnishing your pants, I disagree. With all this nature surrounding you, I'd wager being forced to snooze on the ground kept you from dreaming about your attributes. I know how much you love camping."

"And I know how much you love camping next to me."

Fuck him hard. "What are you doing out here?"

"Why?" The god hooks his thumbs into his belt loops. "Do I get a spanking, my nymph?"

Yep. He couldn't wait for an opportunity to be a hotshot. "Actually, I'm just humoring you like the needy tramp you are."

Although Envy's casual posture doesn't change, an offended light flashes through his eyes. Mortification, perhaps?

Ugh. The chances of that are as high as seeing him in a cotton hoodie.

His self-adoration is historic. During their brief foray into fuckery, they hadn't learned much else of substance about each other, outside of how loud they could make each other come. Over the generations, they've shared about as many secrets as kisses, which is to say, zero.

The goal had been sex. Nothing more.

Never mind that she's right about the grass stains aggravating this god to the point of insomnia. Never mind that he won't admit it. Evidently, this is the reason he'd noticed her absence from the crew in the first place.

Envy has the nerve to cross an invisible boundary, looming forward to get in Sorrow's face. As his scowl clashes with hers, the god slants his head, his breath a whisper across her jaw. "Oh, I can remember a time when you sounded mighty needy yourself," he purrs, the words as thick as syrup. "I remember you twisting my name into so many different cries. I remember it breaking on the edge of your lips. I remember the loud pitch slipping off your tongue, begging for more."

Animosity charges across Sorrow's flesh, chafing down to the cleft in her thighs. She should have seen that one coming. In hindsight, she should have never encouraged his dick, much less her pussy, to begin with.

Lust is dangerous. It unhinges the mouth, the tongue, and the brain until all three collapse in tandem. The effect turns deities into colossal idiots who can't keep their traps shut, all that moaning having split their lips too far apart, leaving them wide open and spewing things they'll eventually regret.

Things like, "Fuck me."

Refusing to back off, Sorrow quirks an eyebrow. "I've got a better question for you. What's it like to be desperate for attention, for the span of three millennia? Now that, I'm curious about."

There it is again. That bolt of light, along with a bonus curl of the lips, some type of hybrid between a sneer and a snarl. Envy does another fresh appraisal of her nude body, dissecting every feature, which is now damp and sticky. When his gaze reaches her lips, words from the past infiltrate Sorrow's memory.

"I like seeing that snarky little mouth parted. I bet every inch would tremble against my tongue."

He said that before they'd first gone feral and pounced on each other. Shortly before. Like, seconds before.

But tonight, the sight of her lips repels this nemesis. He regards Sorrow with flippant distaste, just as he used to regard her prior to this affair and over the course of their lives. As if he's too good for her.

At this point, Envy must be struggling to fathom what he ever saw in Sorrow. Finally, something she relates to.

They're unsuited in every way, with his tailored suits and her gothic attire. They've spent most of their existence glaring at each other, even though they're supposed to be crewmates. That is, apart from the brief spell in which they'd lost their sanity and gotten carnal.

Well, it had been a mistake. It hadn't meant anything. And it's over now.

Envy plucks a limp thread of Sorrow's hair, then flicks it away like a weed. "What's it like to be desperate for attention, you ask? I might counter that attack and inquire what it's like to be insignificant for the same amount of time. With that scrawny frame and loner attitude, it's a mystery you haven't simply disappeared into thin air. Not that anyone would miss you."

Sorrow hikes up her chin. "You'll have to do better than that."

"Believe me, I've tried."

"Unlike you, I don't care what my ex-lovers or anybody else thinks about me."

"Is that right?" Envy slants his head. "Out of curiosity, do you have a matching t-shirt to go with your bullshit?"

"No, but I've got a slap to go with your face," she replies with a fake smile.

To which his eyes glitter. "Has anyone ever told you how ravishing you look when you're pissed off?"

"You know the answer to that."

"Indeed. By comparison, I regret to inform you that slapping me wouldn't change a thing about my face. I'd still be prettier than creation itself. By the way, let the celestial record show that I wasn't out here because of you. In that regard, your assumption was correct. The pant stains were irritating me as much as the notion of camping. Thus, I needed a respite. Ultimately, everything I do is all about me."

"In that case, go fuck yourself."

"Precisely." His grin should come with an explicit content rating. "What do you think I was coming out here to do?"

Sorrow tenses down to her ass cheeks. Based on his prizewinning expression, Envy thinks his cock is a sculpted work of art that needs routine polishing. So that's what lured him here. The discomforts of squatting outdoors like a nomad led to sleep deprivation, which in turn led to frustration, which finally led here. He'd needed to blow off steam.

Of course, it hadn't been about Sorrow. He hadn't noticed her absence after all, hadn't realized she left their outpost while he and the rest of their crew slumbered in their respective corners of the forest.

The silence grates on Sorrow's nerves, tension provoking her to supplement the quiet with additional insults. Now that shagging is no longer an option, how else will they pass the time?

Matter of fact, what are they still doing standing here?

A dragonfly skates across the water's surface. The pond quivers, fluid lapping at Sorrow and Envy's calves. Like chips of glass, constellations pierce the sky, producing tiny gaps in the hemisphere.

One star trembles, as if it's about to fall. For some reason, it reminds Sorrow of a myth that circulates in their world. Something about the almighty stars burning their fiercest only when a deity is ready to hear the truth.

In any case, the firmament has never looked almighty to Sorrow. Instead, it has always resembled scars, a fragile surface poked by too many holes, impossible to stitch up. If anyone but Envy was standing beside her, she might consider sharing this observation.

Anyone else's reaction would be safer.

A shift in her periphery jerks Sorrow from her thoughts. She startles as Envy's index finger taps a spot below her clavicle, where a certain item usually decorates her vest. "No stitching needle tonight. By the way, when are you going to dispose of that pointless accessory?"

She whacks his digits away. "Just as soon as you get rid of yours," she retorts, jerking her chin toward his dick. "Or do you need help locating it?"

"You dare offend the immortal cock?"

"What I do, or don't do, is no one's business. Never has been, and never will be."

"Of course not. That would require you actually mattering to someone."

Hate stings the rims of her eyes. "So that's it. We're back to where we started."

"Oh, my clueless nymph." It's almost apologetic, remorseful, and consoling when his palm cups her cheek, one smooth thumb stroking her lower lip. "What made you think we ever detoured?"

Her teeth are near enough to sever a finger. "Perceptive as ever."

"Marvelous."

"Great."

"Fine."

"Perfect." But as Sorrow thwacks away his hand, she notes the rustle of leaves behind him, her opposite knuckles bending into a fist because destiny has got to be kidding her right now. "Except not really, since we're about to detour."

"Oh?" Envy inquires. "Why's that?"

In the future, Sorrow can reminisce on this moment and gloat that he hadn't distracted her as much as she had him. It's the only justification for why he's not being vigilant.

With that in mind, she levels the pride god with an inconvenienced grin and whispers, "Because we're not alone."

Envy stiffens. Realization sharpens his gaze, the facade dropping like a curtain, revealing something akin to chagrin. Better yet, disgrace.

Nevertheless, the god thankfully gets his shit together. Peering into Sorrow's eyes as if they're mirrors, he scans the reflection of their surroundings.

They stare at each other. Then they dive, dodging the death arrow that shoots toward them.

2

Sorrow

With a twist, she dives into the air beside Envy. Mid-flight, Sorrow registers the synchronized arc of their bodies before crashing through the surface. On impact, liquid thrashes around them like an underwater tsunami, engulfing her upon descent. She plunges, the deluge funneling around her with the force of a vortex.

Her eyelids part, seeking Envy through the cluster of vines, through which another arrow spears toward her, its point a flashing asterisk. Sorrow swerves, avoiding the projectile. It torpedoes past her skull and misses shearing Envy's torso as he pumps his limbs out of range.

Despite the god's monstrous size, he's better at aquatics than Sorrow. Launching ahead, they swim parallel to one another, firing in and out of the water. When they bolt upward, arrows swoop beneath their stomachs, and when they plummet, the projectiles fly above their spines.

Geysers of water slap the foliage. When Sorrow hits the pond's edge, she twirls and rockets back the way she came. That's when— fuck!—the targets change course, assaulting them from unpredictable angles.

While immersed, she keeps her eyes open, discerning Envy's form receding to an area shrouded by glowing pentagram shapes, little starfish who'd been minding their business.

The separation brings her crew to mind. They had trespassed into enemy territory only days ago. So which adversary has managed to spot them this quickly? Have they ambushed Sorrow's crew as well? Are her friends hurt?

In retrospect, advancing her target skill with underwater training would have been a good idea. Learning to wield her longbow while in this predicament could have come in handy.

Then again, her weapons are out of reach, discarded in the grass. If their attacker has seen and identified the ice element of her archery, she's done for. Provided she survives this attack.

Another strike beneath the surface. Sorrow pivots, causing a subterranean tidal wave. After a full rotation, her gaze staggers across Envy, who floats before her, having closed the distance between them. Time slows, pauses, holds its breath. For a second, it's deceptively peaceful down here, the lapse numbing her senses. It's nice not having to feel anything, hear anything, especially when faced with this god.

Envy's collar flutters in place, rippling against the pulse at his throat. His long hair skims through the water, the thick mane lashing around his aghast expression, as if he'd just caught Sorrow picking her nose.

Whatever. In reality, he's still recovering from shock, the audacity that she'd heeded their enemies before he did.

Sorrow jabs her thumb. He blinks and takes the hint, darting out of range from another arrow. They've got few options, seeing as her weapons are unreachable from here, and who knows where Envy left his archery.

Evanescing would be ideal, except there are restrictions. Among the inability to vanish in the presence of their rulers, most deities can't disappear with a companion in tow, and they sadly can't do so while underwater.

In these cases, immortal magic needs an old-fashioned, common-sense alternative. Flipping headfirst, Sorrow pushes herself down and snatches a rock from the sediment. Gliding upward, she breaks the surface, cranks her arm, and flings the rock. The makeshift weapon smashes through the underbrush and explodes into dust against a trunk.

A small gasp resounds from the thicket, its owner on the verge of laughter. And okay, that makes no goddamn sense. Aside from a certain demon god, what predator would cackle as if this were a game?

Nevertheless, the rock surprises their opponent. At the clatter of a bow dropping, Sorrow dives sideways and catches Envy's shirt collar. Hoisting the god upward, she shoves him toward the bank, but he jerks from her grasp.

"Watch the tailoring," he warns, outraged.

"Watch the trees," she snaps, exasperated.

His eyes slit, telling her exactly what the fuck she can do with her orders. His dripping chest heaves beneath the sheer material clutching his torso, the soaked fabric emphasizing those insufferable abs and pecs. Aww, he's gotten his precious garments wet. Such a pity that Sorrow has no time to celebrate.

They surge out of the pond. While racing across the grass, Sorrow swipes her discarded archery off the ground. Belatedly, she remembers her clothes, which she'd left at the camp, electing to stroll naked to the pond.

Garments would have afforded her some measure of protection against the enemy, but oh well. Shit happens, and she couldn't care less about conjuring a new skirt right now. Being naked won't affect her aim.

On the bright side, Sorrow's running a hell of a lot faster without obstructive material. Sprinting through the woodland, they pound past offshoots and shrubs, then spill into the glade where their crew should be—but aren't.

A frantic "Psst" drifts from the sidelines. Following the sound, Sorrow catches sight of pink hair tucked behind a tree trunk. Then a set of black wings bristling behind another. And a clenched jaw behind another.

Sorrow darts behind her own respective tree. With her spine braced against the bark, she takes inventory of the crew, each of whom have claimed various points of the sylvan forest.

Beyond the mist, Merry's shoulder-length pink hair clashes with the darkness. Draped in that frothy pastel dress, the goddess should have been born gift-wrapped and tied with a bow. A neon arrow is nocked to her archery, the shaft emitting a glow only when released. It's a gift from The Stars and a recent addition to Merry's cache of weapons, seeing as Anger has been teaching her to shoot, and she couldn't bring her firstborn pride and joy with her. Driving a motorcycle through this realm wouldn't exactly amount to a quiet entry.

Anger festers several feet away. His nostrils flare as he toggles between checking on Merry—his soulmate—and choking his archery in a death grip. At this rate, he's going to snap the iron in half.

Across from him, Malice smirks. Angel's face. Devil's soul. He's the approximation of a disheveled demon, with that just-rolled-out-of-bed-after-having-hours-of-rough-BDSM-sex hair. His boots peek from beneath low-slung jeans, tattooed letters constrict around a muscled bicep, and he's leering like an asshole, hankering to jump in plain sight. As psychotic as he is calculating, either Malice has a devious reason for the element of surprise, or he's purely in a bloodthirsty mood. When it comes to him, both are legitimate possibilities.

Meanwhile, Wonder—the objective of Malice's passionate obsession—dangles upside down, her curvy legs hooked over a branch fifteen feet above everyone. Stars almighty. Only she can balance a longbow and quiver while in that position.

A corsage of star-shaped wildflowers encircles Wonder's wrist, her billowy pants and off-the-shoulder blouse defy gravity, and chestnut tresses spill around her face.

Across from Wonder stands Love. The goddess perches atop a bough, black wings tucked against her back and a raven dress clutching her petite frame as she kneels, aiming her bow at an unseen target. Presumably, they're surrounded; yet that doesn't stop Love's mouth from peeling into a mischievous grin. Casually, she knocks a pebble from the beech tree with her elbow.

It's a risky jibe, but Love has the most impeccable aim of them all. The pebble lands without a sound, striking where she'd meant it to—the black coat framing her mate's robust shoulders.

Stationed at ground level, Andrew's mouth twitches in amusement. In contrast to the layers of dark hair springing from Love's loose bun, sharp layers of snowy white dash around Andrew's head. Glancing above, he regards Love with a flirty, combative look that promises she'll pay for that later. Because if they weren't about to defend themselves, Andrew would have already lobbed his own pebble at her, shortly before hauling his goddess someplace private to fuck.

Sport is an aphrodisiac for those two. Sorrow respects that.

Anyway. It's not every day that a former mortal finds himself in a deadly realm of mist and starlight, on a mission to usurp its celestial rulers, and about to engage in combat with a legion of Dark Gods. Though, if Andrew's remotely intimidated, he doesn't give that impression. With the sort of confidence that puts immortals to shame, this man wields a human bow with finesse, his grip tight on the weapon.

Since Envy was barefoot at the pond, he retrieves his lace-up shoes from the camp and scales one of the trees. Despite the god's bulk and spiffy clothes, he makes quick work of the climb. The wet shirt and trousers shift in concert to his movements, stacks of muscle contorting under the material.

At some point during their arrival, he'd found time to snatch his glass archery from their encampment. Ascending the offshoots, Envy positions himself and—for the love of fucking Fates—combs through his dripping hair before nocking his bow. Then he puckers his lips, blowing Love and Wonder a kiss.

Unimpressed, the females merely stare at him.

But what does make a unanimous impression is Sorrow as she waits behind her tree, wearing nothing but her archery. Briefly, every head swerves in her direction. Nudity isn't sacred to deities, yet some members in this bunch have prudish sensibilities.

Merry turns away, poppies of red suffusing her cheeks. Anger glares in frustration. Wonder simply raises her eyebrows but quickly gets distracted by the environment as she assesses the canopy, the woods illuminated in phosphorescent jewel tones.

Malice's green eyes trace Sorrow's tits and cunt in platonic camaraderie, his expression the equivalent of a fist bump that congratulates her on being the most creative combatant here. As though everyone else is pathetic for being dressed at all.

Andrew is on par with Merry, glancing away sans the blush. Instead, the snarky human might chuckle if he weren't holding a fatal weapon.

Love shakes her head, tossing out a silent question. *Where the hell were you? What have you been doing?*

In response, Sorrow jerks her chin toward Envy's tree. *What do you think?*

Arguing, bickering, fighting. With her ex-fuck toy, this has become their new mating ritual. Minus the actual mating.

Each crew member aims in a different direction, covering all vantage points. Until now, they'd breached this land without detection, leaving no evidence of their presence. As a connoisseur of research, Malice had concocted an ancient mixture called Asterra Flora, derived from a seed and flower, which had enabled the crew to cross realms surreptitiously.

So how in the everlasting fuck—

A twig snaps from twenty paces away. Sorrow's ears perk.

She pictures Merry's pink eyes and the lavender hem of her dress swishing against the breeze. The grind of Anger's teeth, his windswept hair affixed to the back of his scalp, and the sharp rays in his graphite irises.

The maniacal glint in Malice's eyes, with a touch of kamikaze flair. Only a touch though, since he's got someone to live for. Namely Wonder, who's inverted above with a curious expression as luminescent as the wildflowers she's been picking nonstop during this quest.

Love, aiming two iron arrows at once. Andrew, balancing one mortal arrow and withholding a string of expletives.

Sorrow envisions Envy... not at all. She refuses to envision him at all.

Regarding that god, her eyes take a literal approach. They flit toward the branch bearing his weight. Just as she finds him, his gaze cuts away from her.

Another twig cracks. Bracing her longbow, Sorrow hunts for the source, inspecting the mist lacing through the forest, a network of brooks carving across the earth, some as narrow as strings, others as inflated as Envy's head.

As the group leader, Anger disarms momentarily and raises his flat palm, indicating for them to hold their fire. With a frown deeper than a canyon, he resumes his stance, nocking his bow in slow motion while scouring the arcade of trees stretching from the glade's entrance.

After a minute, he catches Merry's gaze, who nods and mouths an instruction to Andrew, who gestures with an index finger to Love, who juts her knobby chin at Wonder, who signals to Envy with a jerk of her longbow, indicating a massive hedge behind Sorrow.

Despite the distance and shadows, the ferocious contraction of Envy's face is evident. He twists, seeking out Sorrow as if she's a moron who needs to be told.

Mutely, she hisses, *"I know."*

Eventide grows quieter than a catacomb. Sorrow's finger tightens around the bowstring. She licks her lips, her pulse tapping against her chest.

Another crack. Then the harsh flapping of plumes, which don't belong to Love.

Sorrow swerves and looses her ice arrow, which misses a raptor that appears out of nowhere, its slender beak glistening like a blue sword. Since a number of raptors thrive in this realm, including dragonflies and solar moths, this isn't unusual. Except this particular species is rarely spotted.

A lunar heron.

The avian whips around her, then sweeps past the other archers, who follow its trajectory in confusion. As the creature soars away, realization snares Sorrow by the throat. Lunar herons travel in packs. That one had been alone, probably on the way to reunite with its kin, because it had gotten separated, because something must have lured its attention, because that something might have wanted it to fly in a certain direction.

Because it's a decoy.

A bowstring twangs. Sorrow and her crewmates whip around as a projectile slices through the air, heading for the space between her eyes.

A turbulent male growl skewers through the air. Then a glass arrow intercepts the attack, the collision sundering both weapons. Sparks of light blast apart, illuminating the woods in a glaring explosion before the weapons vanish.

Sorrow whips toward Envy, who lowers his bow. Savagery flares in his pupils, an instant before the glint ebbs like an illusion.

She hesitates, then tosses Envy a cursory look of gratitude, then promptly looses her own arrow, which dices through the environment and blocks the shaft heading for Envy's sternum. The impact causes him to reel backward, his frame slamming into the trunk.

More arrows rain from the arcade. Sorrow spins out of a shaft's path, its tip stabbing a bough and flashing on impact, disappearing before she can get a close look at its element. However, from what she can tell, none of these weapons are crafted of moonstone. Therefore, these aren't the weapons of The Fate Court.

Arrows fly, vanishing after every hit and reappearing in quivers. It's a free-for-all, with the rapid fire of Anger and Love's iron, and the lash of Malice's wooden bow as he flings himself into the fray. Like a gymnast, Wonder loops in and out of the bracken while taking shots. Love vaults into the canopy faster than a missile, shooting and dodging strikes while airborne. Andrew plasters himself to a pillar while firing and seething, "Motherfuck!"

Yet it's nothing compared to the rage that skewers across his features when he notices Love in trouble, his crossbow stymieing a shaft barreling for her heart. Distracted by that, he fails to notice an arrow slicing his way until the last moment. At Love and Sorrow's combined shout, Andrew flings himself sideways and rolls across the ground. Sitting upright, his pewter eyes narrow as another projectile rips through the leaves, hell bent on his cranium.

Love drops from her vigil. Her booted feet smack the ground as she lands in front of her mate and swings her forearm, slapping the arrow out of the way. Andrew lunges upright, his irises glinting as she gives him a sidelong wink.

Merry's neon bow gleams through the murk, aiding in visibility. Anger wrests arrow after arrow from his quiver, the motions harsh enough to dislocate a shoulder.

Sorrow catapults to the right, leaping as an arrow whizzes beneath her. Mid-jump, she fires into the beeches. Seconds later, the ice shaft emerges back in her quiver.

There's no telling if her nemesis is down.

There's still no telling who the nemesis is.

Not until a figure hops from the bushes. At which point, Sorrow's reaction is immediate. Her fingers stall, her jaw plummets, and she's pretty sure her allies have similar responses.

The enemy is small and male. The enemy is leering. The enemy is a fucking child.

Another youth pops out from behind the first. Then another one emerges, prancing from the underbrush like a faerie. Then another, and another.

Five archers who can't be more than fifty years old. Two males, three females.

Of the latter, one mini-goddess has metallic hair, another exhibits shimmering tinsel irises, and another bears a cluster of stardusted freckles.

Of the male set, one has bronze skin and a defined jaw that will someday rival Envy's. Whereas the other wears a velvet robe and possesses lilac eyes with a serum threading along his lashes, akin to liquid eyeliner. The buoyant little shits brandish arrows wrought of gems, copper, and other things Sorrow's too dumbstruck to recognize. Clearly, none of the crew had registered the shafts' diminutive sizes, a rookie mistake that will humble them later.

A collective pause ensues. It's the reaction these children are hoping for. And shit. This is why Sorrow detected laughter by the pond.

Are these children fucking *playing*?

A very big maybe. She hasn't forgotten the distinctions between mortal youths and immortal ones. To say the least, her kind are sturdier during their upbringing, and their definition of fun has a sharper edge than that of humans.

It explains why Sorrow and her crew have been spotted so quickly. This part of the forest is tedious to traverse through, not to mention accessible from only a few paths. That's why it's unfrequented. And that's why their crew chose it.

It seems the children had been exploring. Sorrow doesn't recognize the group and can't tell what root emotions they represent. Not that everyone knows everyone personally in The Dark Fates.

In any case, it's possible the runts have no inkling they're facing eight outlawed archers. It's also possible that if they do know, they consider it a thrill rather than a dilemma. Or they don't give a shit either way.

The youths twirl like disks and leap back into the brush with more agility than a flock of gazelles, their creepy, menacing laughter trickling behind them. Echoes of mirth flit through the boughs, the silvery reverberation akin to wind chimes.

One. Two. Three.

Everyone disarms with a collective sigh.

Okay, not all of them disarm. And not all of them sigh.

Anger growls. Malice hisses. Andrew curses. And Envy does whatever the fuck Envy does.

In short, the males fail to pull themselves together, while the females inspect the vicinity with their weapons braced.

Anger's hoop earrings flash as he slams down his longbow, a sign that he's fuming beyond his quota. The rage god strides over to Merry and yanks her against him, clasping the goddess with a strength that would shatter mortal bones, but only causes his mate to gasp and drop her archery. She winds her arms around him, and they remain like that, Anger's territorial expression implying how hard he'll be snapping his cock into Merry later.

Without warning, and without brains, Love and Andrew do the same. The goddess abandons her weapons and jumps on him. He catches her against a body hewn from marble—physically he's one impressive human—the pair checking each other for bruises. Satisfied that the other is in one piece, their mouths crash together. Based on that ferocious kiss, if they were alone Love's skirt would be hiked around her naked hips by now.

Seriously? Malice and Wonder too?

By the time Sorrow glances their way, they've already puckered up. Wonder has vacated her branch and relinquished her longbow in favor of a smooch that's simultaneously vicious and possessive. Malice grasps the roots of Wonder's hair, and Wonder clutches his nape, the wildflower scars on her hands straining as she and her demon go at it. Their tongues wrestle so deeply, they must be licking each other's tonsils.

Although these embraces are sexy as hell, they're also unnerving. Affection is a contagion, each couple in attendance proving that when opposites attract, they turn stupid. It must suck to love someone that much, to become sick with worry, to become so protective it leads to foolish actions. It makes zero sense, this sentimental bullshit.

And yet. It's... nice to see them happy.

A piercing sensation assaults Sorrow's gut, the weight of Envy's gaze not helping matters. As someone who gets off on all things smutty, that he's not ogling the spectacle around them is a testament to the altitude at which he's hovering. The pre-sex fondling between each pair must be difficult to register from such an elevation.

However, that doesn't justify why he's fixating on Sorrow. A quick glimpse reveals his pupils flaring like storm clouds, the discovery producing a feverish itch across Sorrow's flesh. She clears her throat, then does it again.

Finally, the lovers untangle themselves.

Molars clenching, Anger swipes his bow off the ground and jabs it toward Sorrow's naked tits. "Do I want to know?"

"I couldn't sleep," she dismisses. "I went skinny dipping."

"And unfortunately, I went in the same direction," Envy remarks before jumping off his branch. "Alas, fate has a perverse sense of humor."

"Gracious, how romantic," Merry swoons. "A rendezvous in the midst of our quest. A secretive, unbridled moment between—"

"We should be so lucky, dearest," Wonder quips.

"Speak for yourself," Envy objects.

"It wasn't a booty call," Sorrow stresses. "It was the passionate equivalent of a fender bender."

Nonetheless, Wonder ceases listening. She tilts her head toward The Stars and consults their pulsating light as if something is hiding within the constellations.

Malice coils a lock of the goddess's hair around his finger. A raspy tenor slithers from his lips. "Hmm. If you ask me—"

"Only if we have a death wish," Anger bites out.

"—we should all be fighting with our cunts and cocks exposed. Imagine how much added destruction we could do if we fought like bare-assed heathens. I'd like to be a heathen for a day."

"As opposed to your angelic self?" Love quips, wiping dirt from her plumage.

"Tsk, tsk." Malice raises a digit, his taloned fingernail stabbing the air. "Didn't you know? Devils are wingless cherubs in disguise. It's the ones with feathers we need to be careful around."

Love narrows her maroon eyes. "I'll show you careful."

"I certainly hope you will. Now that I've been accepted into the crew, I'm having withdrawals from the lack of hostility."

"Guys," Andrew draws out while peering at the woods.

Wonder hands Malice his leather jacket. "Get dressed, Demon."

"Only this once, Wildflower." Dutifully, he thrusts his bare arms through the garment, the open flaps displaying more abs than a titan, then waggles his brows at Wonder, who suppresses a bashful grin.

"That goes for you as well," Anger barks at Sorrow, sweeping his hand up and down her form. "Do something about this situation."

"I second the motion," Envy says, a subtle bite to his tone.

"Guys," Andrew hisses, raising his bow.

What the hell is his problem? Sorrow would ask, but the way Envy grimaces at her breasts and pussy drives a knife through her tongue. "Aww, I'm sorry," she singsongs. "Are you prudes talking to me?"

"No, we're talking to the invisible goddess behind you," Anger grunts.

Envy puffs himself up like a thoroughbred, his chest expanding all over the forsaken place. "I'm no prude, I'm a whore. Get your facts straight. Now do as Papa Anger said and put on those drab, witchy clothes of yours." He gestures at her hair. "Without them, you look like a gray sewer rat."

"And you look like an asshole, dressed in the suit of a prick, with the grin of a dickhead," Sorrow compliments.

"That's more words than you've said in nearly three thousand years."

"And it's more words than you can spell."

"Make them stop," Wonder pleads to no one in particular.

"No!" Love objects. "Let them keep going. Look what's happening."

Happily, she indicates Anger, who scrubs his face in abject misery. Go figure, since the goddess has always enjoyed antagonizing him.

It would be effortless to point out how often Envy has relished tearing those "drab, witchy clothes" off Sorrow. But that would remind him of their affair, a bygone era she doesn't plan to reminisce about.

Sorrow snaps her fingers, a cloud of badass black instantaneously wrapping around her body, outfitting her in a vest, shredded skirt, and combat boots. Envy can think what he wants. She likes her style, and she doesn't need anybody's approval to wear—

"For fuck's sake," Andrew snarls while aiming at the forest. "Guys, tell me you know how things usually happen in threes."

When the crew squints, he elaborates. "In fiction—especially in fairytales—events occur in counts of three. Herons that come out of nowhere. Children who come out of nowhere."

"Clues in plain sight," Malice and Wonder interpret.

"I was going to say repetition," Andrew corrects. "Which implies foreshadowing."

"So?" Anger and Merry question.

"So while I'm shit at math, I have some practice writing fantasy. In which case, herons and children only count as two."

Alarm grips Love's features. In a flash, she follows his lead and nocks her longbow, along with Wonder and Sorrow.

"Let me put it another way," Andrew murmurs through his teeth. "Deities can't have kids. However, kids birthed from The Stars have mentors. Just a quick reminder of your own world-building."

Silence. Awareness. Idiocy.

Leave it to an erstwhile mortal who pens fiction to call their culture into question. Therefore, Andrew is the only one who hadn't let his tactical guard down, who'd pointed out the obvious. Their crew had been arguing like novices, when they should have been fleeing. Or at least targeting the woods.

The forest shifts in tandem to an army of swiftly moving bodies charging this way. Whether innocent or not, those children had been exploring the woods, toying with a band of insurgents. And like all youths, they do indeed have mentors.

Guardians who eventually go looking for them.

3

Sorrow

Which is why a longer, stronger, faster arrow shears in their direction. Skimming past Malice's head, it punctures a tree trunk, narrowly missing his intestines. Shit, they couldn't have picked a worse god to target.

With a roar, he barrels like a cannonball toward the foliage without knowing how many opponents await him. But unlike the Satanic demon, the rest of their crew focuses on the deities launching out of the bushes, swinging from the branches, and bounding across the canopy. With dexterity on their side, they single-handedly spiral down vines, somersault from trees, and spin around hedges.

Arrows of sapphire, mercury, and countless other elements lance across the sky. Trousers woven of moonrays. Gowns embroidered with starlight. Males and females with clips, wreaths, and beads shimmering in their hair.

Sorrow's unacquainted with this lot. Yet that doesn't stop them from recognizing the mutinous insubordinates who've defied their world and made enemies of their rulers. Despite their ability to each handle numerous combatants, their crew of eight is outnumbered by too many assailants.

Back-to-back, Malice and Wonder brawl with a stampede.

Love and Andrew dodge targets, vaulting around one another and firing.

Anger nocks three iron arrows and takes down a trio in unison, the velocity of his strike blowing them off their feet like bowling pins.

Merry combats half a dozen, taking them down with an apologetic look on her face.

Crimson splatters the grass. Howls of agony slice through the woods from where Malice had disappeared. Fates only knows what he's doing to his attackers, but considering the demon's penchant for violence, his victims will be lucky to retain their cartilage when he's finished with them. Anyone who targets Wonder, much less the crew, automatically moves to the top of his massacre list.

The bloody montage flashes before Sorrow's eyes. She twirls an arrow and lets it fly, then ducks a fist and rams her elbow into a male jaw, the impact crunching bone. The figure spins, several teeth popping from his mouth.

At the whistle of another arrow, she freezes. The shrill noise pierces the night, arching into the sky like... just like...

Prickles nip into Sorrow's flesh. Unbidden visions shred through her consciousness.

A grenade soaring. Exploding fireworks. Helmeted mortals.

Howling. So much howling.

A soldier caught in a barbed net, his lifeless body misshapen like a broken puppet. A vast, smoky field pitted with mines. Another man wailing, his stomach shredded, entrails spilling from his body.

Sorrow's pulse accelerates. It's always the same, always the same, always the same.

Oxygen saws through her lungs. Her temple pounds. She pans her head from side to side until the flashbacks dissipate, the ethereal forest coming into sharp relief.

Amid the tumult, her muscles scream. This is too much, and there are too many of them. And in spite of a deity's imperviousness to temperature, stress and exertion are exceptions, perspiration beading down her spine.

And Envy? He charges through a brook, his hair untethered and his clothes torn. Snatching Sorrow's hand on the way, he ignores her outraged protest and hollers for everyone to follow him. Otherwise at this rate, they'll run out of stamina.

Even Malice is sane enough to concur as he checks on Wonder, who scales another tree and hurdles through the woodland, racing parallel to him.

Andrew slams his mouth onto Love's, kissing her hard and swift before shoving the female away and shouting something. In response, Love nods and spreads her wings, then rockets into the treetops, her ascent ripping a hole in the canopy.

Like a pair of tornadoes, Andrew races beside Anger, both of them crashing through the brook behind Envy. The males exchange rapid glances, which Sorrow interprets as she yanks her hand from Envy's viselike grip. Their crew had plotted their course with diligence, then mapped out a clandestine route. The journey comprises uncharted passages to their destination, which is close enough that it shouldn't take ages to travel, but not too close that they can't rearrange their plan in case of an emergency.

From this woodland, the next part of their quest is supposed to be the mineral caves. Anger knows that geography, which drills through the valley bluffs to the other side. However with an army in pursuit, the trek will get more precarious. And while Anger would be able to lose them in the winding passages, this disarray runs the risk of their crew getting separated.

Anger nods at everyone, signaling a change of plans. Since this area is reachable via limited anonymous trails, including the one from which they'd come, as well as the one to which they'd been heading, there's not much of a chance their assailants journeyed by way of those outlets.

So they must have come from the only other option—the river. Which means they cruised here. And whereas one god knows the mineral caves, the other knows the waterways.

"Follow the brook!" Envy growls.

Sorrow takes up the rear while targeting their chasers. Except she yelps when a hand seizes the back of her vest and hauls her around. She barely has time to glare as Envy pushes her ahead of him, taking her place.

What the fuck? What's with the savior instincts?

She'd had backup under control, but there's no point in arguing unless she wants to slow them down. Their crew sprints out of the wild and tracks the brook into a misty passage, the eddies pouring into a canal. Walkways ornamented with scrolls thread around waterfalls and dense ferns.

They've gained a few leagues from the pack. Out of range, Envy breaks from the rear and bypasses everyone, leading them down a complex network of planks. At the end of one expanse, the sky broadens to a starlit horizon. The canal widens into a river, its surface reflecting constellations and moonlit cliffs.

Envy stalls at the ledge. Love lands beside Andrew, who hoists her against his chest. Wonder drops from the branches, only to gasp as Malice performs a similar alpha move. Merry skids a halt and—naturally—gets hauled into Anger's embrace.

Moored to the walkway, a vessel bobs like a cork in the water. It's shaped like a star, with a silver frame and a pole radiating light from its center. On the deck, a trapdoor leads to a lower compartment for weapon storage, feasibly empty since their enemies presently brandish archery.

Because most deities live on the coast, they often know how to sail, as mortals know how to drive. So yep, the opposition had coasted here. And unless they're cognizant of the other secret trails, the enemy will have to improvise and find another way back home. Either that, or swim.

Sorrow yelps as Envy flings her into the boat like a sack of grain, then jumps in beside her and spreads his arms to the rest of the onlookers. "What the fuck are you beautiful people waiting for?"

Everyone leaps in after him. When Envy touches the pole, it shudders and emits a white flame. Then they're off, the river drawing them in. The deities catch up, halting at the walkways. Blessedly, the little ones tuck themselves out of harm's way, having long deduced this isn't a game. Meanwhile, the elders draw and fire, arrows spitting into the horizon and plunging into the depths.

"Might want to hold on," Envy amplifies, then heaves on the pole.

The boat spins like a turntable, each revolution averting strikes and throwing everybody off balance. Righting themselves, each rebel claims a position along the vessel's circumference, nocking their bows and letting loose as they spin, every circuit blocking the attack.

Maybe it's the remnants of their previous existence as humans, but Malice and Andrew blanch as though their latest meal churns in their guts. The water jostles, creating waves that rock the vehicle. One of the male elders dives into the river, gaining on them as fast as a tidal wave.

Despite his equilibrium, Malice throws his legs over the side and hurls himself into the abyss.

"Malice!" Anger roars. "Get back here!"

"Pointless," Wonder shouts, ejecting a quartz arrow to defend her lover.

The devil's gilded head emerges, his arrow braced not three feet from the swimmer. Without pause, Malice shoots. The weapon detonates into his adversary's face, snapping the deity's neck with enough momentum to sever the head, pieces of his countenance exploding like shrapnel, the male's decapitated body floating across the surface.

Screams erupt from the pack. Blood paints the water, spreading into a crimson puddle.

By the time Malice flops back into the boat with crimson speckling his manic features, the swimmer's remains have been retrieved by one of his female companions. The vessel rounds the hip of a cliff and skims out of sight, livid bellows receding from earshot.

It's a shitty omen instead of a relief. Deities don't tire quickly, and after the rather messy crime Malice just committed, the legion may attempt to haul ass after the boat, purely out of rage. With enough ambition, they'll swim until convinced there's no chance of exacting retribution.

Or nature will randomly get in the way, as nature tends to do in any world.

After a dozen wheezing breaths, their crew slumps into a unified heap. Longbows clatter to the floor. In the dappled light, Wonder wipes the blood from her mate's face while he drags her onto his lap. Merry falls into Anger's flame-tattooed arms, which crush her to his frame. Love opens her mouth for Andrew's rasping kiss.

That is, until he lurches back. Keeling over the edge, the human pukes, the contents of his stomach splattering into the water.

"Andrew!" Love bleats, bending over him and rubbing his back.

"Fuck." Coughing, he gargles water, then slumps and gathers her to his chest. "I'm fine. Nothing a shitload of therapy won't fix when this is over."

Poor guy. As someone who's transitioned from mortality to immortality, he's been coping well up to this point. Routinely, the man's a force to be reckoned with amid deities. He's snarky, tenacious, and hardly the squeamish type, which Sorrow likes about him. But finding himself in this situation, fighting the same types of immortals he writes about from the safety of his office, has got to be traumatizing.

Everyone is waterlogged, the sea having sloshed across the boat. They're also worse for wear, riddled with abrasions, gashes, and bruises.

Anger groans, his shoulder slouching at an odd angle. One of the projectiles must have struck hard enough to dislocate the joint.

Merry waxes poetic about the injury while Envy squats next to Anger and mock flirts, "There, there, sexy god. Allow me to assist. You know, I'm an expert at playing nurse."

"No idea what Anger's supposed to do with that information, other than gag on it," Sorrow remarks.

Without sparing her a glance, Envy replies, "I'm sorry, was I speaking to you? Did I ask for your opinion?"

"I don't wait to be asked for my opinion."

Merry combs through Anger's dark mess of hair. "It's all right, my love. I'm here in your hour of need."

"Same," Envy teases. "Say the word, and Envy shall kiss it better. With Merry's consent, of course."

"For fuck's sake. Get away from him." Sorrow crawls over to the huddle and swats the pride god aside. "If I may."

Unlike Anger, who's too busy grunting, Merry takes that as a signal, burrowing closer to her soulmate in a gesture of support. Without cautioning the god, Sorrow positions his body and pops the shoulder back into its slot. Anger grits his teeth, a bellow scraping from his throat.

Sorrow wipes her hands. "You'll live."

"You call that proper first aid?" Envy laments. "What about TLC? Anger, don't you need TLC?"

"Fuck off," the rage god snarls. "And then go to hell."

"I'll come with you," Malice volunteers. "It'll be fun."

"Hey," Wonder lectures, elbowing him.

Malice nips her chin with his teeth, then swings his gaze to Anger. "Apologies, mate. I'll have to retract that. Can't leave my wildflower any more than you can leave yours."

As the lovers cling to one another, a covetous sensation pierces through Sorrow. She glances through her mop of wet hair, confirming Envy hasn't noticed her reaction. That's one fact to be grateful for.

The stars flicker, chipping away at the indigo sky, which will lighten into a mellow, lapis blue come dawn. That's how Wonder describes the firmament, in museful terms to the point where it has rubbed off on their crew. The goddess has a compulsive tendency to make everything sound like a marvel. That is, when her nose isn't wedged in a reference book, when she isn't staring off into the cosmos, or when she isn't being fucked by Malice.

Though currently, they've got other plans. Her curves fit snugly into his side, and while he fondles her hair, she closes her eyes and meditates.

Minutes lapse. The river calms down as the boat passes tufts of foliage germinating from the cliffside. Although the water's surface is as slick as grease, their drifting vessel creates rings that vibrate outward.

Sorrow wants to submerge her pinky and make the liquid dance. Instead, she catches herself absently checking the stock in her quiver. Not that her cache will suddenly change.

She'll always be one ice arrow short.

When she was young, she lost the projectile. Where, when, and how remains a mystery. And since weapons aren't to be handled lightly, deities can't conjure new ones, not as they can with food or certain inanimate objects. Although Sorrow has accepted the loss, she reassesses her archery occasionally, in case the lost arrow turns up by some miracle.

The weight of someone's attention plies her flesh with goosebumps. With her brow knitting, Sorrow glances over her shoulder, to where

Envy has resumed leaning indulgently against the pole. For certain, his star was feeling ambitious when it birthed him. The god is solid, built like a monolith despite his impractical outfits.

The instant she locates him, his head swerves from Sorrow's features to the distant bluffs.

"Curse them," Love mutters, breaking the intermission. "They'll tell The Fate Court."

"They'll order a hunt," Anger grumbles.

"They'll search high and low, leaving no stone unturned," Merry sighs.

"They'll torture us," Malice says with a haunted edge to his voice.

"They'll leave scars," Wonder predicts, her eyelids still sealed.

"Or they won't," another voice interjects.

Everyone except Wonder glances at Andrew. Tilting his head, the male considers his next words. "Sometimes in stories, and oftentimes in real life, a dumbass who's determined to prove himself takes matters into his own hands. Motivations inform each move a person makes. So what's the difference in this world? Probably not much. Who's to say those cocksuckers won't come after us themselves? Maybe they want to impress The Court. Everyone has a journey of their own, and everyone considers themself the hero."

That's not a half-baked idea. As a writer of spicy fantasy romance, Andrew possesses knowledge of human-fabricated mythology, the extent of which surpasses Sorrow and her crewmates. Perhaps it's because their kind have been too willfully ignorant, too arrogant to take the tales seriously. Yet these days, so much has happened to change their points of view.

"There's no telling what their desires are," Merry summarizes. "Or their hopes and dreams."

Wonder's bright green eyes open. "It could be a window made manifest. If they're the only ones chasing us, that buys us time to continue with our plan."

"Or this could be a different means to the same end," Anger counters, massaging his shoulder. "The Fate Court will eventually know we're here."

"Did anyone leave anything behind?" Envy asks.

Anything that will confirm who they are, as if those immortals don't already know.

Sorrow left her clothes at the campsite. However, since she isn't famous for her style, that's neither here nor there.

As for anything else? No. Before the attack, everyone had the presence of mind to grab whatever would identify them, a precaution before arming themselves.

Andrew had brought a notebook. Wonder had brought her corsage. Malice had brought his mouth.

Thus, all possessions are accounted for.

They'll have to draft a contingency plot, since their original route has been diverted. Although their crew had plotted an alternative before arriving in The Dark Fates, that's being second-guessed too. Meaning, they need a Plan C.

As their boat skates across the sea, each member falls into quiet contemplation. Andrew's fingers twitch. Malice notices and reaches into the breast pocket of his leather jacket, fishing out Andrew's notebook and pen. Malice must have been carrying those items since Andrew's black, high-collared jacket lacks secure compartments of its own.

Leaning over, Malice chucks the supplies onto Andrew's lap.

"Thanks," Andrew murmurs.

"Don't mention it," Malice replies.

Despite the human's original desire to maim the demon god, being mortals in their previous lives has forged a tentative bond between them. That, and their respect for the written word.

Andrew jots notes, but Love interrupts. She grabs the quill and writes a message to him, to which he grins, steals the pen from her fingers, and scribes his reply.

They do this while Wonder and Malice murmur theories to one another, citing research texts under their breaths.

Wrapped around each other, Anger and Merry doze in and out of consciousness.

The scrapes and contusions amid their crew will fade eventually, quicker than a mortal's wounds. All the same, some injuries never fully heal.

Sorrow examines the scars on Wonder's hands. Those markings won't go away, because they'd been too gravely delivered.

Envy fusses over his sodden shirt, pouting when he fails to remove yet another grass stain. What a fucking baby. He could conjure new clothes, if he's so dissatisfied with imperfection.

"See anything you like but can't have?" he drawls, the inquiry abrading Sorrow's flesh like sandpaper.

Checking to make sure their comrades aren't listening, she shrugs. "I see plenty I've had but didn't like."

Like a true pride god, Envy huffs. Disregarding the outfit, he twists toward the pole and steers the boat through a ravine in the cliffs. The edifices glisten with dew, vines crawling up the facades. Sorrow resumes blissfully ignoring him, though she has the urge to sink her teeth into something.

She knows this emotion. It's anger. It has to be.

Because it can't be sadness. Or worse, pain.

Of all people, she knows the difference.

4

Envy

The God of Envy likes three things, and only three things. Males, females, and fucking. The order or combination is irrelevant.

Ritualistic orgies. Experimental kinks. Unfiltered debauchery.

He's done and seen it all. Or rather, Envy once thought he had until stumbling into uncharted, perverted, raunchy territory with a goddess wearing grim-reaper black, her hair and lips pigmented in a melancholy shade.

Envy has never liked gray. Putting it mildly, it's the dullest, drabbest color in existence, the shade of illness and depression. Crying fits and funeral homes come to mind, among other unpleasantries.

Anyway, he hasn't been able to explain himself since the goddess first became a sexual reality. Sorrow may be one-fifth of the most elite crew in history, yet that hardly exonerates her gritty attitude, horrendous fashion choices, or repugnance for the pleasures of life. Stars above, he's never even seen the female enjoy a fucking glass of bubbly.

After every orgasm in his company, she would mope instead of luxuriating in the aftermath. To this day, Envy finds the notion offensive.

There must be something wrong with her libido, because the remorse sure as shit isn't his dick's fault.

In any event, she's Sorrow... *Sorrow.* Neither her origins as a goddess, nor her former status as his consort, excuse Envy for degrading himself with the likes of this female. At some deranged point during millennia of mutual bullying, he tumbled off his high horse, and he'd fucking liked his high horse.

Fates forbid. He'd pounded his exquisite cock into her. Numerous times, in numerous ways, with numerous regrets.

Standing at the nexus of the boat, Envy grunts. No one notices, which miffs him, but so be it. There's no reason to sulk. None whatsoever. He might not have the adaptability of Andrew, but thankfully Envy lacks the short fuse of Anger and the volatility of Malice. Scowl lines on a pretty face are a travesty.

A pair of shimmering bluffs rises on either side as the boat floats down a ravine. Vegetation encrusts the edifices, trimming them in leafy shingles. When the canal forks, Envy twists the pole and steers it down the southern passage, beyond which a third summit looms, its range knifing toward the constellations.

It's refreshing to navigate these waters again. As a youth, and during his intermissions from the mortal realm, he spent his free time enjoying the rivers of this land, learning every secret route and shortcut.

One enclave in particular. To get there, he'd pilot a boat similar to this one, albeit slimmer and smaller.

Whereas Anger prefers the confined fluxes of mineral caves to alleviate his temperamental fits, Envy prefers even deeper recesses. No, it's not his passion. He simply appreciates the water, as he appreciates a fine suit, the wet and willing grip of a pussy, and the sight of a hot masculine jawline. So long as the latter doesn't belong to a face more handsome than his own.

He also enjoys living forever. The privilege has endless perks. For instance, the longer he's alive, the more people get to luxuriate in his good looks, the more widespread admiration he receives, and the more sexual partners he gets to steal from their so-called soulmates.

Fine, then. He might like more than three things.

"Someone tell Narcissus we'd like to know where he's taking us," Sorrow baits.

"I'm impressed," Envy drawls without glancing her way. "You lasted five minutes before seeking me out. That's a celestial record. Only leave the rest of this crew out of your agenda. If they have a request from me, they can speak for themselves."

From her end of the conveyance, Sorrow's tongue lashes like a whip. "Okay asshole, let's get one thing straight—"

"One thing, eh? Can you manage that number?"

"I'd rather hump a reptile than impress you."

"Yet you've given thought to my mythical equivalent," Envy goads. "Narcissus, was it? And now I'm appalled. That mortal concoction doesn't hold a candle to me. Andrew can vouch for this fact."

"Leave me the fuck out of this," the human grunts from beside Love.

"Whatever," Envy dismisses, flapping his hand. "At least compare Yours Truly to the weaving queen, Athena, for textile reasons."

"Fictional or not, I make it a habit of never insulting a respectable goddess," Sorrow fires back. "Especially not on your behalf. Not everyone is destined to perform at your beck and call. Furthermore—"

"Fuck's sake," Malice groans, head resting against the hull. "Anger, shut them up before I do."

"Enough," the rage god snaps with impatience. "You've made your points, however self-serving."

"We're deities." Envy makes an inflated sound. "It's in our nature to be self-serving."

"Is it in your nature to conduct yourself like a three hundred year-old?" Wonder upbraids.

"Narcissus isn't entirely a bad comparison," Merry buffers, glancing between Envy and Sorrow with a hopeful—i.e. pointless—gleam in her eyes. "Only the most distinguished figures are compared to Greek myths. I've heard it's a great compliment to bestow."

"No, you haven't," Anger says with affection.

"No, I haven't," Merry confirms dolefully, sagging into him.

Love prunes her lips. "If anyone ever calls me Eros, I'll skewer them."

"You shouldn't," Andrew murmurs. "You're subverting the myth with your badassery. Goddesses in those tales didn't have much autonomy. They were tools to further the hero's journey."

"I'd rather be Love. Not someone else."

A sexy grin slides across Andrew's face. "I've got no problem with that either."

"Please don't start humping," Sorrow begs. "We're running for our lives. And anyway, I'm sitting right here. Moreover, it's bad luck on this turf."

Shortly following her birth, Merry was ostracized from The Dark Fates. She hasn't returned until now and looks quite panicked. "You mean lovemaking is banned here?"

"She's lying, dearest," Wonder reassures her while nestling into Malice. "It's a ruse to discourage public displays while in Sorrow's company."

"So the hell what? Why would we care if fucking in public was forbidden?" Malice asks. "What are they going to do? Banish us?" He taps his chin in mock thought. "Oh, wait. They've already done th—"

Wonder grabs Malice's face and pries his lips open with her own, sucking the demon into a subterranean kiss that silences him. Tongues flex. Mouths rock. A low growl claws up the male's throat as his goddess pulls away, elated by the glazed look on his face.

Adjusting the corsage around her wrist, Wonder pats the lavender tulle of Merry's dress. "There, you see? Show all the devotion you want."

Territorial Anger tugs Merry closer to him. "Gladly. Once we're out of harm's way."

"Then you'll be waiting a long time, mate," Malice counters, his tone husky.

Andrew crooks an eyebrow. "Define 'long' in immortal terms."

Everyone contemplates, returning to the matter at hand. The original plan had been set into motion when they trespassed into The Dark Fates from the mortal realm. Or actually, it had started earlier. In a handful of years, a shitstorm has transpired. For this trio of couples—Love and Andrew, Anger and Merry, Wonder and Malice—it's a complicated, interconnected story across the board. But ultimately, they have each proven certain deities can feel love.

While their kind consider sentimentality a weakness, Envy's peers beg to differ. They would say love has strengthened them. Their romances led to this crusade, the fight for a balance between fate and free will, an equality between deities and humanity. They've been gathering allies in The Celestial City—the human metropolis where immortal outcasts live—in addition to the ones who revolted from The Dark Fates after being inspired by each star-crossed tale.

The plot had been to trespass into The Dark Fates and prepare for conflict. Despite having allies on standby in the mortal realm, ready to journey here upon the first call, this crew is low on numbers. Nevertheless, they'd chosen a location that offers an advantage in battle.

This, assuming Envy and Sorrow are too entitled to play their parts in this quest. Indeed. That's the only condition Envy has opinions about. Recently, Wonder and Malice uncovered a means to defeat the opposition.

A legend. One with a fucked-up sense of humor.

If two deities choose love over lust, they'll become a force of influence, along with those closest to them.

Because several prior legends played roles in uniting the other couples, this deluded crew has concluded Envy and Sorrow are the remaining match. If they become something official to each other, it will be the final confirmation that all deities are capable of experiencing love. Thus, their people will change. They will recognize they're more like humans than any of them had assumed, that humans deserve a fairer balance of power. Hence, the equilibrium between fate and free will.

Ugh. Kill him now.

If someone had replaced Envy's wardrobe with rags, he would have been less offended. If he had woken up a week ago with his asshole sewn shut, he would have been less surprised. If he had been force-fed a wad of excrement, he'd have been less disgusted.

And yes, he's being hyperbolic. It's a habit he's picked up from Merry.

In any case, this cursed legend is the last solution Envy had expected. Compared to achieving the impossible, he'd have an easier time digesting a gallon of poison. What do he and Sorrow have in common, other than genital compatibility?

That argument is enough. However, his ribs clench. Indeed, there is one other pivotal reason nothing can happen between them. A bit of wisdom the goddess doesn't know about, even though she has every right to.

Nonetheless, the goddess had been the first to concur with Envy on their unsuitability. Since they can't be compelled to feel things they don't—yes, they're aware of the irony—this crew has cobbled together an alternative.

Cue this mission.

Motes drift through the atmosphere, the sight fascinating Andrew.

"The air smells different here," he intones to Love. "And the texture, the pigments, the light."

"Dust in this realm has the iridescence of gemstones," she whispers. "Try and catch one with your tongue, and it will taste like a fresh snowflake."

"I'd rather taste you."

Under her breath, Sorrow grouches to herself. Meanwhile, Anger grins at the marveled expression on Merry's profile, her avid features soaking in the setting.

And fucking fine. Envy *might* be peeking in Sorrow's general direction whenever she's not paying him notice.

As such, he catches the goddess tilting her head. "This place must be a stunner to someone who grew up thinking magic existed only in books."

"It's mesmerizing," Andrew replies. "Or mostly it is."

"Mostly?" his provoked audience repeats in union.

"Mostly," he echoes with an amused quirk of the lips. "I'd still say magic is everywhere. In my world and yours. They're just different shades of the same thing."

Envy's flummoxed. Yet Sorrow nods like she understands better than he does, as if he's ignorant.

Inadequacy pinches his flesh. What the hell exactly does she understand?

"Your confidence puts us to shame," Anger compliments.

But Andrew flashes a wry grin. "Why wouldn't I be confident?" He gestures toward Anger. "Just because I'm surrounded by a broody alpha with a sharper jawline than any of my characters." Then he motions to Malice. "Another god with the smirk of a shadow-daddy serial killer." Then he waves at Envy. "And a god who looks like he stumbled off a catwalk."

Clearly, this hunky specimen doesn't give himself sufficient credit. If Andrew were unattached, and if partners with testosterone did it for the man, Envy would have jumped Andrew's toned ass long ago. Well acquainted with male-on-male rapture, Envy suspects the man's tongue tastes like aged wine—rich and flavorful. To say nothing of his human cock and the savory strings of cum that would pour from the crown.

All right. Perhaps Love once shared this tidbit with Envy over a bottle of cabernet. In any case, it confirms what Envy had already guessed.

He loses track of time, as do the rest of them, silent deliberation lulling the group into reluctant slumber. Envy refuses to rest, dismissing Anger's offer to steer. For once, he wants to be the leader, guiding them where they need to go.

From a brook, to a canal, to a river. The passage expands, changing flow and depth. The mellow tide licks the boat's hull, the sound hypnotic. It drowns out his thoughts for a while, until a splash snaps him out of the haze.

Envy's head loops towards the disturbance. A slender finger dips into the water, creating rings that dance outward and spread like a contagion. With the skirt fanning out, Sorrow steeples her limbs and hooks one arm around her knees as she toys with the water. The action makes her look younger, which resurrects memories of their upbringing, which also resurrects a particular incident in their past.

Words sharper than chips of glass. The sort that forms scars.

An ugly god is easy to spot.

Condemnation. Like a flea, Envy shakes off the recollection.

Earlier, he'd spied on Sorrow as she counted the arrows in her quiver. He knows why, as they all do. Though Envy might grasp more about her lost arrow than everyone in this boat.

What would Sorrow say if he told her?

The wind teases her hair, concealing half of the goddess's countenance. Absently, he leans over to get a better look. When that fails to expose more of her features, the effort produces a disturbing crick in his neck.

Goddammit. Why does he always do this? Either this female has cast a toxic spell on him, or he has an obsessive staring problem. Despite having objectified Andrew earlier, this goddess is the sole reason Envy wouldn't actually jump that human, even if Andrew were unattached. For the life of Envy, he can't stop staring at Sorrow, interacting with this female, and claiming things from her that don't belong to him.

Him, a god who's never had difficulty turning the other way first, leaving every deity in his path frothing at the mouth. For some misbegotten reason, this goddess has robbed him of that ability. And he hates her for it.

"Narcissus loves the water," she muses, her tone as weightless as chiffon, unlike the customarily burlap scrape of her voice.

The delicate sound is foreign to Envy's ears, stupefying to the point where he loses track of the subject. "Who?"

Abruptly, Sorrow grunts. "Stars. Forget it. You're hopeless."

He's *what*?

While Envy searches high and low for a witty comeback, she continues agitating the water's surface. "He was the son of a river god and a nymph. Everyone worshipped his perfect looks and wanted a piece of the pie, but that only made him scorn them."

"I know who Narcissus is," he murmurs. "The assessment sounds only half accurate. I lap up admiration with a spoon."

"Are you saying you're not the least bit vexed that deities are merely interested in your cheekbones? That's all you want to be known and appreciated for?"

"I flatter myself on being a connoisseur of envy. As such, I'd say you're jealous because our people never looked at you with the same ravenous inclinations."

Her finger pauses, then vacates the river. She swivels his way, wiping those unkempt tresses from her face. "No. What I want is for others to look at me and see the truth, not some flamboyant charade. I don't have to pretend for anyone."

Discomfort gnaws on Envy's skin. He abandons his lazy sprawl against the pole, stalks across the deck, and squats before her. "So what makes you such an expert on Andrew's subtext?"

The goddess's lips quirk. "Aww, poor wittle gawd. I wasn't aware that his speech about magic was subtext. Or do you need the gist spelled out for you?"

"Frankly honey, I hardly need you to translate for me. Your mumbling and grumbling, moaning and groaning, cursing and whining, has always been tedious enough to comprehend."

As quick as switchblade, Sorrow flips him her middle digit, the fingernail glossed in the same ominous shade as her lips. "Can you comprehend this, motherfucker?"

Envy chuckles without humor. "You lack originality, not to mention makeup that suits your skin tone."

"Now that you've listed your priorities in a mate, we can rest easy. Our chemistry, or lack thereof, is evidence that this legend is bogus. I'm condescending, crude, and gruff. I don't blush. I don't pine. And I don't mourn the loss of your dick, much less the flash of your pearly whites." Leaning forward, she hisses in his face. "Make no mistake, I tick none of your boxes, and I'm positive you wouldn't even know what my own boxes are."

His retinas crackle like something that's been set on the burner for too long. "Oh, I've located a couple of them."

To his annoyance, she rolls her fucking eyes. "I repeat, I don't blush."

Envy's lips curl. Challenge accepted.

5

Envy

It's a three-step process. To start, his gaze slides to the flecks shimmering beneath her lower lashes, as if she's been weeping stars for an eternity. Then he proceeds to the tear-colored irises. Lastly, he draws out the next words, wedging every syllable into the space between them. "But you still break, don't you? Sad little goddess."

Sorrow flinches. Her eyebrows crimp as if that final part has struck true, though it lasts only a second. Because that's the thing about a trauma goddess. She knows how to recover from a sucker punch.

"You're bitter that I understood Andrew while you didn't," she translates. "You hate being left out, because you want to be taken seriously even though you've got nothing to show for yourself but a glass arrow, a hidden inferiority complex, and a fancy wardrobe that any of us can conjure. That's the extent of your breakage. That's as much as you know about being in pain."

Fuck this. And fuck her.

"You're one to talk," Envy sneers through his teeth. "You wouldn't recognize the opposite of pain if it nibbled on your clit. If I know nothing about anguish, then you know even less about pleasure. Fess up, Goddess of Sorrow. You're a black cloud and a pessimistic killjoy."

For a second, her pupils tremble like thawed ice, and her lips clamp shut.

Shit. Envy hesitates, because why the fuck does it bother him to see that reaction? Worse, to know he's the cause?

It's such a candid reaction that Envy forgets to congratulate himself on the retort, which had come out harsher than he'd intended. And louder. So loud that they could have been overheard in a soundproof room. Loud enough to yank everyone out of their sleep, causing them to gawk in his direction.

Usually, Envy likes being a centerpiece. But not at this moment. Fates almighty, this female has a talent for making the spotlight a regrettable experience.

"Have we interrupted a lover's quarrel?" Merry yawns.

"Seems to me, we interrupted a potential homicide," Malice contests. "Or a dark porno. Or a homicide that segues into a dark porno."

"You interrupted nothing, because there's nothing here," Sorrow vents, gesturing between herself and Envy. "So for the last time, stop getting your hopes up."

"Precisely," Envy concurs. "Look, tropes are fine. I have nothing against forbidden love—" he indicates Love and Andrew, "or unrequited pining and betrayal—," he flicks his wrist toward Anger and Merry, "—or enemies-to-lovers," he gestures to Wonder and Malice. "I don't mind, especially if I'm reading erotica. But if you're spoiling for a marriage of convenience, you've got the wrong deities."

"Courtship of convenience," Andrew corrects.

"Is that a trope?" Merry inquires.

"It's bullshit, is what it is," Sorrow summarizes, her pupils hardening into stones, and the jaded tilt of her lips ascending higher up her face.

Envy rises and straightens his ensemble, which is now dry. All the same, it takes more effort than he'd like to manipulate his features and toss an indifferent look Sorrow's way. Such an irregularity, when he's spent his existence perfecting whatever expression benefitted him. This skill is supposed to come naturally, as it has in the past. He's rarely had to work at subterfuge before.

So in what universe is this suddenly a challenge? And why with her?

Again, that unbidden memory surges to the forefront. A target range and countless witnesses observing Envy flat on his back while a feminine shadow leans over him and speaks under her antagonistic breath. He recalls how the words ground into his psyche and stung his flesh with humiliation.

An ugly god is easy to spot.

Envy leaches the corrosive vision from his mind. Sorrow's opinion has never mattered. Growing up, the surly bitch had been a thorn in his side, as unattractive as her funeral-inspired wardrobe. That's all.

Later—much later—only the decibel of her moans while he pistoned his cock into her held any magnitude. They'd had their fun, her pussy clutching him while they came hard, long, and frequently. The cantankerous goddess had been a conquest, the victory of which he'd repeatedly applauded himself. Not that Envy had doubted his prowess, but he deserves the gaudiest, most ostentatious trophy for bedding Sorrow.

Actually, never mind the trophy. He's earned a crown inlaid with diamonds for splitting her thighs as wide as he had. At least, before inevitably coming to his senses.

As for Sorrow's judgements, viewpoints, reactions, impressions, assumptions, lamentations, and whatever the fuck else he's forgetting to include, it's still immaterial.

Isn't it? Why should any of the nonsense that drips from her mouth with the slow regularity of a leaky faucet bother him?

To the pond, he'd pursued her. Sleeping amid infernal nature had kept Envy awake. When he'd noted Sorrow's absence, two reactions played a tug-of-war, one visceral, the other logical. Either she'd been kidnapped by the enemy, or she went on a private quest, for secret reasons.

Envy hadn't cared for those prospects. The notion of her as a prisoner or a traitor. Either would result in him tearing her captors to shreds or tearing Sorrow to shreds.

Blessedly, his concerns were futile. As usual with her, Envy had overreacted, choosing dramatics over rationality. This became apparent as he went hunting after Sorrow, seeking a glimpse of that bleak hair color, the lingering scent of black tea, smoke, and violet guiding him.

His excuse about visiting the pond, intending to self-medicate his stress with a dose of masturbatory bliss, had been a lie. He'd located Sorrow around the same time he noted a shift in the wind, along with rifts in the brambles.

Already, Envy had sensed an intrusive presence nearby. He should have known it wasn't coming from her, but then this goddess has a nasty habit of redirecting his brain to less productive thoughts. So instead, he chalked up the disturbance to mutual discord, the residue of their animosity lingering.

But why Envy remained to watch the goddess swim remains a mystery. Had he been worried for her? Protective of her? Fuck no. Sorrow can take care of herself.

Perhaps Envy had wanted to ridicule the female for being careless. And maybe spy a little. Just a little, to see what she does when she's by herself.

He'd expected to find Sorrow howling at the moon or engaging in some other cliché. But he hadn't expected to find the goddess swimming buck naked like a dark siren, her thighs spreading with the sort of rhythmic prowess that dredged up more impure thoughts than his cock could handle.

Sorrow, swimming? Enjoying herself? Since when?

The second phenomenon Envy had endured was a demotion of sorts. For the first time in his life, he'd acted like a territorial brute, charging into a female's personal space without being invited. He's unaccustomed to intruding on his conquests. His lovers have only ever flocked to him like pixies in heat. All Envy's ever had to do was stand by and wait.

He has never been unwelcome. He has never felt so thoroughly unwanted. He has never felt the bite of it.

The boat jostles. Where the fuck are they going anyway?

Ahead, the cliffs spread out. Out of nowhere, the river yanks on the boat, the pole spurting white flame. Motes flash through the air, indicating a rushing current.

The summit widens, closer than before. Water expands like a gasping lung, hurling a wet sheet at them, which lands with a vicious smack and drenches the crew. In unison, they veer toward the incoming chaos.

The stars glitter as if disappointed in Envy. Not only should he behave better, but while his comrades were resting, he should have paid attention.

He should have fucking remembered. Rivers have rapids.

6

Envy

No. Fucking. Way.

Masculine shouts erupt as the river swallows their boat. The females are the only industrious occupants, seizing the ends of the star-shaped vessel and fighting to steer it forward.

While that should be Envy's job, he's too busy staring. White fire shoots from the pole, tongues of light thrashing against the sky. The universe explodes into a tempest of sound, sound, sound. Obscenities and bellows from the crew, plus a great lashing roar from the river. Towering walls of fluid strike the boat, shoving them off-route, only for the transport to collide with another curling wave, which flings them in the opposite direction. Water thrashes over the side, dousing everyone and flooding the deck.

The world spins in a vortex, a blur of staggering bodies, raging seascapes, and jagged cliffs. Envy's vision goes rogue, producing a collage of unsteady images. Everything veers from side to side in an erratic mutiny of motion.

Mist sprays his neck. Foam slides down his arms. Liquid clogs his throat.

The rapids snatch the vessel and give a forceful yank, tossing them one way and then another, then another, then another. The boat tilts at an incline, lifts out of the water, rides the tail of a star-spangled wave, and plunges into the brewing flux.

While the females try maneuvering the vessel, the males fight to keep everyone's weapons from disappearing over the rim. Arrows, longbows, and quivers scatter, slick and impossible to grab. Anger dives to catch shafts of iron, then neon. Andrew crushes someone's archery against his chest, wrestling to hold on. Malice hurls several quivers over his shoulder.

Whipping open the lower compartment, Envy hollers for them to dump the weapons inside. Stumbling across the deck, they secure the items into the cubicle. All except for Love, Sorrow, and Envy's archery because the fucking rapids are too powerful.

The goddesses stand vigil at their respective ends of the conveyance. Together, they heave on the vessel, steering without knowing their orientation.

Sorrow bellows something, but the crash of breakers against the bluffs drowns out the words. Everybody careens, grappling to stay balanced. Immortals can last for a while, submerged without oxygen. But not forever. And that's assuming the looming cliffs don't flatten them like crepes before then.

A blotted silhouette traverses the divide. Sloshing through the water, the figure draws near and cuffs Envy upside the head, knocking him out of his stupor.

"What the fuck's wrong with you?" Sorrow spews. "Get your ethereal ass in gear!"

With a backhanded swat of his arm, Envy knocks the harpy goddess aside. "Then kindly move out of my way."

As their transport crashes down the river, he snares the pole and executes a deft twist. They dodge a wave, Envy driving the boat through the turbulence. Up ahead, the range swells larger, closer. Just then, a scanty weight barrels into his side, hauling him off balance. His back rams into the floor as a lanky body lands on top, her sodden thighs astride his waist. Between the seaweed of her hair, Sorrow's silver eyes pop out at Envy, the pupils flashing in exasperation. Simultaneously, their heads swing toward the pole, where an ice arrow has lodged itself.

Shit. The waves must have caused the boat to launch a few renegade projectiles that escaped her quiver. If Sorrow hadn't seen it happen, his head might be a pincushion by now. She doesn't look interested in his gratitude, doesn't act like it either when she fists his shirt collar and drags him upright. Tottering to her feet, she darts back to her position without a backward glance.

Envy lets the mortification roll off his shoulders and resumes his grasp on the pole. Dawn leaks into the firmament, slathering the canopy in lapis lazuli. This conflict becomes a push and pull, a battle without an ending.

Envy's muscles contract as he manipulates the forsaken pole. "Bear north!"

The females grasp and exert pressure on the transport's edges—a less common way to steer—whirling them out of harm's way, then skating another onslaught. The river splits, one route spilling toward the summit and an abutting shoreline, the other extending toward a colony of homes on stilts.

The residences of their people. A guaranteed path to imprisonment, if not death.

Envy opens his mouth to howl another command, but a vicious sheet of water slams into the boat. Then another belt of liquid whips through the air, slams into the stomach of a passenger, and launches the body overboard like a ragdoll.

Like it weighs nothing. Like it means nothing.

Love screeches, Wonder gives a cry, and Merry bawls the figure's name.

Andrew storms into motion, Malice jets forward as well, and Anger thrusts out his arms. All three males snatch their mates, dragging the goddesses backward and preventing them from being saviors. The females keep shouting a name, the moniker swallowed by the rapids. Yet Envy doesn't require silence to hear.

He knows who they're calling out for. He knows who went over.

The boat thrashes in the wrong trajectory. Correction, in the *very* fucking wrong direction. His head dices between one route and the other, eyes cutting from the crew to the sinking puddle.

It'll be okay. She'll be okay.

She knows how to swim. She'll live, and they'll find her later. She'll live, she'll live, she'll—

"Motherfuck!" Envy gives a final jerk on the pole, veering the boat off course.

Then he releases the shaft. Then he mutters another oath.

Then he stalks to the nearest ledge. Then he fucking dives.

The depth snatches his limbs, consuming him whole. A funnel sucks him down, plugging his ears and battering his clothes.

His clothes, which are ruined. He will blame her for this. He will blame that goddess for forcing him to abandon their crew, not to mention his weaponry, the latter of which will likely go overboard.

Yes, he'll do a thorough job condemning that spitfire. Meanwhile, she won't give a shit.

Too bad, because he'll make her give a shit. That will become his life's purpose.

Envy pumps his limbs, descending into an abyss void of sounds and smells. Down here, it's all satiny texture and metallic tastes.

Those sensory details, in addition to sight. Underwater plants glint like rubies. A flash of multicolored, serpentine scales ripple past him.

Diaphanous fins flap through beams of starlight.

Envy floats in place. His gaze skewers through the deep, dashing here and there, hunting for unmistakable traces. The shredded skirt, bloated from the current. Those boots, scuffed and old because she refuses to enchant new ones. The vest, accented with a stitching needle, a tool not meant for sewing but mending gashes.

If she were as flexible as Wonder, as spry as Love, or as alert as Merry, this wouldn't have happened. He wouldn't be down here, with bubbles spurting from his goddamn nose and his mane a nest of knots.

Envy's shoes stifle his progress. Fumbling, he wrenches them off seconds before a wave pounds into him. The impact blasts his body backward, pain detonating beneath his ribs. Groaning, he clutches his throbbing side and kicks his legs.

Why, why, *why*? Why the fuck did he jump?

The goddess would agree, this crew needs Envy more. Yet his gaze scours the murky depths, swerving left to right before landing on a shape floating nearby. Like an eel, the slender female glides his way in a swirl of black. The more distance she covers, the deeper her victorious leer gets.

She's in one piece. She's fine.

Whereas he's a foolish bastard for thinking otherwise. Smarting from his wound, Envy growls. Foam spills from his mouth, which only intensifies that feminine smirk.

But no, it's not a smirk. It's a wince.

And she isn't gliding, she's paddling. Her arms toil, wrestling the current to her last, stubborn breath, and her ice weapons are nowhere to be seen. The rapids must have consumed them.

Abreast of him, Sorrow's joints give. She droops and goes limp like a drowning star.

Envy catches that drowning star before it sinks. His wounded side cramps, protesting her weight, but there's nothing for it. Hefting the female onto his back and linking her arms over his shoulders, he shoots upward.

Breaking the surface, Envy wheezes for air, which magnifies his injury. Blinking the water out of his face, he searches for their transport, but it's gone.

All he sees is a coastline. And the homes of their enemies.

7

Sorrow

There's something very, very, *very* peculiar about the way she wakes up. To start, she's surrounded by water. With her eyelids welded shut, Sorrow registers fluid licking her lips, the taste as pure as melted crystals. Liquid swabs her back and calves, producing a gentle lapping sound. Either she's drooling profusely or engulfed within a deep, dark tank.

Also, she's not alone.

Not entirely unrealistic since Sorrow has always woken up alone. Solitude is her default even after engaging with a lover, the number of which clocks in at a resounding twelve. Though, only one stands out. And he never spent the night, never fell asleep with her, because she hadn't allowed it.

Regardless, someone is here with Sorrow. That someone huffs and puffs like a cranky son of a bitch. That someone is moving beneath her. And that someone reeks of pretension.

Sorrow's body slumps over an expanse of muscles that bend rhythmically against her cheek. The figure moves swiftly while shaving through the water, dipping and rising at a pace equally frantic and effortless. Under her, it's all sleek planes and iconic speed.

Fuck. This had better be some glorious great white shark with hero impulses bearing her weight. It had better not be who she thinks—

"Get your foot off my thigh," a baritone voice pants. "You're pushing us down."

"Mmmph," she grunts.

This inspires a reluctant chuckle from her companion. "Unbelievable."

That voice oozes down her ears like candle wax, hot and slow. Not that she has experience with temperature, but Sorrow has lived in proximity to humans long enough to get an idea. Also, this prick has the unnerving knack for making something like heat manifest, as if he's learned to produce his own immortal form of warmth.

She wouldn't put it past him. He doesn't enjoy being left out of anything, including human capabilities that deities lack.

But seriously, why does his exhaustion have to sound obscenely sexy? Because he's a spoiled brat blessed with more attributes than he deserves. And because, as mortals would say, her eternal life sucks. That's why.

Nevertheless, Sorrow musters her strength and complies with the request. Her body is plastered like a starfish to her rescuer, both arms hooked around a solid throat that swallows hard.

No, she's not riding on the spine of a celestial shark. This is a godly form. Unfortunately, it's a familiar one. Even if he hadn't spoken up, Sorrow knows how he moves, knows the cadence of him, knows the sound of this male breathless, tireless, relentless. He's made these noises before—above her, beneath her, behind her, inside her. Except those lapses of sanity had been accompanied by his hands pinning her wrists above her head and his hips lunging between her shaking thighs. Also, the noises had been wracked with pleasure instead of exhaustion.

What's happening? Why is Envy swimming with her on his back? Why had he sounded panicked when he told Sorrow to get her foot off his thigh?

It had been a simple request. And Envy never panics.

She'd love to open her eyes and tell him where exactly she'd like to plant her foot, however her mouth can't move. What's more, every bone and muscle slumps like a curtain, her body drained of energy down to the atom. Finally, she recalls the reason.

The boat. The rapids. The wipeout.

Sorrow replays the scene, how a raging tide had sent her overboard, along with her weapons. The world had capsized as she'd plunged into the depths. Initially, shock had locked her joints, the realization paralyzing her.

After that, Sorrow had pulled herself together, only for a funnel of water to snatch her, the onslaught clogging her nostrils as if ejected from a syringe. The accident had turned into an underwater combat, with her flailing and the river punching back. She'd scrambled against its grasp, flinging her arms and kicking her limbs. Her teeth had clenched as she fought against the vacuum. Yet the more she did so, the more salvation receded.

As they had in the valley, memories had infested the final vestiges of awareness. Human soldiers screaming, mortal bodies dropping like flies, her arrows failing to strike them in time.

Hospital tents. Severed limbs. Cots soaked in blood.

While submerged, Sorrow had slapped at the water, fighting to outswim the nightmares. At some point, her lungs inevitably gave out. Towed under, she lost her archery to the abyss, and her vision blackened, the loss of consciousness a blessing and a curse.

Yet before that happened, she'd spotted a figure in the distance. In that brief window between survival and defeat, visibility had narrowed to a masculine silhouette, as luminous as a pinprick of light.

Like a flashing star.

Envy must have jumped into the river to save her. Sorrow loathes the idea of him playing the valiant knight, but she's not too proud to be grateful. All the same, she's awful at expressing thanks, so her tongue flops around in her mouth, fumbling for something indebted to say.

By the way, why is he buckling? And did she just detect a hiss of pain?

While struggling to split her eyes open, Sorrow relies on sensations. They've escaped the rapids, since these waters are calm. Likewise, she notes the current's direction, then compares it with his trajectory and mumbles against his nape, "You'll wear yourself out like this."

"Quiet," he seethes.

"Why? What's your problem?"

"Silence, Nymph. Or they'll hear us."

That does it. Sorrow's eyes blast open, the universe flooding her vision with the silvery white of morning stars. Her wide gaze darts from the glossy sea, to the wet layers of Envy's mane, to the landscape at their right.

Fear splashes into her chest. "What the fuc—"

Envy reaches behind, his flat palm clapping over her mouth. Quick thinking but suddenly unnecessary. She's not about to protest when she's indisposed, hyperventilating into his hand.

A smooth coin of water envelopes them, with fringed trees sprouting from the surface, their roots feeding off the sand. Ahead, a network of boardwalks and piers stretch along the shoreline, each platform crisscrossing in various directions. In the distance, a fog-laced harbor docks ancient sailboats, gondolas, and ships.

At the ledge of each pier, circular homes perch on stilts, the shingled rooftops glowing beneath a canopy of dawn constellations. Muffled voices drift from inside, the open windows glinting with ambient light.

They've drifted into the Astral Sea.

Sorrow and Envy know this haven well, because this is where they grew up. It's where they used to live, along with the enemies, who can emerge from their homes at any moment.

Fear splashes through Sorrow's chest. At the same time, wistfulness mists in her eyes, though she can't tell if the feeling stems from awe, fury, sadness, or jealousy. She's pissed off and homesick. Stars, she hates this place and wants it back. And this is what it means to be shunned.

A fruity aroma wafts from inside one of the dwellings. Sorrow's earlobes perk, detecting a friendly chuckle, a rapturous gasp, and a baleful sigh. The twang of a bowstring resounds from another area, followed by the slice of a blade being sharpened.

Armed residents. Countless deities. Gods and goddesses.

If caught, Sorrow and Envy will be taken prisoner, interrogated, and tortured.

Where is their crew? Did they survive the rapids?

Via The Stars, Sorrow calls out to them but receives no reply. It can happen, especially if deities turn their attention elsewhere, if they have other problems with which to contend.

And who knows if they've called out to Sorrow or Envy. She was unconscious, and Envy has been otherwise engaged.

She tries several times more. Presumably, Envy must have as well, prior to Sorrow awakening.

She licks her lips, desperate to ask what's the plan. However, she can't speak. Not here and now. If she's able to discern the slightest echo from this vantage point, their people may detect Sorrow and Envy shearing through the depths.

They're weaponless. Her ice archery is potentially at the bottom of the sea, and Envy's glass weapons are nowhere in sight, which means both of their defenses are either adrift on the boat or have suffered the same fates.

Sorrow inhales, exhales. Yet it's no use. Her pulse reaches critical mass, palpitations slamming into her breastbone.

Envy must feel the inner chaos against his spine. Or if he doesn't, he certainly notices her chokehold on his throat. "It'll be all right," he says, the words as thin as strings.

She clings to that minor comfort and whispers, "I can swim."

"I'd like to see you try," he remarks while pumping his bulky arms.

"You're wincing and grunting."

"Hush. It's nothing."

"I'm slowing us down, you stubborn ox."

"You're as light as organza." He winces, his abdomen seizing up for a second. "Besides, we're almost there."

Where? Because from Sorrow's perspective, the only things they're getting closer to are purgatory and certain death.

With a nudge of his chin, Envy indicates the distant landmass. A moonlit summit crowned by a fortification that surrounds a glass dome, similar in shape to a mortal observatory. Inside stands an ethereal telescope—what their kind call a stargazer. A glimmering film encircles the facade, which soaks up The Stars' radiance.

Fortune's Crest.

The stargazer marks the center of this world, the instrument craning its neck toward the firmament. When the celestials created gods and goddesses, those stars denied immortals the ability to procreate, but not the ability to re-create. The Stars gave deities a tool, a means to channel the magic of rebirth. Every star is a womb that carries the life force of future deities. So to speak, the telescope is the umbilical cord, drawing new immortals from the sky and bringing them into being. It's the gateway to the life cycle of her people.

Sorrow assesses the landscape's scabrous outline. The crew plans to journey to Fortune's Crest and claim it as an outpost, should this crusade commence in a battle.

Or rather, *when* this crusade commences in battle. It's no longer a question of *if*.

To say the least, getting derailed and separated has thrown a wrench into the proceedings. The hope Sorrow had felt withers like a dead leaf.

"We're almost there?" she scoffs. "Are you serious?"

Envy spritzes water as he propels forward. "Oh, I don't know." He addresses the hemisphere and mocks, "Am I serious, divine creators?"

"In order to reach an unexposed trail, we'll have to swim far out of range."

"Again, shh."

Sorrow snarls but bites her tongue. Being overheard is the last thing they need.

And fuck, double fuck, triple fuck. If magic weren't so finicky, life would be simpler. For a start, evanescing can't happen in water. Also, while The Court lives in a palace nestled amid the cliffs, at least one member must be nearby, occupying one of these homes. That would explain Sorrow and Envy's inability to vanish, such a means of escape impossible in the vicinity of rulers.

Okay. So from this immediate territory, the nearest options require taking conspicuous hiking paths. In the meantime, their crew must be in similar danger. Although Sorrow's hardly the doting type, images cycle through her mind.

Love's mischievous grin. Merry's fanciful smile. Wonder's inquisitive gaze. Andrew's sharp stare. Anger's passionate glower. Malice's chaotic smirk.

"When I told you to shush, I had no idea it would work," Envy marvels under his breath.

Sorrow swallows a lump the size of a walnut, her mind fixating on the crew. "They're all I have."

Envy absorbs that statement. A few leagues pass in which he forges ahead, the silence interrupted by shivering ripples and labored pants. More and more, the god sounds off-kilter. Either the breaststrokes are getting to him, or his choppy respirations have to do with something else.

"If they're alive, they'll be waiting," he whispers.

Sorrow pulls herself together. "So will we."

Quietly, she fumbles to unlace and rip off her boots. Then she slides off Envy's back and paddles too swiftly for him to protest. Not that she would listen, and not that it's the right time to voice objections.

Or to voice anything at all. It's possible they've already said enough. Be that as it may, there's no sign of alarm from the houses, no disturbances indicating they've been spotted.

The water sparkles. A fleet of lanterns float in their direction, bleeding light across the surface. Sorrow had almost forgotten this ritual, signifiers of a new morning, their people kindling astral flames and setting them free each dawn. The brighter the flame, the more successful their day will be.

"Huh," Envy bitches. "If I had known I'd be traveling with a mute, I wouldn't have bothered playing the sexy savior."

"Now you want to talk?" Sorrow accuses while they siphon their limbs. "I can't believe you."

"Why not? You of all people should be acquainted with my double standards."

"We're not doing this now. I was minding my own business." Concentrating on the coastline, she makes an ornery noise. "Even in a lethal predicament, you can't resist tooting your horn, and whenever you don't get your way, you piss on the moment. Well, go ahead and flatter yourself, if that's what it's called. Meanwhile, I'll be over here, on my side of the water, fleeing for my life."

Envy grumbles like an entitled asshole. One minute, this prick couldn't care less what she thinks about him. The next, he throws a hissy fit because she's not talking. It wouldn't kill this pride god to sacrifice attention for two seconds. At the very least until they're out of target range.

Sorrow gasps as Envy snatches her elbow. With a muffled curse, he yanks her sideways, the water sloshing and disrupting the lanterns. In a single motion, the god jerks her under a walkway leading to one of the stilted homes, then releases her arm.

Bobbing in front of Sorrow, Envy places a finger to his mouth. In the mottled light, they stare at each other, Sorrow's lungs stalling.

Above them, someone emits a haughty chuckle. "Nice try."

8

Sorrow

Shit. Sorrow clams her mouth shut. Her eyes magnetize to Envy's, which glitter with a ferocious light.

The figure above speaks once more, the voice belonging to a female. "This is a rather grave infraction," she muses. "You wouldn't dare."

"Wouldn't I?" a male teases. "I've always wanted to know what it's like to wield iron."

"Doing so violates protocol."

"See if I give a shit."

Relief sweeps through Sorrow, a whoosh of air vacating her throat. Envy's features relax, though the hostile gleam in his eyes remains. Contrary to the assumption, this couple doesn't register an intrusion.

"We owe them nothing," the male sneers. "Least of all, our respect. Look at what they've done, betraying us, brutalizing one of our own, and fleeing into the sea like cowards... Did you just grunt at me?"

Sorrow rams her palm against Envy's mouth to stifle another puff of umbrage. A lantern floats between them, accenting their shadows beneath the planks. In the glinting light, the pride god's offended glower is unmistakable.

Or it might have to do with his incessant grimacing. Something is wrong with Envy, and it has nothing to do with his general personality.

Graceful footsteps and receding voices indicate the pair's retreat. "Where do you suspect the eight have fled?" the female speculates in a low register.

Sorrow grabs one of the stilts and cocks her head to listen, but she loses wind of the reply. However, one thing's for certain. None of their crew have been captured. Otherwise, the body count would have been different.

She glides to the walkway's rim, ignoring Envy's silent protests for her to *"Get the fuck back here"* and *"Sorrow, so help me!"*

To that, she merely raises her hand in a stopping motion, and his eyebrows catapult into his hairline. His thought-bubble can't be clearer: Did she actually give him a fucking order?

Sorrow curls her fingers over the ledge. Hauling herself upward, she peeks over the side, where two figures huddle together, their arms linked. A cobalt mantel cascades from the male, the textile billowing like blue smoke.

Mercury-forged arrows fill the female's quiver, her body trussed up in a silk jumpsuit.

Based on their attire and weaponry, they're members of the pack that attacked Sorrow's crew. She tilts her chin, but the deities are too remote to hear more of the conversation. Still, this is promising news. The couple had been whispering, so Andrew was right about the ambushers keeping reports of the trespass to themselves. Maybe they're set on becoming the captors, hoping to impress The Fate Court. In which case, the monarchs have no idea about the crew's arrival.

A violent tug on Sorrow's skirt dunks her back into the murk. She hits the water, the splash resounding in her ears. For Fates's sake, that was stupid of him!

She reserves that lecture for later and jabs her index finger over-head. *"It's them,"* she mouths.

Envy's visage tightens. Measuring the distance from here to safety, his irises cleave through the vicinity, then land on her once more. *"West pier,"* he mouths back.

She nods. They paddle at a gradual pace, gliding under the inter-secting boardwalks. Lanterns skate around them, making the water appear deeper and darker. They bypass lilting tenors, animated voices, and embittered grumbles.

Abreast of their designated point, Envy stops. Pausing behind a stilt, he waits until Sorrow joins him.

That's when she lets loose. Exasperated, she shoves Envy back-ward. "Do you have a death wish?" she hisses. "For mercy's sake, any-one could have heard the noise when you jerked me under."

Instead of owning up to this mistake, Envy rolls his conceited eyes. "The octave of your voice would have been a problem, but not the splashing. Assuming they heard a thing, they'll attribute the noise to a different source. Or if you need me to break it down further, other things exist in this sea besides fugitives," he godsplains. "Namely, sea creatures."

Aurora whales. Star serpents.

Valid point, but it still wasn't worth the risk. Nevertheless, Sorrow elects not to browbeat the issue. Arguing this close to potential threats is foolish.

"You said to make for the west pier," she whispers. "Why are we stopping?"

"Pit stop," he murmurs.

Trailing his gaze, Sorrow pans toward a familiar dwelling. On the left pier stands a house. A round, ostentatious, three-story monstrosity with a front door of inky stone.

Envy's home.

In three millennia, the pride god never once welcomed Sorrow inside. Just like she never asked to be invited.

Be that as it may, she knows this place, to which he's got a visitor. A hooded figure slips from the threshold while checking the perimeter, a pair of dark hands wielding a crossbow nocked with sapphire arrows.

Envy unravels the mystery. "Nostalgia."

He pronounces the name between his teeth, mincing each syllable to pieces. Unfortunately, Sorrow has become accustomed to every tone of Envy's voice. The familiarity of this one isn't platonic.

Despite the odd clench in her chest, Sorrow jibes, "Do all your ex-lovers squat here when you're not around?"

"Do I look hospitable enough to welcome a guest when I'm not in residence?" Envy grips. "You're smarter than that."

True, though Sorrow was being sarcastic. "He's snooping."

"Which means he must have been with the pack that chased us, and I hadn't realized it."

"There was a lot going on," she justifies.

What she's incapable of defending is why her nails are presently digging into the stilt. It can't be from learning that Envy and this god banged in the past. Putting it mildly, Envy throws his cock into anything on two legs.

Not important.

When Wonder and Malice quested to The Dark Fates, to breach The Archives and research an advantage to win this battle, they journeyed at an opportune time. Back then, it had been Stellar Worship, a tradition occurring every hundred years, when deities remain at home, paying homage to The Stars with a period of solitary reflection.

Yet it's not Stellar Worship anymore. Otherwise, they wouldn't have been attacked in the valley forest or pursued into the river.

Anyway, Nostalgia could have been ransacking Envy's house for traces of the crew's whereabouts. If so, this deity or his accomplices might have checked Sorrow's home too, as well as the dwellings of Love, Anger, and Wonder.

They won't find anything. Though, if they miraculously happen to locate Sorrow's missing ice arrow, she'd be much obliged.

"Just how crucial is this pit stop?" Sorrow interrogates.

"Relax," Envy drawls. "Have you seen Nostalgia fight?"

"It doesn't matter. He's still an obstacle. We can't get past—Envy?"

In seconds, he's gone. She whips left and right, spotting furrows in the surface, delineating his frame breaststroking underwater. He spears toward his home, shooting to the rocks where his victim stands.

Sorrow gawks. Her jaw hangs loose as Envy slinks out of the sea like Poseidon—dripping, gorgeous as sin, and deadly as fuck. The cavalier god rises to his feet and casually taps Nostalgia's shoulder.

When the male turns, a gasp rips from his throat. Envy flashes a shit-eating grin, grabs his face, and mashes their lips into a harsh kiss. The instant this happens, Sorrow's pupils electrify as if someone has hot-wired her vision. Disgust curdles in her stomach, and she experiences the severest urge to sink her fangs into someone's jugular.

Envy's tactic works. The target's crossbow falls, skids across the planks, and plummets into the sea. Shocked, Nostalgia freezes long enough for Envy to pull back, wink like a prick, and punch the god in the face.

The archer's stunned face whips sideways as he goes down. Sorrow gawks as Envy shakes the droplets from his hair, then adjusts his sopping button-down shirt and trousers. Any harder, and he could have snapped his adversary's neck. Indeed, Envy might have done so, if the intention had been to leave a trail of corpses behind them.

Fuck. The crossbow!

Sorrow dives. Beneath the sea, she jets toward the spot where the weapon had sunk. Flipping her eyelids open, she whirls and scans the depths for a glimmer of sapphire. If they weren't in this predicament, she wouldn't dare seek out another deity's bow. However, being hunted and weaponless puts a new spin on the rules.

The water level is shallow in this area, so the archery must have landed within reach. Sadly at this hour, visibility proves difficult. It would be less taxing to find the weapon at midday, and the clock is ticking.

She bats at a mesh of reeds, in case the archery has gotten tangled there. Instead, a scaly tail darts from the hedge and weaves across her hip.

Sorrow growls, bubbles bursting from her lips. Breaking the surface, she crawls onto the pier like a crab, slogging upright behind the dwelling. Inconveniently, the skirt and vest cling to her body, the outlines of her tits and firm nipples drawing Envy's leer. She would discourage this appraisal if he weren't balancing an unconscious god in his arms.

"We lost his bow," Sorrow whispers. "And he's going to wake up."

"If he rouses before we're done, we'll tie him up." One corner of Envy's smug mouth lifts. "I have experience with that."

Ignore him, she warns herself. Yet the sensuous tone resurrects the memory of Envy using handcuffs on her.

"If we restrain him, someone will eventually see Nostalgia like that," she vetoes.

"Ah. Good point." Envy hustles the god down the planks while keeping to the shadows, then deposits the lump on a neighboring crossway, propping the victim upright on the ground and slumping him against a torchlit pole.

To passersby, it will appear as if Nostalgia has passed out from an alcohol binge. He'll know differently, but he won't go publicizing it, except to the comrades hunting for Sorrow's crew.

Not ideal. But something's got to give.

By the time Envy returns, he's clutching his side. "Condemnation."

Sorrow extends her arm. "What—"

"Just keep watch," he growls, then strides into the house.

Sorrow paces. Although she has never set foot inside his home, she did steal a peek once. And she'd regretted what she saw.

Yet that was eons ago, and he's taking too long, and they shouldn't linger. Anxiety wins out as Sorrow peers through the window. Unlike the only other time she'd glimpsed the interior, she hadn't paid attention to the decor.

Presently, Sorrow anticipates the makings of a brothel. A bathing chamber large enough to fit a harem. A dressing closet packed with so many clothes, it must cost a king's ransom. Beaded draperies. Tiger print. Red satin.

To the contrary, she takes stock of the neutral hues, comfortable sofas, baskets holding bolts of fancy cloth, a drafting table, and weathered renderings of clothing.

All right. Not what she expected.

Envy rifles through the spacious living room, then backs up as he returns empty-handed. "He looted my fucking boudoir."

Sorrow can't resist. "Is that pun on purpose?"

His eyebrows staple together, scarcely in the mood for a joke. "If Nostalgia took my favorite cashmere robe, there will be infinity to pay."

Whatever. The house looked pristine. When she says so, he objects by pointing through the window, where a rug has been partially overturned, in addition to a slanted mirror.

"Did he find anything?" she asks.

"Would you classify extra weapons as anything?" he replies grimly.

Motherfucker. Apparently, Envy had been keeping a cache of arms here. Bows are sacred, but they aren't the only means of combat. Deprived of their archery, Sorrow and Envy could have used alternatives. But like the arrow she lost in her youth, extra weapons are exceptions to the laws of conjuring items. They can't be replaced through magic.

Rules, rules, rules. So many rules.

The fundamentals of wielding arrows are severely complex. The end result depends on a combination of factors including the striker's intention, the intensity of an arrow's power, and the duration of its effects.

But one thing is clear. When a deity is banished, they lose the ability to wield their root emotion. Their arrows no longer hold that influence. This applies to their crew, most of whom have been exiled for their defiance.

Anger and Love are the exempt ones. Due to all the shit that's happened, their weapons are now immune to losing their power.

They slip back into the sea. An eternity goes by, in which she's never moved slower, dreading every splash of water, every sweep of her limbs.

At last, they emerge from under the walkway and melt into the cliffside shadows. As they round the bend, the lanterns fade, and they leave the residences behind. A slender conduit flows ahead. Out of earshot and tucked within the crevice, they swim freely without speaking.

After an hour, Envy's movements grow desperate and clumsy. He's a ship, a wide berth of muscles and flesh. By comparison, Sorrow's more like a skiff, but she's faster at present.

They'll have to devise a new plan for traveling to Fortune's Crest. Their crew would have manifested directly, but it can be a highly populated area, especially during deity births. In such a case, Sorrow and the gang might have landed in the arms of The Court or a cluster of Guides drawing new gods and goddesses from The Stars. That's why the crew had collaborated on an inconspicuous route, combining what each of them knows about The Dark Fates' terrain.

Another hour passes. At which point, they reach a series of inlets.

Sorrow paddles after Envy and bumps into his rigid back, the god's

body pausing mid-swim. She's about to question his trajectory but sti-
fles the impulse, the view stalling her tongue.

One inlet pours into a lagoon. Tethered to a rock, a boat sways above the surface, narrow and long enough for two people. To the right, a condensed bank of bushes and fern trees lines a footpath leading to a cliffside, with a gap in the edifice. The entrance to a cavern, where vines embroider the threshold.

Hidden. Dreamlike. Surreal.

The place robs Sorrow of breath. "What is this?"

Envy stares. "It's my secret."

9

Sorrow

During the first centuries of their lives, bonding hadn't been a priority. They were busy training for their respective purposes. Apart, they learned from their Guides the intricacies of their root emotions. Together, archery practice and lessons held within the misty coves kept them occupied.

Outside of those obligations, Sorrow hadn't been interested in where Envy went, what he did, or with whom. Though, word of his popular antics had circulated. He'd always been surrounded by fans and conquests, and he'd been a regular fixture at sex pageants and oral fests.

Yeah. Not Sorrow's thing.

Aside from training, she had preferred to be a hermit while occasionally enjoying some laughs with Love and Wonder. Even after they left to serve the human realm, shared secrets had been infrequent among their crew, and virtually nonexistent between Sorrow and Envy.

Really, they had only begun to connect after Love and Andrew's story. As such, Sorrow has no clue what to make of Envy's statement.

His secret? Since when?

Envy's expression is one of pure and utter reverence. At the sight, a tight sensation grips Sorrow's womb. It's a queer feeling she hasn't been privy to before, unlike the familiar salt of tears, the cello-like strum of loneliness, and the coarseness of grief. But this foreign reaction, she hasn't been educated to identify. It seizes her stomach, and she doesn't know how to get rid of it.

Somehow, the inexplicable disturbance has to do with his countenance, his features reminiscent of a giddy child. A happy soul.

She shouldn't like the visual of him joyous, the sentimentality of it. Besides, what did he call her on the boat? A black cloud? A pessimistic killjoy?

Well, at least she's authentic. At least reality doesn't skew her judgement, compromise her foresight, or sugarcoat her hopes.

Anyhow. According to Envy, another name for *secret* is *refuge*.

"A secret refuge," Sorrow criticizes. "As if you couldn't get any more self-serving."

Envy knocks his shoulder against hers. "Do I detect the tang of jealousy?"

"Like hell would I do you that favor. What's the purpose of this place? To host exclusive orgies? As if I'd have bent over backward for an invite to one of those."

"I didn't host such commonplace affairs here," Envy dismisses while scanning the vicinity. "I was a guest at everyone else's." Ignoring Sorrow's snort of derision, he adds absently, "And I've never brought any lovers here."

Yet again, his reply clutches an uncharted place in her stomach, but she smothers that reaction before it reaches her brain. No sense in letting that confession go to her head. She may be the exception, the rare ex-lover whom he's brought to this hideaway, however that's because they're on the run and need a place to rest. Which is impossible considering the perfectly functional vessel located near the entrance.

"We can't stay here," Sorrow cautions.

"Nonsense," Envy revokes. "Of course, we can."

"The boat—"

"Is mine."

That's all he says before swimming across the lagoon and hoisting himself onto the footpath encircling the water.

Sorrow hesitates, then paddles after him and sloshes onto the bank, where she drips all over the vegetation. "Care to fill me in?"

"Let's call this my happy place," he tells her.

"We don't need to rest that long."

"I was thinking a few days."

"Not a chance. That's the dumbest—"

A pained hiss slides off Envy's tongue, similar to the noises he's been making since Sorrow's near-drowning. As she leans over to see what's wrong, he twists away with a grunt. "It's nothing."

Typical God. "It's not nothing. You're shaking," she persists.

"Rubbish," he says. "I'm flexing my muscles to their best advantage."

"And for once, you look like shit. You're as pale as an onion."

Envy tries to shoo Sorrow away as she wrestles his hand from his abdomen. Lifting his shirt, she gasps at the welts marring his torso, the contusions puddling across his ribcage, and the disjointed grid of bones beneath. Three fractured ribs. So that's why he'd been laboring through the swim. Unreasonable male! He should have said something and let her help him.

Envy yanks the shirt down. "Do you mind? I'd rather not showcase my ugly to the universe."

"All this time," Sorrow lectures. "All the way here!"

"Oh, leave the dramatics to Merry. So the rapids were a tad aggressive when I dove after you. A rogue wave might have gotten in the way."

"You shouldn't have carried Nostalgia! Lifting is the worst thing you can do in this state. And how the hell did you swim like that?"

Sorrow reaches out to assist him, but he smacks her wrist away like a priss. "Did I have a choice?" Now that they're on solid ground, he's shutting down fast, his large body swaying. "Last but never least, I'm the God of Envy."

For crying out loud. Yes, smashing into a tidal wave will pulverize a human but only nick a deity. And sure, immortal wounds heal faster. But not in a few hours. Human anatomies need about six weeks to mend. For a god, it'll take three days, which means he's useless until then.

"You're in no condition to strut around like a peacock," she admonishes.

"Stars almighty," Envy grits out, spasming again. "I towed you through rapids and our old stomping grounds. I transferred Nostalgia from one pier to another. I swam here without assistance. I think I can make it the last twenty feet into the fucking cavern."

His frame teeters. Sorrow catches him, the weight of all that muscle threatening to overturn them. Looping her arm around his waist, they hobble inside.

"I'm fine, dammit," he mumbles, his mane spilling over his chest. "All I need… is a change… of outfit."

"Get your hand off my ass," Sorrow hisses as they lumber across the threshold. Honestly, it's not his fault. He's already checked out, his reserves officially drained. Thus, he can't control where his fingers land.

Lacy vines tremble from overhead. Upon entering the cavern, Sorrow curses every romance novel in existence. Stunning doesn't begin to describe the cavern. Her feet sink into a soft carpet of moss sprouting, with a lustrous stream carving through. Instead of scabrous, the arched walls are smooth with banners of fine cloth dyed in gem colors looping from the concave ceiling. A set of upholstered chairs, plus an array pillows and cushions, front an intricately carved hearth embedded into the nearest wall, while other hollows lead to adjacent alcoves.

Envy had called this a refuge. Evidently, he'd conjured these details, customizing them to his preferences. The water, flames, and walls give off enough ambient light, yet Sorrow casts about for a practical source. Focusing on the taper candles situated within recesses, she beseeches The Stars.

In response, the wicks flare, illuminating her bedraggled clothes. Her ankle-length skirt and vest are intact, although she'd sacrificed her boots in order to swim. Similarly, Envy's unshod toes poke out from under the tattered hem of his slacks. At some point, he must have relinquished them to the sea.

She glimpses his profile, with its patrician nose and crimped brows. He's debating whether to nurse his shattered ribs first or replace his attire. The choice should be obvious, but this is Envy.

If she makes a suggestion between the two options, he'll ignore it. If she demands his cooperation, he'll whine. If she gives a shit, he'll hold it against her.

This. *This* is why they have zero in common.

Love and Andrew. Anger and Merry. Wonder and Malice.

They're partners who respect each other. Yet they think some legend about two deities choosing lust over love will bring Sorrow and Envy together. They believe it will change this battle.

That can't be right. It has to be another pairing.

Envy stumbles, nearly taking her with him. Sorrow hunkers the pigheaded male to the mossy floor, his body sprawling like a drunken merman, all whipcord skin and sinew. Broad pecs inflating with each heavy respiration, muscles bulging from his arms, more cobbled abs than a priceless statue, and a narrow waist that leads to the most skilled cock she's ever ridden.

Damn him. Tingles rush across the crease between Sorrow's thighs.

And damn her too. This is no time for her pussy to fall off the wagon, especially not when he's in this present state. For pity's sake, sometimes the urges of deities have the worst timing.

Beside him, Sorrow squats and braces her palms on her thighs. "You have a lot of explaining to do, Mister."

"Best to get you out of those wet clothes first," he mumbles.

A traitorous chuckle skips off her tongue. She compresses her lips to stop the impulse, but it's too late. Her mirth slips through the cracks, foreign and humiliating. He was always good at provoking a laugh from her, even if she never gave in, never showed it, never let him know.

Yet this time, this asshole notices the slip. His tired mouth crooks as he listens to the sound, his eyes drifting closed. "I've waited thousands of years for that."

He's delirious. He didn't mean it.

Meanwhile, the flutter in Sorrow's chest is an illusion. A farce meant for sentimental beings like Merry, bless her sweet soul.

The only truth Sorrow knows for certain is they're not going anywhere.

For three days, they're stuck with each other.

10

Envy

Sateen blankets. Luscious. Glorious.

The bedding glides over his skin, caressing the perfect lattice of his abs, which he possesses in abundance. With a hum, Envy rolls onto his back, savoring the heavenly brush of the material.

Vaguely, he has the presence of mind to deduce another fact. He's garbed in nothing but sleeping pants woven of a similar textile, as fluid as water. Silk pants. Based on how the fabric kisses his thighs, it's been sewn from a deep, glossy gulf. The garment's richness also indicates an enchanted quality, achievable only in this realm.

The greater enigma is the mossy bed spanning beneath his weight. Stretching his arms like a panther, Envy notes other perplexities. A lush pillow cradles his head, though he usually sleeps with a minimum of six, preferring the indulgent lavishness of such comforts.

His bare chest contracts with each breath. Familiar spices perfume the atmosphere, and the echo of droplets trickle from nearby.

Envy's eyes whip open to a cavern dappled in warm shadows. He lurches upright, grinding his knuckles into his eyes.

In the Astral Sea, his house contains industrious but luxurious ornamentations. Linen bedding. Plush sofas and mirrors. Bolts of jacquard, damask, toile, houndstooth, and leather. Pelts of fur and spools of yarn.

This isn't his house. Envy's head veers sideways, absorbing the taper candles set into recesses, the wicks twitching with flames, luminescence sprinkling the walls.

His refuge, the other end of which resides...

Hope filters through him. When? How?

Envy consults his fractured memory. But it's the actual fractures that rouse him fully, his ribcage constricting, pain gripping his consciousness. He seethes, resting his palm against the ladder of bones covered in strips of gauze.

Wicked clarity returns. Needing a moment to regroup, he claws through his mane, the infernal layers snarled from the journey here. It's going to take him a while to tame the mess, particularly by his standards. To say the least, he'd have an easier time shaving a fucking warthog.

Envy audits more details. The interior stream. The hearth. The pillows, cushions, and upholstered chairs. The cloth banners looping from the ceiling. Upon periodic returns to The Dark Fates, Envy would often retire here, deeming it his private sanctuary. But after being ostracized, he hadn't anticipated seeing it again.

Presently, he relishes this moment, which alleviates the agonizing pangs of his injury. Yet he can't recall tucking himself in, nor disrobing, nor dressing his wounds.

An ominous presence infiltrates the moment, a grim and sinister essence disturbing the atmosphere. He senses evil nearby, reeking of pessimism and misery.

Envy curls his nose. He peers around, searching for a horrible outfit and unkempt hair the shade of anguish.

The cavern's threshold extends to a lagoon. His gaze lands on a figure perched at the water's edge, where the bank rises higher, producing a natural rim. Settled there, the goddess's profile consults the dome of stars and planets. Her tresses quiver in the breeze, and her skirt puddles around her thighs, enabling her limbs to dip into the pool.

Sorrow.

The grumpy goddess is here, infesting his refuge. For no apparent reason, the vision sends a prickle across his shoulder blades. She should look out of place, yet she doesn't appear that way. In fact, there's something appealing about Sorrow ensconced in his domain, surrounded by All Things Envy.

He shakes his head. Something must be wrong with him. For whatever reason, he can't stop staring at this morose female.

Though, it wouldn't be the first time. Since their youth, he'd been dealing with this unhealthy obsession, frequently stealing glances at Sorrow when she hadn't been looking. To this day, Envy has no clue why he expels so many reserves antagonizing her, like a perverse addiction.

Damnation. Of all the immortals to be sequestered with. At least, the goddess had opted to nurse instead of hex him while he slept.

Yet fuck. Why her? Why is it always her?

Despite millennia of interactions, plus one doomed fling, it's hardly unusual that he knows so little about Sorrow. Apart from the basics, at least. While the same rule applies to numerous other sex partners on his roster, none of the gods and goddesses he's fucked have ever provoked him. None have ever crawled under his skin, nor been unimpressed with Envy, even after their lust faze began.

He grimaces. He must be drowsy if he's making little sense.

Outside the cavern, his tethered boat floats in the lagoon. Beyond that, a sliver of water reveals the inlet from which they'd traveled.

It's eventide, the constellations chipping at the hemisphere. According to a rumored myth among his people, The Stars will shine their brightest when a deity asks for the truth. But a deity will only receive the truth if they're ready to hear the answer.

There's another condition attached to the myth, but Envy's too lazy to review it.

He supposes a declaration of gratitude is in order. Not that Sorrow wants such a thing from Envy, or that she's ever wanted anything of substance from him. That is, aside from his cock.

Really, he can't blame her for that. He possesses a glorious cock.

Envy sweeps the blanket aside. Gaining his feet, he saunters to the threshold, careful not to exacerbate his ribs as he leans against the frame. The instant he does, Sorrow tenses from scalp to ass.

"Sexy view," he murmurs, his husky voice rumpled from slumber.

Sorrow purses her lips. She kicks her legs through the pool, waves swatting a rocky outcropping. "Flattery will get you nowhere."

As if it ever has with her. Not when it's come to anything meaningful.

"I meant the lagoon," Envy clarifies blandly, savoring the chagrined flush that stains her cheeks. For good measure, and perhaps out of genuine curiosity, he adds, "Even if I'd been referring to you, do you even know how to take a compliment?"

"You're welcome for the bandage, by the way."

"Much obliged, by the way."

Nothing but her signature grunt. They'd gotten here at dawn, which means he spent the day blacked out. She must be exhausted from their trip as well.

"The cavern has plenty of alcove chambers," he invites.

"I'm not tired," she lies. "I tried but can't sleep."

Look at me.

She won't do it. That's not her style. During the one-hundred-fifty-and-a-half times they'd gotten pornographic—yes, one-hundred-fifty-and-a half, the latter due to a broken bed frame that interrupted the fun—not once had she looked at him for longer than necessary. The residual sting of resentment snaps at his vertebrae like a rubber band.

He shouldn't say it. Really, he shouldn't.

But he does. "Can't sleep? Sorrow, I've told you before. The monster under your bed is just a mirror."

Her head lances toward him. "Well, you own enough of them to know, so I trust your judgement. What?"

There's that look. That direct look.

Her eyes on him. Her attention, all his.

Those metallic irises flash like supernovas, their radiance soaking into his pores. With the potency of an illicit drug, the effect sends a charge through Envy's blood, the influx rushing to his dick and flooding his balls.

That is, until an unexpected detail consumes his gaze. She's not wearing her customary, melodramatic outfit. Instead, Sorrow has chosen an ensemble that mentally knocks him on his ass.

As he struggles to process the flannel getup, Sorrow's eyes widen in realization. The garments are a mortal style, with clouds printed on them. Fluffy little clouds the likes of which only one fully-grown, immortal soul would don with a straight face.

"Those are Merry's pajamas," he balks.

"So what if they are?" Sorrow defends.

"Why did you enchant Merry's pajamas?"

"Several months ago, before we set out to conquer the world, she hosted an all nighter—"

"To which I was not invited?" Envy asks with mock offense.

"It was for goddesses only. Regardless, I loathe such parties," Sorrow confides. "They're nothing but an excuse to stuff your intestines with cake and paint each other's toenails some shade called Kismet, so everything stinks of acetone, plus you have to sleep in the same room. And don't get me started on the mock-battles, in which participants are forced to use pillows instead of actual weapons. Seriously, where's the fun if you're not drawing blood?"

"I never pegged you for someone who enjoys blood play. To my everlasting regret, we never tried it." But when she doesn't rise to the bait, he inquires, "Are we talking about the human or non-human versions of overnight soirees?"

"The Merry Version. Music played from a record that never seemed to end, we challenged each other to see who could conceive the most ridiculous sleepwear in history, and there was all this… this talk about *feelings*, and 'fate this' and 'free will that,' and 'my soulmate' and 'your soulmate.'" Sorrow frowns at Envy, those eyes two sharp, silver droplets in her face. "Well? Aren't you going to stop me?"

"And miss this rare opportunity to hear you complain?"

"All that bonding swoonery."

Bonding swoonery. His mouth twitches.

Sauntering into the fresh air, Envy contemplates the empty spot beside her, then changes his mind and sidesteps Sorrow. At the adjacent end of the lagoon, he lounges across from her, rolling up his pants and submerging his limbs.

Sorrow's eyes veer from his naked chest. "During the sleepover, I couldn't think of what to put on. The motorcycle queen got ambitious and charged to her dresser."

"And you obviously got attached," Envy concludes.

Sorrow juts her chin toward her skirt and vest, both garments sprawling flat on a boulder jutting from the bank. "My clothes need to dry."

"You could have manifested an outfit suitable to your witching hour."

"For your information, I didn't feel like wearing anything combat-worthy. Not if I was going to try and rest."

Granted the ensemble would look cute on Merry, it's wrong for

Sorrow. To correct the matter, visions of her outfitted in lace panties, pashmina corsets, jeweled eye masks, and haute couture bondage crowd Envy's head like a soft-core silent film. Or better yet, her body draped in one of his oversized shirts.

Though, the star of the show would be Sorrow in nothing at all, her naked skin feverish with exertion, varnished in sweat, and spread out across his mattress.

Fuck. Envy shifts before his enthusiastic cock has a chance to react. "So this is the best you came up with? Ever heard of chic loungewear?"

"I usually sleep naked," she announces.

"At last, something we have in common."

Of its own volition, Sorrow's gaze skates down his torso as if she wouldn't mind seeing proof. And fuck him to hell. Because yes, Envy's impure thoughts also went there seven seconds ago, the confirmation doing nothing to rescue his bloated nether regions.

He pinches the waistband of his low-slung pants. "Rather astute, choosing mulberry silk."

"It wasn't hard to gauge," she says. "Your arrogance has a high thread count."

"If I have arrogance in my DNA, you've got self-deprecation clogging your own. In terms of wardrobe choices, you could have done better for yourself."

"Get over it. I've had other things on my mind than fashion."

Ah, style block. He's been a victim of that in the past. Nevertheless, Envy longs to conjure a camera and document this visual. If anything, so he can use it to bribe Sorrow later. She may not care what others think of her, but she won't want to be reminded of it either.

Moreover, it's impossible not to smirk. "The clouds are pink."

"You need to go away," she sighs.

Envy leans back on his palms. "Need I remind you, this is my refuge?"

"Since when?"

"Since forever. I used to come here often. During my last intermission from the human realm, I spent most of my time in this place. When the period of rest was over, I simply evanesced back to the mortal world from the cavern."

"Who else knows about it?"

"Other than my Guide? You, hon."

Sorrow emits a chafed noise, and her legs disturb the lagoon. For a while, they content themselves with silence, listening to the water mop against the bank.

Envy considers the surplus of things she'd just said and takes a wild guess. "The Goddess of Sorrow is cranky because she's hungry."

"I lost my appetite at the river," she retorts. "But if I had wanted food, I'd have fed myself."

Fine. That said, nourishment requires proper motivation instead of sucking all the positive energy from his abode. It involves nurturing instead of depriving oneself.

Envy audits her clothing on the boulder, his eyes squinting at the pointless stitching needle affixed to her vest. The accessory unnerves him, as if something about her life constantly needs mending. Furthermore, she has never told him the reason for it.

Likely, Love knows the story. And Wonder. And Merry.

But while the thought of Sorrow having confidantes reassures Envy, the notion also plagues him with an emotion he's all too familiar with.

Envy disregards the stitching needle. "Suit yourself."

Channeling The Stars, he envisions an alfresco meal, and the divinities answer the call. A woven mat appears, laden with figs, a cheese board, a breadbasket, thin slices of salmon, a platter of crackers and caviar, decadent pastries that ooze with preserves, and a jug of wine.

From her corner, Sorrow surveys the fare. "You forgot the fourteen karat goblets."

"Would it shock you to discover I drink from the bottle?" Envy inquires, dropping a fig on his tongue, chewing, and swallowing. "Besides, this setup is low maintenance."

"Except you're about as low maintenance as cashmere."

"Cashmere is worth the effort." Plucking a miniature fig, Envy drapes the fruit onto his tongue, noting how her eyes follow the motion. Taking advantage of that, he chews the thing to a pulp, his teeth sinking into the flesh. Then he swallows hard and tilts his head. "By the way, I'll give you sixty seconds to take back the comment about not being hungry."

Her gaze leaps from his mouth to his eyes. "By the way, you'll be disappointed."

"Then I'll go easy on you and rephrase." He quirks an eyebrow, the question a challenge more than an invitation. "Care to join me for dinner?"

11

Envy

If Sorrow's eyebrows dig any deeper into her face, they're going to leave marks, physical evidence of Envy's folly, mementoes of this rather momentous proposition. She peers at him as if he's just invited her to a poison tasting, unappetizing and unlikely to end well. Not that Envy blames her for this visceral response since he can't comprehend where this impulse is coming from.

Even so, his respirations halt in unaccountable suspense. Then his lungs relax, a reflex he's not about to analyze, as the goddess rises and drizzles a path toward him. Her limbs drip onto the flat stones, the pajamas accentuating every shift of her hips, rotating in a manner he's seen before, except while bobbing on his erection.

Envy would pursue this bedeviled train of thought, if he weren't busy amusing himself. Here she comes, heading toward his picnic, crossing the notorious divide. It's like getting an elusive creature to approach after eons of incentives and come-hither gestures.

Miraculously, it has only worked now that he's stopped trying. As such, he can't shake the victorious tingles rushing across his flesh.

That is, until the fragrance of salty, sweet, bitter, and sour reminds him she's merely answering the siren call of food.

Still, let it go on the celestial record. Sorrow was the first to break from her corner, not him.

Envy fights to withhold a smirk. Oh, how quickly one surrenders when carbs, protein, and sugar are near.

The hem of her flannel pants drags across the ground, emitting a gentle brushing noise. Although Merry is just as slender, that glittery goddess is taller than Sorrow, the ensemble dwarfing the latter's thin limbs.

Fates. She'd enchanted pajamas in the same size.

Sorrow drops next to him, cuffs the pants up to her knees, and dunks a single leg back into the water. "So what is it with you and clothes?"

Envy offers her a steaming, buttery roll. "It's an essential part of life, and a beautiful one. Much like shelter and delicacies such as these, preferences that express who we are to people."

Sorrow accepts the bread, tearing it apart like gauze before sinking her teeth into the crust. "Express who we are to people," she quotes. "I can see how that notion attracts you. The opportunities to make an impression."

"Yet I'm no fake when it comes to my tastes."

"Are you certain? Deities curate their lives the same as humans."

"Why shouldn't we? It's a delight."

She scoots closer to the feast. Picking up a silver fork, she spears a wedge of camembert and waves it absently in the air. "But you're still contriving the world's perception of you."

"That's assuming you can control everything others think, which is only half true. But what about pleasure?" Envy debates. "I'm also indulging in these things for myself. For simple enjoyment."

"Considering the textbook definition of envy itself, I don't get how your thirsts are quenched in any given situation."

"How dare you call me one-dimensional," Envy exaggerates with feigned umbrage.

Sorrow mashes her lips together, plugging a reluctant grin. The marvel lasts a mere second before she sobers. "Pleasure is never simple. It comes with consequences and false hopes that happiness is permanent."

"That's a *sorrow*ful attitude. Aren't you overcomplicating the gratification of, say, biting into a succulent fruit or wrapping yourself in silk? What are the consequences of that?"

"The experiences don't last."

"But the memories do," he murmurs as their feet graze beneath the surface.

Sorrow trembles, concealing that enticing reaction by snatching a fig and nibbling on its flesh. Envy studies the grind of her mouth, her lips puckering in a manner that scorches a path up his dick.

Fuck. He scoots several inches back, reprimanding himself for noticing.

Back to more crucial details. Not only does she keep quiet, contemplating his response in silence, but she swallows the fruit as if the sweetness fails to penetrate her palate.

Does this goddess know how to relish anything? To savor anything?

Their kind are skilled in wielding emotions, but they're not meant to be slaves to them. Yet based on the histories of Love, Anger, and Wonder, this isn't as true as Envy once believed.

On the flip side, Sorrow is hardly a drama queen. To the contrary, she's withdrawn. This goddess might be as broody as Anger, as caustic as Malice, and as sarcastic as Andrew. She might be as wry as Love, as resilient as Merry, and as tenacious as Wonder. But Sorrow doesn't lament or throw fits.

By the same token, Envy can't recall an incident in which she has cried. Or laughed out loud.

Beneath him—above him, in front of him—she'd moaned on countless horny occasions. That aside, Sorrow hadn't once shouted with mindless abandon or sighed with contentment in the aftermath. It had been primal between them, an expulsion of energy, and oftentimes over quickly. Seconds after coming around his cock and hooting like a steam engine, she would stare into space. Then she'd scramble into her clothes, uncomfortable with Envy's lingering caresses.

Perhaps this is why they've never kissed.

Envy scarcely calls himself sentimental, but a few minutes of fondling hurts no one. Except *this one*. It must be a defect on her part, because it's certainly not his fault. He's an unparalleled lover, to whom she'd returned for more, demanding he go harder, faster, rougher.

Then again, what does Envy expect from someone who has spent her existence managing human suffering? Does she own her hurt? Or does it belong to her mortal targets? How have they known one another for millennia, without actually knowing one another?

Motes drift through the air like fireflies. While Envy discerns Sorrow's defense mechanisms, for some discomforting reason, he also wants to learn what Sorrow's laugh sounds like. That, in addition to the basics.

Her comforts. Her favorites. Her vices.

"You think pain is a consequence of pleasure," he summarizes.

The goddess shrugs. "The more enjoyment you get from something, the more hurtful it is to lose. Being jaded is easier than being in pain."

"How would you know unless you've indulged? Instead, you avoid pleasure."

"You avoid pain," she shoots back. "That's a cowardly, lowbrow way to live."

Envy wavers, the first adjective striking dead-center, puncturing a hollow place in his chest. Yet despite this, he leans forward, eager to probe. "What's lowbrow about treating yourself to the gifts of life? Why do we have senses, if not to explore and satisfy them? Taste, touch, sight, sound, smell. It's not purely so we can reign over humanity and target mortals."

"It's shallow because you add no value to it beyond the present moment. All you're thinking about is, 'This feels so good,' and then you dispose of the feeling after you've gotten your endorphin hit, and you move on to the next best thing. That leaves no room for lasting gratitude or appreciation." Sorrow loops a strand of hair behind her ear, light from the lagoon embossing her cheek. "I have a theory."

"Oh?" Envy quips. "I'm not sure I'm ready for this."

"Real pleasure doesn't exist unless pain comes with it. You can't savor one thing unless you know what it's like to be deprived of another. Loss is inevitable. When we hurt, those comforting moments—those delights, as you say—are more meaningful. They're treasures, but only when we understand and experience the opposite. Otherwise the pleasure is pointless."

"That's hardly a groundbreaking theory," he replies mildly.

She's nowhere near discouraged. "To that, I have another theory."

"Do tell." He shuffles closer. "I'm all ears."

"The simplest ideas, or the most basic ones, the rules we know," she lists. "We live by them as if they're a given. Yet they're still the hardest to remember and the hardest to live by. And when we do take these things into account, we become scared or threatened, as if they're suddenly new ideas again.

"My theories might not be revolutionary, but that doesn't lessen the impact. After millennia, people are still relearning the same lessons, drawing the same conclusions. It's an endless cycle, both ancient and current."

Sorrow picks through the assortment of goodies. Selecting a cut of salmon, she layers the fish atop a slice of bread and douses it with lemon, citrus drizzling onto the flesh. Rapt, Envy watches her take a thoughtful bite, those lips undulating.

Gulping down that mouthful, she says, "We have the hardest time learning the oldest lessons."

It takes a shitload of stamina to withdraw from the sight of her swallowing. Envy retrieves the lemon, buries his canines into the pulp, and sucks on the remaining juice. Aware of her eyes on him, he drains the orb and then deposits it onto the platter. "Again, how would you know what it's like to forfeit pleasure if you're too skittish to experience it?"

She sets down the remaining portion of salmon. "Again, how can you appreciate pleasure if you're too afraid of experiencing pain?"

Residual acid leaks into his tongue. "What makes you think I'm afraid to experience pain?"

"Oh, please. Because envy itself is a component of pain, and blind pleasure is the coping mechanism. You always make sure to *have, have, have.* You use the senses, compliments from lovers, witticisms, flirtation, and sex to avoid the hard stuff. That's you, spoiling for pleasure and validation.

"You compare yourself to others. That's your purpose. That's your nature. I'm guessing for you it would suck to have less than someone else, to feel less fortunate, to acknowledge the realities of your life if measured against someone else's good fortune. That would be painful."

She might as well have jammed a dozen needles into his skin, each stab deeper than the previous one. "Well, well," Envy jeers. "You're all talk tonight. You think you have me pegged. Except what if I told you this isn't a new idea for me?"

Sorrow wipes her hands. "Sure, you might know this. You might even fess up to it. But are you going to face it?"

"Are *you*?" he throws back. "Are you going to confront all this self-awareness? Or are you just going to sit there and eat all my food?"

Despite herself, Sorrow bites back another grin, yet again denying him the rare visual. "Some host you are."

"Hey!" he banters. "I'm a superb host. I don't care what you say."

The goddess snorts with mirth. Her teasing alleviates Envy's bitterness, the quick gleam in her irises easing the blow of what she'd said. Though indeed, this only proves her point that he uses wit to mollify any darker inclinations.

Sorrow peeks at him. "By the way, thank you. For not letting me drown."

Envy stares at her, thunderstruck. "I wish I'd gotten that on video."

When a muffled laugh tumbles out of the goddess, he considers it an encouragement. Might as well take advantage of the thaw. "I refuse to believe you're immune. Come now, I'm bored and need distraction from my wound. Tell Illustrious Envy, and he promises there will be no bonding."

"Tell you what?"

"Your pleasure, of course." Envy soaks up her gaze like an addict. "What's your pleasure?"

She hesitates. Perhaps this goddess is thinking what he's thinking. Miraculously, they're having a civilized discussion, and it's too late to turn back. The suggestion—among many suggestions tonight—has tripped out of him. Now that they've started talking, he can't keep his fucking mouth shut. Not especially when a full-blown laugh from Sorrow has become a real possibility, the prospect dangling before him like a temptation.

Nonetheless, Sorrow fidgets, the dark lacquer of her fingernails chipped in certain areas. "I don't know what I like."

"That's preposterous." Envy would chuckle in disbelief, but he's not in the mood to get smacked. "Very well. I never object to going first."

"You can't say fashion or fucking."

Goddammit. "Fine. You can't say black taffeta or witchcraft. That's—"

"Getting. Really. Old."

"I disagree. As to my fancies." Envy clears his throat and impersonates a maudlin romantic. "I like long walks on the beach."

Sorrow compresses her lips. "Nice try."

Yes, it was. And it worked, because there's that cusp of a smile.

She conceals the grin, stashing it away like a secret. Envy is stunned that he's come remotely this close to witnessing the phenomenon. Stunned and proud. It's a ridiculous achievement, even more so that he considers it an achievement at all.

Yet he wants to try again, and again, and potentially again. More than once, she's been on the verge of letting it out, so why not make that his new mission in life?

When he prompts the goddess to speak first instead, Sorrow wrinkles her nose. Another thing Envy wants is to see her features relax, to smooth out the grout lines in her countenance, so that she can't hide.

Physically, he'd made an effort with her once before. Sex aside, it's a different experience to engage with her mentally, intellectually, and personally. He has an itch, which he's hellbent on scratching. If Sorrow has trouble identifying her pleasures, he'll push her out of that comfort zone.

Measuring his words, he persuades the goddess to consult her memories, the tastes that she's never forgotten, the ones she returns to whenever she's in a particular mood, the ones that stimulate or soothe her without fail. And before they know it, a pair of chalices fill their hands, a rich liquid sloshing from within.

Envy's pulse skips. Without looking closely or smelling the contents, a guess formulates on his tongue.

"Currant nectar," he says without preamble.

Sorrow blinks, suspicion crimping her eyebrows. "How did you..."

Making a show of nonchalance, he lifts one shoulder. "Saw you take a swig once. You took your sweet time, as if you were downing some artisanal brew."

Bullshit. Yes, it's the truth but only half. Envy has seen her partake of this drink precisely two hundred and fourteen times during feasts and revels. Because also yes, he'd been paying attention. Just as he knows every article of clothing in Sorrow's closet, down to the trimmings and hardware, each garment a different shade of black or grey.

Essentially, currant nectar is juice. Despite guessing right, Envy has always balked at the commonplace choice, tempted to question her about it. Finally, he's getting an exclusive peek into this female's psyche.

Still, any feasible reaction escapes him as Sorrow's irises do something weird, freakish, and spectacular: They light the fuck up.

Those rings of color—the pigment of tears—brightens. Licking her lips, she tips back the vessel and chugs like a pump. A deep and resonant sound curls from her throat, as if she's guzzling a flute of champagne.

Envy's mind detours along with his groin, the stem thickening and shoving against the front of his pants. With supreme effort, he warns the troublemaker to behave as she explains herself.

The nectar is a "comfort drink." Envy is familiar with the human term. He's just never associated it with her tongue.

That rosy, wet tongue.

He shakes himself once more, listening avidly as she describes the tart-but-sugary quality of the drink and the refreshing sharpness of its aftertaste. No matter how curious he'd been over the years about this penchant, Envy had resisted the urge to sample it. As trite as it sounds, he'd wanted Sorrow's description, her impression more than his own.

Sorrow sighs in contentment. "As soothing as a fleece blanket." When confusion pulls across Envy's face, she motions to his chalice.

"For Fate's sake, just try it."

When he does, the effect is striking. The nectar is a delicious balance between sweet and earthy. He takes another gulp, then another, draining the chalice.

"That wasn't vile," he concedes.

She gives him a nod of approval. "How's that for pleasure?"

Envy sets down the empty vessel and swings toward her fully. "What else?"

They experiment. Sorrow enchants a barrage of mortal comfort food, such as stews, pies, and casseroles. He joins her as she samples the choices mindfully, each of them rating the pleasure-factors of every option.

Sorrow's top picks include meatballs and mashed potatoes. Her enthusiasm about it is… cute. Though, the currant nectar remains her favorite.

Envy studies the goddess's flushed countenance. He can't decide if it makes him uncomfortable, or if this feeling is reminiscent of her precious drink. Satisfying. Refreshing.

Sorrow catches him watching her. When he doesn't look away, she averts her gaze and rubs both biceps as if there's a chill. "What I wouldn't give for a walk right now."

"Would that *please* you?" he jokes.

She gives him a dry look of concession. "Very well, you've made your point. The Goddess of Sorrow takes pleasure in some things. Happy?"

Elated. "Only if you are."

"Since when do you care?"

Excellent question. "It's been a long journey. Let's agree that I'm not myself these days. Frankly, neither are you, especially in that outfit."

Sorrow mumbles to herself. Is it Envy's imagination, or is he developing a fondness for her grouchy disposition?

Is there anyone in this realm capable of breaking down that wall? Anyone who would be her exception? Who would always succeed in disarming her?

If he doesn't speak, this night will end. If that happens, they'll revert back to mutual discord.

This female anomaly would like to go for a walk. Envy could do with one as well, so long as he's vigilant about his injury.

Besides. While a stroll would be adventurous with a lover, it's strictly practical with this goddess.

Right. It's settled.

Envy dares to flick her pajama sleeve with the tip of his finger. "I know a place."

12

Envy

Another marvel occurs. The goddess blinks, her eyes widening with intrigue.

Like everything that has transpired in the past twenty-four hours, Envy hadn't expected this. Rejection is Sorrow's forte, and being on the receiving end of a brush-off is an uncommon occurrence for Envy.

By Fates, it takes fossils less time to develop than it does for his companion to reply. In the meantime, pins and needles jab his skin. In the past, Envy wouldn't have given this interlude a second thought. Tonight, it has a gravity that makes no infernal sense. But thankfully, he's got reserves of pride to rely on when she inevitably refuses him.

At least, Envy hopes he'll be able to recover. These days, he's not as confident.

Yet she doesn't snub the offer. Nor does the goddess jump to her feet. Rather, her face crinkles as if he's giving her no choice.

"Sure," she says. "Whatever."

"Well, well, well," he congratulates himself. "Did I just provide you with an enticement? Fabulous."

"Envy, I'm tired. Are we going to this 'place you know' or not?"

"Liar. You haven't been tired since I joined you."

"You're something else, you know that?"

"Originality was the plan. But that's a rhetorical question, correct?"

Also, he's not that colossal of a fool. Trained in the art of covetousness, Envy knows the signs of feigned indifference when he hears, sees, smells, tastes, and feels it. Many humans conceal this defense mechanism behind masked dismissal, and while deities can't read each other the same way, his intuition remains on high alert. Thus, the end result is no different with her.

Sorrow lifts those shapely legs out of the pool, tossing enough water onto the stones to drown a baby seal. How she manages to move slowly yet create a tidal wave is beyond him.

Together, they stand. An awkward pause follows, then he swings his arm ahead, and they trail the footpath back to the cavern. Crossing through, Envy leads Sorrow deep into the hideout, bypassing shimming tunnels and passages that illuminate the space.

They resume their talk, speaking about their homes in the Astral Sea and the places they've lived within the mortal realm, including the worst and best of locations. They compare stories about humans they've targeted, the power trip and the guilt of it all.

When that becomes too much, they return to the subject of pleasure versus pain. Though, mostly pleasure. It becomes increasingly easy for Sorrow to elaborate on her favorite sources of enjoyment, branching off from currant nectar to steam billowing from a cup, the glow of a nightlight, and the nutty whiff of bread just out of the oven.

Envy details his own indulgences. Spiced dishes, melted chocolate, and the sight of water splintering against the breakers.

Actually he's not done. Also, the sound of a cork popping from a champagne bottle, sumptuous bubble baths, the snugness of a well-fitting suit, and the briny spray of seafoam against his cheek.

And sex. Lots of it.

The tight clamp of a goddess's pussy. The brush of her swollen clit against his cock. The fractured sounds she makes while coming.

If Envy has a specific female in mind, he's not about to publicize it. Neither is he interested in asking himself why this lineup doesn't include previous male partners.

Sorrow rolls her eyes at the list. Though, it's congenial rather than mocking.

"The stars when they're not shining," she adds.

"The translucence of glass," Envy intones.

"The glaze of ice."

He glances askance at Sorrow. "Humor me. Why did you choose ice arrows?"

"Why did you opt for glass?"

"To see my reflection, of course."

"Not to see the truth?"

Envy braces his palm against the small of her back, guiding her around a dangerous rift in the floor where fragments of stone have split. "If I recall, you accused me of fearing the truth."

Gingerly, Sorrow steps around the obstruction. "But our choice of archery elements doesn't lie."

"Fine. I like transparency." He tosses her a swanky grin. "Better yet, I envy it. What about you, smart ass?"

"Ice is the closest I'll get to temperature. Theoretically, it numbs you from feeling things that are too harsh. It sterilizes them, protecting a person from anguish."

"Except you said pain is essential."

"It is. But it's also essential to survive the pain."

"Are you referring to humans or yourself?"

"Either applies," Sorrow acknowledges as they slosh through a puddle. "Do you like them? Humans?"

What Envy likes are the strands of hair that caress her suckable little ears. Matter of fact, he's getting rather fucking engrossed in them, to the point where he might have their likenesses secretly commissioned on canvas, to mount next to his own self-portrait. Or maybe in place of it.

Of course, Envy would rather cleave off his skilled tongue than confess this aloud. And this female would rather swallow dynamite than receive praise from her social nemesis.

Anyway. Does he like humans?

"I wouldn't be a member of this crew if I didn't," Envy murmurs. "I wouldn't have sacrificed my place. I'll have you know, forsaking popularity among our people is a great sacrifice in favor of rebellion. But then, it's worth the risk. If we win this thing with our limbs still attached, monuments will be erected in our name, and literary geniuses will pen retellings. In my case, the statue will be naked down to its platinum cock, and the retellings will be x-rated."

"Naturally, that's the whole point," she wisecracks.

"Oh, absolutely," he exclaims. "Won't it be marvelous?"

"We have different definitions of glory."

"I should hope so. Otherwise, our conversations would be dull. We'd talk ourselves into a wall or go in circles, never to discover a thing."

"We'd also never realize we don't know a damn thing. Deities like to think they're wise, but maybe the smartest people are the ones humble enough to admit they're not smart at all."

A chuckle rumbles from his chest. "Look at us, getting philosophical like gods. May I speak honestly?"

"As opposed to all the lies you've been feeding me tonight?"

She's teasing again. Two times in one evening. An event worthy of anthologizing in the Archives. Or if not there, maybe Envy will take up journaling as a new hobby, if only to document the occasion, for his eyes only.

Oh, right. She's waiting for him to continue.

"I think the best of our nature is to be contrary," Envy says, stalking into a corridor trimmed in platinum foliage. "We're walking, talking paradoxes, full of ironies and double standards."

The star flecks beneath Sorrow's lower eyelashes glint. "In other words, full of shit."

"In other words, fluid like water. Or more to the point, like humans. Meaning, neither of us should have power over the other. Meaning, I'm here because I want to be. I'm fighting with our crew because I believe in what we're doing, even if that involves redefining my purpose."

"Which would be?" she inquires.

"To begin, I'd have to declare what it means to be a deity in the first place," he muses.

"Maybe it's a blessing." Sorrow halts, her hair in disarray around her face. "The clincher is, we've misinterpreted what that blessing entails. It could be about embodying magic instead of forcing it on others. Maybe we need to wield that blessing from a different angle."

That option doesn't sound half bad, if a tad ambiguous. But then, Envy's beginning to grasp that life itself is ambiguous.

They reach a second threshold at the opposite end of the cavern. After indicating a narrow lane that stretches from the hollows, he takes the female's hand and leads her through.

At the contact, a short, low noise gusts from Sorrow's throat. And fuck almighty, that sound is about to become the soundtrack to his voluntary downfall. Provided he doesn't get his head out of his shallow ass.

Yet her reaction is nothing compared to the gust of air that vacates her lungs when they emerge into a new setting. Before them, misted cascades fall into numerous pools and baths, with trees sprouting from the depths. Paths web through the shrouded environment, arching like bridges over the bodies of water and vanishing around bends.

Don't look. Do not fucking look.

Fuck it. Envy looks, peek at the goddess's rapt profile. Apparently, his tongue has decided to stop working, the appendage gluing itself to the roof of his mouth. This has less to do with the fetching picture of Sorrow—though, she does look quite pretty when enthralled—and more to do with the hive of bees swarming his gut.

He's nervous.

"It's a waterfall enclave," he explains stupidly.

Sorrow gawks at the scenery. "I've never been here."

Her admiration knocks a few of those bees from his stomach. "In which case, watch where you step." He nudges his chin toward a tree trunk neighboring a pond, an X cleaving into the bark, the marking hewn from an arrowhead. "If you see that, don't go into the neighboring water or any adjacent area. Do so, and I'll resent you for life."

The goddess raises an eyebrow that plainly states, *As if you already don't.*

Oh, if she only knew how right—and wrong—she is on that account. Nonetheless, Sorrow waits for an explanation.

"There are riches as well as dangers to be found here," he says. "Camouflaged coral reefs that will cut through flesh like a knife through butter; stained-glass eels that coil beneath the surface, blending with the atmosphere until their fangs strike; and water reeds that release a drugging perfume, intoxicating to the point where a victim will stumble over slick terrain and crash into a deadly abyss."

The nymph appears more perturbed than surprised. "In other words, this innocent stroll you had in mind is actually a trick."

Envy cringes. They've hazed, taunted, and pranked one another to the same spiteful degree over the ages. But honestly, does she believe he'd bring her someplace dangerous purely to fuck with her?

Guilt riddles his insides. Yes, she fucking does.

Well. Once upon a time, that wasn't exactly farfetched. However, that was before lots of other things happened.

He scans the outcroppings, aware of her eyes on him. "I wouldn't do that to you."

Something in his tone silences the goddess. In his periphery, a rueful blush sneaks up her neck. "Good to know," she says quietly, a tinge of vulnerability creeping through her voice.

Her intonation straps around his chest and gives a subtle tug. Unsure what to do with this visceral response, Envy clears his throat. "Step into the wrong misty corners, and it'll cloak the jagged rocks, each one sharp enough to shred you like a carrot," he cautions. "And one of the pools is not water but liquid glass, though you'd never know it just by looking, which could end bloody if you try submerging yourself."

"How do you know all this unless it's happened to you?" Sorrow questions.

His mouth tilts into a grim line. "Who says it hasn't?"

He glimpses the shivers trickling across her flesh, though Sorrow nods in comprehension. When you live for thousands of years, that's plenty of time to get into trouble. Besides, every wilderness from here to the mortal realm possesses its share of perils, in addition to marvels. This enclave is no different.

Envy has learned his lesson about which parts to savor and which to avoid. Although he's memorized each corner and doesn't need the guidance, the arrow carvings had seemed prudent in case... well, in case he ever brought someone here.

Heedful, Envy guides Sorrow along the walkways. Yet while he's done a masterful job of labeling every fatal terrain, he knits their fingers together, locking Sorrow to his side, baffled why the hell this gesture feels critical when this female excels at protecting herself.

At a safe cul-de-sac, Envy finally releases the goddess and reclines against a tall rock filigreed in vines. "See? There are sublime areas too." Mischief slides across his tongue. "Matter of fact, the ancient celestials used to say if you fuck in these waters, you'll be changed forever.

Wanna try?"

The goddess shoves his shoulder. "You knave. Stop ruining this."

"Does that mean you like what you see?"

"Maybe. I'm still working on my so-called pleasures, remember?"

"Need more help with that?"

"You wish—"

Sorrow yelps when his arm snakes around her waist and tugs her against him. Their chests collide, her breasts mashing into the naked muscles of his torso. "That wish came true once," he croons into her ear, relishing the way her muscles tense and her eyelids flutter.

He remembers this, how their bodies fit. Fucking Fates, he remembers it well.

Waterfalls crash and toss fog around them. After a pivotal second, Sorrow meets his gaze with a wry aspect of her own.

"Railing me wasn't a wish," she declares. "It was a lack of options."

Envy can't decipher if the goddess sounds dispirited or pragmatically dismissive. Yet as always with her, spite chews a deep hole into his patience, the result flaring his nostrils.

Back when he discovered Sorrow missing from their camp, when he'd gone to find her, Envy had sworn he was done playing nice. And he hadn't been lying.

So be it. He swaggers closer to the goddess, primed to strike.

13

Envy

"Was it now?" His flat voice stalks across her mouth. "You're quite right. Exile from any other choices was the only motivation for sticking my cock where it never wanted to go."

The insult would repel any other deity. But not this one.

Sorrow leans further into him, her reply driving a chainsaw through his ego. "Same. I never would have had the stomach to open my thighs for you if it hadn't been for our banishment."

"Really?" Envy flings back. "Except you're used to being a loner, so that incentive doesn't track."

"You don't know what I'm used to."

"On the contrary, I know some things of note. Like the snide looks everyone used to throw your way, despite being a member of the elite crew. And the way you pretended it never mattered."

In fact, Sorrow did that so well, no one but Envy noticed. Because no one was smart enough to pay her as much attention as they did to rare Love, commanding Anger, friendly Wonder, or gorgeous Envy. By comparison, Sorrow was reduced to an afterthought among their people.

The goddess expels a harsh breath. "Not that I'd expect a more illuminating reply, but it's still a paltry example. And it's not the extent of my familiarities."

"So educate this god," Envy appeals, more eager than he cares to admit, a challenge hissing from his tongue. "And don't forget to include your actual excuse for hate-fucking me."

Feigning an apologetic tone, the goddess shakes her head. "I'm afraid that's personal."

Damn this nuisance of a goddess. Those oversized pajamas are becoming more appealing by the fucking second because he knows what's underneath them. Soft tits, firm little nipples, a freckle on her right hip, and an arrowhead scar on her outer thigh. Straight hips that know how to slant high. A ticklish waist, which he only discerned from accidentally brushing his fingers there once. And a deep, dark, drenched pussy that grabbed his dick until he lost the ability to pronounce his own name.

They stare, oxygen shearing from their lungs, her breasts pumping like a lever against his torso. All this time, they've been muttering in low, tight, conversational tones. Every jibe clamors for dominance, the animosity stifling, irritation gripping his cock and stroking it like a fist.

Abruptly, Envy lets her go. "As we were. Back to the..."

What the fuck were they talking about?

Sorrow also recovers from the contentious trance, her pupils dimming as they fumble to recall the subject at hand. "The meaning behind us and humans."

Right. For shit's sake.

"To answer your earlier question, I like humans," he imparts. "I favor them even more after being a voyeur for this long. Their unapologetic passions and how they feel a multitude of indulgent things simultaneously, despite their short lifespan. The concept of families and how much they cherish that custom."

"It would be nice to have a family." Sorrow scoots atop a neighboring boulder, her limbs hanging over the side. "At least, it appears that way from the outside."

"Fascinating, isn't it?" Envy inquires, propping one hip against the same rock and twisting toward her. "To be linked to someone through blood? To thread your life with theirs, in spite of your differences? Not every human dedicates themself to that, and sometimes I don't blame them. But for many, the bond is strong in a way I can't fathom. So much compromise. Such emotional turmoil paired with emotional bliss. All that pain and joy."

"The word for it is love," Sorrow says quietly.

Another inexplicable itch crawls across his skin. Envy forces a laugh while rubbing the back of his neck. "Only Love herself can confirm that."

"Or she and Andrew. Or Anger and Merry. Or Malice and Wonder."

Point taken. The reason Envy and Sorrow are the exception in their crew is the same reason they're no longer lust partners. This, despite that legend claiming if they commit to something beyond a collaborative stress-fuck, something deeper and supposedly profound, then they'll have better odds of winning this war.

Not a chance. Plus, as his stinging conscience reminds him on a consistent basis, he's got no right to expect anything. That door is shut for more reasons than just their mutual animosity. And that's his fucking fault.

Anyway. Love and Andrew fell hard over the span of two weeks. Anger and Merry in the same amount of time. Wonder and Malice in thirty days.

For a deity? That's nothing. In fact, that much can also be said for humans.

Their peers are phenomenal in that respect. But otherwise, no deity would lose their hearts in only a few days, assuming this was possible for two divine rivals. Even if he hadn't made a grave mistake—and still hasn't fucking told her about it—there's no way Envy and Sorrow can make this work. Not in a thousand years, much less in less time than it takes to host a decent orgy retreat.

The enclave of pools percolate around them. A school of dragonflies flits past on organza wings.

Envy straightens a crease in his low-slung pants. "On second thought, we may not know what it's like to be smitten, but we've witnessed it enough to detect the warning signs."

"We'd recognize them," she asserts.

"We'd see them coming," he agrees.

They watch each other, trailing off into the sort of blasted silence that contradicts everything they've just claimed. In any event, Envy and Sorrow at least understand enough about that complex emotion to stop it from happening. When all is said and done, a sinner and a saint would make a more promising match than them.

For a gritty round of hate-sex, they're compatible. However, that's the extent of their prospects, especially in the long term. And for deities, it's quite a long fucking term.

Envy tapers his eyes in the thought. "If you were a human—"

Sorrow snorts. "Are we playing this game? It's something Merry or Malice would think up."

Bravo to them. But Envy's not in the mood to bring up other people. As usual, only one figure has his undivided attention.

It's a cheeky move, one that requires consent. Even so, Envy sidles nearer. Slowly, the span of his waist nudges between Sorrow's thighs, flaring them apart as he flattens his hands on the rock, his arms bulging on either side of her hips.

The goddess sucks in a gale of air. At the same time, those glacial eyes slit, refusing to quail.

There now. If she had objected, he'd already be nursing a black eye.

His gaze rakes across her face, his voice growing coarser by the second. "If you were human, what—"

"—sort of family would I have?" Feigning nonchalance, Sorrow scoots farther up the boulder. "I admire the human parents who strive to feed, clothe, and house their offspring despite severely limited means. That's the most inspirational level of endurance and dedication. And maybe a little brother would be nice."

"An intimate life," Envy husks. "I wouldn't have thought you'd care for that much intimacy. The smaller the household, the harder it is for you to disappear in it."

Shadows dig into the crevices of her face. "What makes you think I want to disappear?"

Shit. Despite their push and pull minutes ago, that exchange had been on equal levels. Whereas this question wrings Sorrow out like a towel.

Envy hesitates. "What I meant—"

"Just because I don't care what people think of me, and just because I keep to myself, that doesn't mean I don't want any connection at all."

"That isn't what—"

"It doesn't mean I'm incapable of having connections."

"I never said that."

Sorrow throws her arms toward the misty ambience. "You're the one who spent your life retreating here, not me. You're the one who stashed yourself away, every chance you got. *Your* words, remember?"

"Sorrow." Envy cups her knees. "I'm sorry."

Defensively, she jerks her legs away. Regardless, her features constrict, that glower bordering on fragile. For such a melancholic goddess, she's unaccustomed to hearing apologies directed her way, especially from him.

And to say the least, Envy's not used to giving them. Although their earlier antagonist exchange had been business as usual, he doesn't want things to end on a malicious note. Not on this front.

"I'd want a big family, a house full to the brim," he mitigates, hoping to erase the past sixty seconds. "The more, the merrier. My parents would be partners who respect each other, and I'd have sisters. Lots of them."

Sorrow is still bristling, so it takes her a while to reply. "Let me guess," she mutters. "To play dress-up with."

A smirk pulls across his mouth. "Is there any other reason?"

They chuckle mildly. It's a simple sound yet not simple at all, which makes it the loudest one he's ever heard.

It's also a pleasant noise. Indeed, Envy can count on one hand the number of nuanced discussions he's had with others, none of them this unpredictable.

Around them, waterfalls range from vigorous downpours, to modest surges that wash down mantels of rock, to rivulets splitting over the tiered slabs. Tranquilized by the effusion, they withdraw into their own separate thoughts.

After that spell, Envy perks up. "I forgot a crucial pleasure on my list. The sound of a long, drawn-out orgasm."

Sorrow wraps both arms around her upturned legs. "Which sexual orientation?"

"Don't make me choose. They're all delectable."

"That's true."

Which gives him pause. Although her tastes are as varied as Envy's, this female has never revealed the extent of her experience. In particular, the head count, the undisclosed tally of which causes his molars to grind.

"How many have you been with?" Envy grates out, his timbre honed like a murder weapon.

Sorrow balks, her eyebrows cinching. "You've had three millennia to ask that. And you definitely could've gotten it out of me when we were screwing."

"That's not what I wanted to get out of you."

"Why the sudden interest? Hoping to compare yourself?"

"It depends. Did you like fucking me?" He looms so far that her calves scissor apart once more. "Bending your ass for me?" Then he snatches her ankles and juts her forward, spearing her thighs wide and stepping farther into the vent. "Spreading your cunt around me?"

Like a brushfire, her skin pebbles. "You know I did," she confesses with a grudge.

"Hmm. I know you bounced on my cock like a rabbit in heat, came like a comet, and then evacuated the premises like a vestal virgin. That's what I know."

"You had your fun. I didn't leave you hanging." She holds up her hand before he can open his filthy, well-stocked mouth. "Bad choice of words."

"Trust me, I wasn't hanging."

"You relieved tension."

"What about the aftershocks? That's what I'd like to know."

"So this is about you."

"But of course," Envy says without preamble. "I'm a god."

What else is there to say? Self-congratulation is underrated in mortals, not deities. Certainly it's about validation, and of course he wants verification of his prowess. There's no other reason. It has nothing to do with how she internalizes the experience for herself. That's her business.

So why is he curious about her ideas of intimacy and whether she yearns for it? Why is he eager to find out how deeply he can push that button?

And why the fuck is he desperate to know the sounds she'd make if he found that button? If he tapped his finger against it lightly, teasing that spot and prolonging the buzz.

Dense air radiates from the split of Sorrow's legs, her thighs flanking his hips. Because mere inches divide the most controversial, misbehaving parts of their anatomy, Envy's head levitates, taking his senses with it. More drastic, his dick swells from balls to crown at the thought of skimming her clit until she's in agony, begging for things she can't name. Her cries would drown out this enclave, ringing louder than the cascades, the mutinous sounds charging through his veins like electric currents.

They've done everything short of kissing, yet it's as if they've done nothing. Fair enough, since they'd never surpassed anything sexually clinical. Every groan, every pump of his cock, and every stream of cum had been transactional.

But there had been moments, incidents in which he'd taken her hand and skirted his mouth across her knuckles. One time, Sorrow responded by calling him an idiot. Yet she had tucked her face behind her hair and almost smiled.

Almost. Like earlier, when they were ensconced beside the lagoon.

Envy gives a start, realizing his fingernails have sunk into a low branch draping across the boulder. A crack now runs through the bark from the pressure of his grip, the bough's width at least three inches in radius.

If Sorrow notices his overreaction, she doesn't make an issue of it. Instead, the goddess shimmies off the rock and saunters past him. "I'd rather not know what I'm missing."

Challenge accepted. Envy snatches her arm, cutting off the retreat. Yanking her backward, he hauls Sorrow into his torso fast enough to give the female whiplash, his abdomen flush with her rigid spine.

Trapping her against him, he grazes his mouth over her jaw, his molten voice licking across her skin. "I can prove you wrong."

Sorrow tenses, heavy pants chuffing from her lungs. "If you had been any good in the first place, you would've already done that."

So much for keeping things light. Envy swings her around. "I know a plethora of immortals who would testify to the contrary, but no matter. Hear this, my nymph. I gave you the perfunctory fuck you wanted and the superficial release we both needed. I tried to indulge in more, but I'm not about to squander my talents on someone who doesn't appreciate it."

"I thought the God of Envy could seduce anyone."

"He can. He *has*." Envy grins to his best advantage, knowing which kind of sass will infuriate her the quickest. "You put out, didn't you? I wasn't imagining your cunt strapped around my dick, every wet inch smearing me to the sac."

She opens her mouth, but he sets a finger against it, no longer in the frame of mind to be magnanimous but in every mood to attack. "If you'd been more advantageous, I might have engaged. But now, I'm seeing things clearly. From your lackluster attitude about pleasure, I'm guessing you haven't been exposed to that many examples. You may have opened your pussy for others, you may have rutted with me, but you know shit about sensuality. You've only grasped the mechanics of a stiff cock, not the exquisite suffering of rapture just out of reach. And yet, now you're accusing me of blowing smoke. Don't give yourself airs, little goddess. If you had been worth the effort instead of a disappointment, I would've known. Like you said, it was just a bit of fun. I had no one else with whom to lower my standards."

Sorrow sucks in a haunted breath. Those gray lips part in shock, her chin wobbling.

Fuck. That went too far.

To a small degree, they've talked about feeling pain. But they haven't scratched the surface, and they definitely haven't broached the subject of *giving* pain.

That's what this moment is. That's what turns Envy's stomach.

This is the pain of hurting someone. And now he knows what that feels like.

In addition to the slap that follows.

14

Sorrow

His inflated head whips to the side. The wet clap of a waterfall hitting a nearby pool punctuates the momentum between Sorrow's hand and Envy's face, his sculpted torso jerking from the impact, the sharp motion visibly aggravating his wound.

Envy hisses as though Sorrow's knocked him out of alignment. And good. If she struck him that hard, maybe it would reorder his brain chemistry. Or at least pull a few of his interconnected muscles to the point where he'll experience impotency for a solid century.

By the time the miserable fucker has got his noggin screwed back on, she's already torching a lethal path through the foliage and out of the cul-de-sac, feminine rage accelerating her speed. Pebbles crunch beneath her bare feet, and damp soil stains the flannel hem of her pants. Striking across the pathway, Sorrow berates herself. Despite the gratification of putting a blemish on his face, she should know better than to trust her visceral responses to this god. It's never led her anywhere productive.

Yet they'd been having such an amiable time together. At some point, they moved past the discomfort, and she allowed herself to get carried away. Sorrow would go so far as to describe this evening as magical, with its lush lagoon and effortless conversation.

Drumroll. She'd had fun.

After their discussion loosened her reserve, she had been game to see where this disarray took them. Envy said things she hadn't expected, dispelling myths about himself. Normally, Sorrow would celebrate this revelation, if only to verify there's a soul behind the bullshit. Though tonight, it had plagued her for reasons unknown.

All the same, he'd reconfirmed other facts. If that overweening male knows anything, it's how to seduce a conquest. Likewise, how to piss them off.

He had ruined this night. Worse, Sorrow helped him do it. If anything, she should have dismissed his rebuttal rather than flying off the handle, as if his opinion matters.

It doesn't. Like hell does Sorrow give an immortal fuck about his judgements and assumptions.

Really, she should have slapped herself, not him. She should have kicked her own ass for letting her guard down, for believing they could spend a single civilized night in the same proximity.

He'd smelled like dark rum and amber.

With a growl, Sorrow hurls out her arms, beating aside the shrubs. His stench is immaterial, a ploy for the weak who think being a garden-variety dickhead increases the sex appeal of heroes. In her estimation, the more despicable a person behaves, the uglier they get. A chiseled jaw, a pair of full lips, a cock more sought after than the Holy Grail, and a six-pack that deserves its own empire haven't a prayer of amending that.

Over the generations, Sorrow remained conscious of Envy's extreme looks, his handsomeness more a fact than a source of arousal. She's grown accustomed to his immaculate face. As such, she will not fall victim to his crap. Not after the hunky, godly fucker criticized her, seeking to invalidate her worth. That's the deal breaker of all deal breakers.

And yes, she's cognizant of the irony.

Tendrils of mist rise from the depression to her left. Condensation floats within beams of starlight, creating a shimmering prism effect.

While admiring the sight, Sorrow takes another step. Then the ground opens up and swallows her.

15

Sorrow

The scream launches up in her throat, then sticks to the roof of her mouth. A slab of rock sweeps beneath her feet the instant she plants her weight there, the slick foundation shifting with such velocity, she plummets like a sack of grain into a void that wasn't there seconds ago.

The bottomless well stretches its jowls, consuming Sorrow whole. Blackness obliterates her vision, the drop hard and swift, her stomach overturning. Her fingers swipe outward, then slam onto a protrusion.

Reflexes kicking in, Sorrow snatches the chink, her body jerking in place. Every muscle shrieks with pain, a brittle cry lurching from her tongue. The sudden stop would have ripped a human in half. Instead, she dangles like a thread of seaweed, water showering down on her.

After a moment, Sorrow's immortal senses reinforce themselves. Trickles of moonlight pour into the narrow channel, spotlighting crusted walls leaking with miniature waterfalls, the cascades threatening to break her grip.

Liquid clogs Sorrow's nostrils, depleting her of oxygen. She twists her head, hacking up the fluid, the motion drawing her gaze to the abyss. Below, eerie vapors sizzle like a sulfur pit.

Panic soaks into her pours. With the deluge cascading from the rifts, she can't evanesce. And without her archery, Sorrow lacks arrows to stab the walls and boost her upward.

Her gaze snaps toward the hole through which she'd fallen. Beyond the torrent, an X is embedded into a tree, branches tenting over the crater.

Fuck. Envy had warned her not to venture near any areas labeled with that symbol. But while she'd been paying heed to those markings, the prism had blotted out the warning sign.

Envy!

Her psyche latches onto The Stars and calls out to him. Yet a minute passes, and still nothing. He could have manifested here within moments.

Not about to hang around like fodder for whatever lurks beneath, Sorrow tosses her gaze about, assessing the funnel. If her free hand can snare the plate, she can hoist herself upward. However, water sloshes down, beating into her like fists and preventing any chance of gaining leverage.

Past the torrential falls, a ledge juts from the opposite facade. The cascades tumble down from there as well, but with less force.

Heart hammering, she flails both limbs, heels seeking purchase. Yet it's too far, her toes scraping the surface.

If she continues like this, the struggle will deplete her reserves. And seriously, after all that's occurred, she's not about to die this way, following a spat with her greatest rival and forsaking her crew.

Love has given Sorrow insight into mechanics of flying. Wonder has imparted details about balancing on the most precarious surfaces. And Merry has somehow managed to imbue Sorrow with more positive energy than the sun itself. At least, on rare occasions.

Channeling her friends, plus a dose of commonsense and her own kinetic skills, Sorrow swings her limbs forward. The force propels her toward the facing edifice, where she flattens both soles on the rocky wall. Then she shoves away, boosts herself backward, and prays to the almighty Stars.

As she pitches into the air, her fingers release the projection. Taking advantage of the momentum, Sorrow twists and focuses on the ledge while plunging. The instant her feet strike down, she flings her arms toward the wall and seizes the crevices. Her body smacks into the stone, where she heaves in place, her lungs chuffing oxygen.

Then she gets moving, craggy fragments of stone nipping her flesh. Gritting her teeth, Sorrow clambers up the pit, careful to locate each chink before capturing it and hauling herself toward the opening.

One of the slabs shifts as she grasps the lip. Yanked off balance, she wobbles and grasps another, which also scrolls from its position. Sorrow scrambles to grab yet another ledge, this one holding fast.

So that's what triggered the fall. While distracted by that prism, she'd set her foot on one of the plates, driving the bastard into motion like a natural booby trap.

More random slabs shuffle, forcing Sorrow to cling wherever she can. Or perhaps it's not random.

Moonlight glazes each jutting stone that bears her weight. "A lunar path," she whispers to herself.

It's not an official term. But it sounds accurate.

The glinting rays appear to mark the safest route. Hardly a guarantee, but at this juncture, she'll take what she can get.

On a hunch, Sorrow follows the moon, each gleaming slab aiding the ascent. Several feet from the top, anxious hope motivates her quicker. As she reaches for the last stone, the moonrays change course as they normally would with each passing hour. Out of nowhere, the ledge she'd been aiming for veers out of the way.

Sorrow yelps, slips, and jerks to a halt. A male hand snatches her wrist, breaking her fall.

Her head whips toward the god's frantic expression. "I've got you," Envy growls, his pupils flaring. "I've got you, my nymph."

Relief pries a strange noise from her lips. "Envy."

"I'm here. And you're almost free. Now do what you do best and survive."

Nodding, Sorrow clasps his arm and charges forth. Alternating between his face and the lunar path, she bolsters herself higher.

Envy's bicep inflates, hauling Sorrow toward him with the strength of a backhoe. Together, they pull her from the depths, and she spills over the edge.

The brunt takes Envy down with her as they tumble to the ground, landing in a wheezing heap. Flopping onto their backs, they gape at the canopy, their chests heaving like pumps.

Three breaths later, the pride god veers her way. Grabbing her face, he checks for signs of injury and barks out, "You okay?"

Gulping lungfuls of air, Sorrow bobs her head. "I'm all right. The prisms—"

"I know. It happened to me once. Though at the time, the drop was dry, and I was able to evanesce."

"I didn't see the arrow marking until it was too late."

"Oh, I'm sure you were vigilant even while pissed," he tries to joke, despite the harsh lines in his visage. "The prisms are too dense for the marking to be obvious. That's probably what also delayed your call from reaching me."

Sorrow drags herself to a sitting position, with Envy still framing her profile. "Thank you," she pants.

His mouth slants into a grin. "As much as I'd love to bask in the credit, I didn't do much. You were less than a yard from saving yourself. Even when you slipped that final time, you maintained balance. My hand just reacted on instinct, basically as a backup."

"The point is you came."

"The point is you called."

Envy's quiet tone draws Sorrow's gaze. They stare, their attention cementing before the crash of a waterfall jolts them out of the spell.

Gaining their feet, they inspect the stone plates. "They shift only once," Envy provides. "They won't rearrange themselves until the gap seals shut."

Regardless, they pick carefully around the well, their hands clasping. For a while, they walk in companionable silence. In thousands of years, it's not as if Sorrow hasn't weathered battles, skirmishes, or natural threats before. Yet the experience leaves her shaken, maybe because there's more at stake. If she dies, her crew will be one fighter short.

Gradually, her pulse slows, and her body ceases trembling. In a safe zone, she eases her fingers from Envy's and approaches the rim of a tranquil pool. Despite what could have been Sorrow's final hour, the experience stokes her defiant side. It would be a shame to leave this place with a traumatized aftertaste in her mouth instead of savoring its benevolent corners instead. Quite simply, the notion bothers her.

The basin ripples, reachable by a trail extending from the bank, its surface reflecting a netting of fern trees and vines. Bits of the sky leak through the mesh, celestials poking holes through the canopy.

On impulse, Sorrow peels off the pajamas and sheds them on the ground. After stepping from one mossy outcropping to the next, she dives in. The depth catches her, the current swirling around her body. Pumping her limbs, she swims along the perimeter, supported by the deep, solitude easing her cramped muscles.

Crashing through the surface, she paddles around a pair of trees germinating from the water. It's a shallow area, the foundation elevating so that she can sit with her back against one of the trunks. Resting there, she kicks her legs in front of her, lightly splashing.

Being ambushed and targeted for death several times in one night. Combatting with a legion of furious Dark Gods. Plummeting down a violent rapid and falling overboard. Almost drowning in the Astral Sea. Hiding from detection near the residences of her former kin. Washing up in this undisclosed location, estranged from the crew, unaware of what's happened to them. Nearly plunging to her demise in this enclave.

All in less than two days.

But there's been good parts too. Friendlier ones.

Closing her eyes, Sorrow coaxes herself to think about pleasure instead of pain, life instead of death. If she doesn't, the latter will win and trample all over this night.

Time ceases to exist, minutes or maybe hours passing. At some point, hyperawareness radiates from nearby. As always, she senses when his shadow looms close.

Sorrow's eyelashes fan apart. The hedges shift, brushing like fingers as he steps into view, that large and powerful body laminated in the shades of eventide. Propping his shoulder against a banked tree, Envy watches her.

Nothing more. He just watches Sorrow with an unfathomable expression, as if her discarded clothing isn't puddled by his feet, as though her nudity is inconsequential compared to the fact that she's still breathing.

Sorrow sprawls before him, visible from the collarbones up. Although the water conceals every explicit detail he's seen multiple times, the god's presence provokes an infestation of goosebumps.

The falls plunge from the inclines. Motes glow like fireflies, highlighting his broad face and the mahogany spill of his mane.

She would invite Envy for a swim, since physical activity will keep them busy. But she doesn't have to, for he's capable of disrobing on his own.

Like he's doing now.

Holding her gaze, Envy unwinds the cloth protecting his wound. Twin hipbones vanish into the low-slung pants, and as his fingers pinch the waistband,

Sorrow staples her eyes to his.

The pants puddle to the grass. Even so, she doesn't need to peek to know the size and shape of his cock. Heavy sac. Thick shaft. Wide, ruddy head. A line cutting through his crown.

And yet. While this male has always given the impression of being perpetually erect, routinely treating his dick like the Eighth Wonder of the Ancient World, there's no sign of arousal at the moment. For all she knows, her near-death experience has deflated his dick.

So. His libido has limits, after all.

Sinking into the pool, Envy hums, the water bathing his injury. Settling across from Sorrow, the pride god lounges against the second tree like a spoiled king who's got the world at his feet.

After a beat, he grins that obscene Envy Grin. "Warning. Now that the excitement is over, my naughty side might be getting a second wind."

He's trying to make her laugh. And it's working. "What am I going to do with you?"

"Once you've recovered from this latest episode, I can think of a few smutty things. Though, I'd better be careful what I say, or you're liable to smack me again." His humor drops like a mask. "I'm sorry, for the second and third time tonight. I shouldn't have said what I did, and I shouldn't have fucking brought you here to begin with. If I hadn't..." Hissing, he shakes his head. "I'm a fucking idiot."

"No," Sorrow presses. "My fall wasn't your fault."

Envy tears his gaze away, a muscle ticking in his jaw. "Many other things are."

Her insides twist into knots. "You're not the only one."

They falter, listening to the cascades. Although water separates them, the distance is insufficient. They sit near enough for Sorrow's toes to graze his. Moreover, for their limbs to tangle, if they so wish.

Once upon a regrettable time, they found themselves in such a predicament. Isolated in a similar setting, they'd been too fed up to ignore one another any longer. That's how they got into a nasty, lusty mess in the first place. The dalliance began a year and a half ago, shocking them to the core. But in the end, taking leave of their senses hadn't panned out well. And it won't now.

That doesn't mean they must remain at each other's throats. What good has it done? Their cat fights have been exhausting and confounding, and Sorrow doesn't want to analyze why he's the only one who, with a mere flick of that gilded tongue, succeeds in getting under her skin like a splinter.

Sorrow's gaze stumbles across his. Those eyes blaze from her wet mouth, to her dripping throat, to the tops of her breasts. Damn him and that look, which reaches other places he can't currently see.

In hindsight, he idled behind while Sorrow indulged in this pool, giving her some essential alone time before approaching. And it might just be the most considerate thing he's ever done for her, even if the list is short.

"How long were you watching me?" she wonders.

Those vivid irises meet hers. "I'm not sure."

"What does that mean?"

"It means, I'm not sure."

Why does his reply sound almost three-thousand years old?

The enigma sends a reinvigorating rush of blood through her veins. Yet just as quickly, shame and remorse cut through Sorrow. Despite this impending war, she and this god have failed to get over each other's shit, which is the weakest link in the crew. If Envy and Sorrow must spend these days in isolation, and if they must spend who knows how long fighting side by side, kinship will improve their battle skills, the reconciliation strengthening their alliance.

Envy's finger taps the side of his head. "What's going on in there? Can I have a look?"

"It's forbidden territory," she cautions softly.

"Oh, my nymph. You don't know the God of Envy well, if you think the word *forbidden* will discourage him."

"Please don't talk about yourself in the third person. It sets a low bar."

"But the first person POV is cliché. As to the third, it's the height of pretension. Hence, I'm the ideal candidate."

"Have you ever been humble? For one day in your existence?"

He leans forward, his strong fingers encircling her ankles. "Perhaps I need someone to teach me." He presses his thumbs into her arch, massaging the pressure points. "I've been trained in many things, so my portfolio speaks for itself. I'm an apt pupil who learns fast."

Tension melts from Sorrow's joints, relaxing her to the point where her pussy reacts, a faint throb building in the crease. Her voice liquifies along with her limbs. "I hate to break this to you, but you couldn't be humble to save your wardrobe."

"Mmm. I'm hoping you'll be there to save me instead. I could pass out in your arms like a damsel and everything."

"I'll rephrase. You couldn't be humble or *platonic* to save your wardrobe."

"And my offer still stands," he husks, that resonant baritone stroking flesh with as much finesse as his fingers, which skim up her calves. "You could teach me to be serious. To be the wounded, brooding hero like Anger."

Sorrow emits a sigh of contentment. "For that metamorphosis to occur, you'd need to face off with your pain. And to do that, you would have to endure sadness. And to do *that*, you'd have to know humility and sacrifice." She extends her legs, granting him permission to knead higher. "You'd have to lose something precious to you." Despite the budding pulsation in her cunt, she whispers sweetly, "And baby? Your closet doesn't count."

The whisper ends on a gasp as her body fires into motion. Snaring her knees, Envy yanks Sorrow across the pool. Her breasts slam into his torso, his grip splitting her thighs around his waist.

Shock robs her of speech. Embers crackle across her flesh, emulating heat in that singular way only Envy has ever achieved with her. Despite the number of times he's taken Sorrow roughly, this former lover has never gotten dominant.

The lips of her pussy abrade a broad ledge of flesh that's now fully erect. Beneath the surface, his cock stands high, the water emphasizing every smooth, turgid inch. Shackling her legs apart, Envy produces an aggravating type of friction, the bud of her clit rubbing his frenulum.

Envy's eyelids hood, a rumbling sound grits from his throat. At the reaction, a whimper pushes against Sorrow's teeth. Her breath skates across his mouth, which parts a fraction, exposing that sly tongue.

Fuck. If she scoots her pussy any closer to Envy's dick, her vision will blur, and she won't be able to see anything clearly.

By some miracle, Sorrow has the presence of mind to gather her wits, rationalizing past everything that's occurring underwater. Maybe it's the boundary he just decimated, but she takes a second to reflect before choosing how to respond.

This pride god is unreserved, decisive, and doesn't allow others to use him. When he wants something, he says so. When he wants something even more, he gets it. And when someone like Sorrow looks him in the eye, someone like Envy looks back.

Ultimately, he's a good person. No matter how much they've fucked each other over, and although he's morally grey when it comes to ridiculing lesser deities and casting off lovers who inevitably bore him, this swaggering one-man parade is an otherwise decent soul. She's not too hardheaded to deny this. In the midst of forthcoming bloodshed, the God of Envy savors life and lives to his fullest capacity.

What's that like?

"What's what like?" Envy murmurs, his voice as smooth as velvet.

Droplets fall from her lashes. "Did I just say that aloud?"

"I'm afraid so. Do it again." His hands slide to her ass, cupping the swells and nudging her cunt further into him, the effect turning his voice to gravel. "Express something without thinking."

Fates almighty. Arousal drips from the slit between her thighs, the water's gentle lap magnifying the effect.

Apparently, her waist has a mind of its own, slowly jutting forward, grinding at a languid pace against his cock. "I'll only say this once," she pants. "I'm not a toy."

"No, you're a planet," Envy hums, his own hips jutting upward, the point of his dick striking her clit. "You're uncharted territory, an unexplored land mass that would take years to reach."

Oh, fuck. He has said filthy, graphic things to Sorrow while pounding inside her, but his words have never held this seductive lilt, the reverence in his baritone throwing her off balance. Wetness pours from her cunt, drenching her more than this pool. Even if her nipples weren't pitting, Envy scents her desire, his nostrils broadening.

Flattening her palms on the tree behind his head, Sorrow uses the leverage to burrow down, chafing their flesh together. "Thank you for the compliment."

Envy's chuckle comes out guttural, infusing her veins like a cocktail. "You're welcome."

"You know, we suck at this, right? At being friends?"

"Is that what we are?"

She sinks into him, her lips grazing his own. "That's what we should be."

Allies, they've managed. Albeit with a grudge.

Friends has always been an impossibility. Over the ages, perpetual hostility was the culprit. These days, the defect has just as much to do with bodily cravings, impulses that don't seem to give a shit whether either of them is mentally on board. Deny it all they want, but bickering and turning the other way has done nothing to resolve the problem.

To make matters worse, they're currently in the wrong place at the wrong time. They've been spoiling for a hot release since their estrangement in The Celestial City, and the dormancy is wearing thin, to the point where she could fuck just about anyone right now. Doubtless, it's the same for him.

Truth. This will only end badly, as it already has once. The origins of their hate-lust are untrustworthy, not to mention unstable.

Sorrow's drenched skin flanks the hard planes of his waist. She drips all over him, liquid raining down his torso. Another inch, and his sac will skim her opening, and they'll fall victim to sexual mutiny.

He seethes across her mouth, trapping her thighs and jabbing his thick cock in shallow, teasing motions. "But you still hate me."

"Yeah," she whines, so low it's barely audible. "I hate you so much."

Envy nods in agreement. "So fuck it."

Then he grits out a violent noise, shackles her ass, and hauls her forward.

16

Sorrow

Her body slams against his. The force knocks their mouths against one another, furious sounds belting off their tongues and then engulfed by the mist like a filthy secret. As if this place won't tell a soul what's about to happen, the mayhem they're about to cause one another, because they just don't know when the fuck to quit.

Sorrow's tits mash against Envy's torso, her nipples tightening into his pecs. Beneath the surface, their pelvises strike together, the abrasion pulling a whine from her lips. Her clit taps his long cock, the friction assaulting her in a way it hasn't before. Silken and weightless. Despite their physical history, they've never railed each other in the water.

As her labia skates across the bridge of his dick, a groan crawls from Envy's throat. The predatory noise flares Sorrow's skin with goosebumps, and the walls of her cunt pulsate, liquid seeping from the crease. Since deities have potent senses, he deciphers the difference between the pool lapping against his erection and her arousal pouring onto him.

"Fuck almighty," Envy husks, clasping her ass, tacking her pussy to his cock. "You're soaked more than this pool."

"And you're harder than stone," Sorrow pants. "So who wins?"

"Hmm. To find that out, we'd need to get a lot closer." His voice crackles across her flesh like static. "You hate me, you say? Then do it, my nymph. Hate me hard."

Clamping onto her backside, he jerks Sorrow into him. From the brunt, an insubordinate sound jumps off her tongue. It's something between a whine and a growl, needy and resistant. But while that makes no sense, neither has anything he's ever made her feel.

With serpentine motions, Envy rows Sorrow back and forth, reeling her pussy against his standing cock. "Hate me so much, it makes you come."

Another rickety sound leaps from her mouth, and her fingers dig into the trunk balancing them. The pride god has pounded her in every way but this. Languid. Lethargic. As lazy and sensuous as this pool, with the cascades washing around them.

Despite his aggressive hold, Envy takes his time, pacing her hips, lulling her into him. He tows her cunt sinuously along his cock, guiding her from his balls to the wide crown, the gliding motions enabling her to feel every inch of them rubbing together. In tandem, moans trip from Sorrow's mouth, which falls open in astonishment.

Envy's dick bloats further, expanding her soaked groove. He rocks her gently into him, his attention riveted on her, the challenge flashing in his irises.

Try resisting this. Try breaking it off. Try it hard.

Sorrow gives a low, stunned cry when his tip hits a place that throws tingles up her spine. Fluid licks her skin, the balmy air varnishing her breasts and his torso, rendering every movement sleeker. Desire floods from her core, the flux pouring onto Envy's erection, every leisurely drag of her pussy smearing him to the base.

The god hums. Locking their hips, he gyrates into motion, rolling his waist up and down. Matching her tempo, he synchronizes every slow beat, heightening the abrasion. His cock and her pussy slip and slide, swaying to and from one another. This produces a ripple effect, the eddies trembling, which accentuates the pleasure.

Yet the teasing is too much, far too much. Pressure grabs her cunt, the result gushing from her slit. Sorrow bites her lower lip until the taste of brine seeps into her palate.

With a famished hiss, Envy leans into her and draws his tongue across her mouth, consuming the blood like wine. At the flavor, a satisfied purr curls from him. Oh, he knows what she's trying to do.

To push her limits, Envy changes angles. Groping Sorrow's ass, he raises her slightly off his lap, then sinks her down, altering the direction of their thrusts. This lowers her clit along his cock, blasting her with embers.

"Oh," she keens. "Oh, gods."

"Fuck, yes," he mutters, watching her, always watching her. "That's it. Hate me good."

But when he says this, he means it differently, indicating a drawn-out, torturous kind of fuckery. That makes it new and unfamiliar, as though they've never done a single, carnal thing to one another. As if this is the first time.

And damn this motherfucker. Sorrow fights to keep it in, but loses that battle, a long-suffering moan dropping from her mouth like a plea for mercy. Her forehead lands against his, her muscles going limp, helpless as he takes over.

Relishing this window of dominance, Envy croons with triumph. He bobs Sorrow in place, rhythmically sketching her pussy up and down the front of his cock, from the roof to his heavy sac.

Oh. Fucking. Fates.

Somehow, her listless posture intensifies the stimulation. Her cleft softens, accentuating every pass of his erection. Easing the muscles of her pussy ratchets up the stimulation in a pivotal way, enhancing sensitivity like voltage, the tension augmenting worse than before. Like this, Sorrow absorbs each brush of movement, each long track of his cock, its height and width sweeping in the trench of her thighs.

Yielding should make her feel submissive, no better than one of his defenseless and shallow admirers. But instead of powerlessness, Envy's haggard response imbues Sorrow with authority. His knuckles bend, gripping her firmer, territorial yet drastic, as though he fears she'll change her mind and end this, as though he can't stand the notion. From the beholden way he clings, Sorrow isn't being feeble.

No, she's being generous. She's letting this god service her needs, allowing him the privilege.

Even so, Sorrow's undiluted cries contradict her. To her own ears, she's delirious, out of control.

Only this time, it's not just an even exchange. Rather, it's shared. Instead of one figure giving in, they're both plunging down that hill.

Needless to say, it's a delayed fall from grace. Patient. Seductive. All the things he's attempted with her in the past, all the things she's denied him out of misguided self-preservation. It's clear now, her prior choice to shrug off foreplay had been foolish. She'd been doing herself a disservice by not exploring.

This whole time, they could have rutted in this provocative manner eons ago. It's not as if Sorrow had lacked the fortitude to resist any residual aftereffects, emotions like fondness. Sensuality wouldn't have weakened her. She wouldn't have grown attached. Definitely not.

Just like she's not about to get attached now. They've merely tumbled off the wagon, drunk on one another, too intoxicated to see straight.

And fine. One more round won't kill them.

"Someday, you're going to kill me," Envy grits out, allegedly reading her mind.

Another moan spills from Sorrow, as easily as her cunt spills onto him. "You're assuming this will happen again."

"Won't it?"

"Fuck, no."

He chuckles through his groan, that gruff baritone too sexy for his own good. "I do fancy a challenge. But if that declaration is true, you're enjoying this more than you should."

"And you're relishing this more than you deserve," she throws back, her words ending on a yelp as the roof of his cock taps her oval just so.

"Tsk, tsk," Envy pants, his frame swatting against her own. "Never tamper with a pride god's sense of entitlement."

"Only because pride gods don't know how to earn what they want."

His pupils blacken like mine shafts, their depths immeasurable. "Is that a fact?"

Uh-oh. That glossy, bottomless look means business.

Envy's silken threat dances into the balmy night air. "Then I'll just have to fucking prove you wrong."

His prowess sufficiently questioned, he fastens onto Sorrow's backside and exaggerates their movements. Slower but steadier. With affronted vigor, he rolls into her, putting his entire physique into the effort, his whipcord torso flexing.

An aggrieved cry detonates from Sorrow, the calamitous noise traveling far, feasibly reaching uncharted dimensions. He steers her atop his dick, boosting her above him, siphoning Sorrow's cunt along his crown, the flared head rubbing, stroking. Magnetic charges streak from her calves to her clit, neither delicate, nor tender. On the contrary, the tingles are sharp, the pressure thick. This god might as well have plugged her into a socket and amped up the wattage.

And Stars eternal. This is what it feels like to blend pain with pleasure.

The hybrid sensations assault Sorrow's consciousness. However unwelcome, this epiphany rouses her to another zenith, as mind-bending as a psychedelic. It's the most exquisite form of torment, splicing agony with ecstasy.

Sorrow wants him to lay into her the way he always has. Faster, harder, rougher. Yet she also wants nothing of the sort, wants him to keep pacing this, keep drawing out the slow-motion anarchy.

The sinuous pump of Envy's ass has Sorrow spiraling, his dick on the verge of plying her cunt apart and pitching deeply. Temptation scorches her flesh. His erection and her crease are too close to one another, on the brink of attaching. It would scarcely require Sorrow to angle herself forward, then lower onto him, the radius of his cock splitting her in two.

That's all it would take to crack her in half. That's all it would take to ruin them.

Too intimate. At this focused, unhurried rate it would be far too intimate. Everything about their motions is intentional, fixated, enduring. It's a harsh and dedicated type of feverishness that can't go further. Because if it does, they'll smash through a dangerous boundary from which they can't return.

They won't just hurt and repel each other. They'll disappoint each other.

The former is nothing new. The latter is not.

Someday, you're going to kill me.

Ditto. This god might be right, providing they push this as much as possible.

And yet. Sorrow's moans hang by a thread, and Envy appears just as unhinged. For all their determination to see this through, they might wreck one another before reaching the finish line.

Envy's sculpted body is a monolith. Condescension races across his burnished skin, the cobbled muscles rippling. Broad pecs. Dusky nipples. Stacked abs. His dark mane pours down his shoulders like velvet, one of his favorite textiles.

Shit. The vision makes it more difficult to resist outright fucking instead of partial fucking.

Sorrow can't say who takes the initiative. Either way, her head flings back, strands of hair dashing down her back. Her spine coils into an arch, her glistening body surfacing from the pool and craning toward the branches. Exposed and splayed around Envy's waist, she clasps his nape, riding the agile slope of his cock.

In this position, with her figure bowing from the water, Envy has an unhampered view. His dick, sliding along her cleft. Her pussy, dripping down to his sac. The sight unleashes a heavy snarl from his chest, his hips snapping gently, jolting her into the air.

Muttering an oath, he bows into her. And the clamp of his lips seals around one tight nipple.

Sorrow chants a shitload of noise. The clamor of sensation attacks her on all fronts, his mouth cinching around the kernel and tugging. His drone vibrates against her flesh, sucking her deeply, his tongue licking the peek.

This goes on, and on, and on. All the while, his waist doesn't let up, probing back and forth.

At length, Envy transfers his mouth to the other breast, fusing his hungry mouth to the other waiting nipple. Every indulgent pull yanks a weepy noise from Sorrow, the volume increasing, the cascades swallowing it whole.

Envy swabs her nipple raw, cursing into the bud, lapping on her. Sorrow's fingernails bite into his neck, cleaving until the god hisses in delight, blood rising from where she's broken skin.

And well, it's the least a Dark God can handle. Certainly more than she's handling the deft slides of his tongue.

The need for added friction overtakes her. Spread apart, with both knees outstretched, Sorrow plants her cunt against Envy's abdomen.

Braced there, she punts herself into him, her soaked center rapping over his torso, smearing her arousal on his flesh.

The god pries his mouth from her nipple and seethes, "Fucking hell."

Then he lugs Sorrow forward with a speed that defies immortal logic. Her breasts smash into him, one palm returning to her ass, the other shackling her skull in place. Wrenching her limbs wider, Envy moors Sorrow to his lap and slings his cock until she's writhing.

His eyes pin her down, their foreheads nailing to each other, mouths ajar. His groans drench Sorrow more, open her more. As a result, disorderly noises stumble from her vocal cords.

He's always been an expert at this, chipping through her like a thin layer of ice. But at some point, between their previous dalliances and now, he's gotten even better, if that's remotely plausible. Either that, or she has no excuse for the desperate moans expelling from her lungs, toppling over the precipice of her tongue one after the other, as if on a conveyor belt.

Envy humps Sorrow to within an inch of her sanity. And it's so monstrously good, she's quaking from head to toe.

Her eyes flutter, threatening to seal shut. Catching that, Envy utters feral noise.

"No," he rasps, snaring her jaw with one hand while squeezing her naked ass with the other. "Eyes on me, Nymph. See who's wetting your pussy. Watch how much he hates you back."

Despite the context, this god makes the demand sound erotic, the opposite of its literal implication. Sorrow is in no mood to think straight. Yet in the midst of chaos, the command works as efficiently as a mechanism.

Sorrow's torn between violating his order and welding her vision closed, blocking out this vain deity or satisfying his wish. Struggling past the pulsation in her cunt, she gets her ass in gear and settles on a compromise, much like a bargaining chip.

She wavers, procrastinating her decision to the point where a barbarous noise vacates Envy's lungs. This reminds him that no one tells this goddess what to do. Once that becomes clear, the reality creases his features with need, only then does Sorrow obey.

Naturally with another twist. Meeting his avid gaze, Sorrow swivels into motion. Using the trunk for leverage, she matches his grip on her backside, actively taking part. Her waist contracts, laboring in concert to his hands, shearing her cunt up and down.

A strangled sound carves a path from Envy's lips. His pupils dilate, the golden brown of his irises disappearing like a magic trick. That glorious, godly cock distends past the brink, the head swelling to full capacity, so that Sorrow feels the tip toughening, the veins blowing up.

Countless deities have had this male. Yet the destitute expression slicing across his features is another type of pleasure, the discovery that she's making him feel something he hasn't in three thousand years.

Fueled by the knowledge, Sorrow chases that wave, riding the outer edges of his bare cock. He's not inside her, and she's not about to let it go that far, but it doesn't need to. The magnitude is equally destructive, just as dire.

Envy's devious lips slant. He does enjoy being taken advantage of, as much as he fancies playing the possessive lover.

Simulating the act of fucking, they charge into it. Screw tomorrow. Screw the rules. And screw him hard.

Envy growls, lashing his hips. Sorrow grunts, vaulting her waist up and down.

She bounds onto him, and he launches against her, tails of water spritzing about. Steam climbs from the surface, coating Envy's muscles in a brilliant sheen, his abdomen contorting. Droplets drizzle down the vent between her tits, the nipples ruching, aching.

Envy's thrashing cock flings her thighs apart, tearing her whines to shreds, peeling back the last vestiges of rationale. Blood courses through Sorrow, surging to the narrow rift between her legs, arousal sopping from her cunt and running down Envy's solid flesh. With a shout, her body flies into movement, landing on his lap and whipping forward this time.

The pride god husks, giving as much as she takes. They go on like this, baiting one another, battering into one another. Riled up and fed up, they establish one more common ground on which to spar, attempting to outdo the other, to make the other come first.

So help her. Sorrow has lost too often to this male. Mere days from potential death, she will not lose this time.

In short, Sorrow doesn't simply turn the tables. She fucking capsizes them.

Sorrow pitches her knees, hooks her calves over his shoulder, and rides his waist like a goddess. Tireless, she bucks into him, pelting the outer ledge of his cock. With each grind of her pussy, she wipes that smug-ass grin from his mouth, then wipes the metaphorical floor with him.

Envy's groans twist into knots. The sort he'll never be able to untangle. The kind he'll remember. Because by Fates, she won't let him forget this, how she owned him once.

His dick lifts higher, the head thickening. She pictures cum leaking from the line in his crown, mixing with her arousal.

And she can't. She just can't take it.

Crying out, Sorrow swivels her cunt quicker. Envy's eyes tense, and his balls tense against her pussy, a surefire sign he's about to come.

Always, he's demanded she climax first. Not this fucking time. She doesn't need him doing her any extra favors.

His features constrict, teeth clenching, gaze trapped within hers. And it's all she can do not to bite his lower lip. So she doesn't bother resisting.

Bending forward, Sorrow snares her incisors into his flesh. She nips until he growls, the salty taste of blood washing across their palates. Dragging her tongue along the wound, she bobs her cunt fast and sighs at the flavor.

The tidal wave crests. That's when he shatters like a cliff.

Envy throws back his head and howls to the trees, his dick spasming, cum shooting along her aching clit. Sorrow watches him, watches the orgasm rip his perfect face to bits.

The sight makes her come seconds later. Her cunt seizes up, then convulses like a tsunami, shouts tearing from her lungs. Sorrow's thighs shudder, slickness gushing from her slit and coating Envy's twitching cock. Their bodies go wild, hearts pumping like engines, their hips slamming together.

Her pussy contracts, latching to the edge of his cock, feeling every shake. Clinging like film, Envy roars, and Sorrow screams, the sounds combative.

Deities last a while. As such, they holler until they have no voices left, and there's nothing more to say.

17

Sorrow

Envy winces, the press of their bodies visibly afflicting his ribs. It's proof that he should back off. He shouldn't be clasping her naked like this.

Yet the broad expanse of his torso against her breasts isn't what provokes another clench in her pussy. It's when his forehead lands against hers, the gesture bordering on playful.

Too late, Sorrow registers her hands landing on his shoulders. For all intents and purposes, she has attached her fingers to the muscled ramps as if letting go means she'll fall.

She doesn't want to fall. She will never fucking fall.

To an outsider, they must look affectionate. However, that outsider would be very wrong. She reduces this to a horny whim, because Envy takes joy in horny whims.

With his cock still braced against her clit, the pride god raises his head, those eyes lowering to half-mast. "Do you still think we should be friends?" he rasps. "Do you think that's all we can handle?"

"I think that's a lot to handle," Sorrow professes, winded. "I think handling it will keep us pretty busy, so I think we should give it a try, and I think we should start now, because I think if you don't let me go, I think your other cheek will get smacked."

"I think I should call your bluff. I think I should ask you again. Is friendship the most we can handle?"

"It's the most this war can handle."

Envy dissects her poker face. Like a clairvoyant, he picks apart every chink, his demeanor shifting. All at once, some type of burden strains his features, as if he's seeking confirmation of her statement. In fact, Sorrow would call his expression repentant, which doesn't track.

After a moment, the god grunts and releases her. Sorrow floats backward, plagued by the aching throb at her slit, whereas the promiscuous god appears less than affected.

In reality, they don't really want each other and have made that abundantly plain. This is merely their instincts hankering for a convenient method of relief, dealing with an itch when there's no one else around to scratch it.

Still, now that it's left her mouth, what Sorrow had said about this war doesn't actually feel right. If they want the upper hand in this conflict, they should take the legend seriously. What's more, they shouldn't let Malice and Wonder's struggle to find that legend be in vain.

In a perfect world, it would be doable. The problem is their hearts can't be controlled that way.

Envy's expression folds like a house of cards. He nods, deliberates something, and fixes her with a scandalous grin. "Friends show each other their playgrounds. Do you want to see the rest of mine?"

No, no, no, no, no, no, no, no, no, no, no, no—

"Yes," she says.

Because that's what a friend would say.

Sorrow averts her gaze while Envy sloshes out of the pool and steps into his pants. Once dressed, he extends his hand to her. It's a gentlemanly action, because Envy prides himself on gallantry and refinement. Regardless of his promiscuity and penchant for sex parties, he'll offer his arm, open the door, and pull out the chair. It's usually a form of role play for this god.

Be that as it may, Sorrow wavers. Stumped, she examines his hand as if the offer is a prank, as though someone has dared him to woo the loner.

Envy cocks his head. "One, sheepishness doesn't become you. Two, I don't have eternity."

Despite herself, she muffles a laugh. "Three, are you sure about that last part?"

"Why? Has no one ever spoiled you like a goddess?"

The instant she winces, his eyes narrow. "Or maybe someone disappointed you to the point where common courtesy is mistrusted." His voice tapers like the edge of a meat cleaver. "Who were they? Which casualty do I have the pleasure of disfiguring for letting you down?"

"This coming from my oldest bully. It's a little late to play the defender."

"We're deities. It's never too late for anything."

Even so. Sorrow wasn't a virgin before Envy, but chivalry is for the "he-loves-me, he-loves-me-not" adolescents with big dreams and even bigger, starrier eyes.

Besides, so what if she doesn't have experience being catered to or adored by her lovers? Who needs that? It's clingy.

"Actually, I'm waiting for you to turn around," she says. "I appreciate the hand, but I'm not about to give you a show."

Mercifully, Envy doesn't comment. But he does sigh—a theatrical drawn-out expulsion of air that he inherited from his ego. Dropping his hand, he twists around, stuffing his hands into his pockets.

Sorrow climbs out of the water and hustles into her clothes. While she's at it, she adds another thing to her list of pleasures. Namely, the visual of Envy's taut ass in loose pants. Sleek. Firm. He may as well be hiding a pair of apples under there. By the Stars, she wants to name a holiday after that ass.

A suave chuckle reverberates from his chest. Sorrow pauses to glower at him. Shit. How the hell did he know?

When she's ready, the god rounds on her once more, glimpsing the Merry-inspired pajamas hanging off Sorrow like an oversized suit, the hems puddling to the grass and concealing her toes. Combined with her drenched hair, she could have conjured something better. In short, Sorrow has never looked less attractive in her life.

Yet Envy's eyes glow like volcanic glass. "I stand corrected," he says with relish. "By some force of magic, you look all sorts of cute in that outfit."

"If you tell anyone about this," she threatens, pointing at him. "If you spill to the crew about this night, or these clothes, or anything else, I will drive an arrow through your bloated skull."

"My, my, my. Such violence from someone who wants to be friends and doesn't care what others think of her. Just conjure your standard, ghastly attire, if you're squeamish about pink. There's no need to torture yourself on nobody's account."

So true. "Where are we going?"

For the second time, Envy takes her hand.

For the second time, Sorrow lets him.

Needless to say, the bastard is gloating, basking in the knowledge of how hard and long he made her come. Yet at least Envy's unaware of the aftershocks assaulting Sorrow's cunt. If it were otherwise, he'd never let her live it down.

While hiking amid the cascades, the god is vigilant, ushering them toward safer locations. He points out the secure landmarks that invoke memories. The bath where he taught himself to swim. The shallows where his Guide, Siren, first explained the discrepancies between egotism, conceit, and vanity. The pond where he learned to shoot an arrow underwater. That day, he almost speared a fish, who then bit a chunk out of his ass.

Sorrow chuckles at Envy's wry tone. The recesses emit mist, which sprays their clothing, and a lane of rocks tracks over a running tributary. As they walk across, he peers over his shoulder in time to witness sprigs of gray escaping from her lazy bun, an appreciative smirk crooking his mouth.

They gravitate through an alcove flanked by downpours and precipitation, illuminated from above by a spool of light. The Dark Fates possesses numerous marvels, both deadly and enchanting, from the starry cliffs to The Archives. The latter is Wonder and Malice's treasured landmark, now reduced to rubble after the carnage against The Fate Court. That her friends have lost their sanctuary plagues Sorrow with sympathy. Moreover, the possibility that Envy might lose his own sanctuary cinches her chest, a state of affairs that's never happened before.

The path widens, the falls receding into a cove. Surrounded by a ring of water, a small island of grass presides at the center. At its peak, a tree looms, its transparent leaves covered in a brilliant glaze.

Sorrow and Envy pause at the threshold, the copse packed with ferns. More ethereal motes drift in the air, one of them landing on her thigh.

Radiance from above draws her gaze. Glancing upward, she discovers the umbrella of branches where mobiles of blue glass dangle in funnel-shaped arrangements. The effect is reminiscent of a dozen chandeliers.

But they're not chandeliers. They're lunar herons.

Fates. They're sleeping, their wings emitting a prismatic glow, their slim beaks glinting blue.

Sorrow opens her mouth, but Envy's index finger presses flush against it. "Wait," he whispers. "They're waking up."

He cups Sorrow's shoulder, urging her to squat behind a hedge. She's glad he prevented her from speaking, because she would have said the wrong thing, made a declaration that doesn't live up to this scene. Ultimately, she would have filled the space with noise and disturbed the setting.

"Remember our first lessons?" Envy asks in a hushed tone. "The stories about the fauna of this land?"

Sorrow nods. "About the coves where lunar herons live in packs."

"The lectures on nature were my favorite, because nature doesn't justify itself. I fancied how something as enigmatic and unpredictable as The Stars existed. Yet in a more tangible way, like its own form of divinity."

"It scared the shit out of Anger."

"But it blew my mind," Envy admits. "I relished learning the history of nature, of anything that couldn't be fully determined by the celestials."

While whispering, he studies the avians, their shadows slicing across his jaw. For once, his expression isn't painted in a false veneer. No, it's just him, taking pleasure in the setting and sharing it with her. This moment doesn't have a greater meaning, a grand function, or a moral. Rather, it's just enjoyment for its own sake.

Deities are born from The Stars. Lunar Herons are born from the water, always during a new moon.

With a single glint of light, they awaken and spread their wings. According to the tales, they live near sacred pools, but no deity had ever found or witnessed such a spectacle.

They also shift to massive sizes when beseeched by The Fate Court. Though, the necessity is rare.

One by one, the avians break away and dash through the air. They sail about, chasing phosphorescent motes in a beautiful dance.

It's magical, a term that has grown bland to Sorrow, so commonplace that its resonance has been diluted. When was the last time she saw or felt something that was truly remarkable? Anything to which she hadn't developed an immunity? Anything that reminded her how breathtaking magic can be?

An ambiguous emotion scrapes her throat raw. "I had no idea," she exhales. "I've never seen anything like it."

"I was a stripling when I first came upon this cove," Envy murmurs. "I got lost in the enclave and ended up here, where I almost drowned in a bottomless vortex. Like in any realm, no environment is ever fully safe, dangerous, grim, or divine. It's routinely both. You can know all there is about your world, but you'll never understand everything. This place reminds me there's infinitely more to discover." He huffs under his breath. "It sounds trite, I'm fully aware."

"No. It isn't," she says. "But even if that were the case, don't you mind sounding trite in front of me?"

His voice sobers, as does his expression. "Not tonight."

So either this god feels comfortable being transparent in her company, or she's just that inconsequential. Envy curates the universe's impression of him. Everyone but her, perhaps because she matters so little.

The herons drop and fly around the cove. Some of them skate along the water's surface, scattering translucent beads of liquid.

Sorrow does her utmost to ignore the strange grip on her ribs. "It doesn't sound trite," she repeats. "It sounds like you're an outcast, like the rest of us."

"A fashionable outcast," Envy improvises, placing a finger against his smooth mouth. "Shh. It will be our secret."

"It's only been several hours. Are we already leveling up which secrets we share?"

The god tilts his head, his eyes squinting in a way that's too sexy to be tolerated. "Dear me, was that another quip? Is the Goddess of Sorrow teasing again?"

She shoves his shoulder. They twist, reclining across from each other, their backs lounging against the rocks. Speechless, they admire the scene, piebald in a swirl of darkness and lightness.

Envy once chastised Love for idling in the evergreens while she served the mortal realm. Maybe his judgment had been a front back then, a persona he'd adopted, the picture of a haughty god.

Case in point, the closer their crewmates grow, the less Envy ridicules Love's fetish for climbing trees. In fact, he commends it these days, just as he endorses Wonder's habit of meditating.

The herons rotate. As they spiral, the whole place ignites.

Sorrow's profile feels the tangible caress of Envy's gaze, the force brushing every inch of her skin. She peeks behind her hair and finds him maintaining an indolent sprawl.

"What?" she says, defensive.

"You're smiling," he answers, serious.

She would have expected him to gloat, to praise himself for diverting her. On the contrary, the god appears perplexed, as though he's never seen anyone smile and doesn't know how to interpret it.

Sorrow can't fathom what to do with her grin, invisible to her eyes yet balanced precariously on her face like a puzzle piece that has come loose. Getting a grip, she reassembles the muscles of her countenance, rearranging them into an impervious expression. Something sarcastic, dignified, or both.

Yet he's still watching her. His broad features absorb Sorrow like a sponge, consuming every facet.

She smacks the grass. "Stop doing that!"

His lips twitch. "I can't help it. Your face is doing such peculiar things, lifting in places, crinkling in others. I've never seen it change structure like this. Tell me, is the smile heavy? Or was it weightless until I pointed it out?"

"You are the most pompous motherfucker in the galaxy."

"That may have to do with my being—what's it called? A deity? A pride god?"

"Just watch the fauna, not me."

"As a youth, I tried talking with them." Envy slants his head, a lock of his mane slipping off his shoulders. "Not that they understood me."

"You never know." She surveys the avians as they soar through the cove. "What would it be like to live as fully as animals do? To live as unbridled as nature does? Do you think we would thrive or collapse?"

"You sound enthralled," Envy remarks.

"Yeah, I must be in a sappy mood."

"You must be. Either that, or it has to do with present, masculine company."

"Don't let this night go to your head. That cranium is already full enough, and I doubt anything else can fit in there."

"Wanna bet?"

Fates forbid. He's been granted the expansive features of a river. Flawless, smooth, and vast. Destiny spoiled him, which is saying something considering deities thrive on perfection.

Sorrow is hardly ignorant of her own looks. Despite Envy's harassment over the millennia, she's aware that she's pretty. Yet she doesn't care. For her, it's a trivial fact, not something to celebrate. And she'd rather be honest than beautiful.

Tucking a loose strand of hair behind her ear, she says, "Thanks for this."

Impressed, Envy quirks a brow. "I'm all ears. Thanks for what? Dare I say, you've experienced a moment of serenity in this cove? Pleasure?"

"Quit while you're ahead, asshole."

"One more request, and then I vow to hold my tongue, provided you don't use it for other purposes."

She shifts in place, suddenly restless. "What's the request? And you had better not say a lap dance."

"Show me pain."

Sorrow reels back. If she had been drinking something, she'd have spit it out. Or if she were eating something, she would have choked. "What kind of request is that?"

Envy turns away, his eyes landing on a distant point. "You ponder what it would be like to live as fully as nature. Alas," he mock-sighs. "That means relinquishing control. Thus, what you said about me avoiding pain, the same way you avoid pleasure? Let no one call the God of Envy a coward."

That's probably the closest she'll get to him admitting she was right.

"I showed you a decadent evening," he prompts. "Now it's your turn. Show me pain as only you can."

"This is madness," she insists. "This whole night is madness, all the things we've been doing and saying. We're in the middle of a war."

"Correct me if I'm wrong, but war hasn't begun yet. Our people have no clue we're here, save for a few ambitious deities. For how long? Who knows. But the fight hasn't started, and something tells me it won't in the next couple of days."

"A year ago, we would have predicted it would take generations for us to finish negotiating, before resorting to battle. Look how fast everything is happening."

"That depends on how long this has been brewing under the surface. It took The Court eons to create a Goddess of Love. At which point, that very goddess turned out to be a renegade who fell for a human, changing the course of our people. Perhaps The Stars had this plan in mind. Thus, this was always our destiny, and we've been preparing without knowing it. Otherwise, yes, it would have taken ages for the negotiations to fail. That we're susceptible to such a rapid change of heart can't be incidental."

"Fine, but teaching you about pain isn't as easy as teaching me pleasure."

"I'll do my utmost not to take offense to that," Envy drawls.

"I can't just map out a lesson plan," Sorrow insists.

He raises a single obsidian eyebrow, illustrating what he thinks of that statement. Yet no deity in their right mind should make this request, asking the Goddess of Sorrow to show them grief, melancholy, and sadness.

Be that as it may, pragmatism sets in. They could do this, become friends, show each other pleasure and pain without involving physical contact. As she theorized earlier, it might supply them with a new kind of strength to benefit this campaign.

It will also take their minds off that infernal legend.

This challenge won't be about the latter. It will be practical, an efficient kind of training. If Sorrow and Envy establish an alternative connection, something that evolves from antagonist rivalry to genuine fellowship, they will have more to contribute. If they're unwilling to force amorous emotions, this might atone for that decision.

When Sorrow communicates this, Envy nods. Maybe he'd been thinking along the same lines.

Technically, she should start slowly. However, they don't have that kind of time. In less than three days, he must leap, crash, and break.

Like a waterfall. Like a rapid.

On that score, she'll have to do it with him. This needs to be consensual, the lessons of pleasure and pain.

Herons commune amid the foliage. One winged soul sneaks up on Sorrow and settles beside her on spindle limbs. Then without a farewell, it launches into the air and rejoins its allies.

She's aware of the shift in her features, the smile that manifests. Sorrow turns to Envy, who witnessed the exchange, who's waiting for her answer.

"Deal," she says.

18

Envy

They travel in silence from the heron cove. Sorrow picks around the hedges, blades of hair sticking out of her unruly bun like straw. Such a mortal updo. Grungy isn't his forte, yet it's inexplicably endearing on this female.

By contrast, her perky goddess-ass looks downright edible in those pants, the oversized fit offering only a teasing hint of the swells. For fuck's sake, it's more alluring than a peep show. This goddess has a talent for turning subtle into salacious.

While trekking through the enclave, Sorrow walks ahead of Envy, granting him an unhampered view. Despite how things stand between them, he can still look. It would be a scandal not to appreciate the tantalizing details, to recall how those ovals contracted every time he bent her over a furnishing. To say nothing of an hour ago when he dry-fucked the anxiety out of them both.

Or more to the point, wet-fucked.

From the moment Envy heard Sorrow's frantic call tearing a hole in his head, to the fear that dug its talons into his lungs, to the terrifying sight of her dangling like a sacrifice over a well loaded with sizzling vapors, to the blast of relief when he extracted her, to a view of this goddess at ease in the pool, to the hot-as-fuck vision of her coming on his lap. Putting it mildly, Envy's head, blood, pulse, and cock have been operating on cosmic overdrive.

The memories thicken his appendage until it's as hard as a spear. Her in the water, the tops of her naked tits glistening. Better still, the creases in her face softening, relaxing after that near-plunge to who the fuck knows where. Dampness curling the ends of her hair. The star flecks gleaming beneath her eyelashes. Her complexion flushing.

Then her thighs clasping his jutting waist, her open mouth unleashing chaos, her breath skidding across his lips like a supernatural hallucinogenic, her soaked pussy rushing up and down the taut line of his dick. The sublime visual of her bouncing, crying, coming like a fucking—

"Cut that out," Sorrow rebuffs. "I know what you're doing."

"As do I," Envy replies, admiring how the tension locks her ass even tighter than it was in the pool when she rode the edge of his cock.

Muttering an oath, the goddess wheels around and snatches his chin between her thumb and forefinger. "We can start with your introduction to pain right now. Just say the word."

"What a dominant-submissive implication," he exaggerates with wide eyes. "In which case, your wish is my command."

"That's not what I meant."

"But we already set a promising precedent back when you slapped me. Not to mention everything else that happened under the drenched surface." Yet when Sorrow merely blushes through her scowl, Envy flaunts his grin like a portrait. This nymph is just too adorably sexy when she's pissed off.

"Suit yourself," he sighs. "To compensate, I'll take what I can get."

"I should be so lucky," she retorts.

Mist permeates the air, dampening their flesh. One would think they've spent the night sweating together, which would have been the next sexual step after their recent bout of water aerobics.

That aside, these hours have been full of revelations, including the knowledge that she enjoys sensual fucking. Matter of fact, she'd gotten downright rogue about it, rolling her cunt into him with the patience of... well, of an immortal.

But the most ravishing discovery is this: His surly goddess knows how to crack a smile. Behold, it's now been scientifically proven. In the heron cove, any signs of cynicism or mockery had vanished. Fates eternal, he'd never seen anything so enigmatic.

Another word for it is *attractive*. A more accurate term is *mesmerizing*.

On the flip side, that which is denied increases in value. Give a cracker to a starving person, and it will taste like a brownie. Hence, Sorrow's galactic smile might be profound merely because it's rare.

Envy shakes off the confusion. With his brain currently short-circuiting, he's in no condition to evaluate this mess. Doing so will only result in frown lines. He's determined to look his best, especially while ailing from shattered bones.

According to the dawning blue tint in the sky, they've been reveling all night. Apart from the fuckery, he replays other highlights. Not least of all, that jovial expression in the heron cove as the raptor perched beside her. Those eyes fixed on Envy as she agreed to his proposition.

These marvels trigger a puncturing sensation, the onslaught taking root in certain vital organs of his body. But when he can't conceive why, The Stars twinkle as though asking, *How many guesses do you need, Envy?*

Oh, fuck them.

Though, maybe because the answer resides in their history. She doesn't know it, but Sorrow had shown Envy pain long before he requested it.

His fingers scrape through his mane. If friendship with this goddess leaves him perplexed and inconsistent, he can't predict the mayhem love would cause. Yes, he's seen what it does to his crewmates. Instead of rendering the couples absurd, they're happy, empowered, and sexually fulfilled. Their bonds are passionate, born of desire and respect. Each pair fluctuates between arguing, laughing, and eye-fucking one another, to say little of how often he's overheard them actually fucking. Perhaps all that emotional fuss is an aphrodisiac, which enhances the smut like a perk. Considering how often they each go at it, those enterprising couples would put a warren of rabbits to shame.

In addition, Envy has witnessed plenty of intimate gestures between the lovers. Despite having fucked countless deities, he struggles to comprehend the brush of Love's hand through Andrew's hair, nor the unconditional flash of the human's eyes whenever he looks at the goddess. The way Anger and Merry entwine while sleeping, with the god strapping his mate to his chest as if she'll disappear. The raunchy tenderness between Malice and Wonder no matter what the fuck they're doing. Every touch and gaze between these pairings are instinctive. Some would say elemental.

Regardless, it must eventually grow tiresome. To be with the same partner forever, shagging only one person for eternity?

Envy and Sorrow make a swift journey to the cavern, the lagoon emitting a veil of steam. Their picnic sits there, abandoned. Envy waves a hand, the dishes and platters disappearing.

Inside, candles pulse from the recesses. The interior stream winds through the moss-carpeted ground.

Shoving his hands into his pockets, Envy rocks on his heels. "We might have to draft terms. For example, I should be permitted to request my pain like an appetizer from a menu. What options do you have in mind? I'll choose."

Sorrow leans against a wall and crosses her arms. "What's your most embarrassing moment?"

His offended brows slam together. "Either I'm giving you too much credit, or this is the most you think I can take."

Her irises flash. "If we're going to do this, I have one condition. Don't bullshit me. You'd be surprised the lengths people will go to avoid humiliation, the pain they'll endure." Her regal transformation is nothing short of astounding, her voice radiating with authority, confidence, and experience. "You're the God of Envy. Like it or not, our root emotions are more synonymous than we want. You know to what lengths humans and immortals will go, just to spare themselves of disgrace. So again, what was your most embarrassing moment? And if you answer like a smart ass, or if you concoct a lie as high maintenance as your face, I'll know. That's my job, pretty god." She taps his lips. "Sadness never lies."

Her prompt spurs agitation, a sudden urge to either flee like an imposter or make a naughty pun. But like the goddess already said, she'll see through his shit.

It wouldn't be the first time. Or the second. Or the fucking third.

At any rate, who the devil asks to be educated in the mechanics of pain, unless it's for bondage purposes? And unless that person's name is Malice?

Who dares to risk this? Evidently, someone who wants to be conditioned, to be prepared for this war. Someone who wants to learn how *not* to break. Someone who aspires to be more like a certain trauma goddess. Of every crew member, Sorrow will recover from torment the quickest, because that's how she was trained.

What was his most embarrassing moment?

Envy opens his mouth. But Sorrow's finger presses firmer on his lips.

"Don't say it aloud," she instructs. "The point is to think about it first. Tell me later, if you want to. Until then, pain is a private thing."

Her touch launches a thunderbolt through his abdomen. "A private thing," he echoes against her soft digit. "Pleasure is the same, unless we're keen to share it." Then he bites her finger, his teeth nipping the flesh.

It's a gentle graze. And it's only fair.

With a gasp, Sorrow yanks her finger away. Envy grins as she wipes that slender, trembling appendage on her pajamas, jostling the patterned clouds.

This goddess doesn't know the half of it. For he scarcely needs time to identify that legendary embarrassing moment, circa adolescence. The instant she had propositioned him, the answer had infested his consciousness.

An ugly god is easy to spot.

Beneath the banners of cloth looping from the ceiling, Envy hesitates. Outwardly, he remains calm, debonair as his hand swings toward the hearth. "Care to sit?"

Dawn breaks, the hours bleeding from one to the next. For a start, Sorrow redresses his wound while explaining the various ways to nurse injuries. Fixing what's broken and watching it mend provides her with solace.

Envy says nothing, because he can't say anything. All he can do is examine her bent head as she ministers to him.

Who knew first-aid could be this surreal? Or this engrossing?

Afterward, they huddle in front of the flames, settling among floor cushions. Indeed, the hearth is merely decorative. If Envy is one thing—although he'd call himself many flattering things—he's aesthetic.

Despite their inability to feel temperature, Sorrow acknowledges the brimming flames are a comfort. If this goddess is one thing—and historically, she has often declared herself only a handful of things—she's an advocate of tranquility. That fact is becoming patently clear.

She wouldn't have betted on this setup from him. Ah, but there's a lot she still doesn't know about Envy, as there might be secrets he's yet to uncover about this female. He reclines against an ottoman, ready to peel those layers from her like a satin chemise.

The glowing candles and swaying blaze illuminate her in whites and blues, while she sits cross-legged beside the sizzling logs. The visual is marvelous, loose strips of hair falling around her face and a relaxed expression gracing her features.

The topic of aesthetics leads to a discussion about practicality versus frivolity. Envy and Sorrow compare notes, supplying one another with the objects they deem necessary and unnecessary, ruminating whether they're as valuable as the baser needs. Mostly they disagree, their voices rising to the rafters, but the argument isn't venomous or goading. It's congenial.

For once, Envy isn't eager to be right. He's too busy wondering what she'll say next.

By afternoon, they've ventured into rocky terrain, debating what they think of this campaign on behalf of humanity. They're not like their crewmates, who each have tangible experiences with mortals. Love fell for a human. Anger fell for an immortal outcast who grew up in the sphere of humans. Wonder fell for a human-turned-god.

But Envy and Sorrow? What compels them?

"Being in love isn't the only foundation," Sorrow answers, tucking her feet beneath her ass. "Some just change on their own."

"Or because of friendship." Envy gazes at the flames. "Seeing Love, Anger, and Wonder like that? It was enough for me. Wasn't it for you?"

"But what about fate and free will?"

"I think they're the same from different angles."

"How poetically evasive."

"I'll amend, you hussy. I think they can exist in harmony, but figuring out how to compromise is where it gets tricky."

"That's why our crew keeps arguing about the methods," she agrees.

Even if Envy and Sorrow were to accept the legend binding them together, leading to some grand inspiration across the board and resulting in a truce, The Dark Gods must still conceive a balance between destiny and chance. And they'd have to do so with The Stars' blessing.

This, assuming the other reason they can't enact the legend didn't exist. Guilt worms through his insides. Envy's been intending to confess this part for eons, yet he's a coward. A greedy, foolish, clingy god.

Worse, this dilemma is intensifying the longer they spend time alone. The confession stretches off the edge of his lips, desperate to leap out. At the same time, fear splashes through his blood, because this closeness with her feels too fucking good. If he opens his trap, Envy will lose that.

He shifts, but the liability adheres to him like static. "You didn't answer my question about our crew."

Sorrow glances away. "I'd sprint into a monsoon with them."

"But?" he prompts. "Come now, tell me something you would never tell them. I sense it coming."

"I don't want to follow them into war. A traitorous part of me wants to stop them."

Shit. His tongue stalls as if she'd tightened a rope around it.

Sorrow's profile contorts. Her eyes jump across the fire, her pupils glazing over. The seconds extend into minutes, her throat bobbing like a loose chink. "I've had enough of war to last a thousand lives."

She sounds old and exhausted. As though a dam has ruptured, she confides about the mortal wars she's attended, the wastelands where she was stationed, and the death tolls she witnessed. From what Envy knows, those battles kept Sorrow, Anger, and Love busy. Them, in addition to Grief and many others.

There were countless souls, and Sorrow had attempted to strike as many as she could, to alleviate them of agony. Not the physical pain, since that's out of her hands, but the emotional torment. Yet their numbers were great, and she couldn't get to all of them before they died.

"I tried," she whispers, her tone as brittle as bone. "I tried so hard."

As the goddess recounts the horrific details, Envy loses sense of time and space. Both narrow to Sorrow's haunted features as she drags out each word, uprooting them from a place buried so deeply, he's surprised the sentences don't cut her on the way out.

"There was a soldier," she croaks. "A boy of maybe seventeen. He was gutted on a mine field, and he was crying for his sister." Her anguish cracks Envy's ribs. "There's pain that's essential because it strengthens who we are. But there's also pain that just hurts like fuck and kills you. Like the slow stab of a blade, I felt every ounce of his suffering."

Tears collect on her eyelids, but she sniffles, refusing to shed them. "You don't want to know that side of pain, Envy. I only sampled a fraction of it, but if we fight, we might... it might... That's not a pain I'd wish on anyone." She grunts, wiping those unshed tears with the back of her arm. "Whatever. It's selfish of me to wallow, as if I have a right to claim their misery as my own."

"There's a disparity between selfishness and compassion," Envy intones quietly. "Just ask Compassion."

Sorrow's trembling lips tilt. "We're not supposed to be talking about my history with pain. I'm supposed to be helping you find yours."

Envy straightens, leans forward, and cups her cheek. "I think you just did."

She wavers, resisting his pull. "I don't... I don't know how to..."

"Now, now. Come on, relax those arms," he says, then demonstrates. "Like this."

She surrenders, allowing him to tug her closer and weave their fingers together. Their intertwined hands rest in the space between them. They stay like that, inhaling, exhaling.

Envy registers the abrasive texture of her despair. He wants to wrap this female in cotton, a soothing textile he's certain she likes.

But then he realizes. That sensory hint isn't coming from her, which shouldn't be possible anyway. Not between deities.

No. It's coming from him.

This hurts, because he can't relate to her past. This hurts, because he doesn't know how the fuck to make it better for her. This hurts, because it just does.

Envy glances down to where his thumb strokes the pulse in Sorrow's wrist. When had he started doing that? When did he roll up her sleeve?

He doesn't care to acknowledge this, and she keeps her comments to herself. They recline awkwardly onto the moss, adjusting to the rarity of her head pillowed on his chest, his palm clasping her hip.

Sorrow speaks in a hushed voice. "Some pain, like in those wars? It's about loss. But the paradox is, I can't describe such horrors to you. At least, not in a tactile way, because I can't relate fully. I have the power, and I've exercised the shit out of that power, yet identifying with it is impossible. What kind of person does that make me?"

"That doesn't mean you're not susceptible like the rest of our crew," Envy murmurs, combing his fingers through her hair. "The opportunity just hasn't happened to that degree yet. We may embody our root emotions, but I doubt any of us have felt the palpable brunt until recently. Love never loved until she met Andrew. I would bet that Anger never internalized his short fuse until it became personal with Merry. And I'm pretty certain Wonder never marveled at the universe more than when she encountered the demon we call Malice."

"And you?"

"Drag your hand any lower, and I'll be damned if I'm able to answer."

Sorrow freezes, her digits having made a roundtrip from his sternum to his navel, a sure path to the swollen rascal located farther south. That she hadn't known what she was doing becomes indisputable as her fingers recoil, fleeing into the cove of her neck.

"Sorry," she mutters.

He's not. At least, not unless his dick gets the timeout it desperately needs.

"I've been bitten by the envy bug several times," he admits. "To cope, I sulk until I get my way or steer the advantage back in my direction. Comparing myself to others is pure instinct, but I don't think I've hit my limit yet. According to mortal tales, the gods are viciously prone to grudges, bitterness, and resentment. It's not far from reality, so there's no telling how far our emotions can go or whether it mirrors the nature of humans."

Sorrow lists the jails, hospitals, battlegrounds, graveyards, orphanages, homeless encampments, group counseling sessions, bathroom stalls, and, yes, drunken parties, in which she has aimed ice arrows at her quarries. People fraught with loneliness, bereavement, and hopelessness.

Whereas Envy has made the rounds in bars, competitions, games, marathons, ceremonies, classrooms, offices, and weddings. People consumed by frustration, prejudice, petulance, rivalry, or lust.

Mortal holidays tend to swamp them both.

As they talk, Envy belatedly realizes that Sorrow's aversion to this war, as it harkens to her prior experiences, should be a reason enough for her to accept the legend. As the lesser of the two evils, she must know this, but perhaps she's too scared to choose.

That makes two of them.

As the afternoon darkens to nightfall, an idea sparks in his mind. At his behest, Sorrow describes her home in The Dark Fates, including an assortment of lamps.

Warm lighting. Envy adds that to the currant nectar, comfort food, and fleece bedding. Plus, her black attire. Reassessing the latter, her overall style is more Celestial Vigilante than Woeful Witch.

Sorrow resumes her task, reminding him to think about that embarrassing moment. Oh, but if she only knew. He's never stopped thinking about it.

An ugly god is easy to spot.

Envy's flesh stings, each word lashing him like a whip. He avoids going there, divulging some of his lowest points instead, such as shooting the wrong humans and watching mortal jealousy turn into self-loathing. In the end, he's drained yet oddly reinvigorated by this deep dive.

But Sorrow has one more request. "Say something you don't want to say."

Shit. He sidesteps that as well. "I don't have a thing to wear for battle."

"Something of substance!" she chides, bursting into laughter.

That laugh. That fucking smile.

Envy mumbles something about needing time to reply. When really, he needs time to recuperate from her.

Always. Fucking. Her.

Because they've worn themselves out, Envy ushers Sorrow to a chamber that will appeal to the goddess, bypassing several adjacent hollows. "It's just down another tunnel—wait! Not that way!"

"What's this?" Sorrow tilts her head, detouring toward an open recess.

"It's nothing," he hastens. "Just a storage cubicle. No witchcraft items for you to peruse."

Hardly deterred, Sorrow ventures into the alcove before Envy can snatch her. "If that's true, then there's no reason... oh."

Hovering on the threshold, he watches as the goddess surveys the assortment of clothing sketches spread across a drafting table, including renderings of a midnight blue gown with chain embellishments, a maroon leather vest, and a tiered black skirt.

He braces himself when she pauses on that last drawing, then swipes it from her fingers with a forced laugh. "I was dabbling."

"And clearly I'm intruding," she comprehends. "Sorry, I... I didn't expect to find anything personal."

He stalks around her and sets the paper back on the table. "I tend to experiment with ideas when I'm not busy shooting humans."

"They're really good. Our people would appreciate the inspiration, even if tailors are—"

"A mortal trade?" Casually, Envy overturns the skirt design, facing it down. "More's the pity."

"It doesn't have to be. Not if you choose."

Huh. The notion appeals to him.

Even so, Envy waves Sorrow from the room, torn between pride that she likes the images and uncertainty that she'll criticize the rest. This, provided he succumbs to the conflicting desire to give her a tour.

Plus, if she musters another generous, out of character compliment, the goddess will find herself thrown across the tabletop. At which point, his fingers will rip the pajamas from her body.

A growl rustles up his throat. Picturing the least attractive images possible—seaweed, a broken mirror, a rayon shirt—Envy's budding frustration recedes, taming the infamous wild beast, also known as his cock.

While leading Sorrow to her chamber, he beseeches The Stars to conjure a few adornments in her honor. Swinging open the door, Envy gives a quick gesture toward the room. "You'll be pleased to know it's the farthest one from my suite."

Sorrow chuckles. "Good thinking."

"Excellent."

"Wonderful."

Spec-fucking-tacular. It's harmless banter, yet it still bothers him to be right.

Envy twists away, then pauses at the entrance while gripping the frame harder than necessary, her earlier request striking him like a hammer.

Say something you don't want to say.

With his back turned, Envy lets the words drop from his tongue. "You intimidate me."

19

Sorrow

Before she can respond, Envy leaves without a backward glance. For minutes on end, Sorrow stands motionless. The candles glow, and firelight tints the cavern in a brilliant sheen, each source kindling for as long as desired.

Has it only been two days? Is tomorrow really the final one?

When was the last time Sorrow asked about his ribs? When was the last time Envy gave her a status report?

His wincing has declined, and the bruises across his torso have faded. Visibly, he's on the brink of recovery. Whereas Sorrow is not okay. Her stumped gaze blurs, the contents of her brain jumbling together, and she's pretty certain her jaw has landed somewhere on the ground.

"What did you just say?" she whispers to no one.

Specifically, to the one who'd been standing there not long ago. Yes, she's late finding the words. As to his confession, the words had sounded as though they'd wiped him out. It certainly was having that effect on her.

At this point, Sorrow's been tarrying in a daze for long enough.

Envy's probably snoring by now. Either way, it's more productive to think of him emitting those gritty noises instead of envisioning the god sprawling naked on his bed.

His muscles contracting with each respiration. Those masculine, throaty rumbles. His mouth at her disposal.

How deeply does he sleep? Does his cock tighten in slumber?

Sorrow groans. If she had stuck around longer after their smut fests, she might have witnessed the unconscious rhythm of his breathing and the rippling contractions of his torso. She hadn't bothered paying attention to these facets while camping in enemy terrain with the crew. Back then, Sorrow had kept her bedroll as far from Envy as possible.

Okay. She needs to put a stopper into this emotional upheaval. Right now.

Idling on the bedroom threshold, Sorrow wheels toward her chamber. Then she halts, blinking through a haze of shock. The sight before her must be a hallucination or a hoax.

Either that, or this is real. Fleece blankets cover the bed, across from which a stack of shelves hold multiple lamps with pull chains.

Sorrow's heart trips over itself, confusion slowing her pace as she tiptoes inside. Atop the mattress, a garment rests across the blankets. Swallowing, Sorrow runs her fingers over the black, hooded robe. It's the softest cotton she has ever encountered, the type of fabric that might dance on air.

The last touch is a glass of currant nectar, propped on a table beside the bed.

Sorrow should feel dubious, since it's not the first time he's pranked her. Yet the considerate details lay those doubts to rest.

This is nice. More than that, it's thoughtful.

While beseeching The Stars, Envy had gotten everything right. He'd remembered.

When has a deity done something like this for her? Something this selfless, without an agenda?

Typical Sorrow would call this weird. So fucking weird. But she'd passed *so fucking weird* about five conversations ago.

Now, Sorrow is simply worn out and overwhelmed. Maybe she's also a tad bashful, as it takes several attempts to touch anything, her fingers reaching out before lurching backward.

Closing the door and stripping off the pajamas, she musters the courage to wrap herself in the robe. The material caresses her skin, the tailored measurements an exact fit, seeming less conjured by magic and more handmade.

Sorrow sips the juice with indulgence, the essence of tart berries soaking into her tongue. Moving with tentativeness, she sinks beneath the sheets, a sigh floating from her lips.

Unfortunately, the reprieve doesn't last. Hours pass, during which she tosses and turns, obscenities crowding her mouth like gravel. Her mind races, doing a mad, sacrificial sprint back to that moment.

Back to that thing he said. That *thing* he admitted.

You intimidate me.

Is this why he never got sensual with her? Is it the true reason he's never tried to seduce Sorrow in the past? Because she intimidates him?

Dismayed and unsure how to digest his confession, she drags her sorry ass out of bed, unravels her hair bun, and combs through the tangles. An embellishment she'd once admired comes to mind. The painted eyelids akin to liquid liner, worn by a young male deity in the valley forest, one of the children who attacked her and the crew.

Inspired, Sorrow invokes a similar flourish, except the liner is pigmented in blue. Just a hint. Just to see. Twisting toward a full-length mirror, she appraises the effect, her lips tilting in appreciation. So this is what it feels like to add color to her face.

Using additional magic, Sorrow refills her glass, then drifts into the main cavern. From there, she wanders to the lagoon. Leaning her hip against the vine-draped entrance, she takes in the tranquil water, secluded vegetation, and surrounding footpath.

Constellations twinkle, dotting the pool with light. She inhales deeply—and a glass shatters from behind.

Sorrow whirls. Envy's silhouette stands arrested, his hair cinched at the nape, the silk pants replaced with a new, loose pair. The plains of his bare torso flex with every outtake, about ten-thousand abs climb down his lower frame like stones in a riverbed, and the slump of his waistline accentuates a steep set of hip bones.

Shards from a fluted glass litter the ground by his feet. As his eyes rake across her body, Sorrow recalls her neckline gaping down to the navel, exposing a ravine of flesh and the crescent shadows of her breasts. Worse, her nipples have ruched against the night breeze, the tips pinching through the material.

There's that, in addition to her unbound hair and blue-lined eyes. The evident attempt to spruce herself up, as if she's trying to impress him.

Sorrow yanks on the sash. She debates whether to flop the hood over her head as well. Not that it would make a difference. Envy's gaze shutters, disorder crowding his face and nailing her to the spot.

Self-preservation gets her moving. She takes a cautious step backward while gesturing to the vestment. "I appreciate the robe. But for the record, wearing it has nothing to do with you."

His dilated pupils jump from her curves to her face. "I may be clueless when it comes to the Goddess of Sorrow, but I'm shrewd enough to know none of your actions have ever had to do with me."

Her eyebrows punch together. "Meaning what?"

"Meaning I'm never the cause. Just the obstacle."

"Is that bitterness, I hear? Well, sorry if I've rarely ever woken up thinking, 'Gee. How can I rearrange my life for him today?'"

"No, but you've certainly rearranged your morals, as well as your bodily positions, to accommodate my cock."

Her blood percolates. Evidently, his assholery knows no bounds.

Here, Sorrow had been preparing to thank Envy for what he did to her chamber. Instead, gratitude flakes to ash on her tongue.

Never mind how wrong he is. Never mind that Sorrow's actions over their history have been provoked by him more than she'd care to admit. And never fucking mind how his comment cuts to the quick, at odds with the hospitable god who outfitted her sleeping quarters with such care.

Sarcasm. Acrimony.

Well, fine. She can handle that. They've had more practice with those sentiments anyway.

"Huh." Sorrow folds her arms. "I'll counter by pointing out that our raunchy affair was for my benefit, not yours. As you accurately described it, I used our trysts to get the randiness out of my system. It wasn't about intimacy. Fucking you has always been a cheap solution to external frustrations."

Envy's pupils alight like furnaces. She can't tell if it's rage, offense, or something more dangerous.

You intimidate me.

There it is again. That thing he'd said.

It had hurt when Envy made callous assumptions about their fling. Mainly because he'd been right. At least, in the beginning.

Not that Sorrow had expected Envy to interpret it differently. He might not know how to internalize pain, but he sure as fuck knows how to cause it. Plenty of memories have proven this, regardless of how Sorrow had affected him in kind.

Agitation crawls up her spine. Meanwhile, Envy stews in silence, observing Sorrow from the darkest corner of the living room, the notion out of character for him. This god never passes up an opportunity to exercise his vocal cords, to be heard and seen, to have the last word.

Sorrow dumps her hands into the robe pockets, juts out her chin, and lays it on thicker than oil. "The universe might salivate over you, but if you had tried seduction with me, your dick would have rusted before you succeeded."

Envy's affronted features scrunch like a wad of paper. "And what about the enclave pool when you bounced so enthusiastically against my cock, it threatened to shear off a layer of foreskin?"

"That was…" She makes a show of shrugging. "It was fatigue."

"You didn't sound fatigued. Upon graphic reflection, I recall you howling like a she-wolf in heat."

"I almost died and was too worn out to speed things up, much less to deny you."

"Deny. Me," he repeats through a set of canines.

"Deny you," Sorrow confirms with an airiness she doesn't feel. "You were so eager to prove yourself, remember? Besides, I required a quick fix. It was only for my benefit."

No, it wasn't. What happened in the enclave wasn't just about her. For once, they hadn't been copulating out of convenience.

Yet Sorrow's mouth keeps moving, fueled by recollections too gut-wrenching to admit. Ultimately, it's easier to be spiteful than wounded. This vicious waltz, she'd perfected generations ago with him.

"Pride gods," she reflects. "You're all the same, in need of constant pandering."

With a hiss, Envy whips around. Through the murk, he stalks over a pile of glass shards and into the tunnels.

Sorrow startles. Where is he going? It's not supposed to be that simple.

Well, great. She told him off. She showed him. She gave him what he was asking for. She—

Fuck. *Fuck,* he's changing his mind. He's not leaving. He's charging back to her, thrusting his fingers through his hair, ruining that fantastic mane. And oh shit, he's not stopping. Fuck, fuck, fuck!

With a shout, Sorrow breaks from her spot. Like prey, she bolts across the cavern as if someone has lit dynamite to her heels, skirting Envy's arm as it lashes out to catch her.

Yelping, she jets into the nearest corridor. It's the wrong direction, but it's too late to turn back.

Mid-dash, she whips her head over her shoulder. Envy's pounding across the chasm like a pissed-off grizzly bear, closing the distance, ailing ribs be damned. If her parting shot has injured him, the god doesn't reveal it. Rather, the ambitious look on his face is neither friendly, nor playful. The only suitable term is *carnivorous*, his features narrowing like a predator hunting a target.

That hell-bent expression is a straight shot to the clit. Frustration scorches a path up her thighs, the tight slit of her cunt throbbing, wrath-induced arousal breaking the folds wide open.

Sorrow's pulse hammers against her chest. Anticipation thrashes beneath her breasts like a caged animal.

Sprinting into the alcove where he stores those fashion renderings, Sorrow backtracks, passing her chamber. Grasping a corner wall, she catapults around the bend, barreling into Envy's wardrobe alcove just as he storms inside behind her. They leave the space in shambles, shirts and belts flying off shelves, wall hooks littering the floor.

Everlasting Fates! If he doesn't give a fuck about the wardrobe's state, that means shit has gotten real.

Speeding into his bedroom, Sorrow leaps across the mattress, then hustles back toward the entrance. Envy shoots after her, aiming to cut her off at the pass, but she dodges his swinging arm.

Reaching the main cavern, Sorrow hotfoots over discarded cushions and flings a set of chairs in his path, which he whips aside with a backward swat of his hands. At this rate, she wouldn't blame an outsider for mistaking this for some destructive mating ritual.

Clamping a hand over her mouth, Sorrow muffles a laugh. The repressed noise must reach Envy's ears, which spurs him to move faster.

Okay, then. It's indeed possible to feel thrilled, terrified, and horny at the same time.

Sorrow one hundred percent knows what this is. And what shall happen if Envy gets his hands on her.

While pounding across the expanse, she bats the hair from her eyes, her gaze landing on the one and only saving grace. The boat!

She flees past the threshold. Scrambling into the tethered vessel, Sorrow yanks on the cord with such force that it snaps. There's a pole similar to the one from the star-shaped vessel that carried them through the rapids, except this shaft towers at the prow instead of the center.

Amped up on stress hormones, Sorrow twists the column, light glinting from the vessel as it shears across the lagoon. Easing up on the lever slows down the conveyance, providing balance while still moving quickly enough to ditch Envy, who halts at the rocky base and hisses like a steam-powered locomotive.

On a whim, Sorrow flashes her middle digit and mouths, *"Aloha, motherfucker."*

The god scowls. Then he's gone, diving in despite his ribs and torpedoing after her.

20

Sorrow

Shit! The god accelerates through the tide faster than an Olympian on steroids.

Sorrow whips around to seize the lever, her grip faltering as the transport gives a violent shudder.

The boat leans sideways with Envy's weight as he splashes onto the vessel like a livid sea monster. He rises to his full height, that cobbled body glistening and gorgeous, his spiteful features dark with intent.

Her eyes balloon from their sockets. She turns to dive, then growls as a powerful arm slings around her waist and hauls her backward. Her spine smashes into his wet chest, the slab of his body as solid as asphalt.

Envy heaves, his wound smarting from the impact. With every choppy respiration, his torso pumps like an overworked machine, his breath striking her throat. Towering from behind, he drips all over Sorrow, rivulets coursing down her limbs. Water dampens the robe, droplets splattering onto her clavicles and sliding into the neckline, teasing a path from her breasts to her stomach.

The scents of dark rum and amber suffocate Sorrow's lungs. With a long-standing axe to grind, his free fingers lock over her hipbones, bolting them in place.

"Say that again," he rasps, the harsh intonation capable of splitting concrete.

"Say what again?" she bites out, struggling to get free.

"All this rubbish about seduction and rusty dicks." Envy's mouth skids up the curve of her earlobe. "Go ahead, tell me what I can't do to you."

"You... you've never... you'll never..." The snide threat dies on her tongue as he swipes Sorrow's hair aside and bows his head into the crook of her neck.

Thick air churns against the sensitive area, his breath ghosting across her flesh, the silken graze of his lips throwing firecrackers everywhere. And just like that, Sorrow's sense of discipline takes a beating. Her inhalations quicken along with his own, chuffing deeper than a set of busted pumps.

The assault produces a chain of events. Her nipples toughen into rocks, and her pussy clenches.

Then his infernal tongue strokes her pulse point. It's a singular move, the flat driving across that spot with evil intent. As if he's turned a dial, a whimper drops from Sorrow's mouth, slipping out too fast to restrain. The noise spills from her like a confession, as tremulous as the sea.

Damn this pride god. The avalanche continues, her joints tensing, her cunt swelling. Each visceral response clashes, at odds with one another.

Pull away. Press closer.

Flee. Stay.

Envy croons against her neck. "Go ahead," he provokes. "Tell me to stop."

"Stop," she hisses. "You need to sto..."

"Again. Try again."

The flanks of her core slicken. Inhaling the scent, Envy utters a gratified I-told-you-so noise. Validated, his torturous mouth sketches the column of her throat, the maneuver less contentious now, the deliberate glide of his tongue dampening her skin.

His lips punish her, chide her, bully her. His merciless tongue laps at her nape, the result torrential, causing a flood of sensation that wets her fully. With each flick, Sorrow's pussy compresses, growing hollow under the robe. Open. Empty. It's a greedy thing that needs friction, the frustration soaking the inner rims of her labia.

Phantom heat steeps into her veins, down to the bloated clit. Identifying temperature should be limited to the other crew members' testimonials. Even so, Envy provides a scalding demonstration.

His hands torch a path from Sorrow's hips to the robe's neckline, where they disappear inside, the panels fluttering apart for him. The god's palms are smooth when they should be calloused from archery, his thumbs etching along the arcs of her breasts, outlining their shapes.

Sorrow's tits pebble, hanging heavily as her chest rises and falls. It's yet another first. For he's never done this either, turning her into such an insatiable creature. During their lust faze, she'd maintained control, extracting herself from the aftermaths like mortals who wrap up the ends of their work days.

Job done. Productiveness achieved. Time to clock out.

Envy has never wound up Sorrow like this, pulling her inside-out so thoroughly, her blood simmering to a boiling point. As in the enclave pool, this is seduction, foreplay, pleasure.

The stars glint. The lagoon swishes against the boat, the vessel heading to who the fuck knows where. Distant cliffs cut into the sky, the edifices crowned in foliage, tails of water flowing from the crevices.

Envy's leisurely touch is close to spanning her breasts, but he's ruthless. He denies her, drawing out the self-indulgent exploration as if it's a luxury. Such decadent cruelty stiffens her nipples further.

Sorrow squirms. She gnaws on her lower lip while arching, forcing his roaming fingers nearer to the peaks. This only serves to prolong Envy's ministrations and incite a revolution, a deprived grunt of frustration skidding from her lips.

She needs to scream. She needs, and she needs, and she needs.

Him. She needs him.

"Say it," Envy commands into the recess beneath her jaw, tipping her skull back, exposing her throat to his sweltering mouth. "Say it, you infuriating little nymph."

"Fuck you," she blusters. "I'm not little. I'm larger than life."

Trauma deities don't merely regulate the afflicting parts of one's emotions. They shave back the layers, exhibiting vulnerabilities. When people cry, it means the truth is coming out, confessions raining down like storms. That leads to catharsis, which then leads to healing.

Envy knows this. She doesn't have to spell out the implication.

"Such moxie," he observes. "Yet true enough. I'll give you that." He intensifies his grip, fingers clamping onto her jaw. "Say. It."

Tell me to stop.

Because if she doesn't, he might crumble or lose his mind. It's a plea as much as a demand. One she can relate to.

Yet she can't do it. She can only choke out, "Envy."

As the name floats off her tongue, it activates something inside the god. Whereas he sounded rash a moment ago, the plaintive side of his request dissipates, and the possessive side takes over. He hums like a satisfied deity. As if rewarding Sorrow, his mouth cuts a line up her throat, running open-mouthed kisses from her collarbones to her chin, then down again.

The novelty floods her with arousal. The simulated warmth oozes from her pussy.

Fates, she has missed this. Fates, she has never known this.

"Do you feel that?" she pants.

Envy slows his ministrations. Sensing she has something particular in mind, he gauges her silence, picking it apart like he's picked apart her resolve a thousand times. Given their unsympathetic and unfriendly history, they shouldn't be able to read one another. They've been so at odds, it's a marvel they can even agree the sky is blue.

Yet Envy's cock lifts high, its girth thickening. After a moment, a word burns across his tongue. "Yes."

Somehow, he knows. This pride god knows what she's referring to, the knowledge stumping him just as much as it does her. How they're able to experience this in tandem is strange. Maybe it's because they're closely linked to the crew. Either way, his reply ratchets up the temperature, incinerating any lingering resistance to ash.

If this is heat, let them melt.

A scorched noise kindles from Envy's lips, then he bows his head once more, going in for the kill. The hot swab of his tongue sketches her throat, the blaze urging Sorrow's eyes to roll back. She sags, reaching behind and clutching his scalp for support.

Mark her words. He'll pay for this later. But for the time being, her head lolls onto his shoulder, inviting him to do his best. Or rather, his worst.

Envy's a multitasker, sucking on her flesh with insistent tugs that pry moans from Sorrow's lips. Air brushes her skin as her robe shuffles, the upper half parting beneath his fingers. Her breasts rise from the material, her nipples puckering into the eventide.

The pride god mutters a gruff, "Not dark enough. Let's fix that, shall we?"

The pads of his digits circle the points. He works the disks until they're raw and pigmented a deeper shade, and she's senseless, her ass grinding backward into his inflated dick.

Somehow, she manages to say, "All this time, I thought you weren't serious. I thought you didn't want me anymore."

Envy rips his mouth from her neck and twists Sorrow to face him. "Isn't it obvious by now?" he growls like a starved god. "I fucking lied."

He's barely finished speaking when he hoists her forward, her breasts punting his bare pecs, the momentum forcing her arms around his nape. Swooping down, Envy attacks her collarbones, his teeth sinking into the delicate flesh.

On a gasp, Sorrow flings her head back, her peeked nipples jabbing his torso. Her fingers knife into his mane, grasping the roots for dear life, for balance, for stability. This, lest she should descend into madness.

With a ravenous groan, Envy wrestles her grip away, sinks to his knees, and takes the robe with him. The garment peels from her body, then splashes to the deck. A salty breeze coasts across her shoulders and sails between her thighs, caressing the lips of her pussy.

Along the way, Envy marks her with his insolent mouth. Languid kisses and gentle licks travel from her tits to her navel, each one branding her. The sensations are unlikely to fade, similar to numerous harassing memories of him, episodes that frequently prompted Sorrow to strike back.

Yet apart from those incidents in which they'd waged war on each other, or every shared fuck prior to arriving in this enclave, Envy's touch is almost reverent now. It's concentrated. One might describe it as selfless.

Sorrow can't fathom how to process that. Neither does he grant her the opportunity. Instead, his knees hit the deck, the position leveling his gaze with her throbbing cunt.

The view sets his pupils alight. Her clit projects from a small patch of hair, the crest pink and swollen, and her core leaks glistening fluid.

Envy mouths something she can't pick up. The words end on a serpentine hiss, as if he plans on taking a bite out of her.

Looping his arm beneath Sorrow's thigh, the god hitches her leg over his shoulder. Then he cranes his head toward Sorrow. "In case my intentions aren't clear, I'm going to swallow this pussy whole."

Holy. Shit.

And the hits keep coming. Envy lowers his gaze, shackles Sorrow's ass, and veers her hips toward his waiting mouth. Then his hot lips seal around the small root of flesh.

Almighty hell breaks loose. The cry that launches out of Sorrow could blast a hole in the stratosphere.

His tongue flits around the crest, then sucks it between his lips. Embers shoot from where he siphons her, cinders flitting through the sopping crease of her body.

No, he hasn't done this to Sorrow in the past. No, she wouldn't have let him.

And yes, she fucking regrets it.

At the taste of her, a famished sound chops Envy's voice to pieces. He feeds on her clit with the devotion of a zealot, as though he's never licked a goddess in his life. Yet the noise aside, his mouth lays siege to the kernel like a god who's had thousands of years of practice.

To prepare for this. To destroy her.

Inarticulate moans peel from Sorrow's throat, each one in cadence to Envy's mouth. His lips purse, exerting the right pressure, an inebriating balance of firmness and softness. Strapped around the peg, he executes a sequence of gentle but insistent tugs, a gravitational pull that threatens to buckle her stance.

Her fingers dive into his mane, yanking so hard she's likely to leave a bald spot if she's not careful. The damage this does to Envy's hair accomplishes the opposite of what she'd expected. Instead of wincing, the god groans around her clit, the stimulation cleaving her apart, the sting of her grasp invigorating him.

So he sucks harder. Clasping her ass and cinching his mouth, Envy drags her clit toward him, bobbing his head. And Sorrow loses all sense of reality.

"Oh, fuck!" she shouts.

Envy rumbles, the vibration rustling across her raw flesh. His audible reaction throws another gust of warmth toward her pussy, which escalates the volume of her cries. Never had she thought, imagined, anticipated...

Yet he's not done surprising the hell out of her. Next, Envy flicks the edge of his tongue, swatting the tip of her clit.

Sorrow's mouth falls open on a devastated sob. Her thighs collapse, and her eyes fly to the back of her head. Heat and compression radiate from her cunt, his mouth encasing her, fitting so well to the apex of tender skin.

More. Less. She doesn't know which will serve her, spare her, save her.

As if he's got all the time in the world—technically, this is true—Envy luxuriates in her pussy. His tongue flexes, toggling over her clit, the clutch of his mouth increasing.

Claiming her. Possessing her.

Catering to her. Pleasing her.

Unfathomable heat washes down Sorrow's limbs, the novelty rinsing centuries of discord from her mind, dissolving it like blood in water. Fates, he's eviscerating her, drenching her.

The assault isn't one-sided. With another fractured moan, Sorrow glimpses Envy through fluttering eyelashes. She watches his bent head take what he wants, all that dark hair showering around his face. The god's eyes shut as he swabs her with a mixture of skilled concentration and flagrant need, his lips clinging to her pussy like a delicacy.

A word splinters out of Sorrow. An elemental impulse.

Lots of things have tumbled from her during sex with this male. His name. Demands for more. A flurry of curses.

Envy. Harder. Faster. Make me come. Fuck.

But this word is new, shoveled from the pit of her stomach like an illicit thing.

"Yes," she weeps.

Yes. When so much of their interactions have insisted, *No.*

The second those three letters edge from Sorrow's tongue, the god hisses in triumph. To her disgruntlement, Envy releases her swollen clit. Then everything happens in quick succession.

First, he smirks like an asshole, enjoying Sorrow's aggravation. Next, the hubris vanishes as he savors the view of Sorrow's clit, the flesh glistening, distended, and flushed a dark pink shade. Finally, the deity growls like a well-dressed monster.

Tacking her ass to his face, Envy hauls her pussy to his lips, and slopes his tongue between her crease. The sleek penetration is the final nail in her coffin. Sorrow hollers, the shape and length of his tongue spreading her open as he launches in and out. To enhance the sensations, the god hefts her back and forth, every forward motion lodging him deeper.

As it had been in the enclave pool, she can't, she just can't, she can't take it. Yet she does. Because he *makes* her take it.

Slowly but insistently, he fucks Sorrow with his mouth. And now she knows what the hell this feels like.

Brittle moans thrash from her lungs. Over and over, Envy pumps his tongue, spearing into her pussy, catching every droplet of arousal. Wetter than she's ever been, Sorrow saturates his palate, her right thigh still slumped over his shoulder.

Mouth, mind, and body unhinging, Sorrow palms the back of his scalp and cranes her pussy into his face. Every long, hot slide soaks her more. It stirs her interior muscles, fiber by fiber. Dammit, he knows where to search, how to seek out the hidden places no one else has breached.

Even then, this god plies Sorrow's cunt deeper, the silken pump of his tongue elevating her to another dimension. Each molecule sparks to life. With abandon, she keens to the sky and pours onto his tongue.

Envy swallows, drinks from her, and probes higher. He thrusts his mouth against her pussy until she's reeling from head to toe, the rapture mounting, firing to a breaking point.

"Yes," she shrieks, flinging her pussy at him. "Fates, yes!"

Envy rasps, his tongue vaulting, lancing fully. Trenching into her slit, he hits a compressed spot, a slender place that has Sorrow spiraling. Broadening his lips, the god charges, wedging into that space, the stimulation pinching her with rapture.

He slams his tongue, pushing Sorrow's limits, pushing into her so hard. And then she's coming, her screams launching into the heavens like missiles. Her pussy convulses, rupturing around Envy's mouth and tongue, the muscles pulsating, the climax gushing down his throat.

The parched god hums, swallowing her cum, devouring her pussy to the last drop. The orgasm prolongs itself in the manner of immortals, stretching to an indecipherable length. Until finally, Sorrow goes limp, hunching over him.

But like every Dark God, they've barely begun. Eating her had merely been an overture.

Envy lets go of her cunt, then snaps his head toward Sorrow. His irises have disappeared behind two wells of black, their surfaces gleaming with ambition.

Spent but hardly depleted, the first orgasm was a warm up. Conditioned to last, they glower hungrily, helplessly. Then they lunge.

Chaining Sorrow in his grip, Envy latches onto her thighs and gives a mighty pull. The movement boosts her off the floor, the world tilts on its axis, and then she's falling. Her spine rams into the deck, the vessel jostling, sea water sloshing over the rim.

To be clear, deities have the strength to handle this. While a mortal would have fractured their vertebrae, the equivalent for Sorrow is akin to crashing on a springy mattress.

Scrambling to a comfortable position, she tosses Envy a Try-Your-Best sneer. Then she splays herself wide and wet.

The god tapers his features, part sportive scowl, part salacious grin. It's a look that promises extensive retribution. Shaking his head with an If-You-Insist expression, he crawls between her thighs, the width of his body sprawling her farther apart.

Sorrow's stomach lurches. So many whipcord muscles. So much to sample.

Not giving a solid fuck about his injury, he spans himself over her, bracketing his weight on both palms. Sorrow grapples for his shoulders while he hitches one of her limbs over his hips, the thick ledge of his cock flush against her naked pussy, nothing but the fancy layer of his pants separating them.

Although they've never kissed, Sorrow isn't sure if she wants that. However, this god has other things in mind, his pupils pinning her with a dangerous light. Holding Sorrow's gaze, he trails an index down the line of her body, teasing her nipples into firm disks, then scrolling along her pelvis.

At length, his touch skims through the dark curls shrouding her cunt, outlining every throbbing groove. Sorrow's mouth parts, whimpers fleeing off her tongue while he draws out the sensations.

Finally, Envy scissors her lips apart, flaring them around his fingers. His features stretch into a predatory mask as he sketches her walls, another flux of arousal coating his knuckles. Those smooth hands collect the slickness and locate that tiny nub once more, lathering the top of her clit. Rhythmically, Envy swirls his thumb over a million nerve endings, lightly scraping, patiently dabbing at the ridge.

Overhead, The Stars pierce the firmament. Out here, there's so much open space in which to yell.

So she does. Sorrow digs into his shoulders and tosses an entreaty into the welkin.

"Well done, my nymph," Envy urges. "Swell for me."

Then two of his fingers slip between her crease. Heat and hardness fill Sorrow, rousing her muscles for a second time.

Envy grates out a primitive noise, which overlaps with Sorrow's cry, both sounds coming out harshly. She has no clue who's louder, and she doesn't give a shit. All she cares about is the steady pump of his digits opening her pussy wider, deeper, longer.

The tempo steals another turbulent moan from her, and another, and another. She's lost to the measured thrusts of his hand. Yet it's the most lucid type of pleasure and pain in existence.

Envy's features twist. Watching her, watching her, watching her. Below his waistband, she glimpses the solid width of his cock, the outline of his crown heavy.

She wants it. So badly does she want him lashing that cock into her. But she can't speak, can barely think.

The hours flash by, with no end in sight. At one point, Envy's free hand fumbles with a closure in the deck and withdraws a makeshift dick.

While bobbing across the boat, Sorrow moans, "You have a fucking sex toy compartment here?"

A corner of his insolent mouth curls. "I stash my toys everywhere."

"I thought… I thought you never… oh," she whines as he skates the tool around her clit. "I thought you never… bring anyone here."

Shadows sink into the perfect crevices of his face. "I don't."

Before she can parse through that statement, Envy angles the apparatus to her clit, using pressure and rolling the flesh like a marble. Sorrow's lungs empty, the contents of her vocal cords shooting into the ether. While his fingers fuck deftly into her, the god traces every contour of her pussy, a disastrous amount of fluid trailing in his wake.

The dildo quests from her clit to the oval of her cunt. For a while, it accompanies his fingers, driving inside her while oscillating, the surface etched with small beads for added stimulation.

And when Envy has tormented Sorrow to within an inch of her eternal life, and she's muttering and threatening to slay him, he glides the instrument from her cleft and returns to the peg of flesh rising from her body. The multitude extracts a frenzy of howls from Sorrow, the brunt of his fingers and the toy slogging her across the deck.

Swaying her hips, she lands on both. As her spine bows off the floor, his arm sprints between her spread thighs, which fall farther apart as he accelerates the pace, her body jutting from the impact.

You intimidate me.

Say it again. Tell me to stop. Come on.

Right there. His finger works her right *there*, slipping, retreating, and again, and again, and again. All the while, the crown of that incredible torture device burrows down on her clit.

Sorrow's about to pass out. The Stars burst, fragments raining from the canopy and crashing into the lagoon.

She locks up, then tumbles over a precipice. The orgasm rips her into filaments, cum leaking from her pussy, the muscles clenching Envy's fingers. Her body vaults into his bare torso, bellows rocketing from her lips.

The god's mouth splits, his eyes exploding like black celestials. "Fuck, yes."

Yes.

It's hot, and it's wet, and it's impossible, and it's confusing, and it's exquisite. Sorrow convulses around the lunging tips of his fingers, her frame wracking against Envy. And just as her screams of ecstasy calm down, she begins to cry.

21

Envy

He freezes. With his fingers primed inside her and the dildo pressed to her clit, Envy drops back to earth, the muscles of his face slackening from rapture to bafflement.

Is this resilient goddess fucking weeping?

He reels back, snapping upright from between her split thighs. Sorrow's shoulders tremble, and she flings an arm over her eyes. Tears drip through the star flecks beneath her lashes, drip past her temples, and vanish into her hair.

The sight punches Envy square in the face. Thunderstruck, he loses his mental footing and takes a nosedive from the heavens. Like an idiot, he's clearly done something wrong. Although she's hardly the delicate type, unlikely to chip like porcelain, he must have hurt Sorrow. Considering she can take the harshest of blows, the damage has to be dire.

Fuck. Envy can't recall an incident in which he's lost control with his conquests. But then, he'd been so lost in Sorrow's moans, caught up in the undertow of them, who knows where the devil he messed up.

As it is, he was a goner the moment he found Sorrow in the dark, her silhouette filling out that cotton robe—his bright idea of a gift—with her loose hair and peaceful expression.

The flannel sleepwear had become endearing on this goddess, but that mantle? And her quiet profile angled toward the vista? And the blue tinting her stardusted eyes?

She had looked nothing short of breathtaking.

Deities can ingest substances beyond that of humans. Seconds before that moment, Envy had just finished chugging the twelfth glass of cabernet, which he'd prayed to The Stars would finally knock him the fuck out. Anything to blot the image of her sleeping in one of his chambers, her body stretching like a buffet across the bed, in reaching distance, so bloody near. Anything to deflate the raging hard-on this visual had produced. As if he's ever been so lucky.

That's when he saw her. The robe he'd designed with Sorrow in mind. The hint of color threading across her lashes. By Fates, the glass had slipped from his grasp, and his tongue had unspooled like a red carpet.

Then she'd whipped toward him and opened her mouth. And so had he. Envy's ribs must be nearly healed, because he hadn't felt a sliver of pain since that moment.

Her jibes. That chase. This boat.

Her neck. Her rapid pulse. The orgasms.

Envy had been so hung up on her disjointed cries of pleasure, so drunk on them he almost levitated like an incubus. Up until that point, he'd never touched Sorrow with erotic patience, nor begged permission to. He hadn't so much as beheld the beautifully soaked slit between her legs, because in the past they'd been too busy getting the job done, getting their clothes out of the way, and getting to the main event in record time.

Yet tonight, he'd discovered the satin cinch of her pussy and the succulent taste of her clit. The effects had acted like generators to his pulse, in addition to his throbbing cock, blasting both into overdrive.

It's never been like this with anyone. He's never made a lover sob through the aftermath.

Envy lurches upright, his stomach curdling. As her drenched cunt contracts around his knuckles, he fixates helplessly on her stricken features.

Was he just that good at making her come? Or that bad?

Self-consciousness wrings him out like a towel. Concern spurs him to withdraw his fingers from Sorrow's tight grip, then hoist her off the deck and strap her in his arms. She doesn't resist, her tear-streaked face landing against his chest as he clasps her there.

Sorrow climbs onto his lap, twining her legs around his waist as if he's a nest. She cries like she mocks, like she owns it. This brave goddess doesn't wail but drains herself freely, accepting the sensations without fear. To her, tears are nothing to be ashamed of. They don't make her weak or fragile. Rather, they turn her into the truest and strongest deity he's ever known.

When the noises subside, Envy speaks into her scalp, marginally terrified of how she'll reply. "What's wrong?"

"I'm j-just overwhelmed," she hiccups.

"Will it help if I say you're not alone there?"

"I don't cry."

Incredibly, this moment is a blend of painful and pleasurable. He can't help the pride of knowing she needs him, that his embrace gives her the slightest measure of comfort. On the other hand, he wants to slay himself for making her weep.

Bliss. Anguish. Solace.

Somehow, he's incited all three in less than an hour. And he doesn't know how to feel about any of it.

But as much as Envy could get used to Sorrow crushed in his arms, he boosts her chin and levels her face toward his. "You can cry all you want in front of me." He swipes a tear with his thumb. "In every way."

She matches his position, cupping his face and studying it. "I think... so can you."

The words chisel through a crevice in his chest.

What The Fates is happening to them? What is this?

The boat coasts on its own. Stars and cliffs rise over the fern trees, banked by clouds as sheer as organdy.

They need to laugh. Right this instant, they need to lighten the mood.

"So, you're seduce-able." Envy quirks his eyebrows. "And I've still got it."

Sorrow blurts out a watery laugh. "Bragger."

"You're worth bragging about."

"Do I really intimidate you?"

What's the use? She's already ruined him ten thousand times over.

Her wet pussy rests on his thighs, slathering the pants and bloating his cock to epic proportions. At the same time, those dried tears have his sternum trapped in a vise grip.

Envy would feast on her cunt for breakfast, lunch, dinner, and dessert. Then he'd go back for seconds. He would make her come again, and again, and again. If she desired it, he would draw out the climaxes until she's wetter than the sea, and her throat is raw from shrieking, her octave rattling The Stars.

Yet she needs something different from him now. Something he's less experienced in providing.

Do I really intimidate you?

Envy closes her robe, hiding all that edible skin and tying the sash. "You always have," he murmurs, forcing himself to meet those silver eyes. "My most embarrassing moment was with you."

It's her turn to freeze. "You're lying."

"I'd call it denial. Does that count?"

"What do you mean, it was with me?" She veers back. "Tell me or go to hell."

"According to Malice, the weather is reportedly fantastic in hell."

"Malice is a part-time lunatic."

Her astonished glare refuses to let Envy off the hook. A three thousand year-old sigh of resignation blows from his lungs. "You were the only one I ever failed to impress. Even Love, who wanted to ram her fist into my face on numerous occasions. Even she caved once or twice, forgiving my sly remarks." He swipes a lock of hair from Sorrow's cheek. "But not you. The reigning Goddess of Sorrow intimidated me, every scowl whittled down my vanity, every judgement reducing my confidence to nothing. Then one day, I experienced my most embarrassing moment in your illustrious company. Full transparency, I've been jealous of you ever since."

"That's impossible!" she protests.

"Oh, lucky me. I've gone and felt an impossible thing."

"You know what I mean," Sorrow amends, allowing him to catch her hands and lace their fingers together. "When did it happen? What did I do to you?"

Envy stares at Sorrow until her pupils widen. "You can't be serious."

"Can't I? I'm glad you cleared that up for me."

"We were young. We hadn't even come of age yet!"

An ugly god is easy to spot.

He slides her closer. Those marvelous thighs open farther around his hips, her breasts rest on his pecs, and their breathing syncs. "Adolescent memories with sharp edges fuck us up. Lately, I wonder—and really, I should verify this with Wonder—whether I haven't been jealous about anything else since that day, because I'm still triggered by the first time. I've based an extensive life on a small moment." His palms sneak into the enticing gap of her robe and cup Sorrow's bare ass, her skin pebbling against his palms. "I can't resist comparing myself to everything you say and do, stacking myself up against it."

Sorrow's eyelids hood as he traces her hipbones, then the dip of her tailbone before returning to her backside. "I don't know what to say," she admits.

Envy leans in, the rush of her breath making his cock and heart jump in tandem. "Don't try," he mouths against her lips. "I'd rather leave you speechless. If it helps, I'm starting to enjoy being jealous of you, being intimidated by you, being inundated by you, being offended by you. So perhaps you started showing me pain a long time ago."

Her head lags backward when he grazes her shoulder blades with his fingernails. "Maybe you started showing me pleasure a long time ago too. Except not like this."

The boat rocks, knocking her clit against his pants. Envy's dick responds, the crown lurching to the hemisphere, as it had until she'd started weeping. "If that's true, we've been building to a crescendo," he intones, nipping the soft concave under her earlobe. "I tried, but I've changed my mind. I don't want to fucking stop."

"Neither do I," she utters.

A victorious groan scrolls from his throat. So that's it. Pleasure and pain.

All the way. All or nothing.

In a flash, Sorrow's back where she started, flattened beneath him. And he's back where he started, hovering above her, his hips spanning between her thighs, about to get himself into a heap of sinful trouble.

"Good," he husks, bracing her arms above her head. "Now, stay down. You're not done coming yet."

His mouth brings her to orgasm for a second time, then a third time, his tongue working her to a glorious chant.

His name, his name. Fuck yes, his name.

Her moans are as sheer as mist. Her flushed pussy tastes sublime, like a sour-sweet fusion of red wine and figs. Envy puts his whole body into sampling that dark budding place nestled within her, skimming and sucking on the shape of her clit and the flanks lining her slick opening. Matter of fact, he won't stop until he's heard every type of tumultuous sound this goddess is capable of making.

Sorrow writhes and wrecks his hair, and Envy vocalizes his approval. Their movements threaten to capsize the boat, water thrashes against its curvature, the prow's pole tossing white flames across the lagoon.

By the time Sorrow spasms once more around his wet tongue, her arousal dripping down his palate, Envy learns a new kind of pain. To be succinct, his balls are as heavy as cement, and his distended cock is on the brink of detonating without the aid of friction.

To cope, he plants kisses on the exposed skin peeking from the robe, exploring the sacred corners of Sorrow's anatomy while introducing her to sensuality. She falls limp and trembling, her legs hooking over his shoulders, her fingernails digging into his back.

Lucky him. At this moment, she's all his.

However, this goddess must notice his erectile discomfort, because she skates her palm down his navel, paving a dangerous path to his dick. Hissing, Envy drags himself away. Ah, ah, ah. While he'd like nothing more than to let this vixen strap her fingers around his flesh, the pressure and pump of her dewy mouth encasing the turgid head, he wants to savor this decadence, not clutter it with hasty bonus rounds. Seduction should happen in stages, progressing at a rate that builds anticipation.

So instead, Sorrow reclines inside the boat, tucked in his arms. They exhale while staring at the sky. Somewhere beyond this inlet, the great stargazer at Fortune's Crest cranes its metallic neck, marking the future site of an impending battle.

Over the past few months, the crew attempted several conferences to debate fate versus free will with The Court. They met in the human realm, with Anger and Wonder's Guide, Harmony, in attendance. In advance, their crew prepared examples of humanity ungoverned. Anger and Harmony had cited people their crew hadn't targeted over the millennia, illustrating that mortals can handle more than they've been given credit for. Their campaign made a case, advocating how the mortal world won't collapse without the intervention of destiny.

The meetings had proceeded to no avail. They went in circles, unable to reach a dignified compromise with The Court. The rulers hadn't budged, reiterating a major principle of their kin: The power of choice is an illusion.

Serendipity can never be outrun. Even if deities can't target every mortal, the ones who do get struck incite a domino effect, rigorous enough to influence many others.

As for the ones not triggered by arrows, The Stars must have alternative plans for them, agendas that don't require immortal intervention.

The Court had deemed this subject non-negotiable. And what had their crew really expected? It takes years, decades, or sometimes centuries for mortal nations to figure themselves out and draft resolutions. Why shouldn't it take Dark Gods infinitely longer merely to broach the subject?

Nonetheless, events have progressed this swiftly, beyond anything the crew could have fathomed. Thus, their campaign has evolved into a military affair.

Yet war seems far away, for one more day.

This approaching dawn. The last one they'll have.

The morning celestials will emerge. By nightfall, they'll make haste. Until then, Envy bolsters himself on his elbow and sketches

Sorrow's pointed nipple through the robe, drawing it with the tip of his finger. "There's one more place I want to take you."

Sorrow seizes his digit, chiefly to hold it close. "Okay."

He returns them to the cavern, then hauls the vessel with him, anchoring it atop one shoulder, and ignores Sorrow's lecture about his ribs. At this point, the injury has mostly rectified itself.

Returning to the waterfall enclave, they float through pools and past waterfalls, which throw steam into the air. Prisms of color arch through illuminated motes, and the occasional lunar heron ventures from its sacred cove. Envy and Sorrow travel beyond the compact peninsulas, where he directs them through a cascading curtain, the onslaught drenching them.

Not having expected that, Sorrow laughs and slaps his calf in retaliation. But she doesn't stop gazing at the atmosphere, beaming at their surroundings.

Floating behind the waterfall, Envy points out a secret tunnel. Upon first discovering it, his Guide, Siren, had verified it to be a shortcut to the Astral Sea. To this day, Envy hasn't tried getting through, due to the shifty stalagmites and noise-sensitive stalactites, in addition to the explosive corners and sharp-as-fuck rocks. Because it's a perilous trek, he hadn't led Sorrow that way during their escape.

Not even The Court is aware of this passage. All this time, only Envy and Siren have known of its existence.

Sorrow nestles her spine into the wall of his chest. Envy encircles her midriff and coos into her nape, "We'd better go back before I get X-rated ideas."

"Ugh," she grunts. "Not yet."

"Ughhh," Envy imitates. "Hiss. Mumble. Snarl."

"I don't sound like that, you asshole."

Minutes later, they dock the boat. Stepping onto the bank, Envy stalls at the shrouded footpath and offers his hand.

Sorrow takes it. When she disembarks onto the soil, he twirls her under his arm and sways her into a slow dance, balling their hands against his chest.

"Well?" he teases. "Am I wooing you? Compliment me. Say I'm irreplaceable."

Even while she rolls her eyes, Sorrow's complexion flushes a beguiling tint of red. That's plenty for Envy. While she's the only goddess skilled at driving him crazy, apparently he's the only god who can make her smile. It reminds him of his manifesto on sensuality, how it needs to be savored in doses. The same rule applies to being with this female.

For millennia, he couldn't stand her. Recently, he'd just wanted to fuck her.

Now he's discovering Sorrow in bits and pieces. Indeed, he likes each of those pieces, most especially the jagged ones that hide nothing.

While dancing with him, Sorrow gazes at his mouth. Desire brims in those incandescent orbs, that look plus the scent of black tea, smoke, and afternotes of violet imbuing his senses. Never mind that no one has ever stared at him with genuine fondness. But has anyone ever done that for her?

After a moment's thought, Sorrow's grin falters, and her voice turns fretful. "I don't know how to feel like this."

The confession brings Envy up short, because he understands. Like tenacious little vines, apprehension slips through the cracks of his facade. He's not doing any better than she at identifying what they've become to each other.

Emotion is one thing. Action is another.

All he can do is clasp the goddess against him and growl softly across her mouth, "But you know how to feel *this*."

22

Sorrow

She has witnessed millions of embraces between millions of mortals. Yet Sorrow can't remember being on the receiving end of one. At least, not one of this nature.

To her surprise, Envy is right. Despite her lack of personal experience, she does know how to feel a hug. And she knows how to reciprocate.

Nuzzling into his hair, she closes her eyes and draws his dark-rum-and-amber scent into her lungs. Her chest siphons with his, their respirations matching. His massive arms envelope Sorrow as if she's a hidden gem. Something rare, evasive, and priceless.

What an infinite moment. She can't put it any other way.

Envy's face burrows into her hair. Like a fleece blanket or a swig of currant nectar, his hold loosens the knots in her shoulders.

Water ripples through the lagoon. When their arms unwind, it's all Sorrow can do to face Envy. Her uncertain gaze clings to his own, and their fingers absently clamp together. It could be a pact, an unspoken agreement to put animosities to rest, once and for all.

Without a word, they enter the cavern and travel to her chamber, lamps pouring golden light across the walls. Envy slides into the bed and takes Sorrow with him, then continues introducing her to the most vivid forms of pleasure. He massages every inch of her anatomy until she melts into the mattress. He feeds her currants, then licks the juice from her lips. He enchants an eye mask, so she can't anticipate which route his mouth takes across her flesh. By the end of that arousing journey, his head sinks into the nexus of her cunt for a fourth time, sifting on her wet flesh to the point of unconsciousness, her moans cataclysmic.

At last, Envy folds Sorrow into him. Days, months, years, centuries, and millennia merge into a single moment. The embrace must have magic, sapping her of energy. Fleece blankets whisper across her skin, preceded by another embrace from behind as the vainest god in the universe aligns his torso with her back, their sodden clothes forgotten.

Her lips curve upward. Blackness floods her mind before her smile can lift fully.

Yet it seems like seconds when Sorrow's eyes drag open. The motion takes effort, with her eyelids glued and caked together. When she blinks awake, the deepening blue of afternoon fills the hollow. They've been asleep for nearly the whole day.

Sorrow rolls over, intending to nag Envy. But she stops. He rests with half of his visage mashed into the pillow and puffs through a partially open mouth. He's wrinkled and unkempt, and dammit, it would be fantastic to get this evidence on camera. If only those contraptions worked on deities, she would produce one.

The cloth around his injury rises and falls with his outtakes. By tonight, he'll be able to remove the dressing.

Her mouth compresses, a frightening sensation pouring through her like syrup. That, along with pride. The God of Envy has risked her seeing him like this, when he wouldn't be caught dead letting anyone else have the uncensored honors.

Carefully, she tests whether he's a light sleeper, brushing a swatch of hair from his chin. Nothing. He barely stirs, the blanket slumping low across the V of his hips.

For a while, she watches Envy until her fingers grow restless. Either she leaves now, or she'll fondle something hard, long, and thick. She could draw down those trousers, admire his dick lifting from the hem, the slender crease over the dark head. She could bow her mouth and pucker her lips around his girth, licking the veins until the head flares, a salty drop of cum beading from the top. She could suck him awake, pull on his cock until it annihilates Envy. She could do all this and more. When really, Sorrow wouldn't dare without his knowledge.

Deities usually don't object to this invasive behavior. But she does.

Nonetheless, Sorrow groans, her pussy clenching at the fantasy. With reluctance, she slogs from the bed and straightens her robe. Padding from the chamber, she coaches herself not to look back, lest she should give into temptation and rouse him from slumber.

At the cavern's threshold, a breeze sails through the foliage, and the cliffs rise to the sky. Settling at the lagoon's rim, Sorrow dips her feet into the water and takes a moment to replay last night. The things he'd done to her. The things she'd allowed him to do. The words they'd spoken. The places they drifted to afterward. The secret tunnel leading from the enclave, which he hadn't shared with anyone else.

The dance. His strong arms banding around her.

Gripping the lagoon's ledge, she twists her mouth into her shoulder, muffling another tilt of her lips.

You're smiling.

That's what he recently said. And yes, she is. Raising her head, Sorrow turns to the welkin and lets the grin expand from one end of her face to the other. Impulsively, she goes wild and flashes her teeth.

After that, Sorrow strips out of the robe and wades into the lagoon.

Her entry produces a lazy splash, the glossy surface quivering. The firmament rotates as she unravels and floats on her back, arms and legs scissoring outward.

Has she ever felt this courageous? This happy?

A heavier splash alerts her to his presence. The wave that accompanies his arrival causes Sorrow to bob over the pool. She directs her gaze to the canopy, no longer grinning, but not frowning either. To the contrary, her features are relaxed and rested.

A pair of smooth palms materialize under her. One hand braces the valley between her shoulder blades, the other her lower back. Silent and getting his eyeful of her damp tits and glistening pussy, Envy balances Sorrow and sways her around the enclosure. Overhead, a cathedral of stars glints as he spins her slowly, the afternoon celestials swirling in her vision. The motion alters Sorrow's view, distorting it, changing it, making it new.

Her smile breaks through again. She chuckles and senses him grinning in kind, amused by her reaction as they turn and turn and turn.

Then they stop, gasping as though they've been wheeling much faster. Sorrow's chest pumps oxygen, every respiration shallow and unsteady.

She can't take it anymore.

Envy swings her upright just as she straightens to her feet. Her arms find his shoulders, and his arms snatch her waist. Her gaze makes it as far as his mouth while the angle of his shadow indicates he's doing the same thing, staring at her lips. They're dripping, heaving in damp air.

He's as naked as she is, though the surface conceals everything below the ramps of his hipbones. Above that, he has removed the dressing, the bruised flesh healed and his ribs contracting normally.

Sorrow trembles. As the hard peeks of her breasts slide into his chest, Envy hisses. If she meets those dark eyes, she'll lose her nerve.

They pause, their faces angling inches apart. Shallow pants rush from their mouths, so fucking close. Her eyelids flutter, and a bead of perspiration quivers down her nape. Under the depths, his cock thickens against the contracting flesh of her cunt.

Sorrow's heart beats like a drum. Or is it his heart thudding?

They've never done this. They've never done this one thing.

To hell with it. To hell with all of it.

She lifts her head and brushes her mouth with his.

Envy's torso hitches, his throat unleashing a feral noise. He stalls, his fingernails biting into her naked ass, his reaction dangling off a precipice while she waits, then he returns the gesture with a caress of his own mouth, the contact suffocating her. And then they're teasing each other, their hectic mouths grazing languidly.

Envy's lips are firm and full, as she'd imagined countless times. Though, her visions pale in comparison to reality.

As they withhold from one another, a thrill rushes through her, their heads slanting in the opposite direction. This time, Envy's tongue flicks against her teeth, and a mewl curls from her lips. Pleasure coils up her thighs, drenching her cunt.

This is the longest calm-before-the-storm she's ever known. This must also qualify as the most frustrating, drawn-out incident in history.

Envy's tongue makes another pass, this one along the crease of her mouth. Curse him, the contact opens her walls. On a sigh, she licks him back, swiping the bow of his upper lip. He seethes, one hand scaling from Sorrow's ass to the back of her skull, his digits snarling through her roots and fisting her hair.

He's got her ready. And as she grips his nape, she's got him primed.

They wait. Then they stop waiting.

With a single lunge, they fling themselves into the kiss. Envy growls, his mouth swooping down and seizing hers. Sorrow cries into him, their lips spitting and clutching.

Their bodies go wild, arms clinging, fingers scraping. His tongue pries her apart and flexes into her mouth. Sorrow grapples the muscles of his back, urging him closer, beseeching for more. A pliable moan slips out of her, their tongues sweeping together.

It teases. It torments.

Repeatedly, they switch direction, devouring each other from different angles. His mouth spreads her. Her mouth clutches his, their tongues fusing, swatting against one another.

Sorrow's nostrils flare. Envy fumes, kissing the fuck out of her.

Her hands fall, clinging to his waist. Crooning, he grasps her face in one hand and attacks, his tongue plunging in and out, matching another rhythm they've achieved. Though, it was never as real as this.

It was never this deep.

Breaking away, Envy plants harsh kisses across her jawline. Finally, she catches a glimpse of his swollen, ruined mouth. The sight is too much, just too much, so she grabs him once more. He smirks into the kiss, hungry and wanting.

Where's that fucking tongue?

Sorrow catches it, lapping up each scalding noise that burns from his lips. Her fingers climb his abs and ascend to his profile, securing him in place. With his tongue writhing against hers, Envy clamps her bare ass harder, smashing her against him, ramming their kiss together.

It's mayhem, a beautiful wreckage of lips and tongues and moans. He plows in again, and she yields again, and they start again.

And now she knows what passion feels like.

23

Envy

Fuck him to hell. Like a resplendent blast of light, it dawns on Envy. He hasn't felt this sort of passion before. Not for her.

Or at least, not for a very, *very* long time…

24

Envy

There's a star that flashes proudly in the sky. It radiates amid the galaxy, glowing as opulently as an expensive jewel. The pompous thing should humble itself in the presence of its maker, yet the galaxy excuses this behavior, for the ostentatious specimen is too confident to deny.

The star is also competitive. It outshines its neighbors with finesse, showing off to its best advantage.

Beneath the hemisphere, The Fate Court and an assembly of Guides quirk their lips. Convening around the stargazer of Fortune's Crest, these observant rulers and mentors agree. The celestial is boastful but stunning, a veritable source of jealousy and vanity. Hence, it bears the marks of a pride god.

"He is ready," the Guide of Envy announces.

With The Court's blessing, the female mentor extends a cupped palm and summons the star, which dives from the firmament and lands with a flourish into her hand.

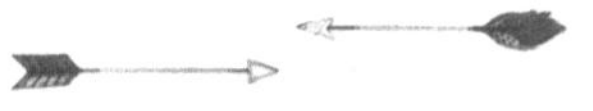

Sorrow

At the same time, there's a star that glints quietly in the sky. Not far off, pulsing with a mellow light, this celestial is lonely. It hovers by itself, solitary yet sympathetic to its environment, from the dull light of isolated planets to the weeping meteors with no place to land.

This star wants to help, to console its neighbors. It tries, it really does. In fact, it sends tiny gleams of hope into the universe, but the offerings fizzle out before they reach their destinations.

It's too much. There's just too many of them. This star bears the darkness like a weight, fighting to hold itself up. Maybe one day it will learn how to thrive. Until then, it cries when it thinks no one is watching.

Yet someone is watching.

Far below, the Guide of Sorrow gazes at the speck. The mentor swallows, aware of how his future pupil feels. And so, rather than wait for The Court to arrive and give permission—they will surely approve later, once they've ceased fawning over that other showy star—the Guide cups his palms, and the star drops, slumping wearily into the mentor's hands.

Stroking the newly birthed deity, the Guide whispers, "Everything will be all right."

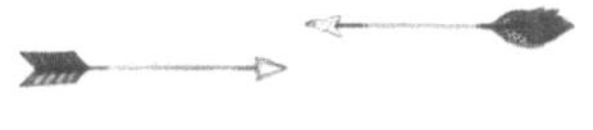

Envy

He grins at the mirror and blows himself a youthful kiss. "Good morning, beautiful."

And later, when it's time to craft his arrows, Envy chooses glass. It reflects his flawless countenance, paying homage to every exquisite contour.

Sorrow

She flops onto her little stomach, mashes her small face into a pillow, and groans until she falls back asleep.

And later, when it's time to forge her arrows, she chooses ice. It's a numbing element, a protective barrier against pain, so that when her time comes to serve the mortal realm, each pierce of her weapon will soothe an ache. Or cause one, depending on what's needed.

By then, she will know the difference.

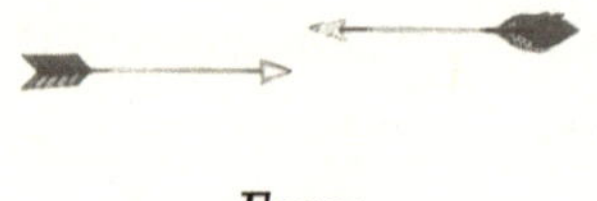

Envy

Despite his fledgling years, he's the only pupil whose feet reach the ground from his chair. Even if his voice hasn't broken yet, at least his height is an achievement.

In a misted enclave of waterfalls, Envy sits with four other youths while The Fate Court promenades around them. The sovereigns proclaim that he's been assigned to the most elite crew of archers in existence.

Excellent. Envy likes the sound of this. The best of the best. The top of the immortal chain, etcetera, etcetera. He won't have to compare himself to anyone, except his crewmates.

There's Wonder, who's a buxom Venus. Plush, perky, and pretty.

Wildflowers ornament her chestnut hair, and she has a wandering gaze, her attention drifting to the clouds instead of Envy's face.

Too bad. He'll need to rectify that later.

There's Anger, all olive skin, sculpted cheekbones, and graphite eyes. Short fuse, for sure. With his nostrils flaring, he's got a furious type of handsomeness. Though his unadorned shirt, pants, and fingerless gloves leave something to be desired, which prompts Envy to smooth over his silken shirt. If that turbulent god gets to claim the coveted title of crew leader, at least Envy can dress better.

Love is a raven-haired spitfire in a black dress trimmed with lace and a pair of wings splaying from her back like an exotic accessory. She represents the most complex of emotions, and because of that, she's the first love goddess to be successfully created in history.

Then there's the banshee seated to Envy's right. The one called Sorrow.

He scoffs at her ensemble. A shredded skirt that has seen better days, a vest dyed in a shade of nightmare-black, and boots with an assortment of metal buckles she must have stolen from a guillotine.

Is this goddess actually considered one of the elite? Look at her. She's no more celestial than a witch.

Oval face pulled down into a dour visage, lower eyelashes dusted in star flecks, and a wry twist to her chapped lips. Tragically, the creepy goddess has painted her fingernails to match her unkempt hair. It boggles Envy to think of how many buckets of slime were sacrificed in the name of that drab color.

And Fates. Does a side of sarcasm come with that morose countenance?

As if hearing the unspoken question, Sorrow cuts her gaze toward Envy. Like a pair of fists, their eyes slam into one another, the impact threatening to knock him off his chair. The goddess pierces him with a stare that pulls no punches, plays no games, and offers zero compliments.

Stars be damned. His confidence withers like a dry leaf.

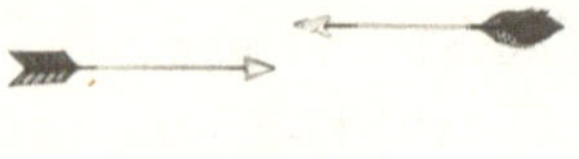

Sorrow

What the fuck is he looking at?

The preening male gawks as if he's caught Sorrow brewing a contaminated potion or speaking a language he doesn't understand. In fact, it takes him a while to get over himself. At which point, the god puffs out his chest like a defensive glory hound.

He's expecting what? For her to blush?

And what a snob. Despite The Court's introductions, they haven't said a word to each other, yet already she can tell this much about the ass-licker called Envy, with his high-maintenance clothes and styled hair. Clearly, he fancies himself the hottest catch in their realm. In which case, he probably jerks off to his reflection each night, as part of his bedtime routine.

Unimpressed, Sorrow narrows her eyes. It takes effort to give him attention, and he must sense this, because her reaction accomplishes the opposite of what she'd intended. Relishing her expression like a morsel of candy, the god flashes her a smarmy grin. Then he winks at her.

Envy

After the indoctrination, their crew travels to the summit of a moonlit cliff overlooking the sea, where the road leads to their homes.

Love invites them to race down the slope, an offer that gets snubbed. Anger twists his mouth in distaste and struts off. Sorrow leaves, tugging Wonder with her.

Because Envy's too good for that hex of a female, he turns his sights on a disappointed Love. She's comely and famous, two qualities that meet his standards. Since no deity their age has failed to melt in his presence, he makes a sly comment to the lone goddess, then leans in for a kiss.

Love responds by tripping his ass down the hill. As he rolls to a stop at the bluffs' base, Envy resists the urge to snarl, pout, or retaliate. Worse, he has company, having landed at the feet of the least desirable female in The Dark Fates.

Looming over him like a wraith, Sorrow crosses her arms and juts out her gangly hip. She must have just parted ways with Wonder. Or Wonder moseyed off on her own, intent on daydreaming. At any rate, he senses what Sorrow's about to say, how she'll mock and declare that rejection looks fantastic on him.

Envy launches to his feet, acting as if he'd meant to fall. Rolling her eyes, Sorrow flips around to leave.

He cocks his head. Well, well. Despite her unspoken insults, silence in his presence won't do, so who can blame him for what shoots out of his mouth?

He says, "So which star shed you like a tear?"

Sorrow whirls and snatches a fistful of his shirt. Yanking him into her, she sneers, "The same one that's going to knock you on your flashy ass. Don't fuck with me, pretty god."

These are the first words they say to each other. And fine, now they've met.

Envy

What is this? Pick-on-Envy Day?

He doesn't like it. He doesn't like her either.

She has made the word *pretty* sound like a cheap trick.

Envy swats her grimy fingers away and mutters that she's going to stain him. By the time he finishes dusting himself off, Sorrow's gone.

Very well. Let the witch go. She doesn't know what she's missing.

It's a reassuring train of thought. His Guide, Siren, would approve.

So why is Envy marching down the nearest trail, hoping to find and rile up Sorrow more?

Hiking past the outcroppings, he fails to locate the goddess. She must have charged in the other direction.

Instead, he finds something else. A secluded inlet.

Curious, Envy rushes home and boards his small boat, the vessel moored to a stilt beside his house. Sailing back to that inlet, he pilots down its course and happens upon a lagoon. Beyond which, vines cover the entrance to a cavern, its passages leading to an enclave of pools and mist.

Sorrow

She grows taller. From her Guide, Echo, the goddess attends daily instructions and learns about the intricacies of sadness. The sound of melancholy, which plays like the strings of a violin, and jagged line between agony and despair.

Sorrow becomes familiar with the facial expressions of a crestfallen soul, cracked voices that signal catastrophe, and the watery quiver of tears.

During field trips to the human realm, she learns how to predict anguish, including every nuance and coping mechanism. So many of them, in such distress. Beggars, prisoners, daughters, husbands, widowers, students, leaders, followers. She coaches herself not to weep, not even when she's alone, curled in a fetal position in bed.

She sucks it up. Otherwise, she'll drown.

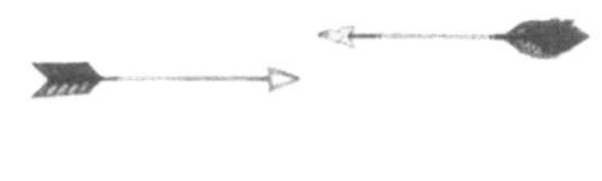

Envy

During archery practice on the hill, he twirls his arrow. The glass weapon flashes, reflecting his visage a thousand times over as the target marker across the range awaits his strike.

Oftentimes, it's difficult to concentrate. Over the decades, he's developed two odious habits. One, a tendency to compare his skill with those of his crewmates, the result only darkening his mood, because Love is the best shot, an accolade she'll carry into eternity.

From Siren, Envy has been educated on the signs of jealousy. The stench of resentment, the tang of spite, and the sting of rivalry. He's been trained to avoid those temptations in himself. Deities aren't meant to be overwhelmed by their root emotions.

However, that doesn't mean they're utterly impervious. At the ripe age of one hundred, these things have become second nature among his peers.

Anger's temper escalates with each failed shot.

Love is constantly preoccupied with the concept of mortal affection, so that she traces her fingers more than she nocks her iron arrows.

Wonder's mind drifts during practice. On a regular basis, either she ends up meditating or daydreaming about libraries.

As for the last female in their crew, the murky goddess mopes every time she misses the bull's-eye, then plugs her disappointment with a dismissive scoff.

Sorrow might be deceiving the others, but she's not deceiving Envy.

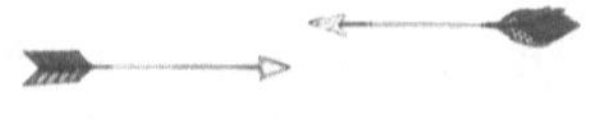

Sorrow

At every target practice and training session, the fucker is there.

He's there, harassing her whenever she misses a shot at the archery range.

He's there, pretending to be a scorekeeper as she competes against herself.

He's there, ridiculing, teasing, and sabotaging.

He's there, his baritone voice oozing like molasses—sticky, addictive, and bad for her.

The god croons and insinuates. He pops his head from behind the target marker and drapes his arms lazily over the bull's-eye, his appearance throwing her off balance.

He pisses off Love as well. But not this frequently.

Ignoring him or making snide remarks only refuels the asshole's tongue. Fates only know why.

By their hundred and fiftieth year, Sorrow's had enough of his shit. She plots revenge in silence, because as much as he's been watching her, she's been watching him. By now, it's obvious what will weaken him the most.

When The Fate Court hosts a demonstration, Sorrow makes her move. Every archer takes a turn exhibiting their skill. Envy saunters from deity to deity, charming like a rogue, flirting like a whore.

He fancies himself a good luck charm to everyone except Sorrow. With her, he's just a bad omen.

When her turn comes, his shadow looms from behind. Aggravated, Sorrow fists her longbow as he strides past while muttering into her ear, "The wind is fickle today. Play nice with it."

Her finger spasms on the weapon. This must be a deception. He can't possibly be tipping her off.

As Envy strides away, she catches the disparaging lift of his mouth, his tethered mane swinging behind him like a whip, his fitted brocade jacket molding to all those muscles, and his polished weaponry shining like a trophy.

He winks at Nostalgia, who sniggers. Well, now Sorrow knows who Envy's next flavor of the month will be.

She gulps, realizing she was right the first time. She's a joke to him. Instead of being a true comrade, he's only pretending for the crowd, faking his consideration, wearing it like a varnish. When in reality, he's mocking her as usual.

More bully than crewmate. More critic than ally.

Everyone waits. A legion of deities. Archers-in-training. Gods and goddesses.

Her Guide, Echo, stands on the sidelines. He nods at Sorrow with encouragement.

From a dais, The Fate Court presides over the event. A pale goddess in snowy lace. Another with amethyst hair. Another with dark skin draped in iridescent fabric, the gown bearing resemblance to a galaxy. A god with a hawkish nose and long braids. And a cloaked male with planks for eyebrows.

Each one of them had witnessed Envy strut past Sorrow like a parade float, his proximity plying her flesh with an infestation of goosebumps. Under a dome of stars, she clenches her teeth.

Before he can take another step, Sorrow whips an ice arrow from her quiver. The projectile cleaves the air, spearing across the distance, flying toward Envy's back.

He wheels an instant before the weapon slams into his chest and blows him off his feet. The motherfucker cannons backward, the arrow ramming him into the bull's-eye. Momentarily, the impact pins him to the facade, then the arrow vanishes in a flash of light and reappears in Sorrow's quiver.

A collective gasp stirs across the field.

Anger curses. Wonder gasps. Love snorts.

Echo drops his face into his palms. He and The Court will give Sorrow all kinds of shit for this later. Lack of comportment. Lack of dignity. Lack of marksmanship. Lack of respect. Lack of camaraderie. A disgrace to her crew and a far cry from the elite unit they're supposed to be.

As Envy hits the ground, a twinge of remorse assaults Sorrow's conscience. She let him get to her. And yes, she debased her crew and her mentor, not to mention she betrayed herself.

But hey, at least Sorrow hadn't loosed the arrow harsh enough to shatter his bones. Only the god's most viable commodity will languish. Namely, his ego.

That is, if she's not counting his dick. And on the flip side, so be it. She's done being his target and will gladly take the punishment, including a stint in solitary confinement.

Sorrow stalks across the grass, the toes of her boots mowing through grass. Squatting before Envy's dumbstruck face, she amplifies for the congregation to hear, "There's a good reason you get so much attention. An ugly god is easy to spot."

Then she marches off the range.

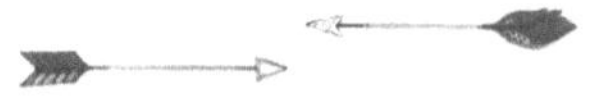

Envy

An ugly god is easy to spot.

He lays there, his nuts thoroughly shorn. A tide of blood scorches a path up his throat, a recognizable visceral response he's seen in others but never felt in himself. He senses the dark shade of crimson infusing his complexion, but he's unable to squelch it in time.

Mortification. That's what this is.

He's the God of Envy. The object of lust by countless deities. Unparalleled charm. Abs to match his abs. A smile that deserves its own constellation. Never a cause to be covetous or jealous of anyone. He's sex on legs, a paragon of perfection.

An ugly god is easy to spot.

Yet he's never been so thoroughly, mercilessly embarrassed. Even Love—who shoved him down a cliff when he tried to steal a kiss, who wanted to claw his face off when he teased her—has acknowledged his attributes. He grates on Love's nerves, but he doesn't repel her, and her gaze doesn't peel him layer for layer like a fucking onion.

Sorrow is the exception to every rule. To her, Envy is ordinary at best.

Such a bizarre event, to desire the approval of an elusive bitch who denies him at every opportunity. It chafes like burlap. It stings like a deep whiff of pepper. A suffusion of blood rushes to his jugular, reminiscent of a river rapid, swift and savage.

That. Immortal. Cunt.

He'd been trying to help her by making a tactical suggestion about the wind. Yet she demeaned him for it.

An ugly god is easy to spot.

Perhaps Envy should care less about her opinion. A lot less. He'll show her what dismissal feels like. From this day forth, she's beneath his fucking notice outside of their crew.

Envy scowls at his surroundings. The crowd glances away, either out of sympathy or awkwardness.

Several leagues off, he locates Siren. She's curvaceous, her wrist bangles clacking together. Thank Fates, she hadn't witnessed this humiliation. Currently, she's conversing with Wonder's mentor, Harmony.

Envy picks himself off the grass like roadkill and strides to join the females. For the rest of the proceedings, he makes flippant comments about the incident to anyone who reflects on it.

Later, as attendants gather in the reception pavilion, his boot knocks into an item. Envy halts, a beam of light catching his attention. Kneeling, he swipes the blossoms aside.

An ice arrow rests in the soil.

Sorrow had grabbed her archery and trudged off in a hurry, the quiver's contents rattling against her tailbone. She must have failed to notice one of her arrows falling.

Envy should catch up to her, then fling the weapon at her chest, thus illustrating her negligence. He should embarrass her the fuck back.

Either way, he has to return the weapon. According to their creed, it's bad form to do otherwise.

An ugly god is easy to spot.

Then again, fuck her. Rising to his feet, Envy checks the perimeter to make sure nobody's watching. He twirls the arrow like a baton, then jams it into his quiver and stalks away.

Sorrow

As the sky darkens, Sorrow stands before his home. She'd forced herself here to apologize for what happened. Partly, Echo had insisted. Mainly, Sorrow hadn't been able to stomach the guilt, once her temper subsided.

Tapping on the front door yields no response. In what morbid fantasy would he ever answer the door to her anyway?

Irate, Sorrow rams her fist onto the facade, harder than she'd intended because the door swings open. She freezes, her hand arrested midair. For some reason, the scene inside causes her breastbone to clench.

The flesh. The groans. The thrusts.

Nostalgia is plastered to the opposite wall, his head flung back and his mouth open in rapture. Envy's the reason. He stands behind the god, with his dick waist-deep inside his houseguest. Although the carved muscles of Envy's back are visible, he's kept his pants on, the waistline slumping low, the front clasps undone to bare his cock. Not that it affords Sorrow a glimpse, but the angle of his body and the violent thrash of his ass tell her enough.

She stumbles backward. Before she can flee, Envy swings his gaze toward her. His lunging hips cease for an instant, shock flickering in his eyes before they taper with ridicule.

Resuming his thrusts, he continues railing the other god while mouthing tightly, *Get. Out.*

Sorrow gets out, though not before tossing Envy an unbridled die-in-a-ditch glare, which falls the second she slams the door behind her, shutting out the crude sounds of fucking. She storms down the pier, saltwater prickling her eyes.

Why the hell is she upset? What's the matter with her?

On her way, Sorrow trips over a rock. When her quiver overturns, she stoops to collect the arrows. That's when she notices one is missing.

Panicking, Sorrow races across the boardwalk. Barreling into her house, she chucks her longbow and quiver aside. Then she tears through the lamplit dwelling, rifling amid cupboards and yanking fleece blankets from the linen closet.

Nowhere. The arrow is nowhere to be found. Either she has misplaced it, or someone is playing a trick, or they've stolen the weapon from her.

It's a celestial offense. A measure of disrespect. A slap in the face.

No way. No one is vindictive enough to take another archer's weapon.

No deity is that selfish.

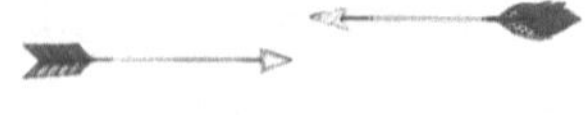

Envy

After Nostalgia leaves, Envy paces. Curse that female for interrupting.

Damn himself for growling at her. He hadn't meant it.

Not to mention, he's scarcely certain why he's keeping the arrow a secret. It had been a retaliation at first, a vindictive need to deprive her of something sacred, the way she'd deprived him of his pride in front of everyone.

He should give it back. He really should give it back.

Claiming a deity's weapon isn't just a grave transgression. According to celestial law, it prevents the thief and victim from establishing a bond. Not that Envy takes that part seriously, since becoming mates with Sorrow is as plausible as Anger serenading a lover or taking up romance poetry.

Ultimately, returning the weapon is the right thing to do. No dignified immortal would encourage his actions.

Envy stalks through the house to where he's mounted the arrow on a wall. Yet the moment his fingers wrap around the ice shaft, an indistinct and uncompromising sensation blitzes through him like lightning. Something akin to desperation and yearning.

Call it curiosity. Call it selfishness.

But whatever Envy does, he'd better not call it obsession.

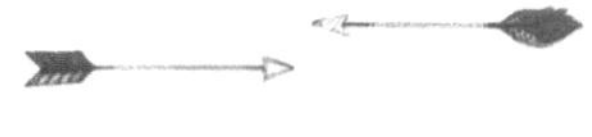

Sorrow

Over the decades, she learns from Echo that every soul experiences three types of suffering. There's the suffering of oneself, the suffering of strangers, and the suffering of a peer.

Wonder has been caught breaking celestial law. According to The Fate Court, she's been making clandestine trips to the mortal world, to communicate with a human. Since it's impossible for mortals to see or hear their kind, the goddess has been writing letters to the man instead.

From what the naysayers report, and from what little their crewmates know, it wasn't a rousing success. All it did was terrify the mortal into madness and land him in an asylum.

As for Wonder? Right now, she's screaming. She's screaming so hard and so brittle, it rattles Sorrow's bones. Because their crew is responsible for each other, they've been tasked with the gruesome chore of exacting Wonder's punishment.

Within a rotunda of immortal spectators, they've tied the goddess to a chair. Her hands have committed the misdeed, so they're the focus of retribution. While Anger, Love, and Sorrow keep Wonder strapped down, Envy slashes the female's palms with a blade. As ribbons of red form wildflower shapes across Wonder's flesh, her howls flood the area.

Each of her cries slices a rift into Sorrow's chest. She hates this. She hates this so fucking much. And she hates that she's a coward who's not stopping it.

Instead, that becomes Love's job. Unable to take it anymore, the winged goddess flings herself in front of Wonder, shouting for the horror to stop.

"Stop!" Love bellows.

Envy reels back to avoid lashing the wrong female by mistake. The intermission is a welcome relief. Privately, Sorrow exhales.

Love puts up an impressive fight, kicking and screeching as Anger vacates his post and drags her out of the room. Being the crew leader, it's clear why he takes action. If he does nothing, the treasonous outburst will endanger them all. By celestial law, defying The Court's orders amounts to deadly consequences.

However, since Love is a rare and precious commodity to their rulers, keeping her in one piece is paramount. Most likely, Love will serve a term in solitary for the disruption, rather than physical torture. Yet she hadn't cared about that, and good for her.

Shame on the rest of them.

Sorrow bites her tongue until it leaks blood, the rancid taste assaulting her palate. So this is what it's like to feel guilt without having to ask Guilt. This is what it's like to witness someone else's pain, to have it slide between the cracks of your conscience. This is what it's like to be powerless, unable to help.

As Wonder whimpers from her chair, Sorrow yearns to stroke the female's cascade of rich, brown curls. Reaching out, she takes the risk. Covertly, her fingers comb through the roots, brushing her friend's scalp.

Wonder relaxes with each pass of Sorrow's hand. And this is what it's like to comfort someone without the magic of an arrow.

Sorrow's eyes water. She peeks at the assembly, making sure no one notices.

Except her gaze stumbles across a pair of caramel irises. Envy stares, witnessing her on the brink of tears.

Maybe he understands. Because yes, the private flinches she noticed from him while he cut into Wonder hadn't been from exertion. No, it had been from remorse.

Envy hates this as much as Sorrow does.

That night, she sinks to the floor of her home. Hunching over, she wills the tears from falling. It isn't fair that Wonder should be broken—her mutilated hands, her anguished soul, her grief over a mortal—and that the Goddess of Sorrow should walk away without a hair out of place.

Sorrow plucks the stitching needle from her bedside drawer. Blowing out a tremulous breath, she presses the tip into the underside of her arm until a pearl of blood surfaces. Then she pushes deeper.

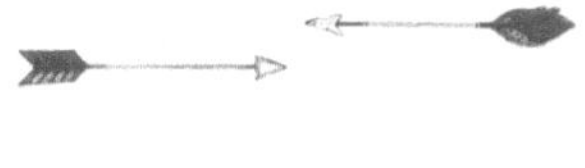

Envy

He doesn't know why he goes looking for her. She would rather eat shit than talk to him, and he's also unsure why this fact causes his molars to gnash.

But he does find her, and he does approach her. She's home, sitting at the dock extending from her front door, with her legs draped over the ledge, her feet agitating the water.

To his surprise, Sorrow doesn't object when he lowers himself beside her and submerges his feet into the pool, wetting the hem of his pants. This isn't a night for arguing. Not after what they just did to

Wonder.

Envy deplores the crusts of blood caking his fingernails. It matches the red of Sorrow's own digits.

Although he appreciates his house, replete with lounging sofas, sewing materials, and barrels containing bolts of cloth, he hadn't wanted to go there.

His enclave cavern had presented a second option, with its hollows and waterfalls, which he'd discovered on that fateful day when Sorrow first spoke to him. But oddly, he's come here instead, preferring to face the memory of Wonder's screams with the female beside him.

"Perhaps deities have no less free will than humans," Envy murmurs.

Sorrow shrugs. "Guess we'll find out."

He nods, then evicts the grim notion from his mind. It's almost time for their crew's deployment into the mortal realm. They'll be stationed apart from one another, in separate areas of the world, wherever their root emotions are needed.

In the near future, Envy shall be targeting humans plagued by fits of jealousy, competition, and vengeance. Perhaps there will be plenty of individuals to distract him from the things he's seen and done. Or perhaps not.

Envy bumps Sorrow's shoulder with his own. "Will you miss me, Nymph?"

She snorts and turns to him, as if he's just that naive. Nevertheless, his breath stalls before she answers, "Get lost, pretty god."

To which his heart constricts in a frightening way.

Sorrow

So he does get lost. As does she.

Sorrow and Envy leave The Dark Fates. In the mortal realm, she serves as she was instructed, targeting the clusterfuck of humans infested by sadness.

Millennia pass. They see each other during trips back home every hundred years, for an intermission of rest. Rarely do they address one another, other than to exchange unpleasantries. Love, Anger, Wonder, Envy, and Sorrow each have their stories, but none are eager to share them. Maybe they all have memories they'd like to forget, plus an eternity to try.

Always, they resume their posts. One year on a minefield, a soldier wails for his sister while an ocean of blood pours from his stomach. Sorrow can't be everywhere at once. There are too many bodies, so many mouths roaring amid plumes of smoke, spilled entrails, and barbed wire. But her speed can't oblige.

Sorrow doesn't reach the male in time. When his eyes glaze over, she kneels beside him, weeping and hacking up bile. She longs to caress his head and apologize for not being there to ease his torment, but her invisible hand only swims through his matted, clumped, lice-infested hair.

So she pretends, brushing his forehead and choking out, "I'm sorry."

The reek of decay is overwhelming, coupled with a thousand horrible noises, from artillery to whistling grenades. Then finally, she stops crying.

In fact, Sorrow stops for good.

Envy

They're approaching three millennia old. In that time, a million things have happened.

Love has fallen in love with a mortal named Andrew. The forbidden union has caused a ruckus, setting their universe into disarray and pitting The Fate Court against the goddess.

To his surprise, it brings their crew closer together. Questions and doubts about fate versus free will rise to the surface, in addition to their individual experiences among the humans, which has knocked them all off kilter. And so, they band together, rebelling against the laws of their world.

In the end, Love and Andrew find their happy end, but it makes her an enemy of The Dark Gods. Moreover, Anger is banished by The Court for protecting Love's secret, for failing to report her attempted treason in the first place.

Later, Wonder, Sorrow, and Envy hunt for their exiled crew leader. Frustrated when they can't find him, Envy infiltrates Sorrow's territory, to see if she's learned anything new. He finds her taking up residence in a human marshland cluttered with water reeds, forming some type of nature preserve for reptiles.

A deck floats like a raft in the middle of the bayou, its wood planks enabling people to sunbathe. Regardless, it's eventide. The mortals and resident fauna are sleeping, the area vacant but for the strumming crickets.

Atop the deck, Sorrow has conjured a four-posted bed with gauzy drapes swaying like banners from each corner. Okay, not the customary chamber of a deity while ensconced in this domain. But then, this female has never made average choices.

The goddess in question reclines on the mattress, one bent limb crossed on the opposite knee. She barely twitches when Envy manifests. Picking her teeth with a length of straw, she drawls to the bed ceiling, "Not a thing."

Envy strides to the footboard and snaps, "How hard have you been looking?"

"In case you haven't noticed, we still have jobs to do." She rises on her elbows, the motion inflating her tits and widening the slit in her skirt. "We can't just abandon our posts unless we'd like to piss off The Court even more. And what are you staring at?"

It's not the breasts or the exposure of flesh that snares his attention most. No, it's the stitching needle. "What the fuck is that?"

Her fingers drift to the instrument. "An embellishment."

Repugnant doesn't begin to describe his scowl. "You consider that an accessory to be proud of? That's your idea of pretty?"

"Envy, for fuck's sake. It's been a long, stressful, debasing few months. Our crew is demoted, Anger is banished, and the rest of us might get exiled too. We'll lose our power if we make one false move, so excuse me if I'm not in the mood to deal with your shallow bullshit. Do me huge favor and fuck off, then come get me when you've made yourself useful and found any clues about our missing rage god. Oh, and when I say clues, I mean the ones Wonder and I haven't already dug up."

"I'll leave once you divest yourself of that absurd needle. Where's your sense of taste?"

"It's jammed up your asshole."

Indignant, he bares his teeth, grips the footboard, and leans in. "Well, then. At least some part of you is attached to me."

Her nostrils flare. She flings her arm toward the swamp. "Go away."

Excellent thinking. He'd like nothing more than to vacate the toxic premises. Alas, Envy bunches his hands into fists, loathing to impart what his addlepated brain only just realizes now.

Muttering an oath, he grumbles, "I have no more energy to evanesce."

Foreboding tapers Sorrow's gaze, as if she's having a close encounter with an extraterrestrial lifeform. "What does that mean?"

Oh, hell no. She knows exactly what it means. Deities can travel in seconds, but that doesn't mean long distances don't tire them out. Minutes ago, Envy had been manifesting between cities in another continent. That sort of migration in a short amount of time tends to have a depleting effect, particularly when combined with urgency.

The price of this hasty visit? Envy needs rest if he wants to flee as quickly as possible. Until then, he's surrounded by wetlands inhabited by unsanitary amphibians and reptiles who don't care where they unload their excrement.

There's only one raft. And one bed.

25

Envy

Fan-fucking-tastic. No way is Envy going to repeat himself. Nor suffer the indignity of pleading.

Sorrow huffs, stabbing her finger toward the deck's hard surface. "On the floor."

Cringing, Envy plucks his shirt. "I'm wearing lunar silk."

"Ask me if I give a shit."

"And it was a gift from Siren."

This isn't a lie. His Guide had the garment custom tailored by The Stars, woven from fine moondust. Reclining on a deck mottled in the residue of nature will hardly preserve the fabric.

The goddess pauses, this new information cluttering her face. If there's one thing she's trained to feel, it's empathy. She respects the relationship between Guides and their charges.

For some reason, pink slashes across her throat. Grunting in resignation, she scoots to the bed's edge. "Stay on your side."

Envy jams his hands into his pockets. "As if I'd cross borders into your lair on purpose."

"Get in here or go to hell."

"Hon, I'm already there."

Tossing him a death glare, Sorrow flips onto her side. An inconvenienced sigh rustles from Envy's lungs. At the same time, his pulse spikes as if it's been laced with champagne. Something with a high alcohol percentage that'll get him drunk fast, liable to make stupid decisions.

Ignoring the sensation, Envy hunkers beside her, crossing both arms behind his head. Because his weight digs a crater into the mattress, Sorrow curls up like a snail, stiffening down to her asscheeks. He doesn't need to peek to know as much, for he's been attuning himself to her kinetics since adolescence.

Silence descends. Despite the drone of insects, the quiet pinches his flesh.

As eventide showers them in darkness, the female's stunted respirations fray Envy's nerves, the effect creeping south to his cock. Very well, he might have envisioned this scenario too many times to count. Albeit with fewer clothes, in a different climate, and with a degree of self-control he doesn't entirely feel.

She insists on shifting positions, the reminder of her proximity gnawing on his patience. Some manner of pressure radiates in the crawlspace between them, restless and thick enough to bury a hatchet in.

This ceasefire doesn't feel right. Sharing a bed with this goddess makes no sense unless they're using it as a verbal boxing ring. On cue, as if looking for a reason to keep fighting, they twist toward one another.

"Cease thrashing," he barks.

"Quit telling me what to do!" she spits.

"What The Fates is wrong with you?"

Sorrow vaults to her knees, grey hair splashing down her shoulders. "What's wrong with me is you! It's always been you!"

A leer spreads across his face, its quality akin to an acrylic sweater—cheap and unnatural. Insolent, he rises on his haunches. "My, my. Now we're getting somewhere. I like seeing that snarky little mouth parted," he hisses. "I bet every inch would tremble against my tongue."

Her pupils ignite like bonfires. If he could measure that fantastic reaction with a thermometer, it would shatter the apparatus.

Ah. Now there's a look he can get used to.

Except this gorgeous praying mantis fires one final, familiar cannonball. Tapping her nose against his, Sorrow warns, "Don't fuck with me, pretty god."

Fury crackles at the tips of his fingers. Maybe it's the shitstorm that's happened since Love's treasonous romance, Anger's exile, and their crew's demotion. Maybe it's all this fate and free will chaos.

Or maybe it's just her.

Sorrow, with all her moodiness, which she conceals behind a mask of cynicism. Maybe it's Envy's inability to break through that cinderblock wall, because she reveals nothing, shares nothing, cares what no one thinks about her, and gives even less of a fuck what he thinks about her.

But he wants her to fucking care. He wants her to think about him. Because maybe they're both wearing masks, and hell if he's not itching to rip off her disguise, among other offending garments. Damnation, if he doesn't want to tear this female apart.

And maybe it's this fucking bed. Maybe he's losing his goddamn mind. Or maybe he lost it ages ago, back when she fisted his shirt and said the same exact thing.

It had gone something like this: *Don't fuck with me, pretty god.*

Yet much later, there'd also been this: *An ugly god is easy to spot.*

Pretty. Ugly.

Inconsistent. Seriously, this flinty bitch should just pick a fucking lane and stay there.

Their gazes lock like weapons. They pant into each other's faces, their exhalations thicker and damper than the surrounding air.

Fuck it. The next thing Envy knows, he's grabbing Sorrow's ass and hauling her against him.

Correction. He's not the only one who loses their shit.

This goddess is no better. She launches across the bed with equal savagery, the pair of them firing toward one another like arrows and crashing with the force of opposing armies.

Sorrow hisses, but Envy plugs the sound with his mouth. Not by kissing her—Fates fucking forbid—but by sinking lower. With the appetite of a cannibal, he slams his lips hard against her neck, incisors scraping a deadly path across the wench's pulse point. And because deities have far fewer concepts of boundaries, the sharp edges of his teeth cross that line, treading hectically as if about to snip her arteries.

Either that, or he's about to make a messy meal out of her. Fuck it all, Envy can't say which.

The instant Sorrow's chest smashes against his own, she attacks with her claws, all ten fingernails knifing into his hair. With hostile relish, she cleaves through every fiber, on a vengeful mission to ruin his mane. The sort that will tangle for eternity and destroy his impeccable reputation, the type of mark he'll remember. As if this heartless, soulless, careless bitch hasn't branded and scarred him already.

When she locates the most vulnerable spot, Sorrow stabs her digits into his scalp, the tips breaking through flesh. Envy snarls, the bloodthirsty noise out of character. In retaliation, his pearly whites nick the goddess's flesh, on a rampage to sever a life line.

They wrestle one another, all teeth and nails. Their arms snag together, waging a tug-of-war, the kind of hate-lust worthy of its own legend.

His hands gun it to her ass and snatch the ovals through her skirt, the contact tipping the scales, another volatile sound cutting from his tongue. On those insufferable nights when Envy succumbed to morbid curiosity, he imagined her stripped and susceptible to his gaze, his scrutiny, his judgement. Though, staring isn't all he'd done to her during those head trips, the figments causing him to sweat through his expensive sheets and nurse an erection harder than granite.

Yet this twisted reality fucks him up worse. Sorrow's curves are more pronounced than he'd fetishized about, her ass filling his palms like they'd been molded for his touch.

And finally. Fucking finally. After giving each other shit for thousands of years, he knows what it feels like to claim her.

Seize her. Taste her.

Christ almighty. The violent beat of Sorrow's heart sends Envy into a tailspin, the vibration of her flesh surreal against his mouth. He parts his lips over the sensitive area and gives a combative suck, demanding to get a reaction, a noise reserved only for his ears, only for him.

On a contentious moan, Sorrow throws her head back and clutches his shoulders. As the goddess's body arches, her tight nipples pit through her vest and wrinkle his shirt. Not that he gives a fashionable fuck.

The harm she does to Envy's promiscuous cock is frightening. From ball sac to crown, every inch vaults upright, solidifying the point where the head might tear through his trousers. It's not the first time she's obliterated his dick without knowing it, but goddamn her. Since when does he forfeit control this quickly?

As always, Sorrow has no idea of the effect she has. Condemnation, those puckering nipples and her disjointed growls are the stuff of unattainable myths. Not to mention sexy as fuck.

And they're his. The resentful lust. The aroused vitriol. Everything she's feeling belongs to him.

It's always been you!

No matter how much blood this female draws from his scalp. No matter how repellant they find each other. No matter how long it has lasted.

She can't take the words back. Like fuck will he let her.

Sorrow's cunt rushes against the engorged outline of his dick. Somehow, the shape of her uncovered clit and the slender cleft between her thighs manifests, easy to decipher, to envision.

As dampness seeps into his trousers, Envy's vision goes black. Fucking Stars, this goddess is leaking through the skirt.

The wet friction obliterates the last vestiges of control. Shoving aside his penchant for seduction, Envy groans from the furious pit of his chest. He flexes his tongue between Sorrow's clavicles, each ferocious pull yanking caustic moans out of her.

She thinks he's worthless? She thinks him unimpressive, shallow, ugly?

He'll show her. When Envy's done with this vamp, she'll eat her cursed words with the same gusto he intends to eat her pussy for dessert.

In a rage, they charge at one another's clothes like animals set loose from their cages. Yet instead of ripping out one another's throats, they slash into panels of fabric, seams spitting, material tearing. The motions are frenzied and competitive, a push-and-pull meant to dominate the other.

Sorrow blows open Envy's shirt, his torso spanning from the textile. Her erratic gaze roves over each packed muscle, those irises glinting like rings of mercury. And despite how many deities have feasted their eyes on him, the impact of her gaze demolishes every bit of admiration that came before, wiping them from memory.

For the life of him, no one's appraisal has ever cut like hers. No one's attention has been this coveted or hard-won. For this alone, he worships and loathes this female.

Seething, Envy rends the buttons of Sorrow vest and hurls the garment to the raft's deck. Her pale tits spill into the sultry eventide air. The shadowed crescents are shaped like teardrops, the rosy nipples dark and cinched, the raw flesh perking.

Envy's mouth waters. A preying noise grits from his lungs as if he's about to shift from a dandified god into an alpha werewolf.

Moderation is his secret weapon. Sensuality is his super power.

Both fail Envy, his patience decomposing in the span of seconds. He's waited long enough to break in this goddess.

Roping his arms around her, Envy sears his lips over the tips. Sorrow bleats, the shocked cacophony peeling through the soggy atmosphere, so powerful it could rustle the shags of moss dripping from the swamp trees. Her fingers grapple his hair, shoving his mouth fully around her nipple. A victorious growl skids from his throat, his lips clamping down and sucking. As the goddess grinds her cunt into his cock, Envy's free palm trails down her skirt, crushing the layers in his grip before ducking beneath the hem.

Raking his hand up her thigh, he tracks the sweltering air radiating from her skin, its damp thickness not unlike the humidity suffocating this marshland. It's an indication of heat, according to speculation among their kind. Though, Sorrow's warmth is far less oppressive than the moonlit bog surrounding them.

Oh, but Envy's theory had better fucking be true. Because that means Sorrow is melting as quickly as candlewax.

His fingers locate the cramped sprigs of hair. Brushing through them, the slender line of her cunt lands in his palm, the groove soaked and swollen.

"Fuck," he rasps.

His breathing frays. Territorial hunger burns a hole in his stomach, to say little of his bloated balls. Stars have pity, her naked pussy is sitting in his hand, liquid splashing from the seam.

So tight. So slick.

Sorrow unleashes a plaintive cry. The reverberation shreds through her as if she's made of paper. Yet he knows better. This goddess had been forged of sterner elements, the kinds that last forever.

Her moan blasts through the treetops. In a maddening reflex, her thighs part wider, opening the rift for his hand to encase that compact pussy.

With a groan, Envy murmurs, "You're wetter than my tongue."

"I..." She licks her lips. "I detest you."

"Are you sure? That's not what this pussy is telling me."

"That's because my body is a traitor. And your hand is an asshole."

"But how much hostile fun they might have together." His angry thumb circles the inflated crest of her clit. "Would you like me to stop?"

He will, if she says so. Yet the bane of his existence whines from his touch, her slim lips glazing his fingers as he dabs at the pleat. Although her expression combusts with rage, that treacherous complexion drowns in pink.

So be it. They're both victims and orchestrators of this havoc.

Between them, a greedy coil of tension springs apart. His cock throbs and broadens, its width shoving against the front of his pants.

Eyes the color of tears narrow on him, insisting, *Fuck you, fuck you, fuck you—*

"Fuck me," she hisses, gripping his collar and biting his lower lip.

With another livid growl, Envy launches Sorrow against him. His mouth assaults the divot between her clavicles, the salt of her perspiration stinging his tongue. Then his aching canines go for the ramps of her shoulders and down the ravine of her tits before seizing the opposite nipple. His pursed lips suction around the bud, wracking her frame with tremors.

At the same time, his fingers do damage to her seeping pussy. His touch runs back and forth along the split, etching her labia and clit until she's good and drenched. Presumably against her better judgement,

Sorrow oozes down to his knuckles, and her cries pour out like steam.

Rather than behave like a skilled lover, doing this the civil and prolonged way, Envy makes a judgement call. Sensuality has no place here. While it's tempting to jam his fingers between those cramped walls and fill her to the brink, to jut his hand in and out like the obsessed closet-maniac she turned him into eons ago, that breed of anarchy isn't going to pacify Envy's craving. For this female has accomplished something no other conquest has. She's drained him of pacing, patience, and pride.

By the Fates, someday she might kill him with a corrosive look, a flick of her tongue, or something more brutal. Something like indifference.

But before that happens, he's going to give this goddess the earth-shattering downfall she deserves. He'll leave his mark on Sorrow, making her come so furiously she'll never forget it, no matter how much she tries to.

Besides, she's just as eager to damn him. So let this be mutual.

Once Sorrow's thoroughly flushed, and her cunt is leaking steadily, Envy's mouth tips into a smirk. But just as fast, his grin drops. It falls off his face as Sorrow makes a countermove, one soft hand releasing his scalp and grabbing hold of his cock.

Through the trousers, her fingers strap around the heavy column, executing a chokehold worse than the one she's had on him for millennia. Her stretched palm encircles his dick, siphoning from the sac to his flared head.

Whereas Envy's actual head explodes. The epicenter of rational thought detonates on contact, blasting to smithereens and morphing him into a fully-fledged brute. Blood races to his erection, which enlarges further in her grasp.

Triumph wrings Sorrow's lips into a smile. Those silver irises gleam with malicious desire. And perhaps a tinge of awe or yearning, those possibilities trembling through her pupils too swiftly to process.

As if this hurts too. As if she's only ever used to hurting.

Envy hates the thought. It makes him want to slash his own throat for causing that look. Though, he can't say why.

Strictly speaking, the only acceptable things she should feel are lust or fury. That will keep her strong and him satisfied.

Sorrow's hand gropes him, her thumb sweeping over the head like a well-placed killing blow. And by the Fates, Envy's defeated.

With a snarl, he digs his hands into her ass. Coming to an urgent agreement, he thrusts her down in a desperate, disdainful craze of movement. The raft and bed jolt, crickets play a jagged melody that saws through the night like a set of broken violins, and muggy water sloshes over the surrounding reeds.

His knees embed into the mattress, the agony torturous and then a relief when he tears open his pants, his cock rising high and hard. Veins pulse from the column, his sac hangs low, and a bead of cum pushes to the surface of his crown.

At the last moment, Sorrow averts her eyes. The goddess twists before viewing a single inch of his ruddy flesh, as though she can't bear to look at Envy, to internalize who's about to fuck her. The action is merciful and terrible, puncturing his chest for reasons unknown.

Envy's nowhere near as repentant. When Sorrow bends on all fours like a feline in heat and flips the multiple layers of her skirt over both hips, there's no way in the fiery pits of hell he's going to divert his gaze.

Those smooth thighs vent open, exposing the trench of her body. The half-moon arches of her ass. The gloss of her pussy, the glistening flanks, the impertinent clit, and that small dark spot in the center. Every plush contour splays out like a banquet, parching his tongue.

Prostrating himself, Envy basks in the sight like an extremist before the altar. This is the part where he'd dip his head and lave that pussy with his tongue, pleasuring her until she's sated and ready to be fucked. Almighty Stars, he would stay kneeling for the rest of his infernal days, for however long it took. That's what would happen if she asked, if she wanted...

With her luscious ass anchored, Sorrow glares toward the swamp. "Hurry."

The demand tears Envy from his stupor, a sinful glower pulling down his features. Hurry, this goddess says? He couldn't agree more.

Get it over with. Get her out of his system.

Now.

Stooping before her, Envy shackles Sorrow's waist. He tilts his cock, angling the pome against the hollow of her cunt, sliding his cum over her opening, smearing his arousal with hers.

A strained noise cracks from Sorrow's lungs. Then it vaults into a wild cry as Envy slings his hips back—and uses the momentum to snap forward.

His cock pitches into her pussy, spearing through her cleft, the lips spreading around his girth. Like a severed cord, Sorrow jolts in place. Her back bows, her head flying toward the canopy, the depth of her body catching him.

The groan that slices from Envy's lips is unrecognizable to his ears. Her walls seal around his dick, gripping tightly, the wet clamp unlike anything he'd prepared himself for. Millennia of watching her, wanting her, warring with her flashes before his eyes like a montage. Yet the reality leaves his prior fantasies in the dust.

This is what it feels like to be inside this goddess. To fill her with his cock, to hear her voice when he fucks her.

Envy can't decide if this is pleasure or pain.

Sorrow's heaving moan gets him moving. On a growl, he charges into motion, snapping his cock. Reeling out to the crown and driving in to the base, he flings his waist, the brunt vaulting Sorrow forward.

With her head craned upward, all that grey hair dashes around her face. Glimpses of Sorrow's profile reveal her mouth hanging open, grunts toppling from those jaded lips. Her complexion reddens, the color as ripe as her cunt.

She likes this. She's enjoying this.

Envy's going to fucking collapse. Only by stubborn willpower does he remain upright, his knees moored into the bed, hard enough to dent the springs and possibly the raft beneath.

Panting, he staples Sorrow's hips in a place and bolts his cock into her. The muscles of his ass clench, waist striking back and forth, rough and fast. He glues his gaze to her pussy, the goddess's desire flooding his cock as it spears into her.

Something like heat climbs up his cock, spurring him to put his entire weight into Sorrow. With every lunge, their grunts come out strenuous, their motions hysterical.

Planting her hands on the wooden surface, Sorrow uses the leverage to buck into Envy. Her cunt meets his cock, both smashing together. With her cries shooting through the marsh, the goddess pumps backward, while Envy pistons forward.

At last, they fuck. Here and now, in this godawful place, the environment as stifling as his present mental state.

Although Envy has ambient standards, he can't bring himself to give a shit. Why? Because like a sorceress with hidden powers, this female makes any place in this universe decadent. A fucking crocodile could surf toward them, and he'd just swat his arm, flinging the reptile across the swamp. He'll have her wherever he can get her, take whatever he's given, offer whatever she needs.

That confession sits on his tongue. To prevent the atrocity from slipping out, Envy jams his teeth into his tongue, drawing crimson.

He rails her like this for who knows how long, his dick lancing, his balls thickening. Sorrow's body contracts, her pussy tensing around his flesh. Her groans escalate with his own, the noise instructing him to go deeper, quicker.

Envy croons and whips his hips, plying her at a rapid pace. "How's that, my nymph? Is this where your pussy wants my cock?"

"Oh," she wheezes, nodding vehemently. "Fuck, right there."

Humming, he rams his pelvis into her ass with such force it's going to break them both. His cock pumps with short, shallow juts, hitting a spot that has Sorrow hollering.

Fuck. Nothing feels like this. Not even immortality itself.

Liquid boils through his veins, the flux converging at the roof of his cock. Sorrow rushes at him, chasing the same vertex, their groans colliding as harshly as their hips.

For a moment, everything stops, teeters over a deadly precipice. They slow, then go still. And that's when they implode.

Sorrow's cunt squeezes his dick, her muscles rupturing as she comes. The scream cleaves through her, loud enough to rattle their bones, the kind of wailing that's felt rather than heard. The noise floods Envy's eardrums, the same way her pussy floods his cock.

That's how she destroys him. Envy stiffens, a roar clamoring from his chest. He comes at the same time, his crown spurting fluid into Sorrow, their bodies pulsating against one another.

Whether it lasts seconds or hours, it's impossible to tell. But his voice is raw and spent when it's over, his cock drained and lodged so deeply in her beautiful pussy he might have trouble finding the appendage later.

For now, they flop onto the mattress, the raft bobbing. Envy's chest slumps above Sorrow, his forehead landing between her shoulder blades, their chests heaving for oxygen.

Perspiration glazes his torso and her thighs. Rumpled and sweaty, they struggle for breath, just as they struggle to look at each other.

Constellations flare overhead, as if scolding the pair of them. There's a myth among the Dark Gods, which declares The Stars will shine their brightest when a deity asks for the truth. But a deity will only receive the truth if they're ready to hear the answer. And that immortal will only be ready to hear the answer if they're ready to change.

No one's ever confirmed this enigma to be true. However, stranger things have occurred.

One of them just did. But as historic as it had felt to fuck Sorrow, it also hadn't... *felt*.

Perhaps Envy's not the only one who thinks so. Without saying a word, he senses them agreeing. It won't happen again.

26

Sorrow

It happens again.

And again. And again.

It happens shortly after they make their agreement. And it happens in different locations of the human world, including The Celestial City, a metropolis of glowing trees, where they find Anger at last.

When they reunite with their crew leader, Anger introduces them to Merry, the peppy goddess who's kindled the rage god's stoic heart.

Not long after, they reunite with Love and Andrew. Then everyone allies with a psychotic deity called Malice, to whom Wonder has lost her heart—and who happens to be the reincarnation of the mortal she was tortured for.

Meanwhile, Sorrow and Envy operate on sexual autopilot, reaping the rewards of casual fuckery. Each time, on each surface, they position themselves so they don't have to look at each other, reaching a concession to be lust partners.

No commitment. No affection. No intimacy.

And never any kissing.

27

Envy

Even when the kiss is over, he's a greedy motherfucker. His appetite has a mind of its own, brushing Sorrow's lips, tracing her skin, laying claim. Indeed, Envy has a possessive mouth, and she has a delectable one, plush and glistening.

Fuck. That's not the only thing that has increased in size since this uproar began.

Growing as hard as a spear, Envy shifts his cock out of range. Any more friction will impair his libido, with no chance of recovery.

Wet strings of hair plaster to Sorrow's cheeks. She clings to the back of his neck, her forehead dropping against his, their chests pumping for air. His eyes sweep over the goddess while she focuses on his sternum, as if searching for his pulse.

Condemnation. Such an asinine sentiment to cross his mind. Though frankly, he's too drunk on this female to care.

Sorrow tightens her grip, demanding more of him. She hugs Envy with her entire frame, burying her face into his throat, where his Adam's apple bobs.

He's lost, speechless. And not fucking done with her.

Uttering a gritty noise, Envy twists his head and seizes her lips again, swiping her tongue with his. Sorrow gasps into his mouth, the pleasured sound floating off her lips, the deathblow that seals his fate. Naked and clinging, they charge at each other for the second time, the relentless strokes of their tongues bordering on desperation.

If this is a buffer to avoid speaking, Envy doesn't give two celestial shits. Not with her succulent tits gliding over his flesh.

The kiss combusts. Her lips yield under his, and his mouth tugs hard, needing her attention, craving it.

On a groan, Sorrow peels her mouth away, despite Envy's famished groan. Standing upright in the middle of a lagoon, they collapse into one another. The water shivers, and constellations swirl, pinwheeling like the backdrop to an immortal acid trip. Indeed, he won't deny the psychedelic effect this female has on him.

This has to be an alternate reality. The universe is playing a cruel trick on Envy. That's the only explanation for why Sorrow hasn't attempted to leave. Stars eternal, she's still clinging to him, holding fast while he grasps the curves of her ass. The contact rubs his cock against her sweet, warm cunt, shivers dancing up her skin.

Plastered against him, she whispers, "Why did you kiss me?"

Envy tenses, every scintillating response in the universe vanishing before he can choose one. All that comes out is, "Because."

Because I'm falling.

The unspoken confession crushes his torso to the point of pain. But if that's true, he's going to fuck this up, because he doesn't know how to fall, much less how to break the landing. He'll plummet, crash to the ground, and break his sculpted jaw.

And he'll take her with him.

If that happens, he'll lose her.

He'll lose this goddess like he has a thousand times, only now it'll hurt her too. Fuck what this will do to Envy's soul. The thought of harming Sorrow is non-negotiable.

Let no one touch her. Least of all him.

Fear knots around his vocal cords, but he snaps the tether in half. He won't let himself go there.

Mine.

As the word infuses his blood with a new sort of power, Envy rasps against the crinkled space between her eyebrows, "Why did you kiss me back?"

"Because," she answers.

Exhausted humor animates her words, forcing a gravely chuckle from Envy. Fair enough, he senses a different reply lingering between them. A truer answer.

But for now, Envy has other plans. In less than five minutes, the force of his thrusts will be jolting her body across his bed. And that's if he goes easy on her.

Based on those silver irises, she craves him just as much. Her gaze slackens, dizzy with need.

"I want you inside me, Envy," she rushes out. "I want that so badly it hurts."

"That sounds like pain," he hisses, his voice a rough-spun baritone. "If so, come to my hollow. Shove me onto the bed and do whatever you want to me. Fuck my cock with your sharp hips and wet little cunt."

"That sounds like pleasure," she whispers.

"As I recall, we had an agreement."

"We didn't bargain for this."

"Then we're excused."

This time, they'll do it right. At least until eventide, when they have to depart and resume this quest.

Banding his arms around her waist, Envy backs Sorrow across the water. She nibbles the bridge of his shoulders while his teeth snatch her earlobe, sucking the tender flesh into his mouth until she's whining. They stumble out of the lagoon, pawing at one another on their way across the footpath.

"You're smooth as glass," she utters.

"You're as slippery as ice," he croons.

Then Envy freezes. The mention of their lost archery, the elements of their bows, carves through him like a stray bullet. Remorse stamps out the heat, replacing it with unworthiness.

He doesn't deserve any of this. Because he'd swiped her arrow all those years ago, Envy has involuntarily fucked up any chance of enacting the legend. Stealing the ice weapon, taking the archery of another deity, has eradicated this possibility.

Fuck him to death. He'd been too inebriated, too besotted, and too damn entranced by Sorrow to think straight. None of this is real. It can't be unless he speaks up. Whether or not she forgives him, Sorrow has a right to know, to reunite with her weapon. That's more important however it affects Envy, whether he'll lose her.

Self-loathing chews on his flesh. It's not the first time he's felt this with Sorrow. But it's the first time his mouth takes the lead.

"Wait," Envy stresses, framing Sorrow's hips. "I have to tell you something." Pushing through the fear and self-disgust, he licks his lips. "I should have done this a long time ago. Sorrow, I took—"

Her baffled squint falters, clarity flashing in her irises. She seizes his arm, going rigid so swiftly that Envy loses his footing. For a moment, her haunted expression takes priority. Something troubles her.

Staring into the distance, realization claims her features like a net. "They have our weapons."

Envy blinks. "Weapons?"

Sorrow nods, angry creases slashing across her face. "Those fuckers have our weapons."

Understanding dawns. Mentioning their archery has led Sorrow to a viable conclusion about the gang of deities who chased them into the rapids. Everyone except Sorrow, Envy, and Love had managed to store their defenses in the boat's lower compartment, seconds before the rapids devoured the vessel.

Sorrow and her archery went overboard, and Envy dove in after her, abandoning his weapons to the torrent's mercy. Also, it's possible that Love lost her longbow and quiver sometime after being separated from Envy and Sorrow.

The maelstrom of water should have swallowed their archery. So how...?

Sorrow replays aloud their swim through the Astral Sea, the words she heard those two Dark Gods speak while stationed on the pier.

I've always wanted to know what wielding iron is like.

Iron weaponry. If the confiscated weapons had been forged of that element, they might belong to Anger instead of Love, though it's less plausible since Anger had secured his bow and quiver inside the boat.

So no, it has to be Love's archery. Either the enemy pursued those arms while swimming after them, or Love's weapons washed up ashore, only to be hijacked. The detritus could have floated into the wrong hands. If so, there's a chance Envy and Sorrow's archery might be in that group's possession as well.

Resolution eclipses relief. It also kills the sex high.

Envy pinches the bridge of his nose. "We were going to make the trek weaponless anyway. We'll figure out the rest later."

"We'll figure out the rest *now*," Sorrow snaps.

"Will we?" His hand drops. "Good luck with that, hon."

"Are you not hearing me, Envy?" She pushes herself away from him, flinging her arms to the sides so that her breasts bounce. "They. Have. Our. Weapons."

He glowers, reading her mind. "Sorrow—"

"I can handle ten deities at once," she states, raising her eyebrows and waiting.

Christ. First, his aching cock gets put through the wringer. Now, his prowess is being called into question. This female will be the end of him.

Envy shakes his head, because he fucking knew it. "Without my longbow, I can't take more than twelve."

"Fine. So we'll—"

"No, we won't."

"Goddammit, Envy!"

Her eyes lance through him. Really? They're going to stand here in their birthday suits, cock-blocked by destiny, fighting about certain doom and even more certain death?

"It's two versus two thousand," he argues.

"Yep," she says, propping her fists on her hips.

"And we're unarmed."

"Yep."

"And it's the opposite direction from where we need to go."

"Yep again."

"And they'll be looking out for us."

She grabs his face, pleading, "Yes. They will."

That's all. And she's right. Their allies can provide them with temporary archery, but it's not the same without their kindred weapons. To that end, this battle won't be the same for any of them. They might lose before they've begun.

Moreover, they already trespassed in the Astral Sea once. So what's the difference between then and now?

Envy shakes his head again. Fine, so the logistics and uneven odds aren't the real problem. "Call me paranoid—"

"That's Fear's job," the goddess snips. "Give it to me straight."

"You want straight, honey? You can take down an army with a single glower, and there's nothing sexier than seeing you nock a deadly weapon. Well, other than watching you come on my cock. That said,

I'm not about to let you risk your savory ass like a lamb to the slaughter. I happen to like your ass in one piece, and skinning alive anybody who touches you will require clothing that can get stained. Overalls or smocks, for example. Neither of which I possess in my wardrobe."

"Envy!"

"Sorrow?"

She throws a fit, thrashing against him while he struggles to hold her. Eventually, she loses steam and deflates in resignation. Kissing her forehead, Envy promises it will be all right. They'll find another way.

He can't blame her for the dagger eyes. Since fucking each other is no longer on the agenda, Envy makes a sly innuendo. Honestly, he's not sure what the comment is once it's out, but it gets her to snort with a grudge.

And fuck. His confession will have to wait until they've slept. Otherwise, the anxiety and stress will tangle everything up, and it'll come out wrong. She needs her rest, first. The second they've awakened, Envy will tell her.

They dry each other off with the towels he brought. Though, Envy might embellish by moving with a tad more swagger, if only to bring levity to the situation, now that his dick has gone flaccid, replaced by antsiness to tell her everything.

Earlier, he'd collected their clothes and brought them outside with the towels, so they dress each other next. Sorrow pulls a V-neck shirt over Envy's head, tucking it into his slacks. Then he slips that long, layered skirt up her limbs, drapes her in that customary vest, and fastens the clasps as if he's got all day.

There's something ceremonial about this. He would call it intimate and far out of his league.

It's one thing to disrobe a female with aplomb. It's another to cover her up.

The motions calm them down. In spite of the argument, the dust settles as quickly as it had escalated, and she relaxes when he purrs appreciatively into her neck.

After folding Sorrow's discarded robe, Envy sets it atop an outcropping, then takes her hand. They gravitate to the cavern's threshold and sit at the edge of the world. He settles behind Sorrow, flanking her with his limbs and encircling her midriff.

She's brooding again, her silence posing a question. Since when has he ever aborted a dangerous plan?

Resting his chin on her shoulder, Envy inquires, "So how many smiles do you have?"

Sorrow holds back, then sputters with mirth. "You piss me off."

"You do much more to me," he murmurs.

They haven't slumbered enough, having woken up too early and then overextending themselves with that kiss.

Fuck almighty. Their first kiss.

Grinning, Envy tucks Sorrow into him and dozes off. Too bad that grin drops like a stone when he wakes up and finds her gone.

Wrath detonates across his tongue. "Fucking Sorrow!"

With a growl, Envy surges to his feet. As he slams into the cavern and cinches his mane into a low ponytail, he considers not only which passage to take, but how tightly he'll strangle that insubordinate goddess when he locates her.

Like an imbecile, the facts only occur to him now. She had given in too easily to his request, melted too quickly from his touch. If Envy hadn't been intoxicated by the effects, he would have realized how uncharacteristic that had seemed.

He's the most gullible fuckwit in history. Of course, the goddess snuck off to be the hero. Because she's reckless and brave and stubborn and magnificent. And because he told her, no.

Also, because he'd shown her the fucking way.

28

Sorrow

Talk about shitty ideas and shittier routes. Sorrow blows out a choppy breath, warning herself to calm down. Otherwise, this jagged tunnel will eat her alive. As she learned upon entering this tomb, the threat isn't figurative.

Picking through the jagged terrain, the new boots she'd conjured splashes through a creek. Slender waterfalls echo down the cavities, the streams questing to unseen channels.

Stalagmites rise from the foundation like tusks, poised to chew on anyone stupid enough to venture down this route. Envy had listed them as one of the many reasons not to pass through here. Get too close, and these formations will sense an intruder and jolt upward, hungry to shear through flesh and bone. So basically, the cave has a mouthful of teeth.

Sorrow wedges through the maze, yelping as her foot slips on a damp rock. With the speed of a fellow immortal, one of the spiked fuckers lifts. It catches her fall, punching a hole through her skirt and puncturing the flesh of Sorrow's hip.

She yips, stumbling upright and scurrying away from the stalagmite, its razor tip dribbling blood. Pressing a palm to the gash, Sorrow clenches her molars, nostrils flaring. If her reflexes hadn't kicked in, she would have belly-flopped onto the thing and been impaled like tonight's rotisserie dinner.

Stuffing her skirt against the wound, Sorrow hisses until the crater in her hip stops hurting like fuck, the pain ebbing from a ten to a solid five. Then she keeps going, hobbling through the stalagmites, the injury compromising her balance.

Every step throws another stabbing lance through her hip. She muffles her cry, because loud noises will shake the rafters, and the noise-sensitive stalactites affixed to the ceiling will plummet like torpedoes. Yet another lovely feature of this cave, along with protrusions in the walls that explode on contact.

The vault drills under the cliff. After he made her come around his fingers, and then around his tongue, Envy took Sorrow on another tour, sailing them through the waterfall enclave. Enroute, he indicated this dangerous abutting passage leading to the Astral Sea.

Needless to say, it's been a crooked and twisted journey. Between the enclave and her destination, this course is supposed to reduce travel time by half. It should take an hour compared with the two that passed while swimming to the lagoon.

More importantly, this shrouded route prevents detection, ideal compared to breaststroking through enemy territory with no cover, exposed to anyone's direct line of sight. Sorrow and Envy had gotten lucky the first time. It's unlikely she would be so fortunate the next.

Envy had classified this cave as unsafe. In reality, that had been putting it mildly. The path is a death trap, chiseled with clammy rocks and slimy indentations. Every fatal hazard verifies why he's never tried navigating it, especially when they fled the Astral Sea, swimming having been the lesser of two evils.

Regardless, time is of the essence. Sorrow can extricate their weapons and make a return trip before nightfall. At which point, she and Envy will set out to meet their crew.

The conduit veers, clouded in a thick blanket of mist. It sprays her clothes, glazing the skirt and vest, the sheen as fine as pixie dust.

Sorrow plants her foot on a bracket of rock and roars an obscenity when the motherfucker shifts as if propped on casters, tripping her and inflaming the hip wound. Though, she's more prepared this time, stabbing her fingers into a chink in the nearest wall, stabilizing her balance.

After a few more turns, the cave teeth fall behind, but the artery narrows. A mantle of stone tears across her elbows and draws more trickles of blood. The sixth wound thus far, including a few on her forearms, another at the column of her neck, and the hole in her thigh. Well, it could be worse.

At last, the conduit expands. The falls dry up as she reaches a border tasseled in foliage. Over the ridge, a panorama greets Sorrow. The dominion of water homes on stilts, with its network of boardwalks and piers. Nighttime incites a slow crawl of activity, most of her kin scarcely active.

Earlier, Sorrow had been faced with three options. One, pull Envy from sleep and ride his cock into the ground. Two, shake Envy from sleep and force him to accompany her. Three, leave Envy sleeping and deal with his fury when she gets back.

By now, the pride god has probably stirred and discovered her absence. Sorrow pictures his face contorted in rage, those full lips swollen from their kiss.

Their first kiss.

Not her only lip-lock in history, but definitely the most toe curling, full-bodied one. The second his tongue had snatched hers, Sorrow's body had detonated like a star, her soul shattered into chips of ice, electricity sizzled through her veins, her pussy throbbed like a pulse, and about a thousand other sensations laid siege to her anatomy.

But her heart…

Sorrow can't comprehend what her wrecked heart had done. The breaking sensation had torn her to bits. Yet at the same time, the clamp of Envy's mouth had stitched those pieces back together.

From this vantage point, she scans the vicinity. The water's surface reflects billions of stars and a cluster of moons. Fronds brush her limbs as she creeps down the slope, to where the sea meets the pebbled shoreline, wafting with ethereal scents including pure silver and fresh white.

Removing her boots and lowering onto all fours, Sorrow crawls like a crab and submerges herself, paddling with her head above water. She pumps her arms, the pool rippling as she quests beneath the walkways.

Palpitations pound at her wrists. Her lungs seize up. But at least the water clots her wounds and alleviates the pain.

Avoiding beams of starlight, she navigates beneath the planks, passing several footfalls and murmured conversations. Someone plays a flute. Another polishes a longbow.

The tension increases tenfold as Sorrow reaches a designated pier. She knows its location well, waxed in moonlight and isolated on its perch. The round edifice has a single story, but rather than candles or draperies, a dusty lamp stands in each window.

Sorrow grasps one of the stilts bracing her house. If her theory is correct, and that group of deities have salvaged Love's iron archery, they might be holding Sorrow's or Envy's weapons hostage as well.

In fact, they might have stashed those weapons as bait. Maybe they're expecting her friends to come searching for the lost archery.

On second thought, when Sorrow and Envy had surveyed his house, they hadn't found a single set of arms, because that group had ransacked everything. So maybe hunting for Envy's glass weapons will amount to zero.

Or maybe Envy hadn't looked hard enough. Or maybe lots of logistical things.

Sorrow presses her ear to the planks. There's no sound of a guard or intruder.

Hooking her fingers over the pier, she hauls herself upward, heedful not to slosh about. Casting the community another glance, she scurries to the door, creeps inside, and snatches the only alternate weapon in reaching distance. A honed letter opener sitting on an entry console, the object a previous gift from Wonder.

Gripping the item like a dagger, Sorrow freezes. No moving shadows. No silhouettes charging her way. After checking the vicinity, she lowers the makeshift blade and pauses in the shadows. For a blessed moment, she consumes the details as if she hasn't been here in a millennium, as if everything has changed that much.

The lamps. The fleece linens. The table where she routinely shared currant nectar with her Guide. The bed where Sorrow used to cry herself to sleep. The floor where she pricked herself with her stitching needle after torturing Wonder. And out the window, the pier's edge where she sat beside Envy, their legs bobbing in the water as he inquired whether she would miss him, once they set off for the human realm.

Back when she couldn't wait to be away from that god. Back when she had known her purpose. Back when she believed in it.

A lump buds in Sorrow's throat. She rushes through the house, auditing the cupboards and closets and chests, rummaging for the welcome sight of archery.

Nothing. Not a forsaken thing.

The subsequent trip to Love's home elevates Sorrow's pulse. Crafted of a dozen mullioned windows, the house stands vacant. Nonetheless, she repeats the process of swimming, sneaking inside, and grasping a fire poker from a decorative hearth to defend herself. After surveying the premises, she lowers the shaft and inspects every room.

Under her friend's bed, someone has strapped a familiar set of iron arms to the bottom of the mattress. At the discovery, Sorrow puffs out a relieved breath. Fuck yeah.

But then she halts, suspicion creeping up her spine. This is too easy. The location of the weapon alone is circumspect, mounted in the most amateurish hiding spot, as if a child had done it. Although Sorrow had to go through the motions of searching Love's home, she'd expected to find the archery in the possession of whoever had confiscated it in the first place.

"It's a trap," she hisses.

Lurching to her feet and wielding the poker, Sorrow wheels toward the windows, the doors, the corridors. Tapering her eyes, she waits but nothing happens.

Well, she's not going to stick around for the cavalry. Hunkering, Sorrow examines the archery, checking for signs of stardusted rigging. After what happened in The Archives with that bobby-trapped book, Wonder and Malice had taken no chances and advised the crew on how to detect such deceptions.

With cautious motions, Sorrow gently detaches the archery. Then she lunges upright again, lest some triggered alarm should sound.

Yet again, nothing. If it's a trap, the culprits would be manifesting here by now. That is, unless the Fate Court is nearby.

At any rate, the small faction of perpetrators might indeed be expecting more than one rebel, as Sorrow had theorized earlier. In which case, they may have stationed themselves at a distant vantage point, the better to target the crew. If only a handful of thieves took the archery, hoping to impress The Court by capturing Sorrow's friends, those wankers will seek guaranteed success. As such, facing off with the elite crew would risk that.

At best, Sorrow's retrieval of the weapons is an unfeasible stroke of fortune. At worst, she's being watched.

There's nothing for it. She harnesses the quiver to her back, the foreign weight tugging down her shoulders.

"Fates eternal," she whispers.

Sorrow has held Anger's weapons before, but this is different. Evidently, the infamous Love carries a heavier burden than the rest of them.

Aligning her spine with the wall beside the door, Sorrow peeks between the crevice and inspects the perimeter. Exhaling slowly, she arms herself with Love's weapons, rounds the corner, and slinks through the partition with the arrowhead nocked.

Then she halts.

Standing beyond the threshold, an archer stares at her. Garbed in a velvet robe and brandishing arrows forged of clovers, he watches Sorrow with a slant of his head, the differences between life and death materializing in her consciousness like a bullet list.

This deity observes her with curiosity.

This deity has painted eyelids.

This deity is one she's seen before.

That's why he was easy to miss when she skulked into the house. Because he stands no taller than her breasts.

Shit. This tiny god is a child.

Craning his head, the fledgling studies Sorrow. His pupils veer from her wet clothing, to her bare feet, to the archery. He's a beautifully tanned soul, with lively sprigs of onyx hair.

Upon closer inspection, Sorrow can't decipher his root emotion. But she can guess, and she can guess well. This youth isn't a pride god, nor a rage god.

Neither is he like Sorrow, Melancholy, Despair, or Loss. He's not a trauma deity.

As she sets a finger to her mouth, his lilac eyes brighten with intrigue. Encouraged, Sorrow whispers, "Are you a wish god?"

Is he Trust or Hope in the making? That can't be, unless those deities have already ascended to mentor status. So is he Desire? Anticipation?

The tyke gives a start. He steps forward and opens his mouth.

Someone shouts. A projectile flies toward Sorrow from the opposite pier, cutting a path across the distance. It's a clean target, which should hit her square in the chest. But the problem with targets is, one can't predict what bystanders will do.

The child is runty, engulfed by the shadows, his presence unnoticed by the assailant. Hearing the whistle, the runt turns on reflex, inadvertently placing himself in the arrow's path.

Son of a bitch! Sorrow shoves the youth aside, hurling him into the safety of Love's house. He yelps and goes flying. Meanwhile, she dives sideways, tumbling across the planks as the arrow slams into the house's facade and vanishes in an illuminated blast.

More voices holler, silhouettes hastening into the fray. Someone blows a horn dangling from their necklace, alerting the residents. Doors whip open, boots slam across the peers, and arrows twang.

Dozens of voices bellow her name. If those conniving deities from the rapids had wanted to catch members of her crew covertly, that plan has just gone to hell.

Sorrow rolls across the walkway, each rotation avoiding a series of strikes. She surges to her feet as another arrow spears in her direction.

After several attempts to evanesce, Sorrow growls. If disappearing isn't possible, that confirms at least one member of The Fate Court is nearby.

Nocking Love's bow brings Sorrow up short, the iron delaying her speed. Dammit, she has to be cautious. Because this archery has retained the magic of its root emotion, Sorrow must render the arrows infirm. And since this isn't her own weapon, that makes things challenging.

Her fingers stall, arrested by the sight of another arrow slicing past her from behind, intercepting the attack. A direct block from a glass shaft.

Sorrow whips around, her gaze darting toward the source. Atop one of the houses, an opalescent moon outlines a masculine frame positioned on the roof. Long mahogany hair tied at the nape. Trousers and V-neck shirt with the sleeves jammed up his forearms. Envy lowers his bow, his mercenary eyes slamming into hers.

How long has he been here? How did he get his archery back?

What had made Sorrow think he wouldn't come after her?

Alarm flashes across his pupils. Awareness jolts through Sorrow.

In unison, they vault toward a stream of incoming arrows and fire. It's a chain reaction, a stampede of gods and goddesses flooding the walkways, the cliffside slopes, and the shoreline. Flabbergasted, the masses identify Sorrow and Envy on sight.

From every direction, projectiles fly. One by one, Sorrow looses arrows, each ramming one into another, thwarting the shots. Bodies sprint along the planks, leap over the gaps, or tumble into the water.

Blood sprays the air and squirts against her vest. Someone takes an arrow through the neck before plummeting into the sea.

Sorrow ducks, evading a punch and retaliating with a jab of her elbow. Envy slashes through a god who springs atop the roof, crimson pouring from the deity's stomach.

While catapulting from one walkway to the next, Sorrow skewers through chests, tears through flesh with her arrows, and spins around random fists. With otherworldly speed, she nocks iron and pelts archers into the sea, red puddling to the surface.

While barreling from one roof to the next, Envy dodges arrows. With each landing, he targets and impales an adversary.

Sorrow vaults to a dwelling parallel to him. They jump between houses, shooting while racing toward the bluffs, where the secret channel leads to the waterfall enclave.

Yet it's a million leagues away. They can't make it, can't outrun everybody.

Not both of them.

Sorrow goes still. The lapse of movement catches Envy's attention. Wielding his longbow, he peers at her, panting in confusion.

They haven't said a word to each other since this morning. She's sorry about that. Already, she misses the depth of his voice, and she misses their honest talks.

There are so many things she longs to say. Poignant things and truthful things.

There are countless feverish touches she should have stolen with him before leaving their sanctuary, endless kisses she's missing out on, centuries of fierce lovemaking and ardent fucking.

But because of this half-assed idea to get their weapons back, she has fucked up those opportunities. So she won't fuck up now.

Committing his baffled expression to memory, Sorrow gives Envy a weak smile. Contrary to what they always believed, they're good together. But not that good.

Understanding dawns on Envy. His eyes widen, those orbs flaring with rancor and protectiveness. "Sorrow, don't you fucking dare!"

Except one of them has to.

Sorrow gives him no choice. She mouths, *Envy, don't you fucking follow!*

Anyway, why would he do that? This is his chance to retreat.

She tosses him the iron archery. As he catches it absently, she blows his livid face a kiss and turns. Unarmed, she jumps into the crowd.

29

Sorrow

The fall is quick. Dozens of outstretched arms break the landing. When the snake pit catches Sorrow, they ambush her. Several deities order the throng to make way, the onslaught of voices drowning out Envy's roar.

Her name, a fractured sound on his lips.

From the divide, Sorrow glimpses his livid face. That gaze storms through the distance, pupils brewing like a tempest as he watches the congregation hoist her overhead, as if she's just stage-dived into her own execution. Beneath the surface, tormented shock burns a path across Envy's irises.

Guess that answers how many times anyone has chosen him over themselves. It's pretty amazing, the way astonishment warps his features, throwing every crack into disarray. If Sorrow weren't being carried to her doom like a sacrificial lamb, she'd laugh.

Envy takes a mercenary step forward, but Sorrow shakes her head and jerks her gaze toward the water. *Get going!*

She's not an extreme sports junkie who took this flying leap for kicks. Her actions have stupefied the masses, buying Envy a window of time before they remember he's here.

He stands frozen, his nostrils flaring, his grip on the longbow about to snap the weapon in half. The motivation to do…whatever he's tempted to do…is short-lived, because this god isn't a fool, despite how often Sorrow has called him one. Raging into this scene will only get both of them trapped.

Savagery burns like an inferno across Envy's face. He grimaces, then dives into the water, the depth swallowing him. Moments later, and from farther away, his upper frame catapults through the surface. Sadly, she can't see his expression.

He's there, floating and watching. Then he isn't.

When he's gone, Sorrow clenches her eyes shut, barricading the tears. She's an expert at not crying. Turning into a busted faucet is the last thing that will save her.

A sense of concern grips Sorrow's awareness. Her lids flip open to where a thin figure idles beyond the crowd, a braid hanging limp over his shoulder, anguish burdening his features.

Echo.

Although she hasn't seen her Guide since this revolt began, the loss is eternal. Since deities are birthed from celestials, then bred without parents or siblings, Guides are the closest thing to family for any Dark God.

He won't side with the crew, not as Wonder's Guide had months ago. Matter of fact, Harmony is the only mentor who has shifted allegiances.

Nonetheless, Echo moves forward, eager to reach Sorrow. But then a feminine hand clamps onto his shoulder, stalling the motion. At which point, Envy's Guide, Siren, materializes. Vigilant, she cautions Echo from making a further spectacle.

Sorrow gives a silent cry. She wants Echo near, but that might trigger him to speak impulsively, exposing his vulnerability and thus endangering him.

Her attention shifts to the child standing beside the mentors, his onyx tresses mussed from when she shoved him inside Love's house. A pair of lilac eyes flit toward the water, then to Sorrow. He saw the pride god disappear, maybe saw the direction in which Envy had swam.

Sorrow sends the child a pleading look, then sets her finger against her lips. *Shh.*

Yet she can't see his response, nor Echo or Siren's. The mob carries her into a channel within the bluffs, a curtain of greenery blocking her view of the only spectators who don't want her head served on a platter.

Because it's pointless to keep bracing her like a rotisserie boar, the world rotates. The company lowers Sorrow to her feet, then restrains her wrists with bonds forged of star-dusted manacles. The god securing her arms behind her back wears a cobalt mantle. He's part of the crew who ambushed Sorrow and her friends in the valley. He's also the one she and Envy overheard from beneath the pier three days ago, boasting how he wanted to try out Love's weapon.

The god fixes Sorrow with a righteous look, rather than the validated one she'd anticipated. Lingering nearby is the female who spoke with him that night. At the time, limited vision had obscured the goddess's face, but the jumpsuit and mercury weapons tip Sorrow off.

With Sorrow detained, the mob travels down a torchlit lane. The route winds into cliffs embossed in minerals, stalks germinating from the summits.

Ahead, the recess leads to a structure embellished with metallic inlays and intricate whorls. Colonnades enwrap the three-story edifice, the obsidian-strewn walls gleaming like a celestial of its own making.

Anxiety prickles Sorrow's flesh. The setting dredges up hundreds of memories, each one so lucid it might have occurred yesterday. Assemblies, feasts, revels, and public persecutions.

The Palace of Starlight.

The crowd recedes, apart from several guards and the major players. An intermission follows in which the mercury-arrow-wielding goddess and cobalt-mantled god step inside The Fate Court's royal seat. Presumably, they're about to give the rulers a thorough report.

After a while, the pair returns to corral Sorrow inside. Winding creeks flow over pebble beds, lanterns dangle from the rafters, and the tune of a windpipe fills the air. The building flows into a fountain courtyard. From there, the group enters an amphitheater of waterfalls, with cascades and a moat spanning the northern cliffside crescent.

A dais rises from the amphitheater's center, the platform housing five thrones hewn of platinum. And five luminous figures.

A pale-skinned female outfitted in lace.

A goddess with amethyst hair.

And a dark beauty everyone likens to a galaxy because of her iridescent gown.

A male with braids as long as ropes and a hooked nose that has always made Sorrow and her crew think of a hawk.

Lastly, an archer with eyebrows so angular someone must have stapled a pair of boomerangs to his forehead.

The Fate Court.

These rulers weren't born into their roles. They were once archers like Sorrow, after which they ascended, becoming Guides to their successors. Later, they were selected by The Stars, ordained to become monarchs of The Dark Fates.

Sorrow used to admire and trust these figures. Even now, admiration wars with disobedience as the guards urge her to prostrate herself, kneecaps crushing blades of grass. On reflex, she inclines her head to The Fate Court, then shoots them an insolent look.

The goddess in iridescent fabric quirks her lips. She approaches, folding her hands and regarding Sorrow with a peculiar expression, which the other sovereigns fail to catch from this angle.

Inquisitiveness? Compassion?

Technically, this female used to be the Guide of Wonder. That had been long before Harmony. And prior to that, the ruler had been the Goddess of Wonder, eons before Sorrow's crewmate was born.

"Welcome home, Goddess of Sorrow," the female announces.

"For how long?" Sorrow wonders.

Another twitch of those condescending lips. "Tell us how you got here."

"Magic."

"I'm afraid your legendary sarcasm will do you no favors."

"Where are your accomplices?" the pale goddess inquires from her chair. "Who is included in the party?"

Right. As if these dictators can't place bets on the answer. "I have a cap on how many questions I can tolerate before it depresses me," Sorrow replies. "Which one do you want me to respond to?"

The iridescent goddess sighs. She nods, and the pair of thieving deities who'd taken Love's weapons disperse with a series of genuflections.

"Our subjects have provided us with enlightening information. It seems not only has your radical band trespassed into The Dark Fates, but some of you lost your archery during a chase into the rapids. We're also told that one of the weapons, which our subjects recovered from the water, is forged of iron." The iridescent goddess hitches a brow. "Yet it is not the iron of Anger."

When Love and Andrew bonded, Love had originally lost her powers, and the rulers claimed her weapons. Sure enough, they hadn't known about Love eventually rejoining their crew, much less that Andrew lost his mortality and became part of this crusade.

A lot has happened since then. A lot has also been rectified.

Evidently, these rulers have begun to realize this. Because of everything that went down after Love, Anger, and Wonder's stories, it has amounted to a number of their subjects defecting from The Dark Fates, to ally with Sorrow and the crew.

Naturally, The Court is aware of that part. They just hadn't been cognizant of a few plot holes.

Nevertheless, the one question they don't need to ask is *why* Sorrow and her clan are here. The reason is obvious. You can't have a battle without a battleground.

"Fine," the hawkish god grumbles, thrusting out his wrist in disgust. "If you refuse to confirm Love's presence among your cult, then we shall come full circle to the first question. How did you get here?"

Recognition alights the iridescent ruler's face. "Wonder and Malice."

Goddammit. As Sorrow's crew predicted, The Fate Court had believed the conflict would take place on mortal ground, since it's impossible for outcast deities to breach boundaries. Provided they lack the means to cross through barriers, exceptions such as Asterra Flora.

As to their plans upon entering this realm, The Court will have to crack open Sorrow's skull like a piñata to get anything out of her. Either that, or torture her with hours of Gregorian chant music.

She remarks as much, embellishing with obscenities and an abridged version of the facts. One, Malice and Wonder are smart as fuck. How many times will it take before the couple proves that? They uncovered all the legends that resurrected Love and Anger's powers, not to mention united both deities with Andrew and Merry.

That's what it boils down to, because love itself is a strength these rulers don't comprehend. Even if Sorrow can't understand the emotion herself, at least she deduces this fact.

Two, even if she knew where the crew was, she's not about to fold.

Three, they can place bets on who's included in the party. These sovereigns are ignorant, but not that ignorant.

Four, fuck them.

Fuck them for disposing of Sorrow and her crewmates like dumpster trash when their values turned out to be different. Fuck them for banishing Love and threatening Andrew's existence. Fuck them for casting off Merry when she was born, just because she didn't fit the so-called immortal concept of perfection. Fuck them for shooting Malice in the back like cowards and almost killing him.

Fuck them for inspiring Sorrow and then disillusioning her. Fuck them for dismissing her. Fuck them for breaking her heart.

The iridescent ruler winces as if she's a mind reader. Maybe the hurt is mutual, because none of these supreme beings act haughty or unflappable. Rather, they appear worn. In their eyes, they feel equally duped.

"All of this effort," the god with winged brows says, clamping his hands behind his back. "Lives compromised. History and destiny forsaken. All this for the sake of mortals."

Ah. That's where the ignorance begins.

"All of this for *all* of us," Sorrow maintains. "Fate doesn't have to involve controlling mortal will. We can find a balance between chance and destiny, a new life cycle, and we might be better for it."

They frown collectively, struggling to perceive her meaning. Pity swells in Sorrow's throat because it's always been this way. It's all they know.

It's all she'd once known too.

"What qualifies you to speak on humanity's behalf?" the cloaked god demands.

"That's rich," Sorrow scoffs. "Mortals can't speak for themselves because they don't know deities exist."

"That isn't what I asked."

"But it's half the answer, while the other half is simple. Our crew includes immortals, humans who became immortals, immortals who became humans, outcasts who grew up near humans, and humans resurrected into devils. And the rest of us have either loved humans or befriended them. That's what makes us the most elite crew of archers. Not because it includes the Goddess of Love, but because we're diverse. It has to start with us."

"Has to?" the cloaked god repeats. "And you say fate has no place in the universe."

"I never said that," Sorrow parries. "I said there's room for every possibility and for everyone. In case you haven't noticed, it's a big fucking sky up there, with a lot of fucking stars. You're just afraid of what you don't know."

The iridescent goddess steps nearer. "And what are *you* afraid of?"

"Tweed blazers. Alien invasions. Romantic comedies."

"Oh, I imagine such triggers would distress anyone." She tilts her head, bringing those exfoliated cheekbones into stark relief. "Or does the answer have to do with the male companion you left behind?"

When Sorrow narrows her eyes, the goddess clarifies, "Envy."

The name produces a cramp in Sorrow's gut. They don't know about the legend meant to empower this campaign. The one that binds her and him together like a pair of barnacles. Yet this female expects the shape and sound of his name to affect Sorrow.

An aurora of color surrounds the female, prisms from the waterfalls floating across into the enclosure. "You claim to have no idea of your crew's whereabouts. Yet you weren't alone on the pier. Or do you not consider the God of Envy an ally? That would be odd, seeing as you tossed yourself into the fray so he could escape. One would think you were petrified of his capture."

"Ugh." Sorrow flips her eyes heavenward. "I was petrified that if he got shackled, we'd have one less fighter on our roster."

"So your platonic history is intact. You were being practical. He's merely a necessity, a crewmate who routinely antagonizes you but demonstrates excellent aim. A comrade rather than a friend or paramour. And a valuable one, if you've chosen him over yourself. Thus, you must know where he's headed."

Who died and made this female cleverer than she deserves? And what's with the benign tone? It doesn't match the insulted, belittling expressions the other rulers wear, the rest of them having lost their patience the moment Sorrow got comfortable talking back.

There's only one response she's in the mood to give. Because her hands are bound, Sorrow glances at each monarch, going down the line. "Fuck you, fuck you, fuck you, fuck you—" then to the iridescent ruler, "*and* fuck you."

As a deliberate afterthought, Sorrow finishes with, "Your Majesties."

"That tongue of yours is quite the coping mechanism," the god with winged brows snarls.

"You can do what you like to me. I'm used to pain."

"Immortality 101," the goddess with the amethyst tresses speaks up, rising from her chair. "There's a difference between pain that's fleeting and pain that lasts. And with us, it can last a very long time."

With the overripe sweetness of fruit on the verge of rotting, the pale goddess elaborates, "Why not ask a certain introspective crewmate?"

Wonder. Sorrow's confidence experiences a quick death. In its place, a charred scent fills her nostrils. Yes, she'd looked up to these figures once, but that fateful day tainted the admiration, the downward trajectory continuing ever since.

"Would you care for a sample of what she endured?" the amethyst ruler suggests.

"Like I said," is all Sorrow replies.

Yet it's the iridescent ruler who Sorrow has bigger trouble facing, especially when the female observes Sorrow intuitively, like a former Goddess of Wonder would. "Your botched escape was rather explicit, including the look Envy gave you before he blocked that arrow on the pier."

The cramp in Sorrow's gut intensifies. The ruler continues rubbing salt into the wound. "Such an exhibition brings to mind other looks. The one Love bestowed upon Andrew as we targeted him. The one Anger directed to Merry when we charged at them in a carnival. The one Malice gave Wonder in The Archives, before he took a shot to the heart for her."

"About that," Sorrow jumps in. "How the hell do you sleep at night? Are you the least bit sorry?"

Shadows of remorse cross their respective features. "Repentant is a better word," the cloaked god with pitched brows acknowledges, since he's the one who targeted Malice. "Chastened to have struck down an unarmed archer in the back."

"That's why we did not bear arms on your crew shortly after Malice and Wonder's destructive actions," the hawkish god defends. "We called a ceasefire and sought to explain the situation to our subjects, only to lose a number of Dark Gods to your side, then to discover Malice survived the injury and you cemented your plot against us."

"The drawbacks of haste are plentiful," the pale goddess judges, her epicene features creasing.

The amethyst goddess steers them back to the subject of Sorrow and Envy, including their attempt to save each other by the shore. "Since your sentimentality has spread like a virus, the susceptibility to love growing into a contagion among your crew, a theory presently festers in our minds."

"You can theorize all you want, geniuses," Sorrow says. "You'd be wrong about him and me. We're not like our peers."

The iridescent ruler drifts off for a second. "How many arrows do you have in your quiver?"

Wow. Talk about a change of subject.

Not to mention, Sorrow's archery is no place in sight. She lost the chance to find her weapons. And since a deity can't replace their weaponry, much less produce new ones, she'll have to deal with the loss. It won't be the first time.

By the same token, the female says, "It seems you've been missing one since youth. In all this time, you've failed to recover it."

The cloaked god twists in his seat and then straightens, brandishing a lone ice arrow between his fingertips. "Would you care to have it back?"

Sorrow blinks. "Where the fuck…"

"In his home," the iridescent ruler supplies. "According to the deities who swarmed your crew, one of them found it while searching the interior."

It's a good thing Sorrow's already prostrate on the ground, because her knees buckle. When she and Envy swam to his home, Nostalgia had been guarding the place. Then after they dealt with him, they found Envy's cache of alternative weapons gone. One of those archers—maybe Nostalgia himself—must have discovered Sorrow's old arrow and taken that too.

All of these years? That duplicitous, double-crossing cocksucker kept Sorrow's arrow to himself the whole fucking time?

Her fingers curl like talons, the breach of trust rendering her speechless. It's one thing for Envy to snatch Sorrow's weapon and hold it hostage for a few centuries during their era of rivalry. But to hide this truth for eons, never once confessing in the waterfall enclave? That amounts to the worst kind of backstabbing.

Another thought minces her to pieces. Claiming another deity's weapon renders both parties incapable of mating, severing the chance for any type of union. The Stars have declared this, and Envy knows this.

This is also why he'd scoffed at the legend Wonder and Malice discovered. Not just because Sorrow and Envy's hearts hadn't been invested, but also because it's a lost cause.

Her insides curdle. Be that as it may, it's stupid to publicize this epic reaction.

Sorrow rearranges her features into a mask of stone. "This means nothing," she lies. "The immortal prick must've taken it to use against me later, to bribe or blackmail me for sport."

"Then he procrastinated for quite a long time. If that's the case, let us do it for him," the cloaked god volunteers. "Since he never mustered the courage to follow through."

"I'm not an easy target."

"I think you are," the iridescent goddess counters. "I think you're the sort who weeps when a human soldier dies in combat, because you couldn't spare him the anguish, because you reached him too late, because your speed has limits, because you can only be in one place at a time. I think you're the type who strokes a crewmate's hair when she's being tortured. I think you're the kind of soul who pricks yourself with a stitching needle after witnessing the pain you've neglected to alleviate in that same treasonous goddess."

Sorrow's jaw locks. Never mind how they know these details. But how dare they belittle Wonder's suffering!

Waterfalls amplify to a deafening roar. Constellations scatter across the firmament like salt.

The goddess draped in pearly lace crosses her limbs. "Love, Anger, Wonder. Haven't prior installments in this series of reckless tales taught you anything? Surely, you didn't think we parceled off our deities to the mortal world without keeping tabs on them. Did you assume we missed your gesture of comfort toward Wonder during her punishment? Or the effect war zones have on you?"

"It harms you greatly to see victims deteriorate" the braided god says, each sentence twisting through Sorrow's gut like thorns. "Such is the nature of a trauma goddess, particularly one susceptible to infernal sentiment. I think you hold those memories so close, if history were to repeat itself, it would be a devastating provocation. Just imagine how it would feel to see your crew befall the same fate, if they should lose this battle. Picture the slow, drawn-out consequences of execution. Visualize the pain they'd go through while you watch from the sidelines, awaiting your turn."

"Envy may mean nothing to you. But will that make it easier to witness us stripping the flesh from his body?" the pale goddess inquires, cupping her hands in front of her. "For your sake, I certainly hope so."

Sorrow tosses her head from side to side. "You wouldn't do something that barbaric."

Wouldn't they? They ordered Wonder's torture. Yes, she endangered the life cycle of immortals. Nonetheless, The Court opted for brutal retaliation rather than mercy.

In fact, Love is the only soul who's too valuable to damage, after millennia of trying to create her. Whereas the rest of them are expendable.

The iridescent goddess knits her eyebrows. "Or when you lose, we could show clemency," she interjects. "We could make it less inflicting, memorable, and permanent. But that is contingent upon you."

Impatient, the amethyst goddess strides across the dais. "You may have recruited a legion, and you may have infiltrated this land, but you were caught within moments of sneaking into the Astral Sea."

"I was there to view the spectacle," the iridescent goddess says, confirming Sorrow's earlier suspicion of why she hadn't been able to evanesce. "Before that, according to the deities who accosted you in the valley—"

"—and who are oh-so willing to take credit for it, even though they kept you in the dark," Sorrow baits.

"We shall deal with their misguided ambition," the cloaked god assures her.

"Be that as it may, you hadn't been in The Dark Fates long before a gaggle of youths and their companions swarmed you," the amethyst goddess recaps. "If you can't get that far, what do you expect? No matter what you think or believe, you are still outarmed and outnumbered, and you do not have the degree of magic to change that."

The iridescent goddess retrieves the ice arrow from her peer and lowers herself to Sorrow's level, presenting the shaft like a sword, its length resting against the female's upturned palms. "You, Goddess of Sorrow, know hopelessness and agony like none of your crewmates. So let's start over, shall we? What are you afraid of?"

Meaning, what are they about to take from her?

Meaning, what do they want her to do?

Sorrow flees into a recent memory. A moment branded on her soul, in which a god had hugged her.

She'd said, *I don't know how to feel like this.*

Yet he'd held her tighter. *But you know how to feel this.*

The pale goddess in lace strides across the amphitheater, joins her comrade, and squats in a bogus imitation of pity. Unlike her peers, this female doesn't wear the same solemn yet disciplinary expression.

No. This bitch is sneering, regarding Sorrow through sanctimonious eyes, getting off on this retribution. Misguided by destiny or not, she's always been a stricter, more dogmatic warden among The Court.

Just like that, it's clear. The iridescent ruler is holding up the ice arrow and voicing an ultimatum. But the pale goddess came up with the idea.

She's chosen to profit from Envy's deceit and Sorrow's pain. All to bring Sorrow and her crew to heel.

Wrong fucking timing. Against her tailbone, Sorrow's bound hands ball into fists. And while she can't use her knuckles to sever bone, her limbs are still free to misbehave.

A red mushroom cloud explodes in her vision. A string of insubordinate vulgarities leaps off her tongue.

The next thing Sorrow knows, her body is rolling backward, her legs are kicking upward, and the soles of her boots are launching forward. A second later, the pale ruler hits the ground, an outraged shriek popping from her mangled mouth. Blood drizzles like sap from the gash, the blow landing so hard it knocks that stupid-ass sneer off her bleached face.

Horror grips the other female's countenance. That, and pity. Because afterward, the rest of The Court is on Sorrow like flies to shit.

The price for her insolence reminds Sorrow of what they did to Wonder. In this case, the monarchs use something far more precious and personal to open Sorrow's skin. But while she' cries out in agony, only one lesson comes to mind.

She used to be scared of pleasure, until him. She also used to think pain was manageable, until him.

The things Sorrow once feared aren't the same anymore. The things she used to handle are no longer the ones she can bear.

He may have stolen from her, then lied about it. He may have committed that act of treachery.

But who's to say Sorrow won't do worse? Who's to say she won't betray him back? And who's to say that won't destroy her?

30

Envy

Fool of a goddess!

Confounding, stunning, self-destructing fool of a goddess. Who the fuck gave her permission to steal his heroic thunder? More critically, who the fuck gave her liberty to play the savior? To risk her neck for the likes of him, as if he actually deserves her sacrifice?

Envy would add reckless to the list, but he needs to concentrate. Otherwise, rage will get the better of him and he'll fucking drown. It's difficult enough to manage his own archery while swimming, but there's also the matter of Love's archery, the antecedent of this turn of events and the reason he's paddling like a lopsided tadpole.

Weighed down, the journey takes him longer than it should. He drives his arms through the sea, thrashing water out of the way. At least it gets his furious blood to pump for different reasons, keeps him from losing control.

By Fates, they had swarmed her like an army of ants. He'd wanted to skin every immortal who came near her, touched her, harmed her. With a bellow skewering up his throat, it was all Envy could do to stop himself from charging, from stabbing through the crowd and committing mass murder on his way to rip Sorrow from their clutches.

Alas, it's only a fantasy. In reality, the enemy would have overtaken him. The God of Envy can handle a dozen fighters, but not hundreds. Such idiocy would have gotten them both captured, and he'd have been no use to Sorrow.

Fuck it all to hell. To rescue her, Envy had to leave her behind first.

While swimming to the coastline, stalking out of the water, and slamming through the foliage, he loathes every inch of distance the route puts between them. Returning to the tunnel, he carves a path along the rocky passage, dismissing every cut and gash this produces until achieving a safe distance. In a cavity behind a waterfall, he deposits the iron arrows, then whips around and retraces his steps. Love's archery will remain hidden until he gets back.

Until Envy *and Sorrow* get back.

Does she honestly expect him to leave her behind? Imprudent female!

Envy secures his weapons, conjures boots for his bare feet, and strides through the misted channels, ridges slicing through his untucked shirt and trousers. Before locating Sorrow on the pier, he had operated on a hunch. Seeing as his home had been depleted of arms, he'd checked Nostalgia's house. That god had been skulking outside Envy's abode days ago, so it stood to reason Nostalgia might have hoarded the weapons in his own dwelling.

Luckily, the god hadn't been in residence. As predicted, Envy found his archery there.

Sorrow had been right. The deities who attacked their crew in the sylvan valley must have pursued them into the rapids. Although the opposition hadn't caught up, they salvaged every weapon that went overboard.

Perceptive goddess. But still, a troublesome vixen he's never been able to shake from his system.

Reaching the tunnel's boundary, Envy scans the vicinity, his gaze tearing across the landscape. All is calm now, residents having returned to their homes, likely murmuring about the news of Sorrow's capture.

Having glimpsed the direction the crowd took her, Envy bleeds into the shadows, then slips through the vine curtain leading to a paved walkway. The path cleaves into the cliff, a route he and his crewmates are all too familiar with.

Torchlight dapples the artery, white flames lashing. He keeps to the crevices, ghosting in and out of corners. Although he hadn't retreated too far into the tunnel, enough time had passed for The Fate Court to act.

To have a penetrating and gruesome effect on Sorrow.

He will not push the panic button. He will not charge like a rhino into danger.

He will not fucking lose her.

The route snakes into the bluffs. At the opposite end, the Palace of Starlight rises from an avenue of trees. Metallic inlays twine through the columns, glass domes reflect the night sky, and walls threaded with obsidian glint like heartbeats, the shimmering veins pulsing with energy. The edifice is mystical to the point of illusionary, captivating intruders and preventing them from noticing the camouflaged spikes, razor-edged pocket doors, and arrow slits hidden amid the layout. Ethereal yet deadly if anyone means this fortress harm.

About twelve armed shitheads guard the threshold, each future corpse brandishing crossbows from various points of entry. Envy veers into the hedges, then grinds to a halt. Shit. Naturally, he should have foreseen this hindrance as easily as he should have anticipated the palace possessing windows. That defenses stand vigil isn't confidential information; it's common fucking sense. So where the devil is his brain?

He knows the answer to that. It's somewhere deep in Sorrow's pocket.

Envy slits his gaze through the shrubbery. He doesn't recognize the sentinels, but he can handle the number with minimal damage to his outfit. The problem is, he'll need to dispose of them quietly.

Such a shame. He prefers spectacle over secrecy. To that medieval end, he was looking forward to making his enemies scream until their lungs bled, until every god and goddess in this realm heard the discord, bearing audible witness to Envy mincing their neighbors into shark bait.

It might still happen. He hasn't yet seen what they've done to Sorrow, the morbid possibilities incinerating his retinas, turning his vision so red he's about to develop nocturnal eyesight.

If they've touched her, he will maim them. Albeit quietly. For her sake, he'll find a way to make them howl quietly.

With fatal calm, Envy slides a glass arrow from his quiver and nocks his bow. Blowing out a menacing breath, he tips the weapons through the ferns, aiming for the first throat. Penetration from this angle will hemorrhage his target slowly, all the while severing the guard's vocal cords.

He pulls back on the bowstring. Then a small hand lurches from the dark and seizes his fucking bicep.

With a hiss, Envy dices his gaze toward the source. His gaze slams into a pair of lilac eyes, the lashes adorned in pigment. It's the moppet who led a team of youths in the valley. Earlier, Envy had witnessed from the rooftop as this runt stood on the pier, exchanging some form of silent communication with Sorrow right before shit got real.

The child releases Envy's arm, indicates a gap in the vegetation, and whispers, "This way."

The shorty flips around, about to hop into the crochet of bushes. Envy snatches the child's hooded velvet robe and yanks him back.

"Ah, ah, ah," he drawls. "Not so fast, Thumbelina."

The miniature god-in-training flashes his teeth in umbrage. Unless he's up to snuff on human fairytales, he won't know what the nickname means. But he does grasp the implication it has on his height.

Up close, the moppet is the textbook definition of immortal perfection. Tanned skin, dark curls that spring around his head, and an exploratory gaze. Indeed, just The Fate Court's type of exemplary.

"Who are you?" Envy asks. "What's your name?"

The little mercenary slits his eyes, his features bunching into a wad of consternation. It's common practice to inquire after an archer's root emotion, yet this moppet glowers as though Envy has accused him of wearing polyester.

The juvenile is astute enough to register suspicion and proud enough to take it personally. He snarls, "Are you coming or not, dickface?"

Envy squints. "How do I know this isn't a trap?"

"You don't."

"How original."

That adolescent's mouth breaks into a sneering grin. "This is a limited-time offer."

Envy tosses him a vapid look. The child's Guide must have taught him all these mortal phrases. "What you see before you are six-foot-four inches, plus two-hundred and twenty-five pounds of male radiance, all amounting to a rather lethal disposition. Don't play games with me."

"Too late." With that, the moppet flounces into the underbrush.

Fuck's sake. Casting another glance at the sentinels, Envy reconsiders the wordless exchange he'd observed between Sorrow and that tiny insurgent. They must have developed a camaraderie with each other.

Since Envy isn't in the mood to show mercy, and since children are hardly unaccustomed to violence in The Dark Fates, Envy has no qualms about chopping the night watch to pieces in front of the interloper. But unfortunately, logic wins out over bloodlust. Getting into the palace without leaving a trail of butchered bodies in his wake will benefit Sorrow more than carnage.

Sighing, Envy stalks after the mini god. The dense lane dissolves into the murk, winding around the fortress like a serpent, its direction and elevation erratic, dipping and twisting and ascending again. Envy mutters an oath while keeping the moppet in range.

At last, a break in the hedges reveals the throne dais. Set within an amphitheater, waterfalls pour from the summit and smash into a surrounding moat. Amid the setting, a lunar heron perches on the central platform housing five regal chairs, all of which stand vacant.

The Court is nowhere to be seen, but they've been here. Envy's thunderous gaze stumbles upon evidence of that fact, the sight draining every ounce of oxygen from his lungs.

She's unconscious and shackled to a tree. Her head slumps forward, layers of gray sloping across her profile, gleaming chain links wrapping around an overhead branch and choking her wrists. With her arms extending overhead, there's barely enough slack, forcing her to dangle on both tiptoes like a broken puppet.

The position exposes Sorrow's arms, where a grid of cuts trail up her flesh. Lines of blood ooze from the wounds, each one stacked atop the other.

Clean lines. Attentive lines made with a deliberate, prolonged purpose.

With an agenda.

Envy doesn't see blood red. He fucking sees death black.

Fury scorches his veins like lava, and his pulse accelerates like a full-throttle berserker. Five more deities patrol the perimeter. He's going to massacre them, he's going to whittle them down to the bone, he's going to... to make this fucking kid pay for restraining him!

The moppet wrestles with Envy, putting his whole pint-sized frame into the effort because, at some unhinged point, Envy had leaped into the courtyard like a rabid mutt.

He rips away from the little menace, the force nearly prying the juvenile's arm from its socket. "Hands. Off."

"Contain yourself, dumbass," the imp hisses under his breath. "They're expecting you."

Indeed. The guards anticipate a rescue, either from Envy or their crew. If he charges in there like a hot mess, it will end in disaster. Sorrow will bleed out even worse than she already has.

The sight of her chars a hole through Envy's pupils. His heart needs to calm the fuck down, his rage needs a timeout, and his fear needs a sedative. Although it's clear those sentinels weren't the ones who laid a hand on Sorrow, they're participating in her agony, preventing anyone from saving her.

Envy snarls. The price they're about to pay isn't going to tickle.

Focusing on the silhouettes patrolling the vicinity, he seethes in a low register, "You might want to look away."

"You might want to treat me like a deity, not a human," the moppet huffs.

Accurate point. Not to mention, Envy made this same conclusion several minutes ago. Carrying a small set of clover archery, the child has already been taught the reality of combat.

Regardless, Envy urges him farther into the hedges, then prowls along the border. Every step propels him faster, until all he sees is more black while slithering behind the first set of archers. His teeth sharpen like fangs, violence detonating inside him like a mushroom cloud.

Two arrowhead jabs to the skull bring the male and female down, blood spurting from the head gashes. Half a second later, Envy twirls one of his glass arrows. The third guard squeals like a chew toy, then shuts the fuck up as the lash of Envy's weapon splits his mouth, widening the gap and spilling crimson. Next, another arrow skewers through a masculine chest, polishing off the cocksucker, more crimson spritzing Envy's torso.

By the time his remaining target registers this slaughter, the god's eye socket meets the tip of a glass arrow. With a maddened growl, Envy jams the weapon through the male's oculus and impales his scalp. Fluid sprays from the guard's orb, his howl cutting off as Envy snatches the male's cranium and executes a quick, serpentine twist. The guard's head spins like a marble, snapping from his neck seconds before he topples.

To be sure, Envy would have preferred to draw this out, torturing them as they'd tortured Sorrow. However, that would delay things. The longer his killing spree lasts, the longer those bonds hurt her.

Sorrow.

Envy storms across the divide. Reaching the unconscious female, he grasps the sides of her face and lifts it gently, red coating his fingers and staining her cheeks. "My nymph."

She moans, lost in dreams. Desperate, he assesses the chains. The stardusted manacles glitter with enchantment, impervious to brute strength.

Fuck. As if a set of inflated muscles and a wrathful temper will get the job done, Envy seizes the links and grits his teeth while shaking, pulling, wrenching. But other than a key, the only thing that will sever the manacles is a dose of Asterra Flora, which wouldn't be an issue if Malice and Wonder were here.

The moppet jogs into the amphitheater. "She's waking up."

"Envy," Sorrow mumbles, her bleary eyelids fluttering, catching sight of something behind them.

The child gasps. Envy vaults around, nocking his bow.

Standing before them is a gangly male with a cleft chin and a braid dangling over his shoulder, his expression heavy as he peers at Sorrow, who blinks with unshed tears. Her Guide, Echo.

Despite the recognition, Envy tightens his grip on the longbow while Sorrow's mentor cautiously withdraws an arrow from his robe, the weapon forged of blue moonstone. An arrow that belongs to a member of The Fate Court. The female known for her astral-woven, iridescent gowns.

Manacles can be unlocked by the tip of an arrow, so long as that arrow belongs to the one who crafted the restraints. Envy and his crew had done this to Malice, back when he was their prisoner, before he became Wonder's soulmate.

Echo must have gone to dangerous lengths, smuggling the weapon from its owner's suite. A treasonous infringement. Nonetheless, Envy is hard-pressed to lower his archery, maintaining aim as the mentor approaches and jimmies the arrow's tip into the bolt.

"The fact remains," Echo begins, his words shaky. "We may no longer agree. But that doesn't mean we stop caring."

He kisses Sorrow's trembling cheek. She gives a choked, half-conscious sob.

The lock shudders open. On a wounded cry, the goddess falls forward. Envy drops his weapons and catches her, cradling Sorrow's limp form to his chest. They must have pushed her to the physical limit, because she passes out again, the scathing cuts along her arms clotting.

"Take care of her," Echo pleads.

"Always," Envy promises.

But the deity smiles sadly. "Siren has a message."

Envy stiffens. A lump forms in his throat as the male indicates the west waterfall and conveys instructions to flee through the cascade. "She said it would take you to a place you know."

An alternate route to the waterfall enclave. One The Fate Court doesn't know about.

Siren isn't here, but she hasn't forsaken Envy. His mentor must have conferenced with Echo sometime after Sorrow's capture. Like the guards, they had anticipated this rescue, prepared, and waited.

Based on the looks between Echo and the anonymous youth, this child is a conspirator. Envy moves to thank them, but commotion erupts from inside the palace. Scooping Sorrow higher into his arms, he nods with gratitude.

The child's eyes glisten. "I'm sorry," he says. "About the valley... I'm sorry."

So the moppet blames himself for making the existence of the crew known. "This isn't your fault," Envy says. "You didn't know us back then."

"I stole the iron archery from those elders and hid it under the Goddess of Love's bed. I was bored and sought to prank them. I didn't mean for your mate to find it and get caught."

"Never apologize for making fools of them. Besides, they were scoping out our homes with or without the archery. In the end, you've given her back to me." Envy musters a half-hearted quip. "And pranks are excusable. Just don't quote me on that. I get blamed for enough."

The moppet's lips crook into the makings of a trickster smile. Then he grimaces and shoves Envy. "Go! Fuck off!"

The shouts ring louder, closer. Envy spins and jets across the amphitheater, splashing through the moat. He glances over his shoulder, only to find the mentor and child have sprinted out of sight. Hopefully, Echo will return that arrow before its owner realizes it's missing.

But why isn't The Court here? If they expect a rescue, why not station themselves close at hand?

Projectiles slice through the air, showering toward Envy. He dodges the first stream and crashes through the cascade, Sorrow nothing but leaden weight in his arms. Jagged rocks pierce his limbs as he runs at a breakneck pace, mist thickening, waterfalls hissing around them.

Envy bolts down the cavity, the conduit expanding into the cave where he stashed Love's bow. On second inspection, this area seems to be a grotto.

The sounds of pursuit ring from behind. Carting Sorrow's weight through precarious terrain means he can't outrun the ones hunting them. Not in the long-term.

"Shoot the rocks," a voice mumbles.

Envy glances at Sorrow's half-lidded eyes. She raises her arm and points feebly at an unstable foundation.

"The rocks," she instructs, then collapses once more against him.

Left with no choice, Envy sets her on a ledge and nocks his bow. Aiming at the crags, he looses an arrow.

A flurry of rocks crack, followed by more, then more, then more. Chunks break from the walls and slam into the ground. The avalanche piles, filling in the gap, cutting off the shouts.

Then it plummets Envy and Sorrow in darkness.

31

Sorrow

It starts with whispers. It continues with shouts. It ends in silence.

The quiet devours everything. Hushed words, hands clasping her face, manacles releasing her wrists, and pain burying its talons into her.

At one point, Sorrow had felt herself levitate. Her body had been encased, resting against a slab of muscle. Water had splashed beneath someone's feet, then she'd muttered something and pointed, a rock explosion shattering her eardrums.

Now, silence. Now, blackness.

And then suddenly, the surge of running water. Mist sprays her limbs, the relief coaxing a sigh from her throat. She stirs, a soft patch of ground cushioning her weight, a large form nestling her close. Sorrow's cheek rubs against a finely loomed textile, and an arm slings possessively across her waist, tucking her in.

Sorrow's eyes flutter open. She's in a cave, a stunning grotto comprising three small waterfalls. The coved ceiling sparkles, and tiny pools beneath each cascade hurl steam across the walls.

From beyond one of the falls, tree silhouettes and more glittering pools indicate an enclave. The way out, beyond the deluge. That means she's behind the veil, rather than in front of it.

Slung across the ground, a strong, masculine body aligns itself with her smaller frame, and a warm palm cups her jaw. She tilts her head, meeting his eyes, sharp amber rings that focus on her.

Envy.

He stares as if he's been doing so for a long time. Then everything comes back, gushing like a rapid. The attack on the pier. The moment she tossed the iron archery to Envy and then leaped into the crowd. The little male deity and the two Guides standing beside him.

The Palace of Starlight. The interrogation from her rulers. The blackmail and torture that had followed.

The cuts. The ladder of deep incisions, patiently made by her own weapon.

As an outcast, her archery has lost that magic. Otherwise, those gashes could have infused Sorrow with her own root emotion, to the point of everlasting bleakness.

The Fate Court had carved into her. Because she had told them, "No."

Her rulers had given Sorrow an ultimatum. With artificial politeness, she had suggested they go fuck themselves, then rammed her boot heels into the pale ruler's countenance, rearranging the bitch's bone structure and splattering crimson in the process.

That's how Sorrow had ended up hanging like a bloody marionette from a tree. After that, she blacked out. Then her Guide's face materialized, along with that runty male god.

But most of all, there had been Envy's voice.

His warmth. His touch.

The escape. The avalanche.

The rest is a blur, except for his arms clasping Sorrow, his breath stirring her cheek. Envy, who stole her ice arrow when they were young.

Envy, who had bullied her. Envy, who'd fucked her. Envy, who did a thousand things to her.

Envy, whom she'd done a thousand things to in return.

Envy, who holds her now. Envy, who must have freed Sorrow from the throne amphitheater, then carried her through the tunnels.

He'd taken Sorrow's drowsy advice and created a landslide, barricading them from their attackers. She vaguely recalls the god picking her up afterward, clutching her like a star, and coming to rest with her in this spot. Covered in moss, the foundation is lush enough for them to sprawl across.

They must have gotten soaked while fleeing. But finally, their clothes are dry except for the glaze from the falls. It's probably been a while, because the injuries on Sorrow's arms have dried into a lattice of red-crusted lines, which peek through a length of silken fabric twining from her wrists to elbows.

Envy's shirt. He'd torn the sleeves to ribbons, his biceps bulging from the frayed seams.

Glass archery resides in an alcove, alongside a longbow and a quiver loaded with iron arrows. The god swam with Love's weapons, keeping them safe. He must have stashed them here before retrieving Sorrow, because he's easy to read.

Yet not easy at all. Otherwise, she'd have foreseen the desolate look on his face, as he presently drinks her in. Like a thorn in her side, this dumbass blatantly disregarded Sorrow's order to escape the masses, to leave her behind. He was supposed to wedge as much distance between them as possible, track down their rebel crew, return Love's bow, and set to battle. All of that, so Envy and their friends could bring this cursed immortal house down.

Insolent god! He was supposed to abandon her. Can't he do anything right?

And motherfuck. She's never been so happy or infuriated to see him. This infernal egomaniac, who has no clue he's got her heart and temper clenched in his fist.

Holding his gaze, Sorrow covers the hand that cradles her face, then traces his knuckles with her fingertips. Envy sucks in a breath. Her touch confirms this is real, she's okay, and he's okay. They're together, stuck with each other as usual.

Relief washes across Envy's features, his gruff tone nonetheless accusatory. "Why the fuck did you distract that crowd for me?"

Sorrow's eyes prickle. "Why the fuck did you come back?"

Clinging like film, they watch each other. Their answers hover in the air, both sentiments the same.

I did it for you.

Envy's features twist, the words splintering from his throat. "I took something from you." His eyes clamp onto Sorrow's, determined to face her, as if nothing less is acceptable. "Your missing arrow. I stole it from you."

Gone is this tender moment. Sorrow's eyes mold shut, the confession twisting into her like a rusty key. She'd wanted him to confess on his own, and he risked his life to recover her, but none of that erases what he did.

When she refocuses, her eyes slit, and her voice comes out flinty. "They told me."

His features cave, bereft to learn The Court got there before him. "Sorrow," he implores through a mouthful of guilt. "I'm sorry."

Imagine that. The God of Envy begging for mercy. Sorrow would never let him live this down, if she weren't gutted to begin with.

"All these years," she bites out. "After we started fucking, and then in the enclave, when I told you everything."

There was a time when she would have spat or hissed that last word. Now it just cracks in half like a twig.

Features crimping, Envy opens his mouth to reply, but she mows through the attempt. "Why?" she demands. "Why did you do it?"

Ashamed, he shakes his head. "At first, I wanted to punish you. But then... I got attached."

"To deceiving me?"

"To having you," Envy hisses softly. "One part of you, at least. That arrow was the only thing of yours I thought I'd ever get to touch. The only thing of you I thought I'd ever have."

"You did have me," Sorrow reminds him, lifting her shaky chin. "Plenty of times."

His pupils hurl fire at her. "That's not what I mean."

The admission twists the rusty key deeper, threatening to break open that beating organ in her chest. Nonetheless, Sorrow's not about excuse Envy just because he's had a change of romantic heart. She aims her nose down on him, silently requesting further explanation.

"The spite lasted millennia," Envy says in a brittle tone, the revelations pouring from him like blood from a wound. "But when we let loose in that raft bed, and when we hit the ground running afterward, guilt clawed its way to the surface. I wanted to tell you, but I was afraid. Then these last few days, the regret and self-loathing ripped me to pieces."

His earlier proclamation spins like a disc in her mind. *You intimidate me.*

Doubt peppers her tongue. "Yet you still fucked with me in the enclave. More than once. That bathing pool, then in the boat, and in the lagoon where we kissed."

"That wasn't about me," Envy pleads. "I wanted to give you bliss, pleasure, joy. Things you believed yourself incapable of, things you deserved, things that would make you happy." He shakes his head. "I know that doesn't justify a cursed thing. I'll never forgive myself for taking what was yours. Fucking hell, I could flay myself."

Better yet, she could do that for him. Punish him. Resent him. Despise him. But the hate of three thousand years has been enough of a burden, and the ways they've inflicted one another have always been mutual. Flashbacks of The Court and their ultimatum infiltrate Sorrow's mind like a glaring reminder of this fact.

That rusty key clicks into a valve, unbolting Sorrow from her rigid posture. Rejecting and detesting Envy is what The Court wants. It's why they presented her with the arrow in the first place, to cause a rift, which would expand to the crew. Giving into this agenda would mean surrendering. Whereas, doing the opposite takes strength, compassion, and something none of those monarchs have ever felt.

"Don't flay yourself." Leaning up, Sorrow bumps her nose against his. "I'd miss you too much."

Envy flinches as if the contact is excruciating. "If I hadn't taken the arrow, they wouldn't have used it to hurt you."

"Because they would have used something else."

"I'm sorry," he grovels. "I'm so fucking sorry."

"I forgive you."

"How? I've ruined our chance to enact the legend. That's how fate works."

"But that's not how free will works," she whispers, then caresses his mouth with her own. "Now show me how sorry you are."

Waterfalls spill over tiers of rock. Pearls of light swim through the fog, the world receding to this grotto.

Them. Alone. Free.

The vainest god in existence rivets his gaze on Sorrow, uncertain, unworthy, yet unwilling to deny her. At a loss, he rechecks her injuries, adjusting the makeshift bandages—evidently, not for the first time— before that immortal countenance returns to her own. Only then does his expression flash, haggard and hungry.

Asking. Hoping.

Sorrow's stomach gives a sweet, anarchistic flip. And she nods. "Yes."

A derelict noise rips from his chest. An invisible coil breaks.

Snatching her body, Envy hauls Sorrow against him. His mouth plants shaky, apologetic kisses over her face—forehead, lips, chin—then down her throat.

Sorrow reciprocates, her mouth desperate, unable to make contact swiftly enough. His collarbones, his jaw, his chin. In haste, her fingers slice into his dark mane, the locks tumbling around him.

Envy inhales sharply. Out of nowhere, he veers back and idles like a motor forcing itself to slow down. As the cascades wash around them, a new look engulfs his features.

Attentive. Gentle. Terrifying.

Stars. He's about to do something unprecedented, fucking up her universe forever.

Panicking, Sorrow swats her head from side to side. "You don't have to—"

"Hush, my nymph." Envy drapes his finger over her trembling lips. "You take care of the world's sadness. For once in your witchy life, let someone do the same for you."

She goes still, unsure how to process that offer, uncertain if she can handle such an experience. But then something akin to warmth trickles through her veins. Yet it's not just the manifestation of temperature.

No. This is trust.

He made a mistake back when they loathed each other. It won't happen again.

Fusing his gaze to hers until the last moment, Envy lowers his mouth and brushes the corners of her eyes, where the star flecks begin. Quietly, he pecks the outer edges, as though kissing her tears.

A hard mass forms in her throat, making it difficult to swallow. The sensation intensifies as he frames her waist and shuffles lower, his lips questing to every wound she endured in the cave. That puncture from the stalagmite, the scrapes and welts, the crusted scabs.

Her breathing stalls, his soft ministrations throttling her senses. Then this hellish god commits the ultimate sin. His mouth runs over each cut across her arms, nursing them through the silk fabric, tending to every proof of pain.

Sorrow's eyes sting. Her soul busts open like a shell. Overwhelmed, she understands what this is, because she's been trained to understand.

Envy's healing her. He's comforting her.

In nearly three thousand years, when has anyone considered her own suffering?

Once the god reaches the final line of blood, his head lifts. Those dedicated features hold fast, hold tight. They tell her she's okay, she'll mend, and he'll be with her when she does.

Legends and myths be damned. She hates this god, and she needs him, and she wants him, and she can't stand him, and she's wild for him.

Envy's pupils flare with molten light. Oh, he knows the look she's giving him. This one, they've had ample practice with.

One pivotal breath, then another. And they vault into motion.

Groaning, Envy launches toward Sorrow at the same time she grabs him by the shirt lapels. Colliding, they gasp into it, their mouths slamming together. Her lips pry open his own, and his tongue swoops inside, licking her into oblivion. The rhythmic flex wrings a moan from Sorrow as she matches him, taste for taste. Her digits claw into his roots and heave the god closer. Their mouths slope, clamping onto one another, opening and sealing.

His weight spanning above her, Envy's knee pushes between Sorrow's thighs. He splays her apart so that his leg grinds against her pelvis, the undulation producing white spots of flame behind her eyelids. In the folds of her cunt, a harrowing clench manifests, pulsating like a drumbeat.

With their clothes abrading, Sorrow hooks her leg over his hip and rocks back, writhing her pussy over the thick outline of his cock. More than her own desire, Envy's serrated growl is the highlight. The more she hears, the greater her need.

She wants to own him, tie him up, tangle him around her. She wants to split him into pieces like no one ever has, make him come louder and harder than he thought himself capable of. She wants his athletic back to arch. She wants those burnished eyes to roll until he can't remember who the fuck he's been with prior, until he can't remember that they've ever done this before.

Then she wants to rile him up all over again.

And again. And forever.

She wants to share herself. She wants to claim him.

Envy rumbles, the noise radioactive, as if he hears her thoughts. He answers that call, flipping over and hoisting Sorrow on top of him, her legs falling astride his waist. Then he rises to a sitting position, the frenzied movement and the possessive blaze in his irises shooting tingles up her spine.

Like this, they pant against each other's lips. Then everything eases up, their mouths trembling with a violent sort of yearning.

They've done swift and rough. Now it's time for a deeper kind of fucking.

An experimental gleam saturates Envy's irises, similar to the only other episode in which they paced themselves. In the boat, when he made her come repeatedly, her cunt rippling against his lapping tongue. With concentrated urgency, they channel that night, mimicking the tempo.

While staring, their hands tug on fabric. The gestures grow measured, fraught with curiosity. One by one, Sorrow unbuttons Envy's shirt, plucking each accessory as if it's part of a ritual.

Envy leans in, hot breath panting against her mouth. The rush sinks low, the lips of her pussy dampening. Chuffing oxygen, Sorrow whips the sleeveless vestment down Envy's arms, peeling it from him.

His torso expands into view, his smooth flesh polished in the half-light. With a heavy groan, Envy lolls his head back as Sorrow dives in, sucking on his neck, drawing the flesh between her teeth until it reddens. Taking a page from his own sensuous playbook, she licks the basin between his collarbones, her lips descending to the ravine of his pecs, catching each flex of muscle.

Motivated by the ragged noises he makes, Sorrow's incisors pinch the dark nipples. Then she swabs the tips until he curses, the wide roof of his cock twitching under the pants.

"Fuck," Envy husks. "You unscrupulous creature."

Sorrow blows against one dusky nipple. "Should I go easier on you?"

"Christ, no." He grasps her jaw and hoists her gaze to his. "Never go easy. Brutalize me. Punish me. Fuck me however you want." Bracing his mouth against hers, the god confesses, "You always have anyway. Because I'm yours."

Envy has barely finished the sentence. He snatches her ass and seizes her mouth, their tongues lashing, beating against one another.

Hers. This unattainable, renowned, infuriating god. He's all fucking hers.

The words seep into her pores, slipping past the narrow slit of her cunt. Sorrow moans into his lips, the vibration trailing across his feverish tongue, her crease dripping through the skirt and onto his lap.

On a hiss, Envy reels away. With deadly calm, he picks open Sorrow's vest, the casual pace teasing her patience. The halting drag of his fingers provokes restlessness, her instincts teetering between speed and moderation.

Yet as his eyes lock with hers, Sorrow musters the will to sit motionless, her thighs straddling his hips.

As he slips off the vest, her breasts drop free. Her nipples toughen under his smoldering gaze, the pegs cinching. Envy's pupils explode, raking over the swells, his fingers sweeping the garment fully from her arms.

When his knuckles trace her wounds for a second time, the affectionate gesture grips Sorrow by the neck. She gulps, a frightening emotion taking shape within her. It's pure in taste and scent, like a clear spring.

When Envy straightens, she grasps his face and smashes their mouths together. Humming, he raises her so that she's suspended higher, crushing her lips down onto his. She licks into Envy, swatting his tongue into a frenzy.

The male groan rolling down her throat amplifies the craving. Her skirt flares around their hips, where his long cock stiffens. That he yearns for her in this way—and that he always secretly has—imbues Sorrow with a heady dose of power.

She sways her hips, matching the rhythm of their kiss. Grinding languidly, her clit sketches his crown, broadening its circumference.

Only when the god emits a guttural sound does she release his mouth. Heaving for oxygen, Envy's hooded eyes rove over Sorrow. There's a strong possibility she might pass out from his expression, or from the circle of his thumbs around her nipples, the raw buds tightening.

Envy tempts her lips with open-mouthed kisses, then sinks to her chin, executing pressure to urge her head back. Snaring her ass, he ducks and hooks his lips around the first dainty tip. Sorrow whines, the reverberation hitting the cave's ceiling, the crashing waterfalls consuming the noise.

She bows, gripping his nape for leverage and shoving her tits into him. The wet tug of his mouth, punctuated by the upward jolt of his dick is a next-level type of misery. The onslaught drenches her, the seam of her pussy soaking through their clothes.

Crooning, Envy seals around the kernel and performs a sequence of tender sucks. Sorrow's pulse goes ballistic, her mewls escalating to cries. Any more of this, and her kneecaps will crack.

Cognizant of her agony, the endearing asshole takes pity and switches to the opposite breast. Not that it calms her down. He works Sorrow into hysterics, works himself into a tangent.

All at once, he surrenders her nipple and gathers her to him, their chests flush and damp from the mist. His skin tints, as ruddy as her own. Their hearts turn into battering rams, plowing through bone.

Envy links his fingers with hers, fitting them together and flaunting a wolfish yet adoring grin. Sorrow marvels at their interwoven hands, the visual dismantling her assumptions. So this is what their obstinance has been missing out on. This is what they've denied themselves.

Who knew it would feel this way? How have they gone without it for so long?

It's never been this lasting with anyone. It's never been this destructively profound.

The pause is fleeting but crucial. They surge into motion again, too distressed to care where they are or if they'll see daylight again. Anticipation builds as Sorrow fumbles with Envy's trousers, her digits trembling to release the closures. All the while, their eyes remain fastened, clicking into place.

They slide the pants down, freeing his cock. The thick column springs from the vent, high and heavy, topped with a wide head. Veins weave up the foreskin, a darker color shading his crown, the slit leaking cum.

Twin hip bones slant on either side, and his abdomen flexes like a grille, every centimeter sleek apart from several battle scars. Fates, he's glorious. It isn't fair to every other deity on the planet, Sorrow thinks fondly. However, she isn't about to gripe, and no way is she going to share him. Not after this.

The feeling appears mutual. Envy's territorial gaze bolts Sorrow to the ground. She couldn't flee that look if she wanted to.

Sorrow scoots closer, her heart pounding. Envy seethes, guiding her buttocks forward, his bare erection skating over her slick pussy. When his frenulum etches the swollen flesh of her clit, the god hisses, and she whines, the friction wetting her further.

While he's entirely naked, her skirt is left, the garment fanning outward. Under the layers, Envy palms her ass, fitting her drenched slot to the hot roof of his cock. With her thighs steepling around his pelvis, the crown nudges her walls apart, standing firm against her curls, nocking at her entrance.

Envy sucks air through his nostrils. His molars clench, and his eyes weld to hers.

Sorrow shivers in his embrace. She's nervous, as if this is their first time.

Because it is. In all the best ways, it's the first time.

She latches her palms around his nape. "I'm going to ruin you for anyone else."

"My nymph." He swoops down, scraping his tongue along the trench of her mouth. "You already have."

And Sorrow falls quicker than a star. The reply comes out like another secret confession, one much older than she could have imagined.

She barely has seconds to react, because Envy braces Sorrow's ass and lowers her onto him. The descent is slow, disastrous in pace. Her mouth tumbles open along with his, the gradual slide of his dick stretching her pussy, so that she clamps around him.

The sensation of Envy's cock gliding into her narrow groove robs Sorrow of breath. The broad tip crests and hits a limit. A prolonged groan of satisfaction—of aggravation—tears from them. The combined echo dashes through the grotto and gets snatched by the waterfalls.

Their foreheads meet. Envy's face constricts like he's holding back, then his features dissolve into rapture as Sorrow gyrates onto him.

Summoning the utmost restraint, she bobs her hips with a leisurely cadence she doesn't quite feel. She wants this fast and hard, but as she'd reminded herself before, they've done fast and hard. With that in mind, she siphons over his cock with furious concentration, turned on by the sight of Envy helpless, powerless as his eyebrows slam together.

Hefting her backside, Envy anchors Sorrow, steering her from the crown to his weighty sac. Every pump smears their arousal together. The up and down slide of her pussy and his cock unfurls a stunned purr from the god.

Then Envy maneuvers with her, synching his waist with her own, his frame undulating as if he's made of elastic. His agile muscles hurl into Sorrow, loosening her with finesse, until she's as flexible as he is. The stimulation goes to her head like effervescence, fizzing every corner, vertigo taking over.

At last, he demonstrates the extent of his skills. And it's excruciating, tampering with her restraint.

"Oh, Stars," she pants, hunching into him. "Oh, my Stars!"

"Shh," Envy husks like a passionate fiend, nudging his cock deeper. "Relax your pussy. Take it slow and long."

With every slow drag of his cock, Sorrow weeps in tandem, her nipples skidding over his pecs. Yet she takes his advice and rides each sharp jut of his hips, her thighs splaying farther.

Envy murmurs his approval. Invigorated, he hauls her up and down, fucking into her leisurely. Then he lapses into another groan as her inner muscles clasp him to the base.

Their open mouths rest together, laboring through this, their stomachs belting. With unhurried snaps, he slings in and out, tapping the edges of her walls. Sorrow's eyes flip to the back of her head, her pussy seeping. It's too much, too harrowing.

Yet they keep going, maintaining this lagging rhythm. Sweat lathers Envy's torso, those strong hips splitting Sorrow in half, his grip on her ass unbreakable, the better for her to take the brunt.

His dick probes, spreading her lips. His vehement thrusts reach deeper, higher, yet never speed up. On each lazy swipe of his waist, her sobs fill the grotto, and she drips down to his thighs.

Sorrow's flesh slickens as though they've landed in a sauna. The illusion of heat permeates her blood, the flux converging at the nexus of her body. Ecstatic, she hugs Envy to her, plastering her tits against him, their bodies flush and pumping closer.

This alters the slant of his cock. As does the tightness of her cunt.

Envy's mouth goes slack, a silent growl hanging off his lips. He watches her through hooded eyes, at her behest.

The vision spurs her on. With a moan, she veers into Envy, urging him backward until his spine hits the moss. And she's got him. She's got all of him. This Dark God, who sprawls before her, carved muscles unraveling.

Envy tracks his sexy gaze over her breasts and face. Black pupils eclipse the irises, the fathomless pool reflecting her likeness, as if she's the only thing that has ever made sense.

Never go easy. Brutalize me. Punish me. Fuck me however you want.

Gladly. Snatching his wrists, Sorrow jams them into the moss, pinning him like a specimen. She angles forward and hovers over Envy, her pussy sloping over his cock.

You always have anyway. Because I'm yours.

Like this, she leisurely rides this god into the constellations. Her thighs clench his waist, her walls cinch his erection to the seat, and she throws her hips back and forth.

As if burned by coals, Envy snaps off the ground, his eyes stapling shut. "Fuck!" he bellows. "Sorrow!"

"Mine," she gasps. "You're mine."

Like an obedient cock, the column bloats, the prow inflating inside her. The increase in size flares her cunt farther, liquid washing out of

Sorrow and streaming to his balls.

"Look at me," Sorrow cries out, bucking onto him. "Watch me fuck you."

Envy's gaze tears open. "I've never stopped watching you."

Her chest squeezes. If that's true, they've wasted more time than she thought.

And so, Envy fucks her back. Continuing this slow precision, he lashes his cock upward, spearing into Sorrow. She writhes, careens on his lap, her fingers shackling his wrists. Truly, she almost couldn't care less whether she comes, so long as he does.

However, it warrants repeating. She *almost* couldn't care less.

Sorrow accelerates her tempo, achieving a subtle bounce, shards of pleasure dicing through her. Her waist flicks at Envy's cock, thumping and dousing him in her arousal. When his crown toughens, sparks race up her shins, and her knees dig into the foundation. With her limbs splayed, the skirt bunches into a mess.

Flattening one forearm along the surface, Envy balances on the opposite elbow. Slanting halfway up, his free hand claims her ass, his grip encouraging her. She gallops above him, their groins punting, meeting halfway.

Envy grins through his moans. He looks proud of her, hot and bothered, and something more. Impassioned. Captivated. Worshipful. That's why he shoots upright and crooks his hands over the backs of her shoulders, fixing her into position.

Sorrow bleats, "No. Don't stop—"

"Not happening," he swears. "But does that mean you like how my cock fucks you? Does it give you pleasure?"

"Yes. Fates, yes!"

"Then don't move," he commands. "Not. One. Inch."

Then he rockets upward. Though they haven't sped up yet, the repetitive snap of his body renders Sorrow senseless. Her joints collapse, yielding to the impact. Becoming pliable magnifies every slant of his dick, so that she feels it acutely.

Now Sorrow lets herself be ridden. Meanwhile, she clings to him, her fingers diving into his mane, lost in a river of hair.

Stars have pity. The god's lips wreathe into a naughty I'm-fucking-my-idol smirk. He pistons his cock into Sorrow with such gentle ferocity that a wail builds in her mouth.

"There you go," he urges. "Take it. Take it from me."

But she can't take it from him, can't take any more of this pandemonium, can't take it without expiring. She claws at his scalp, needing to come, but he refuses to let up, flinging his cock with destructive slowness.

Wild sobs pour from Sorrow, tangling with his groans. Enough is enough. No matter how affectionate, this is a joint venture.

Matching his movements, Sorrow resumes her own antics, her cunt synchronizing with Envy's thrusts. On and on.

In the midst of it, their mouths latch into a dire kiss. The instant her tongue strikes his, Envy's frame shudders. Heaving forward, he reels Sorrow backward, this time fastening her to the moss.

As he does, fresh desire kicks in. He pulls out of her briefly, and they jostle with the remainder of her clothes.

Envy tows her skirt down her legs, then slithers over her, his hips scissoring her thighs wide. After hitching one of her legs over his waist, Envy balls her hand with his and extends their arms above her head. His other palm covers her cheek, and her free hand molds over his taut ass.

"Not done," he hisses, then pitches his cock again, filling her pussy to the brim.

"Oh!" She arches her breasts into him, the sob tearing from her lips. "Oh, Envy!"

"Right there. Let me in there. Open for me."

Naked with him, Sorrow hurls herself into Envy, her pussy soaking his flesh. Growling, he renews his efforts, throwing his cock into her. The hot bridge whips Sorrow up and down, the snap of his waist slinging her along the moss.

The traction of his bare skin is a delicious relief. His abs rub her navel, her nipples skate across his pecs, and their pelvises twist. The ceiling blurs as Sorrow and Envy cling, damp and incomprehensible.

Their moans harden. Their tempo quickens.

Envy's depth turns shallow, his dick probing a spot that wrings a shout from Sorrow. Her hips slant with his, working to reach that zenith, the abrasion inciting a riptide. Envy knows what she likes, and he learns more of what she likes, and he steals it from her, and then he gives it back.

Their fingers lace, then fall apart. He grabs her face, and she grabs his ass.

She could keep this god here forever, but it's impossible to keep him here forever, because she's not going to last forever. This is too good. All of it is too good.

And still, it's scarcely over. Envy's barreling his cock, spreading her cunt, the sopping clutch of her body tightening around him. His impending orgasm thrills her, an intoxication buzzing through her veins.

A human would have fainted by now. Yet Sorrow's not far off. When Envy's base grazes the top of her clit, pleasure bursts from her toes to her skull. The result is inebriating, like she's drunk on lust.

Or rather, something grander. Maybe passionate sex or poignant fucking.

Both seem right, yet it's not the whole story. What they're doing has no definition she can fathom. None that does it justice, blending this much pleasure and pain, an emotional fusion that delivers a warning: They won't be the same when this is over.

Sorrow is fine with that. For they've never left one another's company without being changed. The effect they have on each other isn't just magnetic, it's persevering. This relentless fucking shows no end in sight, which is bliss and its own form of punishment.

Beads of water splatter the rocks. The half-light illuminates their glistening flesh.

Envy growls something against her lips, but she can't hear the words, because her mind has been reduced to the place where they're joined. All senses—sight, sound, taste, touch, smell—converge in the merciless spot where her cunt meets his cock.

Once more, their foreheads press. His black pupils consume her, and she can't get enough of this visual, no more than she can get enough of his body. This deity whom she's hated, befriended, fucked. This god who pumps that long, hard cock deeply into her, his ass flexing with the motions, his face tensing on the cusp of release, holding out as if to say, *You first.*

The God of Envy, who pleasures everyone and pines for no one. That very god, pleasuring her and pining for her.

Her toes curl. Her knuckles curl.

Sorrow freezes, then ruptures. She cries out, her cunt fluttering around his erection, coming long and loud. Envy roars his own climax, his features clenching, his cock spasming.

Their shouts bulldoze through the grotto. The knot of tension breaks. The muscles of Sorrow's pussy convulse and spill down his length, and his dick pours into her, fluid streaming from them. Her body contracts with Envy's, her insides fracturing with his own, the orgasm ripping from their lungs.

In all this time, not once do they look away from each other.

And now she knows what that feels like.

32

Envy

Afterward, he kisses her slowly. Still encased between her thighs, still breathing hectically, he seals her mouth with his own.

And so, Envy gives what's left of himself to this goddess.

Her skin is fleece, as soft as this moment. A gorgeous profusion of pink trails over her body, beckoning his lips to map out each blush until she chuckles.

When she combs through his hair, no intimacy has ever felt so enticing. With his cock still lodged in her glorious pussy, nothing has ever felt this agonizing.

Refusing to pull out of Sorrow's drenched cunt, he nudges deeper until she whimpers. Wrapping themselves around one another, they stare while waterfalls pound against the rocks.

Mustering the courage, he marvels at Sorrow, who peers back through vibrant, pleasured eyes. From that look alone, a landslide of emotions tackles his heart to the foundation. Over millennia, countless deities have lusted after him, but none have ever looked at Envy this way.

Dipping his head, he skates his nose against hers. "You are my pleasure and pain."

She gulps. "Back atcha."

33

Sorrow

Afterward, they dress one another slowly. Their eyes remain pinned as Envy tugs Sorrow's skirt up her limbs, then as she drapes his shirt over his shoulders and buttons the material. Their movements are tender, languid, private. This turning point is as priceless as the harsh and heavy sounds they'd made together.

Sorrow gazes at Envy, at a loss for words. Every smile from him drills another hole into her chest.

How can one feel pleasure while enduring pain? Maybe both are synonymous.

She should know, yet she doesn't. In fact, she's unsure if she knows anything at all.

Possibly, her blackmailing sovereigns had understood better than Sorrow. Because that's how destiny works, predicting the moves and countermoves before the players act. Because until this moment, her answer to The Court's ultimatum had been no. And until this moment, she had expected it to stay that way.

34

Envy

Fuck. It happened in a way it never has before. Fates almighty, they've been missing out. He's been a fool for millennia, taking every moment for granted.

Armed with this second chance, Envy wants to do and say shit out of character. He wants to spoil Sorrow, make her come at least two dozen times, and keep her in this spot, hoarding the goddess like a treasure. He wants to learn more about this all-consuming feeling and figure out how it works.

Barely cognizant of where the fuck to start, Envy swaggers up behind Sorrow, pausing as she contemplates the blurry landscape beyond the waterfall. Encircling her middle, he flirts, "I've always liked gray hair."

She tenses, then curls into him. "I bet you have."

Funny. He would've expected a snide reply or a caress of his forearms, something either typical or intimate. Well, it's all new, and they'll improve over time.

Envy confirms for Sorrow the details of their escape, including

Echo's help, Siren's message, and that unnamed moppet's assistance. Then Envy wheels Sorrow around, locking her in his embrace and hissing, "What did they do to you?"

"You've seen it," she says, referring stoically to the ladder of cuts. "They wanted to know how we got here, who's with us, and where they are." She dissects his lack of reply. "Aren't you going to ask me what I told them?"

"No," is all he says.

Not only is he too busy counting how many limbs he'll rip from the rulers' bodies for touching Sorrow, but Envy also doesn't need to ask what she told The Court. Injuries aside, she would never betray their crew. They mean too much to her, as does this crusade. That's why she rescued Love's iron weapons, because she won't turn her back on any of them.

Had she taken action for Envy too? Flung herself into harm's way to protect him?

Yes, she had. By some intuitive connection, Envy had felt this truth merely from the way Sorrow shared her body with him. The primal arch of her back, her hands gripping his ass, her lips clinging to his, her pussy rippling softly around his cock. Stars almighty, the sex had been transcendent.

However, the magnitude of the past few hours has since dissipated, a new vulnerability emanating from Sorrow. In fact, she flinches at the implication that he doesn't need explanations, no details about her conference with The Court, other than whom to crucify on her behalf.

Envy cradles her jaw. "I trust you."

For some reason, his words accomplish the opposite of what he'd hoped. Those silver irises flicker, the affirmation haunting her.

Well, fine. She's no more used to these unconditional declarations than he is. Regardless of how they hit the ground running when she awoke, how they pounced on each other and fucked like fanatics, they need to pace themselves. Despite Envy's desire to mash Sorrow against the nearest facade and grind his cock into her waiting cunt again, and again, and again, best to get control of his sex drive before it sends them off a cliff.

This, in addition to everything happening north of his dick. Chiefly, the sight of her somber features and the vise grip it has on his chest.

Envy strokes his thumb across Sorrow's cheek, smoothing out the rough edges. "All I want to know is what happens next."

She leans into his touch. "I want that too."

"I would say this is the sexiest truce in the history of truces." He levels her with a serious expression. "I'm all in, if you are."

There it is again. That glimpse of uncertainty diluting Sorrow's expression, her features wincing. "Envy, I—"

"Well, I'll be fate-fucked."

They spring apart. Swinging toward that diabolical voice, they come face-to-face with six flabbergasted figures.

Love, with her black wings smudged in dirt and her mouth agape.

Andrew, his white hair a beacon as he expels a ragged breath.

Anger, his turbulent features slack for once.

Merry, in her bedraggled tulle frock, beaming at the scene as if she's waltzed into the pages of a romance novel.

Wonder, with her verdant green eyes sparkling, those hopeful features lifting into a grin.

Malice, trussed up in devilish leather and smirking as if he knows exactly what shenanigans Envy and Sorrow have been up to. For good measure, and because he has fun being an asshole, the cocksucker leers as though watching a holographic porno come to vivid life.

"Look at you two, doing the immortal walk of shame," the demon god congratulates them.

"Kindreds!" Merry chirps, racing across the divide, her pink ponytail bouncing. She flings her arms around Envy and Sorrow, squishing them against her. "I'm dizzy with glee." Flouncing back to give them air, Merry seizes their hands. "How we've searched high and low for you after being torn asunder!"

"You guys are one hell of a sight for sore eyes," Andrew says.

Everyone embraces, their voices overlapping with inquiries. Relief filters through Sorrow's expression, yet the enthusiasm sits awkwardly on her face, as if the reaction doesn't quite fit and she can't fully enjoy this moment. Not when some other troubling notion is fighting for her attention.

Envy frowns. One might go so far as to say the crew's presence troubles the goddess.

Nonetheless, Sorrow covers it up well, and Envy shakes off the misgivings. It's likely due to everything that's happened since the separation. From her captivity and torture to the copious amounts of orgasms she and Envy traded, fucking to the point where his cock almost broke, the poor specimen in dire need of a sling.

On that score, it's a marvel Sorrow is capable of walking straight. And this isn't counting the tender words they had exchanged in private. At any rate, this is uncharted ground for them, so he must be misinterpreting, and she's merely frazzled.

Sorrow glances at everyone. "How did you know where we were?"

"Can't you guess?" To mollify the tension, Envy flashes his teeth. "My charm and animal magnetism lured them here. The frequency is just that strong. All they had to do was follow the path to greatness."

"Or the path to bullshit," Malice says.

"Or pretension," Wonder amends.

"Or snobbery," Love suggests.

"I second all of these options," Andrew deadpans.

"I do not," Anger grunts. "Appraising Envy's shortcomings is a waste of time."

"That's because you're jealous, hon," Envy jibes, to which the rage god flings his eyes skyward.

During a break in the conversation, Sorrow hastens to retrieve the iron archery. She hands it to Love, who accepts the weapons in astonishment. Since it's clear Sorrow isn't going to expand on the matter, Envy takes it upon himself to convey what Sorrow went through to get the longbow and quiver.

Meanwhile, Sorrow and Love stare at each other. The latter goddess gives Sorrow a wobbly smile as she tucks the archery against her, then kisses Sorrow's cheek.

Once the shock of the tale subsides, Anger interjects, "How about a trade?" He produces Sorrow's archery with a mild grin. "Like you, they don't go down easily."

"Anger rescued the weapons after you went overboard," Merry rhapsodizes as Sorrow accepts the longbow with a humbled expression. "He dove in to save both of you, but you had vanished, so he braved the rapids and saved the archery instead, preventing them from sinking to a dismal end."

"Pure luck," Anger informs Envy. "I tried to find your archery too. It tumbled from the boat, but visibility was scarce." He glimpses the set of glass arrows resting in the alcove. "Though, it appears you sniffed the weapons out on your own."

Envy recaps the past seventy-two hours, omitting the smutty parts when he and Sorrow went feral. Even so, Anger grimaces as if the concept of Envy and Sorrow stuck together is cataclysmic.

Sorrow gives an abbreviated report about their rulers, being captured, and the subsequent interrogation. Is it just Envy, or does he detect a note of contrition in her voice?

No, it's not just him. One mastermind of subtext notices as well.

Malice tilts his shrewd head. Surveying the goddess, the demon god's ashy eyes glitter like a set of polished switchblades.

The crew take turns breaking down their excursion. After the rapids, they washed up on another side of the cliff and discovered a conduit, which was their only option, since none of them are as familiar with this summit as Envy.

Battered and bruised, they rested and then sought an outlet or lookout point, a place where they could search for Envy and Sorrow. Or at least locate the path leading to their original destination.

Neither had panned out. They sojourned for three days before stumbling upon the waterfall enclave hours ago. From there, they located the cavern and recognized the signs of Envy's residency. Essentially, the hollow filled with his wardrobe tipped them off.

By then, Envy and Sorrow were gone and dealing with The Fate Court. On a hunch, the crew had backtracked through the enclave, suspecting Envy and Sorrow might be nearby. It appears the belly of this cliff has a number of arteries beyond what Envy had comprehended.

"We might've found you two sooner, if the grumpy god to my left hadn't bitched about taking the east tunnel instead of west," Malice remarks, then erects his index finger, its nail as sharp as a talon. "I sayeth, we went round and round more times than a fucking prayer circle."

"Will you please let that shit go?" Anger snaps, as if they'd been over this more than once.

"Sorry, mate." Malice levels him with a devil-may-care grin. "Beating that dead horse is what you get for not listening to me—or Wonder, or Andrew, or Love. It's also what you get for turning down my original Graffiti-the-Palace idea."

Ah, yes. Prior to entering The Dark Fates, Malice had suggested that as some form a military tactic, the logic making sense only to him. But because he's Malice, no one had been able to gauge whether he'd been serious or not. Either way, Anger had shot down the proposal, to which Malice had branded him a "cockless killjoy."

One guess how the rage god responded.

As for their outlook, everyone agrees. Although The Court knows of their presence, it doesn't change the plan. Sorrow hadn't given any-thing away, after all.

Envy had intended to sail his boat with her to Fortune's Crest. From the enclave, there's a waterway that will take them there. However, the vessel isn't big enough for everyone, which means they're traveling on foot.

They clean themselves up, drink their fill from the waterfalls, en-chant fresh garments, and set forth. Skirting sideways through a pas-sage that spares them from getting drenched by the cascades, they emerge into another cavity. Eventually, it connects with the secret groove—naughty Siren, keeping this from Envy—and deposits them into the enclave.

At Envy's direction, the crew hikes along one of the bridges. From there, they bypass baths and torrents leading to multiple niches.

Merry whispers with Anger. Love and Andrew play a guessing game to distract themselves. Malice and Wonder theorize on all things legendary.

During an awkward silence, Envy brushes his fingers against Sorrow's hip and attempts to tease the goddess. Yet her spine goes rigid.

To the rest of the crew, her attitude is business as usual.

To him, it's something else entirely.

35

Envy

Fog belts around Envy's limbs as he guides the procession. His friends admire the mystical scenery and scan the water trees, each member vigilant of an ambush.

Ascending in elevation, climbing higher into the bluffs, they leave their refuge behind. The environment changes, narrowing to a slim peninsula, an estuary snaking along the range. The only way to reach the main crest is via boat or the trail of boulders running down the center. As they step from one slab to the next, a vista greets them.

Andrew stalls atop one of the rocks, marveling at the panorama of moonlit cliffs, sylvan valleys, and metallic shores.

"Welcome to my childhood," Love tells him with a wistful smile.

"Welcome to your history," Anger whispers to Merry, who's riveted by the setting.

"Welcome back to your stomping ground," Wonder says to Malice, who gives her an artful grin.

Envy glances at Sorrow, only to find the goddess gnawing on her lower lip. Once more, a bad omen sinks its fangs into his mind. His thirst for her attention withers to disappointment, then to scrutiny.

Something is wrong.

Stars and moons crowd the sky, pearlescent rays skipping across the water. The journey proves longer than he'd predicted, but they sojourn to Fortune's Crest without incident.

At last, the estuary deposits them at the summit, and the great stargazer comes into view. Multiple levels of walkways and parapets protect the glass dome, which expands from the center at the uppermost level. In that translucent structure, the instrument shines. It's a vessel between The Dark Fates and The Stars, an umbilical cord that funnels the births of deities, as well as a mighty shrine to destiny.

The estuary broadens, spilling into a lake near the stargazer's base. Each crew member pauses on their respective boulder.

"Are we mad?" Wonder asks.

"Only one of us," Anger broods, jabbing his thumb at Malice, who casually flips off the rage god.

"Go ahead and call me mad," Malice says. "I like being mad. Keeps things interesting."

"Wonder meant, are we foolish for doing this?" Love clarifies.

"Depends on who you ask," Sorrow mumbles.

"Meaning?" Envy questions, his eyebrows stitching together.

"As the designated wordsmith, I'll take a stab at it," Andrew volunteers. "There are rules to magic, things it can and can't achieve. Let's thumb through that. What can celestial magic do?"

"Control how humans feel," Love answers, tucking her body into his chest. "In other words, not all magic works for the better."

The sexy corner of Andrew's mouth lifts. Brushing her ear with his lips, he murmurs, "And what *can't* magic do?"

"Control how deities feel," Sorrow supplies.

"Not true," Love objects, shivering from her mate's touch. "If I scratch myself with my arrow—"

"But that would be your choice."

"Could happen by accident."

"But that would be your mistake."

"It's still control." Sorrow swerves toward the group's most erudite pairing. "Malice, Wonder, break out your dictionaries. I'm betting the definition is the same in any realm."

"Magic can't control nature," Envy says under his breath.

But they hear him. And like a telepathic bond, they get it. Magic can control itself, defy itself, and break its own rules. But it can't control or defy nature.

"That's where we come from," Andrew summarizes. "Humans are of the earth. Deities are of The Stars. Both are nature, so we're alike, and we have a right to own our paths. Our choices."

The crew stares at him. For fuck's sake, this man is too damned shrewd for his own good. Like Malice and Wonder's prowess in researching mythical legends, the surplus of fantasy plots originating from Andrew's cranium amounts to its own weapon. Creativity in sex scenes aside, his perceptive skills and mortal origins give him an outsider's vantage point.

Andrew's argument is simple yet critical. No, they're not foolish.

They cross the water. The boulder path veers to the lake's embankment, merging with a stony outcropping. Beyond, high grasses and flowers—hyacinths, according to Wonder—sway in the breeze.

There was a time when they would have passed through the facade's stardusted gate easily. Instead, Malice withdraws a vial of Asterra Flora and smears a droplet onto the foundation. With a shudder, the gate opens.

They hesitate. All except Malice, who saunters through with an exaggerated flourish. "Move your asses, mates," he drawls on the way.

"Show-off," Anger grunts.

Wonder elbows him for the comment and pursues her lover, those chestnut curls swishing around her ample hips. To complement the goddess's corsage, stalks of celestial foliage coil naturally around her scalp like a headband.

Inside, lanterns pulse with starlit flames. Their company mounts the spiral stairs to the dome, where painted recreations of constellations grace the floor. Above the artwork, an elegant funnel aims toward the sky, its weight supported by posts that spiral like vines.

Might as well go for ceremony. Surrounding the telescope, the crew joins hands. Anger takes the lead, glancing at The Stars and summoning their allies.

As outcasts and deserters, they're unable to breach boundaries without the means to break down that barrier. Thank Fates for Malice and Wonder's supply of Asterra Flora. They left plenty behind in the human realm, in the safe keeping of their allies, preparing everyone for when the call came.

A moment passes. Then another.

The ground trembles. Anger's eyes flare open. Everyone bolts, dashing from the central platform and sprinting along the exterior parapet.

Beneath a curtain of moonlight, silhouettes appear. Exiled deities and former loyals glide up the hill, each carrying longbows and crossbows. Star-woven cloaks and gowns billow from their shoulders. Moon-sewn leathers stretch across their arms and limbs. Mortal style coats jingle with buckles and chains.

It's a motley bunch. Deities they've known in The Dark Fates, including Confusion, Guilt, and Hope. Outcasts from The Celestial City and Malice's cult, among them Hate, Scorn, Calamity, Pity, Courage, and Trust.

At the forefront strides a deity with sage-green hair. Her meditative gaze is akin to a certain voluptuous goddess, except this female wields arrows of ivory.

"Harmony!" Wonder exclaims, rushing to meet her Guide at the gate.

Minutes later, their allies flood the monument. Surprise and Kindness are two of Merry's comrades. The former is a veritable disco ball, with sequins enwrapping her skin like glittering scales. The latter's hair is twined into a bun at the nape and fastened with a glowing clip. She has gentle eyes, and a soft velvet ankle-coat accentuates her frame.

The outcasts each have their own tale. In the end, they were all evicted from The Dark Fates, having committed crimes or failing to suit The Court's so-called standards of exemplary deities.

As for the ones who hadn't been exiled, some resent these criteria of perfection. Whereas, others have never cared for assigning destiny, and the rest simply resent having their life's purpose designated to them.

Anger speaks to the crowd, bringing everyone up to speed on The Court's knowledge of their presence. Because this was always a possibility, the pronouncement doesn't surprise anyone. Except for, well, Surprise.

"They may not know where to find us," Anger calls out, scanning the crowd. "But they will soon."

"Scouts," Harmony addresses a unit of warriors. "Make haste."

The troop disbands to guard every neighboring summit. Sorrow watches them leave, her face twisting with restlessness. "I'll go with them."

Heads swerve toward her. Perplexed, Anger furrows his brows. "What for? There's no need."

"For once, I concur." Malice scrutinizes the goddess's profile. "Don't recall that being part of the plan."

"Who cares whether it was planned?" Sorrow snaps. "Forgive me for getting antsy."

"You can't," Merry protests, the quiver of neon arrows clattering against her lavender dress. "We lost you before. And..."

Silence, but for the howling wind. As the anxious goddess trails off, remorse clutters Sorrow's face. "You're right," she concedes. "Never mind."

The fuck? Since when does this inflexible female talk herself in circles? And since when does she cave that easily?

Envy isn't the only bystander whose gaze bears down on Sorrow. Malice's demon eyes probe the goddess like a set of laser pointers, searching for a crawlspace through which to pry her open.

After being assigned to their stations, the warriors disperse, some gathering in clusters on the grass, others scaling statuesque trees interspersed across the summit. Firepits illuminate the atmosphere, including the rock walkway connecting the estuary to the monument.

Now they play a waiting game. The Court will come, leading an army in tow.

Figures tip back cups of enchanted water or sharpen their weapons. As starlit flames swat the air, deities share recollections of the past and visions of the future, no longer forced to keep these private thoughts to themselves.

Empathy slides into Envy's ribcage. After making the rounds with Anger, they hunker with the crew. Each couple nestles around a blaze, whereas Envy and Sorrow sit apart. Dammit all to Fates, he can't handle analyzing why she's giving him the cold shoulder. At this rate, the strain in his body will surely rip a tendon.

He's not alone in his angst. Based on the bleak expressions, this lot could use some levity.

Merry can always be counted upon. Snuggling into Anger's tattooed arms, she asks, "Does everyone know that myth about The Stars shining their brightest?"

Envy recalls thinking about it sometime during their voyage. "The stars will shine their brightest when a deity asks for the truth."

"But a deity will only receive the truth when they're ready to hear the answer," Sorrow adds while fixating on the grass.

"And that immortal will only be ready to hear the answer if they're ready to change," Merry finishes.

Andrew frowns. "What does it mean for The Stars to shine their brightest?"

"Answer, and he'll just interrogate us with a dozen more questions," Love teases, then nips Andrew's ear. "Not long ago, I do remember telling you to—"

"'Pick your battles, you exhausting creature,'" he quotes in a dramatic voice, biting her lower lip in retaliation. "How could I forget?"

"Maybe it means The Stars will shine in an unforeseen manner," Wonder theorizes.

"Or just blind the shit out of us," Malice says.

"Or cast light from an uncharted perspective," Anger murmurs.

"Can we pick a subject that isn't ninety-nine percent random?" Sorrow grunts, earning a bunch of pissed off looks.

Malice sneers. "You're a regular ray of sunshine, aren't you?"

"Hey," Envy growls. "Leave her alone."

Grimacing, Sorrow dices her gaze toward him. "I don't need you defending me."

"Is that right?" Envy leans forward and mocks, "What do you need, Nymph?" Then he snaps his fingers. "Ah, right. Not a fucking thing."

"What will everyone do, once we're victorious?" Merry tries again. "I mean, in addition to establishing a resolution about free will. I imagine we'll have centuries of work ahead. But what about during times of respite?"

Her distraction succeeds. Everyone contemplates, their expressions banked in firelight.

"From time to time, we'll check on things back home," Andrew says while Love curls into his broad chest.

By home, he means Evershire. The mountain town where he and

Love resided during her temporary stint as a human.

"How you must miss it," Merry empathizes. "Your family and friends."

"Everyone." Andrew's voice cracks. "Every day." Then he balls Love's hand in his, pressing his mouth to her knuckles. "But I'm right where I belong. Like hell am I going anywhere without you, Little Myth."

Love turns, nuzzles his lips, and whispers, "Like hell would I ever let you go."

They tangle themselves up in one another. At least they'll have eternity to split their lives between realms. It's not without sacrifice, but from what Envy sees, they have no regrets.

"We'll make returns to Celestial City," Merry says to Anger, who clasps her tighter.

"And make use of that motorcycle," Anger husks, as if hinting at a smutty memory.

"We'll rebuild The Archives. And I'll show you my house in the Astral Sea," Wonder says to Malice, her head resting in his lap. "Remember? I promised you."

He combs through her locks. "Will I be jealous of your bookshelf, Wildflower?"

"You can count on it, Demon."

"Christ," Sorrow grumbles. "All this sap is giving me a migraine."

She collects her weapons, launches to her feet, and flees the scene. Because that attitude isn't out of the ordinary, no one blinks.

Envy's not deceived. She'd looked on the verge of tears.

A gruff noise cuts from his lungs. "Fuck."

Launching to his feet, he stalks after her, the lingering gazes of his crewmates charring a hole into his back. Before their eyes, two unprecedented events occur. To start, everyone witnesses The God of Envy doing something he's never done: chase after a female.

Next fun fact? This isn't the first time Envy and Sorrow have stormed off after a public fight. But it *is* the first time they fire in the same direction.

At the cliff's promontory, a rock wall shields the goddess from the encampment. Shadows cloak her silhouette like a figment holding too many secrets for the light to penetrate. Idling beside the ledge, she audits the distant peaks, elevations so far out of reach.

No, not the peaks. Sorrow gazes at The Stars. She focuses with concentration, as if calling to someone.

"Hey!" Envy demands, burning a path toward her.

She swerves around, strings of hair batting her chin. "Hey, yourself."

"What the fuck?" He flings one arm in the direction they just came from. "What was that shit? What are you doing, Sorrow?"

"If I told you I came here to pee, would you go away?"

"What the hell is going on with you? In the grotto, I thought—"

"That was a mistake."

As though stabbed by an arrowhead, Envy staggers back a step. Not that her striking him down is a new experience. Although he's used to it, his defenses have never developed a thick enough surface, a notion he's finally made peace with.

She takes a shot, he reacts. That isn't about to change.

Regrouping, Envy glowers. "A mistake? Which part?" he bites out. "The part where I came inside your cunt, or the part where you came around my cock?"

"For Fate's sake, get lost!" Sorrow tears her fingers through her hair. "For once, let me be!"

Fury doesn't become him, so Envy changes tactics. He storms forward, eating up the distance in seconds, throwing his weight until he's got Sorrow backed up against the cliffside. Plastering one hand above her head, then flattening the other beside her hip, he burrows down, caging her there.

"Oh, hon," he coos. "If my proximity is so overwhelming that you needed a breather, all you had to do was say so."

"Quit bullshitting," Sorrow spits, her voice shaking. "Your swagger doesn't work on me."

His feline grin drops. "Then tell me you don't want me."

The goddess's features crimp. "I... I don't..."

"Go on," he grits out, burrowing down, seething against her lips. "Tell me what happened in the enclave meant nothing. Tell me you're not still thinking about it." His timbre lowers to a rough whisper. "How deep my cock sank. The way your pussy melted. How we watched each other the whole time."

His voice cracks like a twig. Worse, his heart commits a similar felony.

When Sorrow's fingers drift to his waist, Envy takes that as permission and runs his palm along the side of her breast. "Tell me you don't want that again. Right here, right now." He shears his mouth over hers, their hot breaths clashing. "Say you don't crave that sharp release, my hips snapping between your thighs, your mouth hanging open, your body coming around mine, hidden from view but with everyone less than fifty feet away—"

On a snarl, her mouth snatches his.

36

Envy

The next thing he knows, their lips crash together like firebrands. Ferocious, flammable, and fatal. The collision threatens to detonate the solar system, shattering everything to fragments.

Including his fucking heart. If it hasn't already been demolished.

The violent push of Sorrow's lips throws Envy off the cliff's edge, his head and body spiraling to an inevitable downfall. With a growl, he shoves his mouth into hers. They slam together, lips clamping like a set of vises, locking down in an unbreakable kiss forged of steel. Like its own weapon, something that feels good to wield, but will hurt if the wielder isn't careful.

However, Envy doesn't care about the risk. With this goddess, he's never cared.

Like a hot poker, the point of his tongue slices across the crease of her lips. The answering moan that fires out of Sorrow ignites his flesh, blood rushing through his limbs with the speed of a tsunami. By some elemental force, heat is less an enigma with her, every desperate sound crackling like timbers.

Let me in. Right fucking now.

His tongue swipes over that delicate line, ready to pry her open, begging for that privilege. In response, her lips tremble like an object about to crumble. On a hot gasp, Sorrow spreads for him, her mouth collapsing.

A coarse sound rumbles from Envy's chest as he spears his tongue inside, driving it between the pleats of her mouth. Dampness envelopes him, as slick and deep as her cunt. With pent-up strokes, he rakes against Sorrow's tongue, teasing every nerve to life.

Harsh whimpers dart from her throat. Flinging her arms around his shoulders, Sorrow leaps against Envy's torso and flicks her wet tongue with his.

Stars flay him. She tastes of currant nectar, with the afternotes of a briny sea. As their mouths fuse, black tea, smoke, and violets waft from the goddess's skin.

Dark, bitter, and stinging. Yet sweet and aromatic.

This, he has always known about her. The way she smells, the incense of her body working on him like a drug and its antidote. An eternal addiction.

Envy's fingers itch, then plummet into her hair, fisting the roots. Fixing her scalp in place, he rasps into her mouth. Nostrils flaring, he kisses her harder, deeper.

Sorrow meets the momentum, their tongues plying, jaws rocking. The instant she melts like honey, the kiss combusts. They snarl into one another, distraught, confounded, and desperate.

Fuck, this connection doesn't merely penetrate his flesh. It lodges itself bone-deep, soaks into his pores, infuses his blood.

His features twist, along with her own. Then the kiss transcends from angry to ardent, with every wistful moan, every helpless intake of breath.

The warmth of Sorrow's lips matches the density radiating from her pussy, that tight little pelvis bucking against his straining cock. It's the only way he knows what boiling point they've reached. The only thing that makes sense.

As for the rest, fuck it. The stress. The fury. The confusion. That's nothing new in their history, and he'll take whatever anguish it costs to grab her, touch her, have her.

With the Goddess of Sorrow, there is never a guarantee. And it's worth it.

Groaning, Envy slants his head and crushes his mouth to her own, taking this kiss and shredding it apart. With each fervent tug, he dislodges a whine from Sorrow, the sound rare and precious.

Rare and precious. Two descriptions he's never associated with anyone. Until her.

Fates, she will drown him in this kiss, in her arms, in her scent. So help him, he'll go down willingly.

Feverish and impatient, they paw at each other. As his tongue curls with hers, the kiss blows up, and he stalks forward. Backing Sorrow against the rocky foundation, he plunges his hands to her ass. Trapping them in his strong grip, Envy hoists Sorrow off the ground. At the same time, she bounds into the air, landing against him. Her weight drops into his arms, thighs venting open, calves linking around his waist.

As the shape of her pussy rustles against his aching cock, Envy snaps into motion. Crushing her against the cliffside, he tacks her like a dragonfly, splaying the goddess wide. Only then does he rip their mouths apart, a mutual gasp tearing from their lungs.

In the shadowed cove, their gazes catch. Shaken, they pant into one another, lips ajar and brushing.

Arrested like this, their hands go wild. Sorrow wrenches his shirt from the waistband, then yanks on the trouser buckles. Hardware clicks, clasps loosen, and the material gives. The flaps slump, his dick lifting into the night, the stem broad, the crown ruddy. His sac hangs heavy and bloated, and a droplet of filmy liquid surfaces to the roof.

Sorrow's eyes fall to half-mast. Her fingers strap around his girth, his flesh throbbing in her hand, heightening the sensitivity. With a conniving smile, the goddess pumps the head, the contact shuddering his muscles. But when she thumbs his crease, then jams that digit into her mouth and sucks on his cum, a low roar grinds from Envy's throat.

Seething, he rucks the skirt to her hips, baring that savory pussy, the flanks glossy with arousal. Fuck, she's already dripping onto him.

Humming, Envy draws a free finger along the groove, rowing back and forth.

Sorrow's mouth slackens another inch. "Oh…"

"Yes," he whispers, sketching her cunt. "Make noise for me."

"Too close. They'll hear."

"Since when do you give a shit what others think of you?"

"Never." While she siphons his cock, and he etches her slit, conviction and something protective flash in Sorrow's pupils. "But this isn't just about me."

The words pry Envy's chest open like a clamshell. Understanding floods his being. That anyone will hear them fucking isn't the issue. This goddess doesn't care about the opinions of others, the crew being her only exception.

But she does care about keeping this moment private. Sacred between them, as if they're still cloistered in that grotto. Sorrow wants this bond to be theirs alone.

Envy couldn't fucking agree more. For all the distorted truths they've lived through, this much is real. This one thing, this one moment. It's theirs.

Whatever happens the second they pull away, he'll still belong to her.

Sorrow's eyes cling into his, for once holding nothing back. As eventide conceals them from this battlefield, her irises glitter with a mixture of defeat and defiance, surrender and rebellion.

That candid look sews the gash in his chest, because he feels it too. The determination to claim this, keep this safe. No one is getting in the way of that. If they try, he'll chop them to pieces.

With a passionate hiss, Envy whips his waist. His cock pistons upward, lancing high. In one powerful jolt, his crown spreads her drenched cunt and strikes to the base.

Sorrow vaults from the impact, a rapturous cry lurching from her tongue. Groaning, Envy covers her mouth with his. Sealing their lips, he swallows the noise whole, devouring it like fine wine.

Her muscles clutch his dick, warm and soaked. The effect goes to his head like a fever dream, a fantasy made manifest. But when Sorrow presses firmer against his torso, coiling into Envy as if she wants to bind herself there, the all-consuming sensation reaches farther, snaring that pounding organ in his chest. Owning it.

The feeling is so tremendous, he can't think straight. All he can do is follow it like a devoted participant, giving everything he has. Even if it will never be enough.

Sorrow bends her face into his neck. Her pussy stretches around his cock, her respirations dovetailing with his, from one inhale to the next exhale.

It's terrifying and thrilling, how his instincts know what to do. Envy rubs her tailbone, waiting it out despite the agony this causes his nuts.

While Sorrow quivers, Envy murmurs, "It's okay, my nymph. It's okay."

"No," she whispers. "It's not."

Before he can translate what that means, she drags her gaze to his. Tender and mutinous, she caresses his lips with her own. "Show me pleasure."

The unfiltered plea grabs a hold of Envy. Her wish is his fucking command.

Husking, he rolls his ass, expanding Sorrow's thighs until they're pinned to the cliff, his dick punching into her with deliberate, even strokes.

His goddess mewls, her forehead landing on his, their eyes fastening. With each pump of his cock, her body juts into the sky, and her beautiful tits jostle against his torso. From his crown to the seat, the planks of her cunt clench Envy's flesh, her body pouring onto him.

All the while, her fingers comb through his head, frame his jaw, trace his mouth. She moves with restless abandon, the ministrations caught between disobedient and apologetic. Although, he should be the one who's sorry.

Sorry for bullying her for generations. Sorry for all the wasted years.

Sorry for the ice arrow. Sorry for everything.

Instead, he tells her with each snap of his ass. Hauling his body into her, Envy fucks Sorrow into the mountainside, thrashing at the top of the universe. Because this is the highest spot in The Dark Fates, therefore the closest pinnacle in existence to The Stars, this is where she belongs. This goddess should reign, thrive, and come at the peak of their realm.

Strung out, they launch their hips. Moonstruck, out of his mind with desire, Envy lashes his cock, aiming for that condensed place he knows so well now. The nook that will make her howl from the pit of her lungs.

Sorrow shouts, the noise rocketing across the plateau. This spurs Envy deeper, swifter, his hand flying to her mouth. Each of her rhythmic moans shoves into his palm, flooding his veins until he's strung out on the cacophony like an addict.

In cadence to his waist, Sorrow flings her hips at him. Their pace matches, their bodies working into each other like a single entity. A lightning bolt. A wave cresting. Something about to split open.

It's not just fucking. It's not merely sex.

This is infinite and extraordinary. Their crew would call it lovemaking.

He'd once thought the concept delusional, beneath a deity's consideration. Gods don't lose themselves like that.

How fucking wrong he'd been.

Yet instead of feeling inadequate, Envy's thrilled to be mistaken. It's led to this, here, now. Sorrow bounding on his cock, her drenched pussy lathering him to the base, her cries a rite of passage. For once, it's not about himself. It isn't about what he can get from a lover, but what he can give.

Everything. That's what he'll offer, if she lets him.

To demonstrate, Envy slings his ass between her thighs, spreading her wider. The prow of his dick hits that glorious place over and over and over. Sorrow's teeth grab onto his palm, the sting invigorating, thickening his erection even more inside her.

He'd like nothing more than for her screams to reach the sun, wherever it's hiding at this hour. Yet as she said, this is too special to be public. Everything this goddess wants, longs, and yearns for will be hers, to be treated like priceless artifacts. Cared for. Respected.

Fuck. Envy doesn't recognize his own thoughts. Still, all the benedictions toppling from his mind feel right.

They've hurled enough insults, jibes, and glares at each other in front of their kin. So let this be their private redemption, their own transformation.

With a delighted hiss, Envy releases Sorrow's mouth and smashes his lips against hers. While vaulting their hips, he devours her sobs, and she consumes his groans. Her cunt oozes onto him, the peg of her clit skidding over his frenulum.

Envy growls. Snatching her wrists in one hand, he tacks Sorrow's arms overhead and rams his body forward, lunging her upward with each sinuous thrust. Despite the clamor, they move soundly, fluidly.

Lovemaking. Indeed, he could get used to this new kink. But only with her.

Sorrow's skirt flutters around his legs, the hem sliding off her naked hips, her boots linking beneath his tireless ass. While clasping his buttocks, she weeps into his mouth, the noise caressing him like satin. His pelvis skates over her clit, the little stud poking from her, the abrasion staggering.

Constellations chip into the sky. Below, waves crescendo against the breakers.

The sexiest cries in existence splinter off Sorrow's tongue. Grinning into her lips, Envy laps that quavering tongue with relish, the pleasure-pain hurting so good.

And now they know what the fuck this feels like.

Astride his cock, Sorrow scrambles in his arms. In an amorous panic, she bats at his muscles as though she can't tolerate only one position, one way to fuck.

Envy can't agree more. Releasing her wrists and swooping around, he bangs his spine into the cliffside while Sorrow clambers off his dick, her crease slipping from around his rigid flesh as she scurries to the ground and turns. The separation draws a dissatisfied grunt from Envy, his hands yanking her backward, her shoulder blades striking his torso.

Scissoring her legs apart, Sorrow nestles into his chest. Then she hikes up her skirt, hops back onto his cock, and beats her ass into his groin. Except there's one crucial difference.

Her lovely pussy isn't what seals around him. The tight passage of Sorrow's anus lowers onto Envy, sinking to the hilt and compressing his flesh.

Fuck him to death. Envy's vision goes black. His blood turns into a lava.

Putting it mildly, this is a first for them. And how marvelous to be an immortal with the stamina to indulge without lubrication or coaxing. Rather, this goddess takes his cock like their bodies were molded for one another, a sigh floating from her mouth.

Overdosing on that noise, Envy shoots his waist forward, jutting into her ass, reaching so deep Sorrow arches on a disoriented moan. Extending her arms behind her, she clasps his nape, using it to brace herself. Standing against him, she writhes on his cock, her backside lunging with his waist.

They grind into one another, neither fast nor slow. Sorrow gyrates with Envy while they gaze ahead, groaning with rapture, gaping at the vista of celestials.

Sliding his arms around the goddess, Envy sketches her clit, his finger dabbing the crest. Sorrow whimpers, struggling to keep her octave to a minimum. Her cunt leaks onto his fingers, and her hips buck into him, eager for more.

Fuck yes. Crooning, he rubs the dainty flesh, pressing and circling.

The muscles of her pussy tense, as do her cries. In turn, the head of his dick expands, and infamous heat gushes onto his sac.

Envy hits critical mass. He jabs his cock swifter, and his fingers massage her slit, his body moving in tandem. With each thud of their hips, they chase that apex, racing after it until their limbs threaten to give out.

As his balls tighten, Envy rushes his lips against her earlobe. "Come on, nymph," he pants while swiping his waist. "Come at the top of the universe. Come right here."

That does it. Sorrow bows into him, her head lands on his shoulder, and a shout cleaves from her throat. Her cunt pulsates, hot liquid washing down his fingers, and tremors wrack her ass, the ovals squeezing him.

To protect this stunning climax from being overheard, Envy swoops down. At the same instant, Sorrow twists her gaze, her mouth catching his own. Their lips clamp, kissing and coming in unison.

Blinding lights fire behind his eyelids. His dick spasms, twitching inside her, release spurting from the crown. The orgasm grips him in a chokehold, then lets loose, a destructive bellow carving from his lungs. He comes, going so deeply he can't see the fucking sky.

Sorrow keens, swallowing the noise, feasting on it. Their mouths cling, anchoring them to the bluff. They kiss, and kiss, and fucking kiss. Willingly, they leap into oblivion, disheveled and shattering against one another.

Fates almighty. This goddess.

Crumbling into the jagged facade, they fall against each other. With his cock still encased inside her, Envy nestles Sorrow into his frame. She curls there, slumping in a gorgeous heap, her upper body turned his way.

With their lips clutching, they wheeze into the kiss, fighting to catch their breaths. Their mouths ease up, softening into a lighter embrace. Winded and hazy with pleasure, they skim their lips, tongues flicking.

His knuckles caress her warm pussy, the phenomenon of temperature never ceasing to amaze him. Though, nothing compares to her own satisfaction. Sorrow bundles herself in Envy's arms, which strap around her middle, holding her close.

He can stay like this for a solid century. Matter of fact, with her ass grabbing his cock, he'll be ready for another sumptuous round in a few minutes. Once they resolve why she acted distant after the grotto, they'll be free to indulge in more decadent pastimes, including several impassioned quickies before this war gets underway.

He'll lavish her with endearments, make her laugh, and make her come again. Multiple times.

Husky with elation, Envy smiles into the kiss. Dragging his lips away, he murmurs against her mouth, "This lovemaking business is underrated among deities."

As if he's pulled a trigger, Sorrow's eyes flap open. A haunted light flashes across her irises.

And then she gets moving. Given how they'd wiped one another out, the goddess squirms away faster than he could have predicted. She rolls her waist, her ass releasing his cock, the skirt dropping around her jellied limbs.

It's déjà vu all over again. Normally, he'd haul Sorrow backward with a fiendish, "Ah, ah, ah. Not so fast."

But this time, Envy's so nonplussed and sex-high, he's incapable of stopping the goddess. Stumped, he watches Sorrow yank her clothes into place while gearing up for another... whatever this has become.

A second ago, he thought he finally knew. Because a second ago, he was a smitten fool.

The tender guilt weighing down her features says it all. Deities attune themselves to premonition, whispers of destiny incarnate. Therefore, that look jolts Envy like a knife to the back. So this is how his former conquests felt when he left them without a backward glance.

Envy's spent cock deflates. He closes the flap of his pants, then spreads his arms. "What did I do wrong?"

Retreating to the bluff's edge, Sorrow's eyes mist. "Nothing."

"Nothing?" he barks. "Don't fucking lie to me! You've been treating me like a pariah since the enclave! The second we finished fucking, something changed! Is this about the arrow?"

"No!" she hollers, although he wouldn't blame her if it was. "It's not that!"

They go in circles, screaming persistent things and evasive things he can't keep track of. Sorrow marches past Envy, but he snatches her arm and whips her around. In the piebald light, he glares, wounded, helpless, enraged.

He wants to shake her, kiss her, fuck her again. He wants to wipe that bereft look from her face, then promise a thousand things he's never promised to anyone.

Except these options would be difficult, seeing as their crewmates are jogging up behind them, having overheard the shouts. On the fringes, Love, Andrew, Anger, Merry, Wonder, and Malice skid to a halt. Though, Envy doesn't give a fated fuck who's watching.

All he cares about is *her*.

Sorrow's voice buckles, her features collapsing like a stack of dominos. "I can't do this anymore."

"Can't do what?" Envy roars. "Fuck me back? Want me back? Love me back?"

Stunned silence from the crew. Not even a gasp from Merry.

He stalls, his head catching up with his mouth. Motherfuck. It had just come out.

Sorrow's pupils explode with shock. Her lips quaver until a steely resolve takes over. "But I don't," she says, the words calcifying inside him. "I don't love you. I never have." Her attention darts to the speechless group. "And I'm sorry."

Envy releases her as if she's poisoned him. "What do you mean, you're sorry?"

The goddess retreats, stepping closer to the windswept precipice. "You wanted to know pain."

"What the fuck, Sorrow? Tell me what that means!"

"It means, you should have left her tied to the tree."

Materializing beside Sorrow is a figure with dark skin, her height swathed in a galaxy of fabric and weapons forged of blue moonstone strapped to her lithe figure.

A royal goddess of The Stars. A member of The Fate Court.

37

Sorrow

Nearby, firepits burnish the summit. Below, the sea's rapids smash against the crags. Shrouded from their encampment, the stunned gazes of her crewmates spear through Sorrow like javelins.

The ruler stands alone, the folds of her gown rippling like a sail. She glances placidly at Sorrow's friends, who scramble to raise their weapons.

Stricken, they digest the monarch's presence. More importantly, Sorrow's proximity beside her.

Confusion warps Envy's features. But when Sorrow fails to explain, he does the math. His complexion blanches, and his baritone tapers to a hiss, a shadow of his normal voice. "No."

"You. Can't. Be. Serious," Anger grates, rage climbing up his face.

"It's not true." Traumatized, Merry shakes her head. "I won't believe it."

"Nor I," Love whispers, her black wings tensing, the plumes ready to swat the monarch off the promontory.

Andrew aims his weapon and grits out, "This is bullshit."

In desperation, Wonder pores over Sorrow's countenance. "Dearest?"

But astute Malice is already there. He slants his gilded head, the razor edge of his jaw tightening. "What do they have on you?"

Heads bob toward him, then to Sorrow. Although he's correct, it's merely the hunt for an excuse. Her soul wilts from their conviction, the loyalty she hasn't reciprocated.

Betrayal rips a hole in Envy's face. That's the most agonizing part, grabbing her by the jugular, threatening to shove Sorrow to her knees.

His honed words slice the air in half. "Who cares why the fuck she's doing this?" he growls. "The point is, she's bending over for the enemy like a spineless waif."

"Who *cares*?" Merry repeats, incredulous. Disarming, she braces a palm to her chest. "I do! I care because she's family. We're all family." She pivots toward each of them. "Aren't we?"

Staggered silence. The crew swaps grave looks, the sorts of expressions that bleed.

Sorrow withholds a sob as Merry flounces toward her. "Sorrow?"

As she trails off, the unspoken question surfaces. Why is Sorrow doing this?

Because she has to. Because they're going to lose. And when they lose, the degree of Envy's suffering—all of their suffering—will depend on her. Because she has no choice. Because the moment she fell in love with this crew, and the moment she gave herself to Envy, everything changed.

The reply is simple, yet the words scatter across her tongue like loose marbles. Her stupefied friends shift, torn between disbelief, treachery, and rancor.

This is what wounds do. They taint and fester.

The Court would have rooted out this location anyway, but her actions have erased the crew's advantage, plus the element of surprise.

Sorrow's disloyalty is a ruthless measure, stripping them of faith.

These figures were once her crewmates in name only, then her allies, then her friends. As Merry said, they've become Sorrow's family. To that end, she knows their fighting tactics and vulnerabilities.

Envy's scowl hardens into contempt, the vision chipping at her, piece by piece.

The ruler offers the crew a conciliatory glance, her sympathy genuine rather than patronizing. In particular, this catches Wonder's attention. Which brings to mind something Wonder once shared about her mission with Malice in The Archives, while the pair did bookish spy work. When they'd briefly gotten caught, this reigning goddess exhibited an affinity toward Wonder and Malice, even curiosity about their cause.

"Consider this a parlay," the ruler says. "You're outnumbered, outmagicked, and outranked. Stand down, and we'll show benevolence in the face of treason."

"Compromise with us, and we'll stand down," Love counters.

When the female glances at Love, a twinkle of pride filters through. "Goddess of Love. Our infamous revolutionary spark." She inclines her head. "I'm afraid only when The Stars command it shall we compromise. Yet they haven't. What does that tell you?"

No one speaks. Because why the hell *haven't* The Stars intervened?

"Then a battle, it must be," the monarch concludes.

A massive form soars into view, its great wingspan liable to remove a chunk of the summit. The lunar heron bats its plumage. Its spindle limbs land atop the cliff, its size having shifted at the presumed behest of this monarch.

So that's how the female got here in record time. While the ruler could have manifested, that wouldn't have been ideal, given she isn't planning on leaving alone.

The raptor's appearance startles the company. But not as much as the goddess ushering Sorrow onto the avian's back, then straddling in front.

"Oh, and as to your choice of fortification," the monarch imparts, somewhat apologetically. "Don't you think we know the stargazer's weak points of entry?"

Sorrow's eyes widen. Such a basic fact that hadn't occurred to her, nor to her friends, the announcement stalling their weapons.

The avian vaults into the firmament. Sorrow's insides swoop from the elevation as she grips the female's middle for balance, the wind lashing at their hair. Peeking over her shoulder, the silhouettes of her friends shrink, along with Envy's livid glare. Shingled wings vibrate as she and the monarch fly at a breakneck pace, their shadows oscillating across the sea.

Welding her eyes shut, Sorrow ignores the clench of her heart, lest it should topple her over the edge. Instead, she concentrates on the waterfall enclave, where Envy showed her a new source of pleasure. The poignant visuals feast on her soul, chewing her to bits, so that a cry of pain clots her throat.

The trip passes quickly. They descend in the Palace of Starlight, in the amphitheater's throne arena, back where she started. The Fate Court awaits, nodding to the goddess as she disembarks and inspecting Sorrow with begrudging astonishment.

One pasty pale goddess in particular. Spite clutters the female's gaze, the scarred gash where Sorrow had rammed her boots into the ruler twisting that mouth into a caricature.

Whatever. She'll heal. And so will the wounds across Sorrow's arms.

In any case, Sorrow hadn't wanted to create a fuss, which is why she'd called out to only one of them. That had been shortly before Envy cornered her, mashed her into the cliffside, and laid siege to Sorrow's body.

The next several hours prove disorientating. The rulers question her, though she has the presence of mind to keep both fists to herself this time. Because brainpower is as dangerous as a blade, she plays a mind game, channeling the skills she picked up from Malice to obstruct her answers. Come on, she'd hadn't planned on simply caving without a fight.

If Sorrow must align herself with these fuckers, best to screw with their plans. She provides enough skewed information to satisfy them without offering crucial or authentic details, omitting certain particulars and feigning cluelessness about others.

It's fortunate that Sorrow's a jaded goddess. Her inherent cynicism convinces them she hadn't invested time in bonding with her allies enough to know their private susceptibilities.

Outwardly, she relents. Inwardly, she revolts.

Preparations to conquer Fortune's Crest commence. The rulers assemble at the Astral Sea, summoning all loyals to bear arms. To say the crowd is gobsmacked by Sorrow's participation is an understatement, the deities' gazes ranging from impressed to repulsed by her shift in allegiances. To them, Sorrow's actions render her wishy-washy.

Despite the misinformation she fed The Court, the sheer quantity of fighters doubles her pulse. Over the next three days, thousands of them suffocate the shoreline, questing in droves from their outposts in valleys and bluffs, as well as from the human realm. Others include deities and keepers who had volunteered to rebuild The Archives' most sacred dominion—The Hollow Chamber—after its destruction when Malice and Wonder trespassed there months ago.

Sorrow maintains a vigilant ear, tapping into plots and strategies. Maybe she can reach out to the crew with a message.

Wishful thinking. While she has sided with them, and although she's been eavesdropping, The Court takes precautions to ban her from loitering near their most privy subjects. Some like Pride, Spite, and

Grief give her a wide berth, whereas others keep a skeptical watch.

Apparently, a few outcasts from The Celestial City have had their banishments revoked, in exchange for their fealty. Sorrow and her friends anticipated that might happen. Merry had once pointed out the likely candidates, when they'd been in the human realm. Therefore, Sorrow notes the presence of Cruelty, Fear, and Shock.

Technically, they have no claim to those titles anymore. In the decades since their expulsions, many exiles have been replaced by new gods and goddesses, which means this army has double-booked some of the root emotions. Nevertheless, the former outcasts keep their distance from those who've supplanted them.

Thankfully, Sorrow and her friends haven't been ostracized long enough to be recreated. Except for maybe Malice, although Sorrow has never heard of another god such as he. Sometimes it takes a while to find the right star.

That's not the only reality check. While pretending to exercise her bow at the coastline, Sorrow notices a pair of archers hugging, a goddess rustling the curls of a younger one, and another god singing a ditty to enliven his companions.

She spots the figures who had chased Sorrow's crew. Among them is the pair who confiscated Love's bow. The female wearing a jumpsuit and brandishing mercury archery is Delight, while the male in a cobalt mantle is Bliss.

Presently, they host a targeting game for a school of striplings. It's the same children who startled Sorrow's crew in the forest, minus the small male she's encountered more than once now.

Nostalgia has evidently recovered from Envy's attack and retrieved his submerged weapons. Since he hadn't laid eyes on Sorrow when Envy ambushed him days ago, Nostalgia's got no cause to pay her attention. Instead, he adjusts his sapphire archery, then approaches the cheering clique that includes Delight and Bliss.

Another goddess sits at one of the docks, where she strums a lyre and hums to herself. Another god sketches in a journal.

A water lantern floats across the sea, coasting in the direction of Envy's home. At the sight, a pang of longing swamps Sorrow anew.

Which is more overwhelming? Having him or missing him?

At any rate, the image of Envy in one piece is the only visual she can tolerate. To think of the alternative, of him hurt, mutilated…

A slender hand cuts into Sorrow's view, an ice arrow poised between the female's fingers. "I believe this is yours," the iridescent ruler says.

Refusing to genuflect, Sorrow seizes the arrow with a harsh swipe. Refusing to express gratitude, she jams it into her quiver.

Calmly, the luminary goddess scans Sorrow's profile. "What can I do to help you?"

Shit. Is Sorrow's pining that transparent?

She snarls, "I want nothing from you. Not anymore."

"I imagine that's true. But don't suppose this is easy for us," the ruler cautions with delicacy, as though Sorrow still matters to this lot.

"Was it hard to condemn Love, target Andrew, banish Anger, exile Merry, torture Wonder, shoot Malice, threaten Envy, or compromise me?" Sorrow volleys, hitching her longbow onto her back.

The sovereign glances at the constellations. Her expression grows remote, yet her inflection is tangible. "Being a leader demands the ultimate strength of will. We need it to pass judgment, exact punishment, and endure. Yet it isn't without its torment." She casts Sorrow a weary glance. "We don't fight because we wish to."

"But you'll crucify my friends if I don't comply."

"Being ordained by The Stars also means it's our task to defend the lives of many subjects, rather than spare a handful of rebels. When all is said and done, exacting justice is our duty. That does not mean we enjoy it, but such is our destiny."

"And what about inspiring your subjects?" Sorrow presses.

"Destiny created inspiration. Destiny created choice. Doesn't that matter?"

The female's face transforms, flashing with confusion. Her eyes veer to the sidelines, detecting company. The Fate Court loiters behind them, witnessing the exchange. Like this goddess, their quizzical reactions bear resemblance to the ones Sorrow observed in the Palace of Starlight, when she made a similar argument. Despite their upbringing, they had exhibited misgivings back then.

It reminds Sorrow of the minute but renowned traits about these leaders. The pale goddess paints canvases to combat depression. The amethyst goddess pens verse, anthologizing every soul in this realm. The female who wears iridescent gowns is a self-proclaimed guardian of animals. The hawkish ruler performs random acts of kindness to his subjects. The cloaked god makes the rounds, singing lullabies to children who have trouble sleeping. These presumed leaders have fears, doubts, passions, dreams, losses, regrets, and joys. They're prone to double-standards and errors in judgment, as much as to wisdom. If they make mistakes, they might learn from them.

Like any of their people. Like humans.

The goddess delays her answer, then lowers her voice. "Then convince us," she challenges before joining her fellow sovereigns.

Sorrow wavers. Convince them how?

Flummoxed and no longer wishing to be the object of their scrutiny, she retreats in the opposite direction. That's when another feminine hand materializes, brushing Sorrow's elbow. She pauses, stumped to meet the countenance of Envy's Guide. Siren is beautifully curvy like Wonder, except with a penchant for wrist bangles.

The female might also be a tad vain, but she's nowhere near as conceited as Envy. Growing up, Sorrow had been fonder of this goddess than of the god in question.

"Trespassing into enemy territory when your sovereigns expected an uprising in the human realm," Siren recaps with an amused tenor.

"Ballsy, I know," Sorrow remarks, giving the female a wry grin and accepting a hug.

"Goddess of Sorrow."

"Guide of Envy."

"I'm sorry to meet you under less than promising circumstances."

"Not sorrier than I am," Sorrow confides, pulling back. "Thank you for everything."

For conspiring with Sorrow's Guide, for informing Envy where to flee from the throne amphitheater. For taking the risk, regardless of their differing opinions.

The Guide's voice loses its veneer. "Is he well?"

The inquiry grinds a rusty nail into Sorrow. "Last time I checked, he was."

Last time she checked, he also despised her.

The mentor nods. "I know what you're doing for him."

Thrown for a loop, Sorrow hedges. "Who told you?"

"Come, now. Immortals talk. Your conference with The Court is circulating, as are your presumed feelings for my charge."

"It's complicated."

"Banality aside, that sounds like a rather complex emotion. One that the Dark Gods aren't supposed to feel."

Her voice turns brittle. "I thought deities considered sentimentality a weakness."

Siren grins blandly. "Not all of us."

Based on the romantic tales about her friends, maybe Sorrow and her crewmates have been proving more of their kin wrong. Maybe others are coming around, even if they're not publicizing it.

They part ways when Sorrow glimpses another mentor watching her. Rushing toward him, Sorrow meets Echo at the pier by her house, flinging her arms around his slender form. Chuckling, he squeezes her back. Thank Fates, he's unscathed after colluding with Siren. Whatever the case, it appears their sovereigns haven't found out about that.

Nonetheless, Sorrow hasn't seen her mentor since returning. She reels back and shoves him. "Where have you been?"

"What are you thinking?" Echo reprimands in kind, lecturing under his breath, his chin set in disapproval.

"Thinking?" Sorrow galls, her features knitting. "I'm protecting my friends."

"By betraying them."

"And I'm siding with you."

"By going against what you believe in."

Guilt punches a crater into her chest. She deserves this retribution and more.

Kicking off her boots, Sorrow drops onto the deck, then plunges her feet into the sea. In her periphery, she catches movement from a parallel dock, glimpsing the little god with painted eyeliner. He perches several feet across from Sorrow, his short legs lost in the depths while he surveys her.

Sighing, Echo lowers himself beside Sorrow. "I didn't teach you to take sides. I taught you to unite them."

She speaks to their reflections in the water, the surface illuminated by starlight and floating lanterns. "Is that what you want?"

"It's what I'll support," he replies. "I side with fate, and I'll guard it with my bow. But should we lose, I'll accept a compromise, and I shall be willing to learn a new way."

"Why are you here?" the child interrupts, his nose scrunching.

Clearly, he's miffed that his efforts to help liberate Sorrow have backfired. Though, she can't blame the fledgling for being pissed, since she's just as enraged at herself.

Sorrow exhales. "Because I know what pain feels like."

"Just as you know what healing feels like," Echo reminds her with a somber expression. "Just as you know how to resist the former and strive for the latter."

"I've seen enough mortal wars—"

"To remember that anything can happen, at any time. To know they may die on the battlefield rather than by execution. To know they may perish now or later. To know you can only do so much."

Fair enough. However, death in combat will be swifter than by The Court's hands.

Echo takes Sorrow's hand. "You hurt your friends by turning your back on them. More so than by shielding them from the arbitrary point of a blade."

Siren is right. News travels fast.

The question tastes poisonous in her mouth. "Even if it means a drawn-out punishment instead of a merciful one?"

To which Echo turns and frames her cheek. "I don't have to answer that for you."

No, he doesn't. If Sorrow knows her outcast crew as well as she believes, the answer's clear.

We're all family.

As Merry's words cycle in Sorrow's mind, Echo rises to his feet, his braid swishing behind him. Though, he promises to return after convening with a neighboring group.

Left alone with the child, Sorrow casts him a tentative glance. This tyke has a rapport with Echo and Siren, considering she'd seen the trio standing together during her capture. Maybe that's also why the little god had aided her rescue.

With that in mind, Sorrow ventures, "For what it's worth? Thanks."

The male inspects the starry flecks trickling from her lower lashes. "Cute. But my eyes are shinier."

"Hmm. Maybe you can teach me that trick?"

With a snigger, he stands and leaps across the water. Landing on

Sorrow's pier, the child squats beside her and extends his hand. "My name is Faith."

A wish god. Feeling inexplicably bashful, she shakes his hand. "It's an honor."

The voices around them fade. Winged silhouettes fill the sky, their collective cries growing in decibel like the loudest silver instrument in recorded history.

Rising on the deck, Sorrow and Faith search the constellations, moons, and planets.

"Whuuuuut's that noise?" Faith draws out.

It's a rhetorical question. It's a well-known sound coming their way. It's the commotion made by a troop of dwellers with prismatic wings, beaks as long as swords, and the ability to shift sizes.

In the mortal realm, such raptors make a grittier sound. But in this dimension, the noise is gracefully sharp, like an expansive wail. Something that cuts to the bone.

It's a premonition. It's a wild card. It's a war tactic.

Terror ensnares Sorrow's chest, a whisper slicing from her tongue. "Herons."

38

Envy

It's too quiet. Everything about this summit is too fucking quiet, to the point where he hears an arrowhead slicing through the air. Someone is twirling his glass weapon like a windmill.

Ah, right. That's him.

The arrow goes rogue in his grip, spinning out of control as he flips it across his fingers. If he wheels the thing any faster, it's going to fly out of his hand and skewer somebody's intestines. Except he can't stop. He's a caged tiger, prowling the length of the parapet, pacing around the crew, who do their damndest to remain calm.

Or they were doing their damndest until now. Patience exceeded, Love grinds her teeth. Wonder crosses her arms over her chest and lances Envy with a disgruntled glare. Merry frowns, concern sparkling in her pink eyes.

Andrew expels a pent-up breath. Malice balances on a single bent knee, positioning himself on the stone tooth of a crenellation, where he aims a hickory arrow at Envy.

Anger simply gets angry. "Stop fucking doing that!"

"No," Envy snarls, pacing faster and accelerating the weapon.

"I can make you stop, mate," Malice warns, his arrowhead trailing Envy's movements. "I enjoy making people stop."

"That won't help, dearest," Wonder disputes to her lover.

"Let him be," Merry sighs. "His heart is wounded by the tragic loss of love."

Envy rounds on the misfit goddess while pointing his free finger. "Take that shit back."

"Why, kindred? You admitted your feelings before she left."

"Well, I'm taking that back too."

"Christ's sake," Malice mutters, then clicks his eyes to Wonder. "Was I this bad?"

"You were worse," she tells him with affection.

"Stubborn fuck." Anger snatches Envy's arrow and spins it from his reach. When Envy growls, ready to pounce, the god braces one palm against Envy's torso, breaking his stride. "Enough," Anger speaks in a voice that could boil iron. "We need you."

To demonstrate, he flicks his gaze sideways, indicating their audience. Envy's friends and allies shoot glances toward the scene. From a distant platform, Harmony watches, her flat gaze telling Envy that squandering his energy will do him no favors.

Nor this fight. Nor the people relying on him.

Ever the leader, Anger has reigned in his temper, his words striking true. As much as Envy would like to continue fuming, it's not fair to unleash on the rest of them. Very well, so his restlessness is a coping mechanism, preventing him from smashing his knuckles into the nearest edifice and ruining his manicure.

The monotony also spares him from remembering her lying, traitorous face.

Her smile. Her mouth, open in pleasure while he pumped his cock into that exquisite body. Her chin trembling from the weight of her lie.

Sorrow had betrayed him. She'd betrayed them all.

Envy hadn't believed it. Even now, it's incomprehensible, the reality imploding like an atomic bomb in his brain. Despite being the most disillusioned member of the crew, Sorrow is also the most conscientious about inflicting pain. With every grunt, she delivers tough love openly, while internally the goddess agonizes over everyone, concealing this fragility beneath a cool veneer.

Fates, he would have gambled his wardrobe before predicting Sorrow would ever turn her back on all of them. But then, this nymph has always defied his expectations.

After everything they've said and done. After the waterfall enclave. After that night on the boat. After that kiss. After more fucking, talking, and confessing than they'd ever done. After their escape.

After they mated like it had actually mattered.

Yet again, the bitch has deluded him. In the end, the fucking had been no different to Sorrow than their previous shags. Naturally, it had been a farce. What is three days compared with three millennia?

And why the fuck does it feel like his chest is caving in on itself?

Whatever Envy's expression reveals, Anger reads him like a mirror. Which makes sense, given it's Envy's favorite inanimate object, other than double-breasted suits and sex toys. To say nothing of Sorrow's missing ice arrow, which deserves its own shrine.

Anger's palm leaves Envy's chest, only to switch gears and press the glass arrow against Envy's pecs. "You're not the only one Sorrow betrayed," the god testifies.

Envy snorts. "No, I'm just the only one she fucked."

"She didn't betray us willingly," Wonder insists.

The group swerves toward the goddess while she contemplates the remote hills. "Before Sorrow left, she had the look of someone carrying a secret pain."

"They're playing games with her," Malice states. "They've fucked with Sorrow to the point where she was forced to castrate Envy—"

"Must we use that choice of analogy?" Envy pouts.

"—and debilitate the rest of us," the demon finishes with a grim smirk. "And no, that analogy suits you just fine, mate."

"Whatever. If you motherfuckers want to publicly analyze my latest drama, we might as well rope Guilt into this conversation," Envy spews. "She's around here somewhere."

"Oh, Envy," Wonder berates. "You're letting pride get in the way of sense."

"That's not pride," Andrew contests, his tone vapid.

"It's love," Love and Merry say in unison.

Envy grimaces, the declaration reopening a wound that has barely closed. He confessed as much to Sorrow before she hitched a ride with the enemy. Everyone is still getting over that bombshell, but if The Fate Court has somehow pushed Sorrow into a corner, this crew doesn't seem surprised. Why? Because they all know what it's like to forsake their freedom.

Shame and inadequacy snatch Envy's ribcage, the epiphany knocking him over with the force of a thunderbolt. Andrew lost his mother to tragedy. Love lost her immortality, then her memory. Anger lost his place in this world, then melted his iron wings. Merry was exiled from the beginning. Wonder endured heartbreak, causing her mate's downfall and bearing the scars to prove it. Malice was confined, tortured, and resurrected.

And Sorrow...

Sorrow endured millennia of wars, mangled soldiers, and countless lost souls. She's witnessed so much human blood and tears, she can swim in it.

By comparison, Envy is an outliner. He's witnessed fits of jealousy that led to violent crimes, the stress oftentimes bringing him to his knees. And yet. He's never been traumatized or crushed like everyone here. Not by experience, destiny, or his root emotion.

No. Only one goddess has ever been the source of his anguish. And most of that is on him, including but not limited to confiscating her archery, inadvertently preventing them from bonding like mates.

The invisible noose tightens. Despite confessing this breach, guilt clots his throat, a permanent sensation if there ever was one.

Ultimately, his comrades are wiser than Envy. And more rational since he's the only one whose balls had been invested in Sorrow. Unlike him, they've had the breathing space to think logically.

So, yes. They're right. But fuck them anyway.

Envy wants and doesn't want to hear lectures, consolations, opinions, advice, justifications or whatever the fuck else these experienced pricks are willing to impart. Hell, he wants and doesn't want a lot of things right now.

The speculative crew watches him. They understand, and they don't understand, because what he feels is strangely universal and unique.

Regardless, they each have a right to this affliction. Whatever Sorrow was to Envy, she was also their friend. They've lost her too.

We're all family.

An anomaly, perhaps. Or maybe their bond has become just that close, to an intuitive degree. If so, how very mortal of them.

Anger squeezes Envy's shoulder. Everyone regards him with looks of camaraderie. Even Malice, who disarms and offers a devious wink.

Envy still has them. And they have him.

The clenching sensation inside him eases up. He accepts the arrow, nocking the glass stem to his longbow. Then he joins his friends at the rampart, where they line up and scan the perimeter, each of them outfitted in plates of armor. Invoked through magic, the protective shields mold to their bodies, the vestments solid yet flexible.

Overhead, the celestials glow. A gust of air buffets Anger's shoulder-length hair and tousles Malice's golden waves. While casting his grim profile toward one of the moons, Andrew's sharp, white layers glint in stark contrast to the sky.

After circling the sky three times to check the vista, Love lands beside her mate, her sooty wings brushing his shoulder.

Merry stations herself next to Anger.

Wonder bounds atop the crenellations alongside Malice.

The current picks up, swatting the tail of Envy's mane, his hair affixed at the nape. The ominous breeze ruffles every cloak and fletching, whispers from this army petering out.

Hyperawareness of an incoming presence simmers. Thousands of archers stand fast, keeping vigil from every elevation surrounding the metallic stargazer. After a while, conversations pick up again. Harmony approaches their crew at the primary outpost and confers with Wonder.

Andrew and Love hold a conference with Anger and Merry, both couples murmuring. Though at intervals, the former mortal glances at the welkin, his pewter eyes flashing in suspicion. As a fantasy writer, Andrew has trained himself to conceive of numerous scenarios in any given story, including possibilities deities wouldn't think to consider, either out of arrogance or vanity.

Envy would know. So whatever the hell Andrew's thinking, it shoots prickles across Envy's forearms like a fleet of spiders.

Bowstrings vibrate. Hate, Scorn, and Calamity nock their arrows.

Them, as well as a legion of others. Likewise, Envy's crew mimics the action, their movements graceful yet militant like a deadly, synchronized dance.

By contrast, Envy doesn't arm himself yet. He inspects the ground, which remains motionless. Nor does the wind carry the pounding echo of footsteps.

Ever since they aired Sorrow's dirty laundry to this legion, each warrior has been on edge for days, depleting their energy in anticipation of a siege. Perhaps that was The Court's intention. Nevertheless, these troops haven't let their guard down.

The Dark Gods who've remained loyal to The Court know where the rebels are, so their arrival is imminent. Moreover, their sovereigns maintain thousands of allies. Their approach won't be a quiet one. Or rather, it shouldn't be.

With his bow poised, Anger gives voice to everyone's thoughts. "Something is off."

"They can't be here yet," Merry says, her neon arrow set toward the northern cliffs. "We would have heard them."

"The scouts would have returned," Wonder adds from beside Malice, the pair kneeling and angling their weapons.

Voices multiply and overlap in hushed but rapid tones. There might be routes they haven't covered. Or perhaps the scouts were overrun, provided their crew hadn't plotted for every contingency in advance. It's unlikely, but stranger things have happened. Every plan has its limits, even among the wisest.

In war, nothing is a guarantee. Nothing except blood, death, and loss.

Out of nowhere, a steady howling sound reverberates through the landscape. One might call it lilting. That is, until it covers additional ground, building to a shrill lament reminiscent of wind instruments.

Arguments cease. Throughout the battlements, deities tighten their grips, uncertain where to aim.

Once more, Andrew inspects the sky, his fingers locking on his bow. "Motifs," he seethes. "Fuck, I hate being right."

Drawing on their weapons, the crew follows his lead and appraises the vista. It's a radiant night. The glowing motes settle like dew upon the grass, the hyacinths sway, and firepits brim with flames.

"Might want to elaborate right fucking now, mate," Malice growls, his raspy tone liable to saw through metal.

As usual, Andrew isn't fazed by the threat. "What I said back in the valley, when that first group of shitheads attacked us," he reminds everyone. "In fiction, there are foreshadowing clues. The repetitive motifs might mean nothing."

"Or everything," Love adds, her wings bristling.

Her mate expands on that. "Legends, tokens, phrases. Details about the setting like legends, constellations, or... *fuck*."

As he cuts his gaze to Love, she finishes his thought. "Herons."

"Meaning?" Anger queries.

Lunar herons like the one that filtered through the trees in the sylvan valley during that initial skirmish. Sacred avians like the ones in a hallowed cove, located in the waterfall enclave. Fauna, which sometimes grow larger, such as the creature a detestable ruler and traitorous goddess sat astride as they abandoned this mountain.

Envy's head snaps toward the firmament. "Meaning they're not coming on foot."

Heads swerve. Weapons shift. Both of which land on a cluster of silhouettes getting bigger, crying louder. A throng of pearlescent wings swat the air, the motions reflecting on the lake's surface.

Herons. Thousands of them.

Riding atop the fauna sit five armored sovereigns and an army of Guides, including those who've come before them. Millennia worth of leaders and mentors.

The moment freezes. Of all the strategies Envy's crew had anticipated, this hadn't been one of them. This is the only contingency they neglected to see coming.

Apart from a certain goddess's betrayal.

Anger bellows, "Arms!" as the first arrow cleaves through the distance.

The projectile rents the air, a clean shot flying toward a head covered in sage green tresses. The target zooms in Harmony's direction, fast enough to snap her in half, even as she aims to dismantle it.

A length of quartz gets there before the strike, splintering the attack. Light detonates on impact, hurling brilliant threads into the atmosphere like a firework. The weapons cancel each other out, vanishing at the point of collision.

Harmony ducks beneath the illumination. Rising again, she glances at Wonder, who lowers her weapon, her quartz arrow reappearing in her quiver.

Weapons rain from the canopy. Gods and goddesses straddle the herons, some kneeling with impeccable balance, their crossbows and longbows spitting arrows.

The Fate Court wields five sets of archery. Green, gold, blue, white, and silver moonstone. Their capes flap around them, and their expressions display conviction over rancor. Leaders, protecting the ancient pantheon of their world, warring in the name of destiny.

Envy recalls a million declarations, denials, excuses, and affirmations the monarch made over the generations, a bunch of shit he grew up believing. Some true, others false. The mudslide of memories avalanches into his mind, suffocating him.

Anger's next commanding shout plows through Envy's consciousness. He raises his weapon alongside the immortals flanking him.

Merry. Love. Andrew. Wonder. Malice.

Despite their differences, and despite this unexpected means of attack, their features mirror one another for once. Fierce, stunning, focused. This is what they've been training for.

In one unified movement, they nock target and shoot. The projectiles harpoon into the air, blasting down a row of deities. There's no respite from the visual of his kin plummeting, those with whom Envy had once bantered.

Blood coats the air and drenches the terrain. Herons whiz overhead, then split and veer around the stargazer's circumference, slingshotting in and out of the fortification.

Then comes the army on foot. With the rebels' attention diverted toward the canopy, thousands of hollering deities spill across the landscape, flooding the jagged horizon of trees and boulders.

Anarchy ensues. Arrows forged of countless materials lance the hemisphere, half rocketing upward, the other half parachuting downward, all of them colliding. The universe ignites, bodies capsizing from above and below.

As the mounted herons dive, a cavalry of assailants leap into the fortification and land on the grass, where they trade blows with the rebels. Someone's back hits a wall, cracking into the stone. Envy's arrow spears a Guide off their mount.

Flares of light remind Envy of an evening when he listened to a goddess speak about mortal minefields and screaming soldiers.

You don't want to know that side of pain, Envy.

A fist swings in his periphery. Envy's forearm rams against the incoming set of knuckles, and his free hand slices his weapon across the archer's throat, cleaving deeply enough to loosen the enemy's head.

The ally to Envy's right screeches as a white moonstone weapon plows through her stomach, its owner—the reigning monarch in snowy lace—soaring past them on a lunar heron, her attention already fixed elsewhere.

Envy wants to aid the downed female, but Pride and Spite charge at him. He dives, tumbles, lurches upright, and targets them with two arrows at once.

Where the fuck are his comrades?

Frantic, Envy skewers his gaze across the perimeter. The world is a gritty, shaky montage, figments shifting in and out of the picture.

For a minute, he gets a clear window. Merry slides down an incline on her hip, a rapid succession of arrows hitting focal points that impair opponents' vision long enough for her allies to thwart them.

Anger provides backup from the building's highest tier. He alternates, raging against anyone who gets near Merry, then pitting his iron arrows at anyone who targets his crew.

Covered in gashes, Malice tramples a deity jetting for Anger. The two gods scowl at one another, then spin and fight back-to-back.

Love spreads her wings, the panels launching a dozen figures across the range. Then she rockets into the firmament, shaving a path around the herons while firing.

Wonder scales one of the trees, bounding with dexterity from branch to branch. Flitting between the leaves, she dodges arrows while nocking her bow.

No longer needed by Anger's side, Malice licks his bloody teeth and bungee-jumps sideways over the parapet's ledge, dumping himself into the fray, crashing into a group of deities. Lunging upright, the demon flashes a psychotic leer, his hickory bow pumping arrow after arrow. Lack of direction aside, he bulldozes everyone out of the way, leaving body parts and puddles of red in his wake.

Yet even for this god, Malice's bloodlust is too zealous, his velocity uncoordinated. Envy ducks an incoming arrow, then squints beyond the crenellations to follow the demon's trajectory, homing in on the cloaked ruler who shot Malice months ago in The Archives.

The more ground the devil covers, the more violent his speed. The court member doesn't see Malice pounding his way until the demon god slams into him with the force of a sledgehammer. They roll in a flurry of arms and limbs, firepits snuffing beneath their weight.

When the ruler identifies his adversary, the god's brows pitch in shock, then slant in defensiveness. Fuck. Malice has muscles and calculation on his side, but from the looks of it, he isn't about to use either trait wisely. He's too amped up on vengeance to think straight.

"Wonder!" Envy roars, but she's already got Malice in her line of sight. Jumping from the tree, she races across the ground—"Malice!"

she shrieks—and reaches the brawl as her mate cracks the ruler's face in two, crimson splashing Malice's countenance as he pounds in, and in, and in like a wrecking ball, his fury running on automatic.

The monarch bellows, his features reducing to pulp. Though, he's already done a number on the demon as well, both of them covered in gashes.

When Malice staples the male to the field, he steals one of the ruler's gold moonstone arrows and raises it, ready to plunge the tip into his victim's heart. Just like that same victim had once done to Malice.

Wonder scrambles to his side and seizes the demon's tattooed bicep, the words *Dearest Wayward Star* inked on his skin.

"Malice!" Wonder shouts. "No!"

No. Not like this.

At her frantic voice, Malice freezes while snarling down at the ruler. Envy is too far to confirm, but he imagines the devil fighting to leash himself. Eventually, Malice drops the arrow and drives his fist into the male's visage three more times, blood coating his knuckles, rendering the monarch unconscious and disfigured.

Wonder hauls Malice to his feet. The pair launches into one another, the demon seizing his mate by the ass and hauling her mouth to his, commencing in the bloodiest, most vicious kiss in history. Wonder claws through Malice's hair, the demon's red-soaked mouth prying her wide open, their tongues wrapping around one another.

Well, fuck. Not as graphic as Envy would like—for war reasons. However, he'll take whatever battle palate cleanser he can get, even if it lasts mere seconds.

The instant Malice and Wonder's lips detach, they race into the scrimmage while keeping close to one another.

Envy dices his gaze around, assessing the devastation. Piloted by deities, the fleet of herons veer around the stargazer, its telescope craning to the hemisphere. Flames erupt higher from the firepits, blazes slithering across the underbrush. The fortification walls crumble in numerous places, masonry toppling down the edifice.

Andrew and Love are a magnetic pair. The former shoots a rainstorm of arrows, his mortal prowess disorienting Love's opponents, enabling the goddess to dive from the sky, her wings mowing through a line of archers.

Although Love has regained the power to infuse her arrows with her root emotion, she curtails the magic. And Anger, who forsook his iron wings to the sun yet recouped the rest of his power, operates with the same restraint. Although he could defuse his assailants' tempers, he refuses to take such advantage. That would only mark him as a hypocrite.

As iron projectiles fly from his bow, the god dilutes his magic, relying instead on aim, velocity, and fatal arrowheads. He fights steadily, with wrathful concentration.

Until another deity targets Merry. At which point, hysteria pulls across Anger's profile. Roaring, he cuts his longbow toward the archer.

At the same instant, a heron lowers itself before the rage god, commanded by a feminine silhouette wielding a silver moonstone arrow—which punctures Anger's stomach.

39

Envy

Time stops. The scene plays out in slow motion.

Pain tears Anger's eyes wide open, the pupils fattening like blisters while crimson dribbles from the wound. Staring ahead in a daze, he sways in place, then his knees hit the foundation.

No. *No!*

Anger, nodding at Envy in encouragement during training. Anger, keeping their crew calm after Wonder's torture. Anger, believing none of them except Love knows he's afraid of storms. Anger, protecting Love's secret when she defied her rulers for Andrew. Anger, banished for valuing his peers more than his sovereigns. Anger, looking at Merry as if she's every star in the universe. Anger, rallying thousands of deities. Anger, offering a rare laugh when Envy teases him.

Anger. His friend.

With a mercenary snarl, Envy nocks his weapon. The twang of another string looses a second shot toward Anger, which Envy blocks. Then a third shot, stymied this time by a wooden arrow.

Malice's arrow. The demon god lands beside Envy, his bow poised and his breathing erratic. Behind the shredded sleeve of his leather jacket, his bicep tattoo contorts with every movement. Together, he and Envy arm themselves to obstruct additional strikes meant for Anger.

Nevertheless, all it has taken is one. Anger casts them a dazed, sideways glance. Then he topples over.

A roar tears from Envy's lungs. The sound catches Merry's attention, which alerts her to an incoming attack. Her arrow cuts through the archers' shot and blows the male off his haunches.

She beams at Envy, assuming his shout had been a warning. But then her eyes slide toward her mate's motionless form. The vibrant complexion leaches from her face, terror shredding from her lungs.

"Anger!" she wails.

Her irises catch the offending silver moonstone arrow before it vanishes from his stomach. Recognition dawns as Merry spots the ruling goddess, whose arms visibly shake, the monarch's features ashen from what she's done.

The kill had been intentional. Yet Anger was once The Court's most loyal and trusted warrior.

Composing herself, the monarch flies off. Then something happens that Envy hadn't thought possible. Fury suffuses Merry's features. Clear, bright, murderous fury.

The goddess tears ahead faster than her motorcycle back in the human realm, her speed bulldozing every opposing figure who gets in her path. Launching into the air, Merry spins and fires with each revolution, impaling the deities who try to stop her.

She lands, then surges toward the ruler, her teeth gnashing as she executes a dexterous trick, using the stargazer as a ramp to vault back into the air. Rotating mid-flight, she hammers into the ruler with a neon arrow, which punctures the female's abdomen, the gash spurting blood, the impact blowing the monarch off the heron. When she crashes into a wall, crimson trailing down the facade, several fighters gawk at the outcast who brought down a sovereign.

Merry pays them no heed. Landing on the parapet, she hurls herself across the divide and slams to the ground beside Anger.

Envy and Malice blitz toward the havoc, landing on all fours next to the pair, while Merry uses her tulle skirt to staunch the blood.

"Anger!" she cries, tears streaming down her face. "Anger, don't! Please don't! Please!"

"Merry," he coughs, blood drizzling from his mouth as he bolsters her cheeks. "Merry, shh."

"Here," Envy grits out, stripping his armor, peeling off his shirt, and using the garment to stanch Anger's wound. Remembering what Sorrow once told him about tending to injuries, he instructs Merry to keep it pressed in a certain way.

"But we n-need to move h-him," she chokes out. "If s-someone—"

"Don't worry," Malice growls. "I've got your backs."

"Malice," Anger coughs. "Show them who they banished."

All hell breaks loose across Malice's delighted face. "Like I need your permission, mate."

Anger chuckles weakly while Malice blasts off the ground like a carnivore and takes off. When a trinity of immortals besiege him, the demon god barrels around them, ducking repeatedly out of range. Each time he lunges upright, Malice changes expression—crossing his eyes, sticking out his tongue, baffling his adversaries to the point where they end up pounding into one another instead.

With a sneer, Malice jumps over them and makes a destructive beeline for any immortal bent on attacking Anger's huddle. At which point, it stops being a game for him.

Dismembered limbs fly. Voices screech in agony. Red seeps into the earth.

It's not pretty. But then, it never is when Malice is involved.

As Envy helps Merry prop Anger against a wall, the god's

blood-coated fingers grasp Envy's shoulder. "Bring her back to us," he heaves out, grimacing through the pain.

Merry nods, her skin streaked with dirt and tears. "Win her back."

What the fuck? Why in the flaming ashes of hell should Envy do that? What do these two—and the rest of this crew—understand that he doesn't?

Almighty Fates. But it's no use lying to himself. No matter how much he tries extinguishing Sorrow from his mind, she remains at the forefront with every nock of his arrows, with every target, with every corner that he turns.

Yes, he's been searching for her this whole time. No, he doesn't know if she's safe. And yes, it's killing him.

"Curse you," Envy sighs to Anger. "Curse you for looking this pretty while covered in blood. And curse you for taking advantage of this shit."

Anger offers him a slanted grin. "Call me a selfish myth."

That makes eight of them.

Grunting, Envy shoots to his feet. He jumps to the nearest crenellation and spots a heron free of its rider. The sight resurrects a memory of something he'd told Sorrow.

As a youth, I tried talking with them. Not that they understood me.

He shouldn't. He might insult the creatures.

Envy throws himself onto the avian's back. Teetering sideways, he grasps its thick hide and scrambles upright. On a whim, he speaks in low tones because perhaps this winged being had been part of that memory, living in the cove when a younger version of Envy attempted to communicate. Perhaps it remembers him.

Or he's being asinine. Either way, the raptor accepts his weight and flies where he asks it to take him. It speeds up, cutting around each tier of the fortification and slicing over the crest. The air whips through Envy's hair, his blood pumping as he scans the carnage.

One face is missing. Amid the red-soaked vista, he hunts for a glimpse of an ice arrow.

Pity and Kindness wrestle with Cruelty. Courage pits himself against Fear. Surprise crosses arrows with Shock.

A flash of sapphire archery confirms Nostalgia's presence. He must have recovered his weapons from the sea. Presently, he squares off with an archer whom Envy can't identify among the pandemonium.

Echo contends with Harmony, neither of them able to get the upper hand.

Siren's tresses glint as she coasts atop a heron, heading toward Envy. Her eyes dash across his face and waver. With a sad smile, she steers the avian from him, her departure a fracture to the chest, momentarily immobilizing him.

Either that, or the paralysis has to do with the projectile spiraling toward his sternum. Cursing, Envy tightens his thighs around the heron and nocks his bow.

An ice arrow intercepts the strike. It illuminates the cliffs, rendering every zenith inconsequential.

Envy's head snaps toward the source. Scanning the expanse of water, it occurs to him how the lake reflects this war, turning everything and everyone upside down. Including the slender figure in a shredded skirt.

His heart thrashes. Positioned on the opposite side of the water, Sorrow brandishes her weapon, anxiety distorting her lacerated face as she disables Grief.

Grief, who's not a rebel. Grief, who'd been about to annihilate Hope and Joy.

Sorrow has been fighting for a while now. But on which side?

While Grief rolls across the grass in an unconscious heap, Sorrow jogs backward with the same harrowed expression she'd worn while telling Envy about her memories of war. She could have massacred that deity, but she hadn't.

She doesn't want to extinguish anyone. However, she might make an exception. Envy realizes this as her eyes stumble across his.

Despite the leagues separating them, their gazes collide. The jolt produces a chemical reaction. Something toxic, flammable, spellbinding.

Now he knows what pain feels like.

And maybe one other emotion, a persistent feeling that's been shadowing him like a pest, creeping up on him since the day he first lost his mind and touched her. That infamous moment in time when he'd traced the goddess's sarcastic mouth, those lips painted a brooding charcoal gray to match her hair.

In the past, her chronic scowls, dreary clothes, and perpetual middle finger used to nauseate him.

But hidden beneath the tough exterior? The watery texture of hurt. The sweet-and-sour taste of rapture.

Those are the parts he wasn't supposed to discover. Those are the parts that came later.

Yet his transcendence hadn't begun until asking her a question. *What's your pleasure?*

In return, she had thrown one back at him. *What's your pain?*

On this bloodthirsty night, the answers chip away at his soul. Standing opposite from each other, they face off across a chasm.

Rivals to lovers.

Lovers to enemies.

At some point, the two of them chose different sides. He can't remember how it came to this, how they've ended up fighting for different endings.

With the battle raging across the summit, his fingers tighten around the bow. On reflex, she nocks her own weapon. As they aim at one another, he smirks mournfully. This was only ever going to go one way, with only one outcome.

That's fate.

So now he knows what pain feels like, every shift of its curves, every sigh of its breath, and every glint of its irises. It's a permanent emotion, like a stain he can't rub off.

What's a god to do when his match is the last person he can stand? He resists.

And what does that goddess do? Naturally, she makes him regret it.

Yet does Envy honestly regret everything that's happened? No.

By Fates, he wouldn't take back a single fucking moment with her. Even if it hurts like hell.

Their arms shake, and their bows waver, but neither of them fires.

I've had enough of war to last a thousand lives.

You don't want to know that side of pain, Envy.

Sorrow, weeping over the death of a soldier. Sorrow, caressing Wonder's hair during the goddess's torture. Sorrow, wearing a stitching needle like an emblem of suffering and healing.

Just like that, Envy knows. He knows why she abandoned him, what The Court said to coerce her, what they'd threatened to do.

A goddess rams into Sorrow from the sideline. They go down, arms and limbs flailing.

Envy's retinas blaze. Speeding atop the heron, he twirls his arrow and lets it fly.

Blood sprays into the air. In a nebula of light, the goddess jolts in place, then rolls off Sorrow in a puddle of crimson. Sprawled on the grass, his spitfire glances at him with tentative hope, then gains her feet to combat another deity, and another, and another.

She's fast, her skirt fanning around her as she spins. And now he sees.

Sorrow isn't attacking either side. She's on the offensive, defending herself against anyone who targets her. Mid-flip, she looses an ice projectile that flings the last deity backward.

Closer to the ground, Envy dives to the grass, dread pumping him with adrenaline. His weight slams into the earth, but a dozen leagues and the water separate them.

So many harsh truths. So much change.

That earlier conversation around the fire rekindles. The one about a myth.

The stars will shine their brightest when a deity asks for the truth. But a deity will only receive the truth when they're ready to hear the answer. And that immortal will only be ready to hear the answer if they're ready to change.

What truth? What answer? What fucking change?

As questions crowd his mind, he comprehends. Catching sight of one another, they both do. Since this fight began, they've known.

Myths, truths, changes. Legends, lust, love.

Envy meets Sorrow's gaze and calls out to her. Through The Stars, he summons all of their friends.

Are you ready for the truth?

Because he is. He's so damn ready. But he needs them to be as well.

Envy senses the collective pause. Twisting, he locates the crew, positioned at various intervals. As they find his gaze, realization dawns.

But how do they tell The Stars they're ready? And how will The Stars answer?

There's only one way to find out. When the crew inclines their heads, Envy veers back to Sorrow, who nods. Together, they make a choice.

They stop shooting. Eight sets of weapons lower. As the battle rages, their crew waits.

Moments later, the herons slow, their wings agitating in place. As fauna of this land, naturally they sense it first.

Dumping their riders to the ground, the raptors scatter. As the hemisphere rattles like pebbles, every god and goddess stalls.

Trepidation crawls up Envy's spine. Perhaps they've misjudged or enacted this myth in the wrong way.

From a distance, Malice's voice cuts through. "The fuck…?" the demon god draws out while tugging Wonder close and slowly retreating backward with her.

Andrew is less subtle. And much more deafening. "Oh shiiiiit!" the man shouts, hauling his exquisitely sculpted ass toward the stargazer fortress. Snatching Love's hand on the way, he yanks the baffled goddess with him while bellowing at everyone, "Run, you motherfuckers! Run-like-fuck-get-out-of-range-the-stars-are-answering!"

Very well. This isn't the response Envy expected. Staying their weapons, all combatants register the constellations dropping like bombs from above.

Just like that, the world changes shape.

Just like that, The Stars fall.

40

Sorrow

The sky collapses. As the constellations break apart, they plummet like comets. Great globes of burning light arc from the canopy, spearing the universe in white blasts. Thousands of heads tilt, a sea of faces awestricken by the spectacle.

Sorrow follows the celestials' trajectory. Memories string together, freezing her in place.

Grenades whistle above mortal soldiers. Mine fields detonate with smoke. Bodies lay tangled in barbed wire.

Except this isn't the human realm. These aren't grenades. And they don't whistle.

The stars sizzle, the crackles growing louder as they cannon toward the cliffs. Though both are almighty, celestials in The Dark Fates are infinitely smaller than those of the human realm. However, the former possesses a greater radiance.

The tumult is mesmerizing and so magnificent, it takes her seconds to remember. Anything that falls will eventually land.

With the first crash, the ground ruptures. The single star punches the earth, throwing lambent shards across the summit. Embers sizzle, roasting whatever it touches, blistering or torching deities who fail to escape.

The impact ejects Sorrow off her feet. She soars thirty feet and hits the grass with a cry. Her body slams into the ground, molars jostling in her skull.

Batting hair out of her face, she glimpses an incoming meteor shower. The constellations rain down, nosediving from the firmament. Deities roll across the range while others leap sideways, dodging the maelstrom. Some deities tumble over the grass, and others sprint to evade the turbulence.

Celestials spear through the air, drive their ancient fists into the cliffs, and splinter into fragments. Every descent quakes the landscape. Sorrow struggles and fails to rise, then tosses her head this way and that, scanning the panorama.

Where is Envy? Where are her friends? What about Echo and Siren?

Sorrow crawls across the blood-stained grass, scurrying past corpses leaking crimson or baked to a crisp by the Stars. Visibility wanes, flashes of light distorting her vision. Against the glare, she can't tell if the fortification still stands or if it's been blown to smithereens.

Yelling everywhere. So much yelling.

Sorrow pats her vacant chest. She'd lost a grip on her weapons. The longbow, quiver, and arrows lay scattered across the earth like detritus. Scrambling on all fours, she reaches for her bow, then launches backward from the crash of a nearby star.

Ramming onto her back, her bones rattle. She skids across the dirt, pain tearing the flesh of her arm, spots bursting behind her eyelids.

A distant voice bellows... her name. The source is calling her name.

Dazed, Sorrow flops over. She shakes the disorientation from her mind, anxiety streaking through her veins.

Someone is roaring for her. Someone is terrified for her.

That someone is a male.

The bluff vibrates, rippling as Sorrow hauls herself to a sitting position. Again, she scours the vista. This time, she scours through the divide, her gaze plowing into a set of panicked eyes.

There he is, alone. The Stars have thrust him to the ground, where he teeters upright on his knees, his hair a black banner whipping in the wind, his chest bare and littered with contusions.

He's alive. He's alive and in one piece.

Envy's haggard features lock with hers, relief wiping clear the remnant signs of fright. Sorrow understands that relief, which floods her as well.

That, and another emotion. One of numerous dimensions, forged by a million sights, sounds, tastes, scents, and textures. It's the same emotion reflected in his pupils, blessedly accessible from her vantage point. Moreover, it's tangible enough to blot out the chaos.

Balanced on their haunches, they stare at each other. Just like that, she knows what this is. And he must know, because his visage blanches.

This is what the legend spoke of. This is the myth's truth. This is imperfect, sentimental, vulnerable, empowering.

This is love.

The ruler's earlier words return to Sorrow. *Then convince us.*

Fine, because she's not about to sit on her ass and let the celestials flatten her to a pulp or incinerate her flesh. Not when there's so much to live for.

Lights spark around Sorrow and Envy like deadly firecrackers, the onslaught of constellations flaring. They swap gazes, and when he gives her a repentant grin, she mirrors it with a lopsided one of her own.

They run.

Barreling toward each other, they pump their arms. Oxygen saws through her lungs, and pain throbs in her joints, but she doesn't care.

Her boots pound across the summit, bounding to the left, then jetting to the right as she sidesteps falling debris. Although the mountain rattles off its hinges, she keeps steady on her feet, desperate to grab him, to be held.

The lake is the final boundary, its surface reflecting a universe of falling stars. Sorrow and Envy dive. They plunge, come up for air, and crank their limbs.

They swim, and swim, and swim. Over the last few leagues, the water gets shallower rather than deeper. Submerged only to their waists, they're able to stand upright. Drenched, they stagger across the final stretch.

"Envy!" she screams.

"Sorrow!" he shouts back.

"I'm sorry. I'm so sorry!"

"I know. I'm sorry too—"

"I didn't mean it. I would never hurt—"

"Fuck it all, I know!"

"I love you!" Sorrow cries.

That, Envy hadn't known. He really hadn't because he stumbles, slipping on the words and almost going down like a redwood tree.

Getting a second wind, Envy charges. In the lake's center, they collide like asteroids. Sorrow flings herself at his naked torso, and he catches her with a growl, his arms crushing the nymph against him. Throwing their weight into each other, they're a clinging, trembling mess.

Celestials shower around them, fracturing the cliffs and hammering the water. This could be it. Exposed like this, they're clear targets.

But at least they've made one choice. At least they've chosen *this* before it was too late.

Wrenching back, Envy hisses. Then he grabs the back of Sorrow's head and slams his mouth to hers. A cry leaps from her throat, her lips clutching his own, her fingers burying into his mane, drawing him down on her. His tongue spears past the cleft of her mouth, tasting and stroking, every flex wrought with terror and relief.

The world blurs. The strength of Envy's mouth drowns out every pulsating light and ear-splitting noise. While the earth shakes, they hurl themselves into the kiss, tongues fusing, lips rocking together.

Prying himself away, Envy grits against her lips. "It's always been you," he vows, his baritone louder than the cacophony around them. Grasping her face, he shakes his head, ferocity setting fire to his words. "I would race into a fucking volcano for you."

Sorrow lets out a dry sob. "You too."

Bowing their heads into one another, they hold tight. And moments later, more sets of arms sling around them, expanding the circle.

Love. Andrew.

Anger. Merry.

Wonder. Malice.

Tears prickle Sorrow's eyes. As one, their crew forms a sphere of burning light—their own star. They wait, and wait, and wait.

The quaking ceases. The clamor quiets.

And The Stars stop falling.

41

Envy

Nothing but dead silence. They might as well be submerged in an abyss, as if the world has drowned.

As a body shuffles in his arms, Envy stares down at the face peeking from behind a curtain of gray hair. Sorrow blinks, her bottomless pupils reflecting his own. When he strokes her cheek, she nuzzles into him, her breath stirring against the pulse in his throat.

The wind brushes through stalks of grass. Blood and water drench the fabric of his trousers.

Envy lifts his head. Sorrow follows suit, as does the crew. Cavities glazed in stardust pothole the summit, white flames slapping the air. Crimson puddles and charred corpses lay strewn amid the wasteland.

The herons return, cautiously hovering above the stargazer. The great monument, which stands untouched beneath the hemisphere.

Footfalls approach. Detangling themselves, the crew breaks away to inspect the scene fully, their circle the focal point of every rapt gaze on this cliff, including the five injured rulers who stand nearby. Filing along the water's edge, a bleeding crowd of deities marvel at the scene:

a small pack of rebels who held tight under a bombing of stars.

Instead of stoic or regal, the monarchs blink in a daze. Slowly, the hint of a smile draws across the iridescent goddess's mouth, her torn gown flapping in the wind like a demolished solar system.

Envy's gaze travels from sovereigns, to mentors, to archers. The ones who have survived, as well as those who've fallen, their lifeless forms scattered throughout the wreckage. Everyone stares, stricken and awed by the aftermath, though the latter is a strange reaction for what just happened.

Or perhaps it isn't.

If two deities choose love over lust, they'll become a force of influence, along with those closest to them.

Envy glimpses Sorrow's countenance, his heart cinching. He can only describe this sensation as endless, without shapes or borders. It's as calm as the sea, yet as fierce as rushing rapids.

A force of influence. A fucking celestial riddle.

After his theft of her arrow, it shouldn't be possible. Yet in Sorrow's glowing features, the opposite becomes true. Beneath this violent sky, they chose love over lust, enacting a legend that canceled out any other clauses or rules, a possibility they never thought to consider.

That's not all. Envy studies his friends.

Love's mischievous nature. Andrew's tenaciousness and creativity.

The moral strength of Anger, whose olive complexion has blanched from the wound soaking Envy's shirt. The stubborn bastard had risked his blood-clotted gash, just to make it out here.

The unapologetic enthusiasm of Merry, with her theatrical spirit and dazzling eyes.

The curious nature of Wonder. The diabolical intellect and un-hinged devotion of Malice.

Strung together like this, the experience is forged of every emotion Envy has ever known. Because this is what it means to belong to others.

We're all family.

That's what Merry had said. That's what they are.

They're messy. They didn't ask to be thrown together, and they've sometimes made the worst of it, but they've usually made the best of it. They've done brutal things to each other. They've done spectacular things to each other. They've behaved conditionally and unconditionally. They're not perfect, but they're still here, protecting one another.

That's love.

At the heart of The Dark Fates, this is love in its many facets. The bond of friendship, family, and passion. Perhaps it's the final key, with Envy and Sorrow choosing love over lust, grabbing one another under a deadly sky rather than staying apart.

Their destiny. Their decision.

Perhaps it kindled an evolution, with their friends joining in. Each of them, foolish and selfish and vicious. Each of them, flawed by their mistakes. Each of them, empowered by their victories. Each of them, touched, torn, tempted, and transcended.

All of them, no better or worse than humans. All of them, tied to mortality.

This is what they had to do. Unite beneath the falling stars, brave the chaos as one, proving that love is power. It's magic unto itself, which moves realms and conquers wars.

That's survival.

And maybe this is what it takes to inspire, to understand there is no hierarchy between deities and humans. Creating an equilibrium isn't about redefining these things, nor about finding a middle ground between separate entities.

There is no middle ground. They're not separate at all.

To strike a balance is to understand that fate and free will are one power. Recognizing and embracing this fact is the key.

Disarmed, the rulers wade through the lake, their gowns and cloaks trailing moonlit puddles behind them. Nodding with Envy's group, who spread out to admit them into the circle, the ring broadens. All the while, Envy keeps Sorrow close, strapping his arms around her midriff.

For some reason, the iridescent goddess regards Sorrow with a satisfied twinkle.

"Convinced yet?" Sorrow asks.

The female inclines her head. "I think we're about to be."

The constellations return to the sky, having spoken their truth. It's time for their subjects to do the same. Every soul bears the hardship of gathering the fallen and setting the bodies within beams of starlight, where the souls fade peacefully. Some fighters weep for their lost kin, others can't muster a sound. Many deities take it in stride, while some don't.

After an hour of mournful silence, the throng retires for a period of recovery and reflection. Whatever needs to be said deserves time.

Plus, Anger can barely stand any longer.

Envy and Sorrow trade a glance. After the deadly night they've had, he wants nothing more than to staple the goddess to his side for eternity, on the off-chance residual tensions remain among The Dark Gods. However, ordering Sorrow never to leave his sight again will only backfire. If she needs her space, that's her choice. It's what they fought for, after all. And while she'll never be safe enough for his liking, this female also isn't helpless.

After Sorrow flies off with her Guide on one of the herons, Envy engages in a stream of farewells. His friends return to the Astral Sea, he reunites with Siren, then embarks on his own trip home, where he collapses in bed. What follows is the longest sleep in his life, fleeting moments of wakefulness filled with thoughts of a jaded mouth sipping currant nectar.

When their people have refreshed themselves, they return to the site of combat and the place where deities always come into being. They congregate around the stargazer, crowding the telescope's dais. Envy has donned charcoal trousers, a loose ivory shirt, and an ankle-length coat. Though having an impeccable wardrobe fails to restore his confidence, his heart hammering at the prospect of seeing Sorrow.

Time crawls by slower than a slug. Any second, and Envy will start pacing like a beast, which shall wrinkle his ensemble.

The instant she appears on the threshold, their eyes lock. Envy's flesh does something strange. It mirrors the familiar stirrings of heat, pressure building, blood rushing to the surface. By now, Andrew, Anger, and Malice have confirmed this theory.

Likewise, a flush consumes Sorrow's complexion. Their feet carry them across the distance until they meet on the platform, where he struggles to contain himself. A hundred juvenile endearments sit on his tongue, none of them worthy.

Anyway, it's not the right time to make a fool of himself. They have other matters to address.

The Court summons every child, since youths weren't allowed to participate in the fighting. This includes that nameless moppet with the dark curls, who materializes beside Siren and Echo. The former's cramped face exhibits frustration, but the peeved expression dwindles when he spots Envy and Sorrow.

Envy nods. By comparison, Sorrow and the moppet wave at one another.

Envy finds his voice and leans over to murmur, "You've gained an admirer."

"What can I say?" Sorrow whispers back while staring at the crowd. "Faith and I have the same taste in makeup."

"His name is Faith?" Envy feigns insult. "I'm jealous. He told you but not me?"

Perhaps it's too soon for teasing. His attempt falls flat, because Sorrow gives a noncommittal shrug. Although she stands beside him, their crew aligning with The Court, a slow drip of doubt leaks in. What happened on the battleground might have been temporary. This period of rest might have given her second thoughts.

And where the fuck do they go from here?

Siren catches his eye and gives him a dry look, warning Envy not to get ahead of himself or jump to conclusions. One thing at a time.

Anger's gash is slower than usual to heal, but the wound has closed. Let no one call the obstinate god feeble. The opportunity for rest has done him well, restoring his complexion and replenishing his energy to attend this meeting. He shuffles forward, bolstered by Merry and Malice.

The iridescent goddess addresses the congregation. To this day, it astounds Envy that none of their subjects can rightly pronounce the five sovereigns' names, so ancient are their chosen monikers. They are simply identified as The Court.

"In the lifetime of an immortal," the ruler begins, "this quarrel between celestials and rebels has been ephemeral. Yet for many of us, it feels as though it has lasted an age." She spreads her arms. "Perhaps it has. This conflict might have ignited long ago, since our very inception. It is a culmination of our destinies, as well as our choices. Yet finally, all sides have spoken, as have The Stars."

Anger straightens as best as he can. "This is the route we needed to take, born of circumstance and action."

"Fate and free will are matched," Love says. "Neither can exist without the other."

"Neither is faultless," Merry campaigns, lacing her free hand with Love's.

"Both are flawed," Andrew adds, claiming Love's other hand.

"But we're stronger for it," Wonder professes.

One by one, eight rebels clasp palms with five rulers.

"At last, we have reached the brink of renewal," the iridescent ruler calls out. "To see a disparate band of immortals prove that love not only exists among our people, as it does among humans, but that it empowers us. Then we must conclude deities and mortals are equal."

"We have faults and strengths, sentiments and resilience," Sorrow ventures. "And we're still standing."

"And still pretty," Envy says with a half-smirk, inciting somber mirth from the crowd. "Humanity will endure without our intervention."

"A mortal man once taught me not to underestimate his kind," Love confides, smiling at Andrew. "If left to its own devices, the human realm won't fall apart any less than ours will. If we are equal, we forfeit the magic of our bows, the magic of control, in favor of a new pantheon."

"One that inspires instead of controls," Anger finishes.

More talking, more speeches, more debates. What will this new mythology be? If fate and free will are not separate but the same, and if embracing that fact is the key to a balance, how must deities treat their powers? How do they wield human emotions without actually controlling humans? Ultimately, how will that preserve the life cycle of both humanity and The Dark Fates?

Envy recalls one of his talks with Sorrow in the cavern.

To begin, I'd have to declare what it means to be a deity in the first place.

Maybe it's a blessing. The clincher is, we've misinterpreted what that blessing entails. It could be about embodying magic instead of forcing it on others. Maybe we need to wield that blessing from a different angle.

Inspired by those words, Envy makes a suggestion. "I know one goddess with the answer."

Sorrow blinks as he turns his attention on her, then the same memory comes rushing back, a small grin spreading across her lips. "A blessing."

The same magic from another angle. A new way to bond with humanity instead of commanding it. Heads bank left and right, intrigued by the notion.

Merry hops in place. "Gracious, how divine. A dedication."

"A ritual," Anger interprets.

Murmurs amplify as deities entertain the possibilities. They were never given a choice of which root emotions to represent. If they still can't determine which to wield—for that can't be altered, even by The Stars—deities can at least decide *how* to wield them.

Instead of forcing emotions into mortals, what if each strike of an arrow serves as a blessing? A benediction that grants humans the ability to feel those emotions, to embrace the malevolent ones and endure the harsh ones.

Just a blessing. How every mortal chooses to absorb and act on their emotions throughout life... well, it's up to the individual.

As such, deities must retrain their bows. For ages, they've learned the varying intensities of a single strike. If immortals can imbue a minimal amount into their archery, it will be so faint as to yield a blessing rather than a command.

They'll require more practice to master this without fail. But that's fine. None of them are going anywhere.

The attendants weave their fingers together and use the stargazer to beseech the celestials. Together, they ask for approval. In response, the constellations shimmer and toll like bells.

Like an old tale. Like a myth.

Afterward, the room fills with a renewed sense of honor. There's much to consider, even more to learn. But it's a start.

The throng disperses, gods and goddesses departing to their homes throughout The Dark Fates and the mortal realm. The Court and Envy's crew stay behind to address another decision. This new beginning calls for an officiation, in the form of a vow.

As to which kind, they debate. Everybody participates, contributing possibilities.

Actually, not everybody. A crucial detail occurs to the assembly. Namely that Malice has been quiet this entire time.

The group casts the demon god a skeptical glance. To which, he runs his thumb across his lower lip. Uh-oh.

Envy sighs. "I know my face is distracting, but would you care to focus and share the inner workings of your brain with the rest of this clan?"

Malice lifts a taloned finger. "On one condition—what?" he asks when everyone groans. "So suspiciously suspicious. I haven't said anything yet. What the fuck do you take me for? A devil?"

"Malice needs paper," Wonder translates, reading her soulmate's expression. "He's wearing his studious face."

"You know me well, Wildflower."

"Then say it, Demon."

"For a start, anyone have a spare quill and a blank sheet of paper?"

It would be effortless to conjure. However, Andrew presents the notebook and pen he'd brought from the mortal realm. Carefully, he rips out the pages filled with his handwriting, tearing them from the spine's crease and then handing over the binder. "Will these do?"

Malice accepts the notebook. "You sure?"

"You carried it for me most of the time. I owe you."

"I like being owed things." The demon angles his wicked features toward Wonder. "Sooooo how many stars exist in the sky? How many legends came from them? And how many were stored in The Archives?"

She contemplates. "That number doesn't exist, my love."

"That makes for a shitload of potential tales. Think there's any wiggle room left?"

"To what end?" the iridescent ruler inquires.

"Don't leave out the good parts," Envy requests.

A grin slides across Malice's face. "I've got an idea."

No one rests until they have a draft. Malice and Wonder are experts in this area, so they oversee the collaboration and appoint Andrew as their partner, the trio taking turns transcribing the dictation.

Finished, they read it aloud. The abstract is rough, and it will take time to modify the contents, but that's one luxury they have in abundance. When they're done, it's going to be the longest mythical word count ever penned.

Only one choice remains. Where to store this book?

Malice jabs his thumb at Wonder. "Ask my favorite goddess. She might have a solution."

Wonder taps the pen against her mouth, concealing a grin. "You might be right."

After consenting to her proposition, The Court retires to the Palace of Starlight. Meanwhile, eight figures remain, tasked with safeguarding the notebook. They say nothing more tonight, bidding one another farewell. They'll have a job ahead of them revising the draft, then another job restoring a certain former landmark.

Wonder and Malice can't wait for that. Envy's pretty certain they'll prove to be strict generals.

Out on the parapet, Love and Andrew mount a heron and soar to her house. The same goes for Anger and Merry.

Sorrow hesitates beside Envy, one of her boot heels grinding into the floor. "So, um. Enjoy sailing to the enclave."

"What makes you think I'm not going to my vacation home?" Envy quips.

"Because I've spent three days with you. I know your tastes."

His gaze clings to hers. "That, you do."

Silence stretches between them, but for the nearby lapping of water. Eventually, Sorrow clears her throat. "Well, then. Goodnight."

Envy hooks a strand of hair behind her ear. "Sweet dreams."

She walks backward while staring at him, then hitches a ride with one of the winged creatures. Envy watches her shrink inside a full moon. Doubtless, she'll enjoy returning to her house on stilts and sleeping in fleece blankets.

Shoving his hands into his pockets, Envy heads toward the fortress's threshold, then stops. A runty silhouette perches on the lowermost rampart, the figure's limbs swinging over the side. Sorrow wouldn't have gone so quickly if she'd known he was here.

Malice and Wonder are about to depart when Envy asks if he can keep the book for a while. After Malice threatens to castrate Envy if anything happens to the tome, the couple leaves.

When they've vanished on a lunar heron, Envy changes direction and settles next to the child called Faith, who pouts at the moonlit cliff range. His doleful expression contrasts with the buoyant gloss of his eyelids. Also, he doesn't react to Envy's presence.

Together, they regard the panorama.

"What has you in such a pissy mood?" Envy jokes, elbowing the moppet.

"I'm a good fighter," Faith mumbles.

Ah. That's what's bothering him. He's crestfallen about being left out of the carnage. If Sorrow were here, she'd knock some sense into this runt.

"And whose side would you have chosen?" Envy asks.

"Neither," the mini god replies. "I would have fought to stop all of you."

"I know someone who'd agree with that course of action. On that note, I like to think rebuilding is a better use of time than bloodshed. Interested in helping us resurrect The Hollow Chamber?"

It had been Wonder's idea to store the book in The Archives, the great library of their realm. It's a proper location to place this brand-new legend of their own making.

Meanwhile, the library's restricted section currently lies in ruin, following that conflict between Wonder, Malice, and their rulers. With peace on the horizon, they've agreed to rebuild The Hollow Chamber and its forbidden vault.

"I'll tell you what." Envy produces the tome and offers it to Faith. "Mind taking a look at this for us? We could use your feedback."

The child accepts the book and swings his gaze toward Envy. "Why me?"

"Because I like your name more than mine." Ruffling the god's hair, Envy stands and smooths out his ankle-length coat. "Though, I still dress better."

Faith compresses his lips, withholding a snicker. "Then go impress someone who actually gives a shit." To illustrate, he flits his gaze toward the sky, to where Sorrow had disappeared.

Point taken. Envy throws back his head and laughs.

42

Sorrow

Unable to sleep, she flings aside the fleece blanket and stalks out of the house. At the pier's edge, the sea engulfs the stilts of her home. Sea water trembles, its surface reflecting planets and moons. Lanterns float across the depths, each one brimming with flames.

Sorrow inhales the pure aroma of starlight. She's never noticed the distinction before, but Andrew was right about the air smelling differ-ent in The Dark Fates.

A steady breeze whips Sorrow's skirt around her legs, the shredded material sweeping over her bare toes. She crosses her arms and rubs her pebbled flesh, although she still has no clue what cold feels like.

Maybe the sensation is due to loneliness. She's well-versed in that.

Daytime constellations will soon replace the nighttime ones, and the sky will brighten to lapis blue. Sorrow groans, her battle-worn mus-cles aching. Yet that isn't what's keeping her awake. For thousands of years, she's been fine living alone, rising from slumber without some-one beside her.

Is home a dwelling, a landscape, or a realm? Is it eight figures who've become family?

Or is it a person?

Strolling along the boardwalk fails to alleviate her insomnia. To make matters worse, she takes the wrong path and ends up passing Love's home, then Anger's residence, then Wonder's dwelling. Though they should be wiped out, Sorrow detects the subtle but rapturous sounds drifting through the windows of each structure. Allegedly, her crew has been celebrating.

Love and Andrew's chuckles radiate with a post-sex afterglow, the goddess's bed squeaking in what can only be the echoes of play. Likely, they're on the verge of chasing one another naked through the house.

The noises coming from Anger and Merry's love shack harmonize like a song. The god's tempestuous growl defies his injury, while his soulmate's rhythmic cries indicate her pussy's on the receiving end of Anger's tongue.

And Fates, forget Wonder and Malice. Based on the thrashing sheets, the husky taunts coming from Malice, and the panting moans from Wonder, they're competing for who can dominate whom, which means they'll be going at it for a while.

Actually, it all sounds pretty hot.

Sorrow can't take it. The only place she thinks to go is also the only place she wants to be. But since it's not exactly around the corner, she flaps her arms at the next lunar heron that passes by, humbled when the raptor obliges. Manifesting would be faster, but taking longer buys Sorrow time to get her pulse under control. Besides, she likes the view from above.

Sheepish, she expresses gratitude before hopping on the avian's back. When the creature deposits Sorrow at her destination, she steps inside a vacant cavern, ingesting the fragrances of dark rum and amber.

That's when she feels it. The peace, the belonging, and the memories of three isolated days with the last person she'd ever wanted to be stuck with.

Two options. The guest hollow he set up for her, with fleece bedding, a collection of lamps, and that sensual robe, which had made him drop a fluted glass.

Or another room entirely.

Sorrow slips into his empty chamber. Feeling greedy, she crawls into the sheets, linen enveloping her body as she dissolves into blackness. And when she stirs with a grumble, hazy afternoon stars leak through the chasm.

Also, she's not alone anymore. The mattress sinks beneath a muscled weight, which curls like a shield around her. One arm has slid around Sorrow's middle, tucking her spine against his chest, while the other rests above her hair, fingers brushing through the roots.

His shirt sleeves are jammed up his forearms, exposing light brown flesh that clashes with her chalky skin. His knees bend into the backs of her own, and a pair of full lips brushes her temple. She knows the contours of his frame, the pacing of his breathing, and the shifts of his clothes.

Tears spring to her eyes. Maybe she has the same effect, because when he speaks, his tone is haggard. "Have I ever told you I'm a fan of shredded skirts? They're right up there with loafers and ascots."

Sorrow half-chuckles, half-sniffles. "Have I ever told you that you're full of shit?"

Envy's chest rumbles. "That's the nymph I know and worship."

"Who said I was your nymph?"

"You did," he murmurs, that erotic voice oozing affection. "You did in the middle of a star shower, unless my ears were deceiving me."

Those words. Those three pivotal words she shouted beneath the siege.

He's right about that, but Sorrow had been unsure what to expect afterward, or whether they would broach the subject. They've chosen this, fulfilled the legend. So why is it terrifying to acknowledge?

Envy swallows, his whisper trailing down her earlobe. "How long have you known?"

"I think it happened when you reminded me that I know how to feel a hug," she confides.

For such a large physique, the god shudders like fletching. "Fuck, Sorrow. All you had to do was say so."

"When was I supposed to do that? Anyway, what would you have said back?"

"I would have said three fucking millennia worth of things."

The long-suppressed words crack out of him. He cannot mean...

But then she remembers another telling fact. "Why three millennia instead of only three days?"

Contrite, Envy stalls, his fingers arrested in her hair. "Come now, my nymph. You're a perceptive spitfire, if there ever was one. Don't you know?" He tugs her around, those sweltering eyes consuming her features like a life force. "Don't you know that you're every emotion I've ever felt?"

43

Sorrow

Every emotion he's ever felt. By Fates, she hadn't known that. How was she supposed to?

But yes, Sorrow understands. The same tempest has been brewing inside her for just as long.

With her heart stuffed in her mouth, Sorrow fists his collar and gives a gingerly shake. "Dammit, Envy. I don't know whether to slap you for holding back all these years or kick myself for doing the same thing."

"Never harm this body." He drags his fingers across her hip, the corner of his lips ticking up. "Though, feel free to smack me around whenever you'd like. Only make sure I'm tied down."

Laughter slips from her tongue. "Insufferable god."

"Not done yet." He drops his forehead against hers, the digits of his left hand climbing into her scalp. "I've been in love with you since The Dark Fates, when we first parted ways and traveled into the mortal world. I asked if you'd miss me, and you told me to get lost. I loved you then. I love you now. I love your scowls, your sarcasm, and the sensitive nature you keep hidden from everyone. I love your desire to heal others and your courage in the face of pain."

His free fingers undo the buttons of her vest. "I love your witchy wardrobe and the stars dusting your face."

The garment slides from her shoulders, his touch coasting down her breasts, the nipples puckering under his palms. "I love your taste for comfort food."

Envy licks the seam of her mouth, prompting a mewl from her throat. "I love that you hide as much as you reveal." He leans over Sorrow, all that magnificent weight burrowing her into the bed. His fingers slip beneath the skirt, skim up her thigh, and nudge them to spread.

"I love that you don't care what others think about you, but you care how they feel," Envy pants, his pupils exploding as he reaches the intimate patch of hair shrouding her cunt.

When his thumb presses into the sensitive crest of her clit, Sorrow arches into him, her eyes fluttering to stay open. A delicious haze fogs her mind. Wetness seeps out of her pussy and coats his hand, both of them groaning.

He toys with the pleats, coaxing them open. Flexing his fingers, he pries her apart and pistons two digits into Sorrow, the rhythmic pump splaying her wider.

"I loved you even when I couldn't stand you," he rasps, gazing down. "I loved you when I couldn't fucking stay away from you. I loved you when I was jealous of you. I loved you when you humiliated me in front of a crowd, all those years ago on a target range."

His mane hangs around his face, and his lips quirk as they blaze a trail across her body. "I loved you when you compromised my innocence."

On a teary chuckle, Sorrow pitches her knees high. She writhes across the bed, her pussy lurching upward to meet the depths of his fingers, the languid motions drenching her, so that she leaks down to his knuckles.

Ravenous, Envy watches her. "I'm still in love with you." He withdraws from Sorrow's crease and rolls on top of her. As her thighs clamp around his hips, his gaze pins her to the bed. "I plan to fall in love with you every day, for the rest of my infernal life."

"Then let me love you back," Sorrow whispers, undoing the buttons of his shirt, exposing a smooth torso and a rapid pulse at his throat.

Envy's heart rams against her own. He shakes his head in feverish misery and growls, "I'd be fucking honored."

His mouth collides with hers, their lips rushing against one another. At the contact, an outbreak of tremors builds, throbbing deep within her. It's a lit fuse, an aching pulse of adrenaline.

As their mouths fold and rock, Sorrow's tongue dashes against his, each stroke percolating her veins. The craving escalates until they're peeling her vest and skirt, then chucking his shirt aside and kicking his trousers to the ground.

In between these ministrations, they surge into another raving kiss. Envy's tongue rides her own, drawing a series of hoarse whimpers from Sorrow. Their arms and limbs hook together, his pecs sweeping over her taut breasts, the nipples budding for his mouth.

Sorrow cries out when he purses his lips and sucks with force, stars bursting behind her eyes. As she mumbles incomprehensible words, he answers with additional flicks of his tongue, teasing the stud, tormenting her to the brink before taking the other breast.

"I've wanted you my whole life," he hums against the peak. "I still want more of you, but not for what I can take. I want you moaning selfishly, indulgently. I want the painful, pleasurable sound of you coming for no one but yourself."

Ah, ah, ah. As much as Sorrow likes what she hears, the words trigger a different priority.

In one illicit move, she rolls out of his arms, snatches her ice arrow off the floor, then pivots back the way she came. With a grunt, Sorrow swings a leg across his lap, springs upright, and slams her arrow shaft into his wrists. Envy's arms whip backward, the line of her weapon pinning him to the wall overhead.

A half-groan, half-purr lurches from Envy's tongue. His pupils alight with mischief as Sorrow sits astride his waist, her split thighs framing the carved V of his hips. Her body hunches over him, and the high stem of his cock juts high, the ruddy flesh solid and thick.

Leaning over, Sorrow rakes her lips over his. "Together."

Then his eyes soften, hooding with warmth "Together."

And that same balmy temperature floods Sorrow to the core. That he'd find pleasure strictly through her own climax is paramount enough. This god, who has never fucked anyone without aiming to benefit himself.

Until Sorrow.

Her spirit bursts into flames, bright and powerful. She can come for herself any time, hardly needing this deity for that. But they've achieved something greater, stronger, deeper. This is bonding, mating, sharing.

Her desire is his desire. Her fear is his fear. Her torment is his torment. Her victories are his victories.

There is nothing in between. Not anymore.

Sorrow brushes her mouth along his once more, the contact wringing a devoted sound from Envy. When she peeks, his eyes have clenched shut, brows crinkling in a gentle anguish. His muscles loosen, yielding under her, taking and giving.

The disarming sight pulls fresh tears to the surface, only these ones are new. They're from happiness.

"Goddess," he whispers hoarsely.

Sighing, she pecks his lips, tasting the endearment. "I prefer nymph."

Despite their overcome state, a masculine chuckle rumbles from his throat. But then it shudders into a low hiss as Sorrow skates her free fingertips over the flushed head of his crown. Grinding his molars, the god arches into her touch, his eyes flipping over to watch her through blackened pupils.

While nailing his wrists to the wall, she feathers her opposite digits up and down his length, shaping its width, outlining the weight of his sac, then climbing higher. With dedicated ministrations, Sorrow drifts across the swelling tip, coaxing his dick to rise, its girth twitching.

"A pretty cock for a pretty god," she compliments, idling tracing his slit.

Envy's mouth falls open, a strangled noise leaping from him. Still, his irises never waver. They cling to Sorrow like moonlight clings to the surface of the sea.

In that critical look, she's never felt more immortal. No, she doesn't require anyone's approval to validate her, nor does she give a solid fuck about impressing others. But with him, she doesn't have to.

Simply, she enjoys feeling sexy with this male. That's pleasure.

The proof of her touch beads at the prow of Envy's cock, an opaque drop of cum quivering into view. Sorrow makes an encouraging sound, then runs the pad of her thumb along the slim crease, smearing the fluid over the cap of skin.

A guttural noise cleaves from his lungs. His waist jerks on reflex, bobbing Sorrow in place, the edge of her clit skimming his sac.

The light friction throws sparks through her veins. They gasp, their reactions bouncing off the walls and echoing down the cave's hallways. The glittering effect takes a century to recover from, Sorrow and Envy gawking at one another, before she keeps going, keeps stroking him.

Like a naughty thing, her index fingers slide up the ramps of his hip bones, then return to his cock. Veins weave up his skin, blood pumping through them, the surge radiating against her fingers as she twines her fingers around Envy.

"Fuck," he grits out, his waist bucking into her hand. "Oh, fuck. Sorrow."

Her name coarse on his tongue wets Sorrow's pussy, the nexus puddling on his abdomen. From the shadows, those molten irises flash like amulets, two degrees from hitting its melting point.

He's heavy, his erection packed with heat and muscle. The enigmatic ability to sense this hasn't waned. In fact, it's grown stronger, like every mated couple in their crew.

Maybe it's because they were meant for this. Maybe it's their choice, which has severed a barrier, just as they breached celestial law by clutching each other beneath a sky of crashing stars, their hearts uniting regardless of her missing arrow and Envy's thievery.

Maybe it's both. Maybe it surpasses that.

Either way, Sorrow wants more of this heat, more of this pleasure. Circling her fingers around his bare cock, she bows forward and moans against his crown. Then she parts her lips and seals them over the tip.

Not in supplication. But in consummation.

Envy snaps off the bed, his groan dragging through the room. Humming into the rigid flesh, she cinches around him, then lowers her face. On a slow descent, she draws on his sinful cock, engulfing him to the seat.

Stars. The essence of wine seeps into her palate, a flavor she's been missing out on, seeing as she's never sampled him like this.

As if swallowing gravel, Envy grates out a string of moans, in tandem to Sorrow's pursed lips. Savoring this reaction, she unspools her tongue and laves his erection, lapping up every inch, lavishing him with attention.

And feeding her own needs. Because if he wants Sorrow to oblige her desires, this roguish male should have included himself on the menu. For this is how she takes her fill, by partaking in mutual intimacy.

Like lovers. Like equals.

The volume of Envy's response tingles Sorrow's flesh. Her pussy drips, her nipples ache, and her blood races.

Making up for lost time, she puckers her lips and gives a tender suck, exerting pressure up and down his girth. Envy's rapt octave shreds through the chamber, his muscled arms straining against the ice arrow. Mindless, he swivels his waist, lunging his crown, meeting the lowered pump of her lips.

Envy flings back his head, her name cutting from his lungs. Lost, he siphons into her mouth, hurling his waist against Sorrow's flat tongue.

Moaning around his cock, Sorrow swipes his tip, tasting salt. Doubtless, they've had a penetrating influence on each other, because she's in the mood to play, her teeth coming out to scrape the ledge of his dick.

Fates have mercy. The hunger is too much, her canines slipping and breaking skin. Envy hisses with jubilant enthusiasm, because of course he would.

Grinning around his erection, Sorrow licks a mixture semen and blood. Spurred by this, she rams the arrow shaft into his wrists and tightens her mouth, tugging on his dick, working him into a stupor.

All the while, the weight of Envy's voracious eyes prickles her scalp, riveting on her bent head. He whips his waist, hauling into her. Matching the pace of her lips, his growls escalate, and his body flexes, straining like a cord. Then he snaps.

A bellow cracks from his chest, the sound combusting through the cave. His cock jerks, streams of hot fluid washing down Sorrow's throat. The potent mixture of tart currants and dark wine soaks into her palate, an awed hum pulling from the back of her throat. Fates save her, but she tastes their combined essences.

Her vocal cords vibrate around Envy's dick, plying his body with aftershocks. Shackled by the ice arrow, the object of every deity's desire twists, writhes, and grunts from the pit of his chest. Each muscle stretches taut, each joint locks, and each feverish inch of him pulsates between her tight lips. Tipsy from his loss of control, and with this god at her disposal, Sorrow sucks him dry.

She'd always thought of oral pleasure as a one-sided exchange. But screw that, because it's more. It's communal, her pussy leaking onto his calves where she straddles him, his cock releasing for her like the mark of a dedicated deity. This is what happens when two beings are in love, the ebb and flow intrinsic, reciprocation balancing like the tide.

What one of them feels, both of them feels.

So she feeds on this god, and he comes hard and long, their groans filling this cavernous place. Simultaneously, her weapon digs into his pulse, red lines forming on his skin.

However, the ice doesn't chill or numb his flesh. Cold is still a mystery, whereas heat kindles in his pupils, the sensation remarkable.

With his mouth ajar, Envy watches Sorrow drink him to the last drop. Then on a jagged hiss, his arms blast free, and he's on her. Careening forward, he snatches the arrow and launches in her direction, the bridge of his cock popping from her mouth.

Snarling, the god slams into Sorrow. She flips onto her back, an exultant moan shooting from her lips, her heart jackhammering. Envy's massive physique crashes against hers, his body splaying her limbs apart, thighs steepling over his ribs, heels on his naked ass.

The plates of his torso rub her breasts, nipples poking him. And it's wondrous, to be stripped with someone, withholding nothing. That's the look he gives her while towering like an animated Greek statue.

All. Fucking. Hers.

"Yours," Envy rumbles, as if reading her mind. Then he slants his hips, tucking into Sorrow, that strong cock rowing along her slit like a cruel tease. And as she whines, his pupils glint, his voice rougher than a pumice stone. "Mine."

To accentuate the words, he flicks his waist slowly, jabbing his tip. "All. Fucking. Mine."

The shallow probe of his crown throws fire up Sorrow's limbs. Her cunt spills onto him, the flesh achy and hurting so well.

While fixating on Sorrow, the god uses one palm to bracket her wrists overhead, the same way she'd done to him. With his opposite hand, he exhibits the arrow, remorse cutting through his features. Despite the closure they've reached, regret covers him like a second skin.

Although his remorse eases her soul, enough mistakes have existed between them. Enough spite and grudges and offenses.

She leans up, brushing his lips with hers. "No more."

No more fighting. No more resisting. No more repenting.

They'd done plenty of that. It's finally time to heal, to survive, and to celebrate.

A gust of air rustles from his mouth, like a ghost being released from its confines, a latch breaking open, liberating them. With a baritone sigh, he burrows in, seizing her mouth, fitting them together.

Curling over her, Envy sinks his lips into Sorrows, their tongues dragging over another. Then he veers back with a husky grin. Ah, there's the wicked god she knows and adores.

Gazing at her, Envy turns their memory into something better, replacing it with this. He spins her arrow across his knuckles like a baton. She gasps, exhilarated when he etches the arrowhead along her jaw, descending to her neck before scaling to the crook of her mouth. The stimulation goes to her head, a buzz racing through Sorrow.

Angling the weapon, he tilts her lips open. "May I?"

"Fuck, yes," she insists.

The god quirks an eyebrow, savoring this playful side of her, which no one else will ever see. With gentle force, he nudges the arrow shaft against her mouth until she clamps her teeth around the slender weapon.

Palpitations beat in her throat. The expression on Envy's face makes it clear. She'll need something to bite on.

"Watch me," he murmurs. "Only me."

She nods. They have a lifetime of experimentation to account for, but as long as she anchors her gaze to him, Sorrow will always be safe.

Secured. Loved.

The knowledge fills her soul until there's no room left. The impact is greater because she's endured its opposite for eons.

Balmy air coasts through the chamber. Linking herself around him, Sorrow rests her head on the mattress and tenderly bumps her pussy into his cock.

Make love with me. Fuck me.

That's what she communicates. Envy absorbs the silent request, his irises glinting, showering her in light.

Casting his head sideways, he swings his waist, probing her soaked cunt with the broad tip of his cock. "Like this?"

She sighs around the arrow and heaves into him. Yes, like that.

Another agonizing jab, and another, and another. "Does this hurt?"

Decadence glides up her spine like the edge of a plume. She nods again, her nails burrowing into his hand because, yes, it hurts. Yes, it hurts so good.

Yes, it's pain. Yes, it's pleasure.

And no, don't fucking stop.

Hissing, Envy obliges. Braced on his palms, he suspends himself, his abdomen flexing with tension. The V of his hips leads to a prominent sight, his dick standing firm and ready at her slit. The vision of her thighs sprawled around his naked waist, and his cock primed, steals the last of her oxygen.

But it's his face that unravels her.

No artifice. No veneer. No ruse.

In this secret place of their making, Envy gazes at Sorrow with an immeasurable emotion, one that has baffled her for ages. But not anymore.

Whimpering, she agitates her lower body, her slick cunt coating his flesh from base to crown. Envy's eyelids flutter, a curse sputtering from his tongue.

She gyrates a second time, then a third.

And his restraint snaps. And so do his hips.

In a single whipcord motion, Envy lashes his cock into her. A cry snaps from her lips, the brunt jostling her over the bed. Her pussy clutches him to the seat, the hot length of flesh expanding her, the prow tapping her favorite narrow spot.

Growling, Envy charges forth, rocking his ass. Their bodies thrash over the sheets, moisture laminating every flexing muscle. The delirious pace of his cock punts Sorrow upward, her sobs and his grunts inundating the chamber, the noises accelerating.

As he spears his dick, Sorrow spreads wider, encouraging him to go deeper, then even deeper, and deeper still. Her walls seize Envy's dick, and her clit sketches his pelvis, the friction terrible and wonderful. She reels beneath him, his body hunches over her, and they drive against one another.

Envy curses, punching his cock in tune to her shouts. With each pivot, her molars grind into the arrow, a riot of noise escaping her.

She watches him, watches him, watches him. And he marvels at her, reverence flashing in his eyes, harsh gales of oxygen shoving his mouth. Their gazes fuse, and her features twist, and his mouth slackens as they race after that peak.

Envy's all toned muscle, tireless momentum, and vigorous tempo. He sprints his cock, locating a spot that nearly blinds Sorrow. Matter of fact, he hollers as if he hadn't known that place existed.

Thank Fates for that. She can't be the only one who's either going to pass out or detonate into shards.

"Yes, my nymph," Envy rasps, pistoning his waist. "Show my cock where to make your cunt spill."

Oh, she'll do more than show him. On the precipice, Sorrow spits out the arrow, and catapults off the mattress. With this god still primed inside her, they veer upright, Envy landing on his toned ass while she clambers onto his lap.

Astride his cock, she grasps his hair and hoists into him, her pussy swatting his cock. Seething, Envy reciprocates. With the might of a deity, he powers into her, fucks into her.

Facing each other like mates, they haul ass. She slings her hips, loving the clench of his canines, the toughening of his jaw, the heat of his dick, the wild percussion of his heart, the flare in his eyes. Craning back her head, she rides him to the ends of the earth, relishing his speechlessness.

By the Stars. She loves it all, consumes it all.

Clasping Sorrow's ass, Envy tugs her forward and backward, changing the cadence so that she can't do a thing but straddle him. She keens in cadence, her knees digging into the sheets, her thighs branching farther.

While dashing his hips, Envy's mouth steals hers, prying their kiss apart, in the same way his cock pries her apart. Sorrow shrieks into his mouth, and he swallows the reverberation like a glutton, as if the sound will keep him alive.

Breaking from the kiss, he grapples the back of her head with his free palm, holding it in place, trapping her gaze to his while he slings into her with long, burrowing strokes.

They're rushing at one another, she can't tell where it begins or ends, their bodies chasing a new type of eternity. Envy's hips tear between Sorrow's, and they beg for more, and more, and more.

"Oh!" she cries, throwing her head once more to the ceiling. "Envy!"

"Yeah," he pants. "Come for me. Come for yourself. Come on, Sorrow."

With renewed stamina, Envy slams into her cunt, arousal dripping to his sac. The width of his cock broadens, beads of fluid rise from Envy's crease, the cum sliding across her flesh. That she feels this throws Sorrow into a tailspin, into a dream, into a fucking fantasy made manifest.

Together, they go still. Then they explode like a pair of celestials.

Sorrow reels back to him, and he snatches her mouth, and they roar into each other. Clasping, they come with entwined shouts. The cacophony blows through the rocky halls, ripping past the cave. And it goes on, and on, and on.

At last, they collapse into stunned silence. Boneless, she traces his damp ass, and he cups the edge of her breast. For a long time, they're quiet, astounded, exhausted.

Still touching, they tangle themselves up, their limbs braiding. Unable to quit staring, they whisper into the night, sharing memories, clarifying misunderstandings, and shedding light on past actions. They talk over one another, bicker in amusement, and laugh with remorse.

Like they did over the course of three days, the conversation flows from one subject to the next. All in all, it's imperfectly perfect.

Envy makes a gluttonous noise and snacks on Sorrow's jaw.

Sorrow's fingers dip low to fondle the ledge of his cock.

This only gets them riled up again, which is fine. It's going to be a long, smutty night. And a much longer, smuttier life.

By dawn, Sorrow is one hundred percent fucked. And happy.

The bedding is a mixture of linen and fleece, since they combined the two after fucking for three consecutive rounds, after she'd taken his cock into her mouth again and made him bellow, and after he'd licked her into a fainting spell, and after he'd used a number of toys on her, then bent Sorrow in front of him, the deep pitch of his cock making her shriek into the pillows.

Envy sleeps on his stomach. The blankets barely cover the swells of his ass, those indentations tight and smooth. Sorrow traces his slumbering body with her fingertips, then swears affectionately under her breath. It should be against celestial law for one being to look like him. Yet she knows his flaws as intimately as his attributes, and she adores them in equal measure.

Slipping into her robe, Sorrow pads outside to the lagoon. The water sparkles, his tethered boat bobs over the surface, and the ferns sway.

On the opposite side of this refuge, a waterfall enclave awaits them. Envy plans on showing her more hidden crevices today, preferably ones in which she can come as loudly as she wishes while he pounds her against a watery embankment. Because even with all this love business, some lustful things don't change. In fact, the sentiment only spurs them on, their desires hardly satiated if the past few hours are anything to go by.

Sorrow's hair drapes over her chest. Warmth oozes into her cheeks.

Is she blushing? Probably.

Well, that's okay. Besides, only one person is allowed to see her like this.

And that person is coming this way. A tall shadow falls across the ground, a pair of toned arms slant around her waist, and a dangerous mouth nibbles on her ear.

When Sorrow tilts her head to give him better access, a husky voice flirts, "Purrr. I'm getting used to this."

She nestles into him. "Which part?"

"You. Me. Pain. Pleasure."

"You think we can handle it?"

"So far, so good."

"Then it helps that I love you."

"I love me too." When Sorrow flings back her head and laughs, he squeezes her playfully. And when she angles her face toward his, Envy grins. "But I love you more," he vows before claiming her mouth.

Sorrow parts her lips, and her hands vanish into his hair. With every resonating sweep of their tongues, she feels the truth down to the marrow of her bones. And she returns the fervent kiss, because the feeling is mutual.

That's their choice. That's their fate.

Envy traps her against him and whispers in detail all the ways he's going to fuck her while cornered like this, with the open world shimmering ahead of them. At which point, he carries her into the lagoon and demonstrates.

44

Envy

Six archers are already there when Envy and Sorrow arrive.

Love in a black dress, with her raven wings tucked out of sight someplace beneath her skin and a naughty expression on her face.

Andrew, with his white hair, pewter eyes, and snarky grin.

Anger, his shoulder-length hair tied halfway back, those graphite irises glinting with peace.

Merry, in her pastel dress with a sweetheart neckline, her smile wider than the horizon.

Wonder, with a cascade of chestnut hair and a corsage of wildflowers.

Malice, a golden devil in leather, with a perverse but cunning tongue.

They stand beside the bank of a tranquil lake, the great stargazer of Fortune's Crest rising in the backdrop. The water's surface mirrors the sky. Celestials dapple the atmosphere without sequence or order, creating an erratic arrangement.

That's how they've always been. Disorderly but resplendent. Messy but eternal.

The crew waits for the final pair with varying grins of amusement, some more impish than others.

Malice's laser gaze knows a thoroughly satisfied couple when he sees one. "Now that's what I call respectable kink. The evidence is all over you."

On her way past Malice, Sorrow claps him upside the head, causing the demon to belt out an insulted, "Fuck. That hurt!"

Merry offers Envy and Sorrow a set of pulsing lanterns. As they accept them, the goddess's pink ponytail matches the flush in her cheeks as she rejoins Anger, who tucks her close to his side, his injuries newly healed.

They form a ring, each holding a lantern, flames highlighting their faces. Envy stays close to Sorrow, whose smile puts a dent in his heart. He needs to stop this, quit fetishizing the female all the damned time, or his upright dick will be permanently affixed this way, like something that belongs on a fucking trophy shelf.

Then again, he does fancy the notion of his cock on display. He could build an altar for it. Something decked out in gold leaf and marble.

Sorrow rolls those silver eyes at him. Albeit lovingly.

All right, never mind. The only thing that belongs on a shrine is her.

Wonder's gaze brightens. Although the blazes illuminate the scars embedded into her hands, she is more than just her wounds, and she knows it. "Are we ready for this?"

"To a new legend." Malice glances at Wonder, love dominating his devilish features. "Hell, it's about time."

"A legend that won't be hidden," she says. "That anyone can find, because they'll know where to look."

"To gods and goddesses who can love," Love declares.

She bumps hips with Andrew, who smirks. "In whatever messy way they feel it."

"To imperfection," Anger follows, a set of hoop earrings flashing from his ears.

"No more banishment," Merry says. "To a life where all deities may dwell in whichever realm they call home."

Sorrow swallows. "To the past."

Envy nods. "To the future."

In addition to relearning their magic, they each plan on indulging in their passions whenever they can, bettering themselves instead of reigning over humans.

No more control. No more denial.

Blessings and inspirations. Destiny and chance. Hope and trust.

Should immortals wish to control anything, that liberty shall be limited to their own souls. Although deities will endure, they'll be Dark Gods unto themselves. No one else.

With that in mind, they make their pledges and release the lanterns. The vessels of light float into the air, then into the sky. Knotting their hands together, the crew watches until their vows blend with The Stars, until it's impossible to tell one from the other.

The dome glitters, accepting this promise.

Eventually, this crew will each have their own destinations. Love and Andrew intend to live in her old glass house, tucked in the forest of a mortal woodland, where they met. That way, they can watch over Andrew's stepfather, the shopkeeper named Georgie, and their friends, Holly and Griffin.

Occasionally, Love and Andrew will write notes to those beloved mortals. Nothing annotated but enough to affect the ones they care about, to let the humans know that Love—or Iris, as they'd called her—and Andrew are near.

Anger and Merry will return to her observatory in The Celestial City, with every formerly exiled deity who has chosen to remain there.

Wonder and Malice will build a life together in The Archives.

They'll spend their days surrounded by books, perhaps digging up additional legends.

As for Envy and Sorrow, he can't wait to trap her in the cavern, keeping the goddess all to his greedy self. With a surplus of carnal positions and sex gadgets left to try out, he'll spend his days fucking her soundly, making her come until she forgets the world outside.

It's not the end. It's the beginning.

They're a new crew. They plan on seeing a lot of each other, spending time in one another's domains. Because that's what a family does.

First, they have another job. In the valley between the bluffs, The Archives awaits them, along with hundreds of volunteers.

Wonder shuffles in anticipation, her green gown sweeping the blossoms around her unshod feet. "We should head out, dearests. The Hollow Chamber is not going to rebuild itself."

"We have a few hours yet," Anger reassures her.

"In that case, who's up for a swim?" Envy suggests. "I don't know about you, but my splendor needs replenishment."

"A night swim," Merry agrees. "How romantic!"

Andrew and Love quirk their brows at one another. "On your marks," he prompts, leaning into a racing position. "Get set—"

"Go!" the goddess shouts, sprinting ahead.

Love, Andrew, Anger, Merry, and Wonder vault toward the water while howling to the sky.

Sorrow pats Envy's shoulder. "This will require getting your outfit wet, pretty god."

"Think again, mate," Malice says, stripping off his leather jacket, followed by his pants. Wearing nothing but a devilish grin, he charges down the hill, his arms widespread, a quill tattoo blazing across his whipcord back.

"Good point," Sorrow concedes. "Though, that's more of him than I needed to see."

"Don't lie," Envy teases. "He has a remarkable ass. Only not as re-markable as mine."

To prove it, he peels off the suit he'd donned for this occasion and then waits, knowing what Sorrow will do. She disrobes from her vest and skirt, but she leaves on her combat boots.

Envy gawks at the sight, his retinas flaring across her naked curves. Only the reminder that they're not alone keeps his cock from losing control. However, he plans on doing some explicit damage to this goddess later. So he commits the visual of Sorrow to memory, for when he's got her alone in the enclave, where he can spread this goddess wide and fuck her beneath their choice of waterfall.

Sorrow struts backward while crooking a finger. Then she yelps, wheeling around and racing toward the lake as Envy pursues her with a predatory growl.

They reach the bank just in time. Malice pushes Anger into the water. Then Love pushes Malice. Then Wonder pushes Love. Then Sorrow pushes Wonder.

Then Andrew pushes both Envy and Sorrow. Then he jumps in after them.

Malice dunks Envy's head under the surface, then attempts to yank down Anger's pants, then splashes away as both gods charge after him.

Love straddles Andrew's waist, grinning as the man seizes her ass, then claims her lips with his own.

Anger spins Merry in a circle, his mouth sketching her throat while she flings her head to The Stars.

Wonder floats on her back until Malice snatches her into a feverish kiss.

Waist-deep and dripping, Envy saunters up to Sorrow. Taking her hand, he presses her palm to his beating chest. "Go deep."

Sorrow places his own hand against her heart. "Go deeper."

One lingering kiss later, they join their family. Beneath a gleaming sky, the crew shouts with defiance. They dive, swim, and revel in the dark.

And they love. Because now they know what that feels like.

45

Faith

He watches them. Spreading the leaves like a curtain, he peeks through the foliage and spies on the eight immortals reveling in the water.

All that fighting and rebelling. All those captures and escapes. All those flying arrows and fatal battles.

He would have done it differently. Wouldn't he?

With a shake of his head, Faith cannot decide whether to grin or purse his lips at the display. All four sets of fated mates have gone mad. They spray water everywhere, some bare-assed, others with their clothing drenched.

They clasp and kiss their soulmates. Then at one point, they float on their backs and stare collectively at the sky.

Is this what fate looks like? Is it what free will looks like?

Hmm. Faith cocks his head. Although he fancies his clover arrows, the thought of blessing an emotion rather than forcing it on a target is sort of thrilling. Also, it sounds godlier. He likes that.

Maybe he should thank this crew. Maybe he likes them a little.

Okay, maybe a lot. Maybe he's looking forward to seeing them often, whenever their paths cross in The Dark Fates. And maybe it's nice to spy on them like this, wild and happy.

When the eight figures depart together, Faith creeps out from behind the shrubbery and steps to the water's edge. His longbow and quiver clatter against his back. Perching on the bank, he deposits his archery on the grass and dips his legs into the lake, which reflects the summit's stargazer.

But where the hell did the constellations go? They were up there a moment ago, before the crew left.

With a crinkled brow, he cranes his head from the lake and inspects the hemisphere. Suddenly, it's the strangest sky he's ever seen, not quite eventide any longer, nor quite daybreak yet. Then again, he's never been out at this twilit hour, on the cusp of darkness and lightness.

He's not allowed. In fact, his Guide would flay him for sneaking out. Well, fuck that. Everyone is breaking rules these days.

Settling more comfortably, he resumes inspecting his watery reflection. The burnished skin. The wide, lilac eyes. The hooded cloak covering his slender shoulders. Nothing he hasn't seen before, yet the firmament is so vast, he resembles a tiny star blinking in the sky.

There's a star that blinks in the sky...

Right. Isn't that how he began? His Guide once told Faith the story of his birth. Funny that he remembers only now.

Faith swerves his head from side to side, surveying his appearance anew. His eyes glint, the lids inked in a midnight sheen. The ornamentation reminds him of that gray-haired goddess, with silver stars trickling beneath her irises. They're natural on her, but even if they weren't, he wagers she would don those star flecks for herself and no one else. She's authentic and doesn't try to impress others, and he fancies that about her.

That long-haired god is fairly likable too. The male who bestowed

Faith with a chore.

Rifling through his quiver, Faith retrieves the small, leather-bound tome. He'll have to return it to the crew later, when he joins them to rebuild The Archives. But for this next hour, he flips through the pages and rereads the text, transfixed by the contents.

It's a legend.

It's the one those rebellious immortals scribed with The Court when they congregated at the stargazer. At that point, Faith wasn't supposed to be there, since everyone but the rulers and the infamous eight had gone home. But Faith had stationed himself outside during the proceedings, determined to sulk on the parapet.

He hadn't known what they were doing inside the dome. Not until shortly after, when that god presented Faith with the book. Endorsed by The Court and blessed by The Stars, the pages include a prologue of mythic tales.

One is about a star that refuses to shine: a mischievous goddess who falls in love with a mortal.

One tale is about a star that blazes too harshly in the sky: a rebel god who falls in love with an outcast.

One tale is about a star that drifts in the sky: a wildflower goddess who falls in love with a devil.

One tale is about a star that flashes proudly in the sky, as well as a star that glints quietly: a vain god and moody goddess who fall in love with each other.

The book continues with the legend itself, envisioning deities who live alongside humanity, existing in a universe of destiny and choice. Then the final passage declares the most puzzling thing, a string of new words forged by the court and crew.

If a deity falls in love, it shall be a union of fate and free will.

Closing the notebook, Faith cocks his head. "What the eternal fuck does that feel like?"

Then he smirks, because now he'll have the chance to find out. And when he glances toward the celestials, the sky glows with beams of light.

Finally. The Stars are out.

**Thank you for joining the celestial crew on
their star-crossed journey!**

PLEASE REVIEW, so more readers can discover the series!
Then recommend *Dark Gods: Selfish Myths* to your besties and
add it to your Amazon collections and wish lists. This tells
the Zon to show the series to more readers, which keeps the
crew's story alive for eternity.

Never Miss a Release!
Get new release alerts, exclusive content, and wicked details about
my books by subscribing to my newsletter at:
nataliajaster.com/newsletter

AUTHOR'S NOTE

Stars almighty. We've made it, dearest mortals. From the beginning, this crew claimed an eternal place in my soul. I hope they have in yours too!

Each couple brings a special dynamic to this world. The forbidden passion of Love and Andrew. The fierce and volatile light of Anger and Merry. The dark, seductive, and heartrending intensity of Malice and Wonder. The raw, snarky, and honest growth of Envy and Sorrow.

Like every pairing, these two overcame some big hurdles with each other. More than any other crew member, Envy and Sorrow had the greatest challenge identifying (and understanding) their emotions. To say nothing of accepting them. But once the veneer dropped, their story took an exquisitely candid turn.

They're also pretty damn fun to be around. I had a blast creating their sharp, tongue-lashing banter, their fiery chemistry, and their rocky evolution into love.

One of my favorite moments is when the crew holds each other beneath the falling constellations, becoming a true found family at last. I'm so proud of these fated mates, and I'll miss them until the Stars fade.

Will the series continue in some other way? I have no plans for that.

This is the happily-ever-after of the mythical quest. But as Faith's chapter reminds us, hope for the future of deities and humans is as bright as the constellations. The crew has triumphed, and now it's time to revel.

Thank you for joining them on their destined journey.

PLEASE REVIEW, so more readers can discover the series! Then recommend Dark Gods: Selfish Myths to your besties and add it to your Amazon collections and wish lists. This tells the Zon to show the series to more readers, which keeps the crew's story alive for eternity.

All my gratitude, dearest mortals. You are stardust.

XO,
Natalia

ACKNOWLEDGMENTS

Thank you to the court of beta and sensitivity readers—Ali, Jay, and Daniella—who generously offered feedback for Transcend. As always, your real-time responses made me smirk like a deity.

To my family, for your support. And for never reading the spicy scenes.

To Roman, my fated and devious mate.

Always, to the Dark Revelers hype team. I'd defy The Stars with you any day.

Finally, to everyone who has read, loved, and shared The Dark Gods universe with this bookish world. Without your support, I'd be screaming into the void. Literally.

You are kindred. You are immortals.

ABOUT NATALIA

Natalia Jaster is a romantasy author who routinely swoons for the villain.

She lives in a dark forest, where she writes spicy fantasy romance tales about rakish jesters, immortal deities, and vicious faeries. Wicked heroes are her weakness, and rebellious heroines are her best friends.

COME SAY HI!

Bookbub: www.bookbub.com/authors/natalia-jaster
Facebook: www.facebook.com/NataliaJasterAuthor
Instagram: www.instagram.com/nataliajaster
TikTok: www.tiktok.com/@nataliajasterauthor
Website: www.nataliajaster.com
See the boards for Natalia's novels on
Pinterest: www.pinterest.com/andshewaits